Stray
A Femdom Romance

Daisy Jane

Copyright © 2022 by Daisy Jane.

All rights reserved.

No part of this book may be reproduced in any form or by any electronic or mechanical means, including information storage and retrieval systems, without written permission from the author, except for the use of brief quotations in a book review.

Proofreading done by Geeky Girl Author Services.

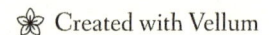

❦ Created with Vellum

Warnings

Warning: this book contains themes possibly distressing or upsetting to some. Before reading, please visit the reading guide on my website for all content warnings.

Please be advised: additional content warnings will NOT be listed at the beginning of each chapter. Read accordingly to have the safest, most fulfilling reading experience.

Note: Femdom is when a woman controls a man sexually, so if you're not interested in that, turn back now.

Roll Call

Didn't read **Where Violets Bloom** but need to familiarize yourself with the Men of Paradise cast? Here's a breakdown of who's who, including all of their nicknames.

Bran: Brian Edwards, "Bran", "Arizona Robbins"
  Van: Donovan Drake, "Van", "The Bodfather"
  Mally: Christian Miller, "Mally", "Malibu", "Boo"
  Batman: Henry Burke, "Batman"
  Robin: Robin Burke, Henry's wife
  Sammy: Samantha Edwards, "Sammy," "Sam"

I can't say it happens often because I stopped regularly dating a few years back. But the few and far between I've been roped into going out since *the night*–the night where I became disabled–the dates have been eerily fucking similar.

Men may be stupid about a lot of shit, but we know when a woman does *not* fucking dig us.

The blonde sitting across from me tucks her hair behind her ear for probably the twentieth time in the past ten minutes. As I lift my beer to my mouth and enjoy the cool amber ale, I realize this chick could be a fucking gif.

Yeah, those little animated, soundless videos on the internet.

She alternates between tucking her hair back, rolling her lips together, and then partially smiling while pushing around limp lettuce on her dinner plate. Yep, she's holding the fork again, moving soggy food around.

Over and over; hair, lips, fork.

The gif of a disappointed woman who wants to fucking bolt.

This whole date is wash, rinse, and repeat. And again, the reason I don't fucking do it.

She's quiet; I'm sure devising an exit plan or strategy. And I'm fine with that. Because I don't want to waste time on a chick that makes me feel worse about the one thing I already feel pretty fucking bad about. I don't know what I deserve, but I know it's better than that. Sammy tells me as much.

I drain the remainder of the cold ale and lower the empty pint glass back down to the table. The waitress comes, and I pay the check–my date making a show of going for the bill. But the last thing I'm going to let this girl do is go back to all her fucking friends and tell them she had to buy her own meal after being subjected to a date with a fucking pirate.

I want to groan my frustration at the situation, but I don't want to *sound* like a pirate to boot. No pun intended.

I sit quietly, resisting the urge to smooth my fingers along the elastic in my hair, the one that keeps the patch sealed over my eye. I fiddle with it when I get nervous. Sammy always slaps my hand if she's with me.

But you can't bring your younger sister on a blind date, so instead, I'm in this booth, parked inside my head, shouting, *don't touch the eyepatch, man.*

I shouldn't be anxious. I knew this chick was disappointed the moment she laid eyes on me. She just felt too much guilt to call off the date. Still, my nerves fly around in my gut like a water hose on blast, spraying every calm part of me until I'm completely fucking saturated in unease.

She declines any to-go boxes. Neither of us finished our food, and I think her lack of appetite made me lose mine.

We met here, thank fuck.

Not a minute after the waitress is out of earshot does she pass me a consoling smile.

"Brian, I–"

I lift my hand, showing her my palm. "It's fine."

She huffs out a relieved breath, and even if I don't care about this woman, it still sets off a small burst of pain beneath my ribs. "Yeah?" she asks hopefully, and my eye meets hers. Her brows are raised, and her face is so hopeful. Seeing her eager and excited to get *away* from me feels... *really fucking great.*

"It's fine," I say, dropping my eye to my lap. She slides

Prologue

Bran

I'd rather be blown off hard than be pity blown

What's kept me from doing this? The answer is glaring. No, the answer is currently munching on a forkful of romaine, doing her absolute fucking best to look at everything *but* the one thing she really *wants* to look at.

And *this* is why I don't date.

I can traverse the tumbleweed flatlands of *"where did you grow up"* and *"how many siblings do you have"* all night long.

I can take Advil to ease the neck pain that comes from mutely bobbing my head to another person's endless chatter all night.

I can stomach the uncomfortable moments of a stranger

and me talking over one another because we don't know the other's nuances and social cues.

I can get through paying for drinks that sound like vacations and dinners that cost more than a grocery trip, even if it leads to absolutely nothing—because it's only money.

I can enjoy having differences of opinion, finding and maintaining interest in a person I know I have no future with just for the sake of having a nice date.

I can blow fucking twenty minutes styling my hair and the effort to get ready for a blind date.

Fine, fine, all of that is *fucking fine*. And those things are *not* the reason I don't date.

It's this moment. *Right here.*

This moment where my date doesn't know how to behave because of my disability. I hate calling it that, by the way. But according to the fucking DMV, it *is* a disability because it earns me a beautiful blue placard to hang from the rearview mirror in my pickup.

She swallows the last of her bite, blotting the corners of her mouth with the wine-colored napkin. Her dress parallels the color, but something tells me she wouldn't like to hear that.

I'm about to ask if her salad is good when she rests the fork on the plate a little loudly. She shudders down with a wince, muttering a quick "*sorry.*"

Not looking up at me, she instead digs through that duffel bag she's calling a purse. This is where she gets out her wallet to pay for her portion. Because even though the check hasn't even come yet, this is when they secure their life raft. Get their wad of cash ready to pass off for the speediest bill pay and departure possible.

out—I can hear her—and a moment passes before I look up and find myself alone.

Again.

I take out my phone as the waitress returns with boxes, staring for an uncomfortable amount of time at the newly vacant seat across from me.

I shove my hand through my hair, pulling at the ends. "Thanks," I say, maybe a little too loudly, trying hard to divert her attention from the fact that I was ditched. I tug out some extra cash and slide it across the table without meeting her gaze. "Thanks again."

She leaves me, and I return my attention to my phone.

Bran: *She couldn't get away from me quick enough.*

Sammy: *[GIF: Sammy from Jersey Shore crying "Ron Stahp"]*

Bran: *Seriously. She fucking bolted after I paid. She was relieved when I told her it was fine.*

Sammy: *What a bitch!*

Sammy: *I'm sorry, B. But you can't quit!*

Bran: *No inspirational speeches right now. Please. I just spent seventy bucks to get blown off.*

Sammy: *Shit, where'd you take her?*

Bran: *Taco Bell. The woman knew how to eat.*

Sammy: *HAR HAR.*

Sammy: *Don't get off the horse, though, B. Seriously.*

Sammy: *Or is it off the wagon?*

Bran: *I think the wagon is for booze-related issues, not women.*

Sammy: *Okay, so keep riding that horse!*

Bran: *You're making me sound like a gay cowboy now.*

Sammy: DON'T STOP TRYING TO MEET A WOMAN BECAUSE THAT ONE SUCKS

Sammy: *There, how's that? Clear enough for you?*

Bran: *Message received. Alright. I'm going home where I belong. Sleep tight, Sammy.*

Sammy: *See you in the AM.*

PACKING UP MY LEFTOVERS—ONLY because it's rude to leave the boxes the waitress brought over—I wipe my hands on the merlot-colored napkin and slide out of the booth.

This was a grapevine blind date—a co-worker of Sammy's at the hospital had a friend whose cousin's sister was looking to date and had a thing for tattooed, strong guys. It was supposed to be a good way to get back into it because even with a loose thread socially connecting us, I didn't think she'd blow me off so hard.

But I'd rather be blown off hard than be pity blown.

It's been so long since I've dated. Somehow I stupidly thought that in the age of no bullying, #MeToo, and cancel culture, I'd have a better chance of meeting someone.

That a good, sweet, kind, loving woman wouldn't look at me and see an eye patch. That in this new world that allows anyone to be anything—even I could find love, too.

Eight years ago, on that fateful night—I knew my life would change. I knew it would be hard moving on missing such an important piece of me. I mean fuck, an eyeball is pretty goddamn important.

Stray

I just didn't know it would affect my heart so much, too.

1

Bran

I have a face people stare at.

"Bro, where are my waffles?" Mally asks from his spot in front of the drink refrigerator in the lobby of Paradise, the spread door being held by his hip.

I understand my mom's harrowing battles over the refrigerator door as a kid more than ever.

"Dude, you're letting all the fucking cold air out," Donovan says.

"And," I add because Mally won't fucking listen without multiple reasons. "That isn't your personal snack fridge. That's for paying fucking clients who like to buy energy drinks and shit."

"Those aren't even good for you," Mally says pointedly, nodding to the rows of colorful cans of energized poison, the door *still* fucking open. The timed light inside the cooler clicks off. Van lifts one thick leg, using his foot to tap the door free from Mally's hip, effectively closing it.

"There," Van says, turning his head to give me a smug grin. "I'm the good son."

Mally snorts, and the two of them begin their almost daily verbal battle over who's stronger, more handsome, the better officer. They're both cops here in Willowdale, and they're even beat partners, too.

With the rag tucked into the waist of my sweats, I smooth over the Mally-finger-shaped smudges on the glass door. When I tune back into their conversation, they're now arguing over which of them would be Macaulay Culkin's character in the movie *The Good Son*.

They've been my best friends since junior high school, but Jesus Christ, they can really be idiots.

"If I let you go, do you think you could fly?" Mally dramatically recites the famous line while gripping Van's hand. He rolls his eyes and yanks his hand free.

"Dude, I'm both Elijah Wood and Macaulay Culkin. You're... you're the dummy they throw off the overpass."

Thank god for my little sister Sammy. She strides through doors that open for her, large black frames covering half her face. Mally and Van abandon the nineties movie talk to greet her.

"Good morning Samantha," Mally smiles as he steps toward her, flipping her sunglasses up to her head. He lowers his face close to hers, narrowing his eyes while... sniffing.

"Are we hungover?" he asks, his tone full of suspicion.

She places her palm directly over his face, fingers fanned out, and shoves him back. "Back off, Christian," she snaps, and *damn*. Real naming at four in the morning means she's either hungover as Malibu suspects, or she had a hard night at the hospital.

"Christian," Malibu repeats his name, a plaintive hand draped over his pecs. "What did I do to deserve the real name treatment?"

"I don't need you to analyze my face up close, that's what," she snaps back as she drops to the bench lining the wall. She toes into her lifting shoes—I got them for her birthday last year when she said she finally wanted to see what lifting was all about. She's a natural, just like me.

"You look good up close, though," Mally says thoughtfully as he swipes his water jug from the counter. My sister rolls her eyes.

"No one's pores look good up close, Malibu," she says, her lightening mood evident from her use of his nickname.

"Yours do," Malibu says, batting one eye in truly a stomach-curling wink. I take the two steps across the lobby of my gym to get to him, then promptly twist his nipple.

"Don't fucking flirt with my sister, man," I say, releasing him just as he squirms away. Pulling the shirt from his body, he peers down the neck-hole at his nipple, blinking.

"It's still there, thank god," he sighs, and I can't help but roll my eyes.

"You're wearing a stringer, you idiot," Van says, using one finger to swipe the thin strap of Mally's tank aside, immediately exposing his nipple. But Mally is a dramatic asshole, so of course, he had to look down his shirt.

"It's fucking ten after four in the morning. I don't want to see your nipple," Sammy says, shielding her eyes as she rises from the bench.

"Your brother wants to touch it," Mally grins, and I refrain from socking him as the four of us make our way into the lifting room and start our session.

Sammy doesn't always work out with us–probably just a few times a month. The rest of the time, she comes to Paradise on her own, after her shift, with a novel blaring through her headphones and her focus solely on the job–lifting. She's got that dedication to things inside of her the way I do, and it's part of why we're so close.

Part of. We've been through some shit together, Sammy and me. And I keep her close to my side as much as I can because of it. She's unexpectedly joining us this morning, but we're cool with it because even though Mally flirts with her, these guys are my brothers and treat her like a sister.

That may put Mally in the *Flowers in the Attic* category a bit, but still, I trust him with her because *I trust him*. We all have earned each other's trust, so even when they annoy the fuck out of me, I'm still fiercely protective of all of them.

Though I'm having a hard time remembering the latter this morning as they poke and prod me relentlessly over the fact that I haven't "gotten back in the saddle" after my shitty blind date a few weeks ago.

"If you think about it, online dating is really the smartest. None of this friend of a friend shit," Van says thoughtfully, stroking a hand down his beard that closely resembles mine.

In fact, the two of us look like actual brothers, with dark hair and cropped beards, muscles, and tattoos. He's taller than me, just slightly, and wears a pair of black-framed glasses. And where his eyes are blue, mine is the color of mud. I guess that would make me the ugly brother. Yet again.

"Online dating isn't just for people who can't meet

people, so don't even start with that shit either," Sammy huffs out as she steps free from the thick blue band she'd had around her thighs. "That's *so* eHarmony."

Mally slides plates onto the bar, prepping for his next set of box squats. "Totally." Damn, he really does earn that beach boy nickname.

Van continues. "Everyone does it now because everyone lives behind a phone."

"And you'd online date, then?" I ask Van because I know he's not seeing anyone. And I know he isn't online dating either. What I don't say is that he doesn't have to try online dating because women look at him and soak themselves. He doesn't look like a fucking *Sons of Anarchy* reject like I do.

He tips his head just once in a singular decisive nod. "I would."

"But you don't *have* to," I say quietly so that the words can't travel to the squat bar where Mally and Sammy are at. Van steps toward me and drops his gaze down, keeping that private, too.

"Neither do you. But you'll be more comfortable, and that's what you need to get you going–*comfort*." Then he gives his attention to the bar at his feet, positions his chalked hands around it, and with a deep grunt, he starts his set of deadlifts.

He's not wrong.

Being able to talk to someone a little online first *would* bring me some comfort. I could, at the very least, warn them that I'm not going to be their show-pony on social media. Seems like that's what a lot of women are looking for these days, anyway. Not a genuine connection, just someone to show off.

I used to be that guy.

And the boys and my sister are always trying to convince me that I *still am* that guy. "You're the total package, Bran, but no one can see it because you're so focused on a tiny little imperfection in the wrapping. But nobody's perfect. Everyone has imperfections." She's uttered variations of that message again and again over the years. It went in one ear and right out the other.

Another frustrating thing about my situation is that—*goddamn it*—I know she's right. Obviously, as a thirty-year-old man, I know that no one is perfect.

But I still can't find the fucking confidence—Jesus, do I sound like a girl—to believe that the rest of me is good enough to make up for the fact that *I now have a face people stare at.*

I attempt to give online dating some serious thought, but the first thing that pops into my head as I do? A profile picture. That's the first thing those accounts are going to ask for.

"I don't want to make profiles for online dating, okay?" I say, forcing some backbone into my tone so that he'll drop it. Van finishes his set and wipes his hairline with the hem of his shirt.

"Okay," he says, after a pensive moment where he stares into my eye.

Van's always been good at figuring me out without going through a lot of deep talks. On the other hand, Mally is someone who thrives on and loves deep talks—he's the sensitive one in our group. Our other best friend, Batman, is the logical thinker out of all of us. He makes sound choices based on statistical relevance and shit like that. I guess that leaves me being the strong and silent type that's there for my people, constant and continual.

And I can do that forever, without a girl.

I've always been a man who dreamt of being married, being a dad... all that shit. I knew life would be very different when I lost my eye that night. I just had no idea how those differences would alter my life vision so much... again, no pun intended.

Instead of focusing on what I don't have and can't obtain, I decide as I watch Van finish his set and listen to Sammy and Mally bicker over God only knows what that I'm going to pour myself into the one sure thing in my life: Paradise.

2

Elsie

It's the good in my day–coming home to them

"Good morning, how are–"

The man reaches over the desk, scanning the barcode on the laminated rectangle hooked to his keys. He doesn't bother meeting my eyes as the scanner turns green, his photo and information flashing across the computer screen in front of me.

"Alright, Scott, have a good workout," I say to the air that *Scott* has left behind because not only did he not let me do my one measly job of scanning his fucking membership keychain, but then he didn't even let me greet him.

Asshole.

As if I want to greet his stupid ass anyway. I don't, but it's my freaking job. It's not like I'd show up at his work–the *stick up your ass factory,* maybe?—and start doing his job for him.

Prick.

The doors whoosh open again, and I see two familiar faces this time. Quinten and Cordelia Wilder, an adorable married couple who joined the gym a few months back. They have a home gym, but because Cordelia works from home as an audiobook narrator, she said she had to join a gym to actually leave her house once in a while. Though we only talk while she's here at the gym, I like her a lot and consider her a friend.

"Good morning," I beam because these are two people that I actually *do* like seeing.

"Elsie!" Cordelia grins, speeding up her pace to make it to the desk before her husband. Mutually, we lean over and exchange hugs.

Dread sears my guts as Cordelia's eyes go wide with impending excitement. The last time I saw her was last week, the day of my and my boyfriend's six-month anniversary. I'd shared with Cordelia that he and I were having a date just by ourselves—something we rarely did.

I hadn't expected much more than a nice meal, but Cordelia had brewed an entire scenario where Jake, my boyfriend, was probably going to propose.

Truthfully, I didn't really want to marry Jake. But the idea of a proposal—it did something to me. It gave me this weird sense of hope. And it feels too good to be hopeful, doesn't it?

I didn't want to get married anytime soon. Hell, I'm only twenty-two. I'm too young. But once she'd floated that out there—her own diamond ring singing her happiness from its comfortable spot on her finger–I let myself get... *excited*.

And now it's time to let her down easy.

"Well?" she asked with a grin plastered to her beautiful face. Holy shit, letting people down never gets easier, even with how much I've had to do it. Quinten sidles up next to her, rubbing his palm along her lower back. Ugh, they're cute. And the part of me that wants that–that is *screaming* for that casual back-rubbing cuteness–forces me to look away.

I give her a tight smile before flicking her keycard in front of the red laser. The computer bleeps, and their account flashes over the screen. Clicking them into acceptance, I hand the keys back to her and adjust my smile accordingly.

Her excitement wanes, and her brows lift to her hairline. "Oh no. What happened?" She reaches over the desk and drags my hand toward her, immediately spotting the bare finger.

"Yeah, definitely no ring."

"No ring," she repeats, and I glance up to Quinten, whose eyes are studying his wife's profile like he can't get enough of her even in plain conversation. My gut twists with jealousy, and it's not because I want Quinten–an uptight shrink, *no thanks*–but because of how glaring his love is.

I take my hand back under the guise of needing to click around on the computer screen, and she lets me have my little lie. Forcing my eyes to her big hopeful ones, I swallow down my nerves and let her down easy. A lot like Jake did to me.

"Turns out, he wanted to break up instead. That's why he wanted a *private* date."

"What a shithead," Cordelia huffs as she adjusts her high ponytail, her head shaking just a little. "I'm so sorry, Elsie. I filled your head with rainbows and unicorns, and he–"

"Rained on the rainbows and murdered the unicorns," I supply, trying to bring levity to the situation. I can feel bad about getting dumped by Jake, but I don't need Cordelia feeling bad about it. How could she have known that my boyfriend would choose our fucking anniversary to dump me? I mean, that's pretty cold.

"And on your anniversary," she supplies like she's reading my thoughts.

I nod but keep a small smile on my face because there is a warmth at the back of my nose and behind my eyes that could easily grow if I let it.

And fuck that.

Jake isn't getting any more of my tears. Truthfully, the tears weren't for Jake anyway. I'd cried for the last three and a half days because of the reasons he'd served up to me in his big speech that night.

"It's okay, honestly," I admit because even though this woman and I are just friends while she's here, she's easy to talk to. "I don't want you feeling bad. I thought it would be good news, too, but I realized after he dumped me that I wouldn't want to marry him, anyway."

She nods at me to continue, sensing there's more. But it's too much more. Definitely too much for a casual "welcome to Globo-Fitness" type conversation. I steer away from heavy toward easy.

"It made me realize... Well, Jake wasn't *the one*." I shrug and ignore the heat still bubbling up inside me. It's only been a few days—I'm still hurting.

"Clearly," she adds, leaning forward to pluck a piece of lint from my Globo-Fitness polo. "Well, I'm sorry." She tips her head to the side, eyes on mine but not really focused. My palms glaze over in sweat because she has a look that I'm really familiar with, and I don't like it.

"You know, Quinten has a friend–" she muses, but I stop her with the universal sign to halt, a palm up between us. If there's anything I know, it's that mutual hookups and forced blind dates never work. I won't put this new friendship on the line for a stab at a not-so-bad date.

"Honestly, it's okay. Jake said some things that really... resonated with me," I lie because *"devastated, broke me, and caused me to binge two pints of Ben & Jerry's"* sounds way more dramatic. As we talk, I check in another two clients who make their way straight to the cardio theater.

Globo-Fitness used to be an old movie theater. All the theater rooms had been torn apart except one. The owners of the chain left one of the huge screens up and added some smaller screens around it, all depicting some television show or movie. At the back of the room, furthest from the screen were the people doing extreme cardio on machines like the rolling StairMaster and the water rowers. They didn't take breaks or split the machine time with someone else–they simply went hard until their time was up and left the back row drenched and smelly. In a gradient, the rest of the machines were treadmills and ellipticals, with one row of stationary bikes closest to the big screen.

At peak hours, the cardio room was packed. In the mornings, like now, it's as empty as it will be all day since most of the early risers gravitate towards the group classes and weight room.

Cordelia apologizes to me again while Quinten fuses their hands together, staying silent behind her as we finish our conversation. It's just a fucking handhold, but my eyes must linger on it a second too long. Because I get a sad goodbye smile from the both of them as they filter into the big free-weight room to start their workout.

My eyes stay on them until I lose sight and thank God for my boss for calling my name, or else I think I was about to let myself wallow, just a little.

And Elsie Francis does not wallow. Francis women do not wallow. My mom taught me that—one of the many fucking empowering and bomb things she taught me.

"Els, hey, there's a situation in the women's locker room. Stop by the janitorial closet before you head in," Karina calls. And the thankfulness I felt when she first called my name vanishes almost instantly when I realize what she's said.

A "situation" at a gym is usually something requiring a mop, and things here that require a mop? They're nasty.

But I'm used to it.

I'm not the vomit-cleaner and front desk keycard-swiper because that's the big energy I want in my life.

I'm here for *them* and only for them.

Eight hours later, I'm turning the key on the front door to my house, my feet sore and my muscles aching. Despite the fact that I've been at a gym for the last eight-plus hours, I'm not sore from working out. Just... working.

A dull throb rolls through my temples, and my stomach scorches with hunger. My feet literally ache, and my hair smells like lemon disinfectant. But as soon as I drop my keys on the table near the door, I hear the most perfect, beautiful sound, and the world is right again.

"Mama!" Effie calls to me, the symphony of small feet on hardwood putting a smile on my face before I even see her.

"Give her a minute to get in the house, babe," my mom calls to my four-year-old from the kitchen. The warmth of Effie pressed to my chest, her little fingers tangling in my ponytail as she launches into every detailed moment of her day, makes my chest expand.

"I missed you, baby," I whisper into her ear, even though she isn't listening at all. She's full tilt as she describes her lunch with grandma today.

"Have you ever dipped chimkin nuggets in honey?" she asks as she tries to pull back from the hug and wiggle free.

"Oh honey. Yum." I wiggle the tip of my nose against hers, so soft and small. "Yeah, baby, I've had that. It was my favorite as a kid." Despite the fact I'm answering her question, I'm ninety-nine percent sure she doesn't hear it because she's back on her feet, racing to the kitchen. I follow her to find my mom looking... *good*.

She's cooking, and Effie is already gripping the edges of the countertop, trying desperately to lift herself up. I always tell her, *you can sit on the counter when you can get up and down yourself.* That's how I know it's safe. And the little chip off the old block has been struggling and groaning in the kitchen for the last few months. She's nearly got it.

Hiding my sigh of relief, knowing that mom and Effie are doing well, I kiss my mom's cheek and smooth my hand down her back.

"Hi, mom. Good day?" I ask, keeping the question as vague as possible. Because sometimes, on her good days, it upsets her if I get excited about it. Reminds her of the bad days and how none of us can really control them.

"Wonderful day," she smiles, sifting her fingers through Effie's hair as she squeezes between us at the stove. "And in ten minutes, it's going to be even better." Her eyes hold mine. She has green eyes, and mine are blue, but we share the same wide, almond shape. She blinks a few times as the anticipation creeps across her face in the form of a grin.

Slowly and dramatically, she lifts the lid from the red metal wok to reveal a sizzling heap of chicken, peppers, and onions. The steam from the hot dish wafts towards me, and my stomach cries out a garbled response.

"Fajitas," she and I drag out in unison, using our most Homer Simpson voice. Because who doesn't love fresh fajitas?

I make a plate for Effie while she continues to do battle with the countertop, all while hearing about their day. It's the good in my day–coming home to them.

Especially when it's a good day for mom.

It makes the vomit clean-ups and pricks who can check themselves into the gym all worth it.

3

Bran

Pity makes me feel like a massively self-indulgent asshole.

Laying in bed, scrolling through social media to avoid getting up, I see a post that makes me wish I hadn't procrastinated. I should've just gotten up at 3:30 when the alarm choked my senses and dragged me kicking and groaning from my perfect REM sleep.

Because this post is not a great way to start the day.

The account belongs to a guy that works out at Paradise. The people that come to my gym usually look me up on social media within the first month or so of training–and then they friend me. It's cool, I like knowing the people that want to know me, and I certainly appreciate their support of my gym.

This guy–his name is Jamie–started coming to Paradise

Stray

when he outgrew the barbell set in his garage. Instead of investing a few grand into the weights he needed, he decided to start coming here. He's a toddler in his weight lifting journey, but I'm fucking stoked he's going to grow his muscles here. He's a good dude. Hard-working.

He isn't, however, *a looker*. And I'm not trying to be a dick or anything, but I can admit when a man is good-looking. And it's not that Jamie is ugly; he's just got an Opie meets the MAD magazine kid vibe happening. There is a gap between his teeth, hair that sticks out everywhere no matter how he smooths it down. He's got a lopsided smile and a goofy disposition.

Why the fuck is this relevant?

Because Jamie, awkward snort-laugh and all, *has a girlfriend*.

And she's fucking gorgeous. But that's not even the fucking deal. It's that Jamie–who, by the way, is no fucking alpha millionaire–stocks the shelves at the hardware store and lives with his mom. By all accounts, the guy is just normal. And that's okay. Nothing wrong with normal.

But even Jamie found a girl; even *he* found fucking happiness. Did I mention he has a barbed wire tattoo around his tricep? And *he* found a girl.

I've got all the shit women want.

I own a business. My body is a fucking temple–partially as an homage to Paradise but also because working out is one of my free meds for anxiety. I own a home, have a great relationship with my parents and sister, have a circle of friends that are more like brothers than anything else, and have an awesome fucking dog. Add in ink–which I know a lot of women love–and I *should* be the perfect fucking catch.

Hell, I used to wake up and enjoy my reflection.

When I lost my eye, I lost more than confidence; I lost myself. I thought I'd find a new me–Sammy and the guys probably thought I would, too. But the more time passed, the further hope drifted. And the longer I went without any good experiences with women and dating, the more the tide dragged my faith out to sea. Without hope and faith, it's hard to become a new person.

One year turned to two, and here we are, *eight years later*.

I haven't been a fucking nun, and it's not to say that I haven't been around.

I've fucked. I've dated.

But I haven't been *in love*.

I haven't met someone who can't live without me, or me for her. I've been the scratch to an itch. Orgasms, bad boy fix, slumming–I've been plenty of things for women in the last eight years.

But I've never been *the one*.

The one they can't live without. The one they think about all the time and make playlists for. The one they show off on their Instagram stories and tell their mothers about. The one that makes them scribble their first name with my last name all over their grocery list or wherever the fuck.

I'm not *the one*.

Because I'm the storied looking guy with a fucking eye patch.

Locking my phone, I flip the sheets back and hop out.

"Come on, man, let's go," I say to my dog, because yep, I'm the guy that has a dog he treats as a personal therapist.

Even though I have an actual therapist, apparently, I've got enough issues to require help beyond the human race. Great.

Stoner huffs out a breath, blinking up lazily at me from his spot on my bed. I pat his head, scratch him behind the ears a little, then deliver the four words that get his lazy ass on his feet every fucking time.

"It's time to eat."

He scrambles to his feet like a drunk man being scared awake, and it makes me smile. It always does. That's why Sammy got him for me after I lost my eye. It's impossible not to smile when you own a fucking dog. Dogs are the best.

"I thought that would do it, you lazy fuck."

The sound of his nails tip-tapping down the hallway behind me provides the emotional boost I need to shake off Jamie and his girl. What kind of asshole am I that someone else's happiness makes me feel bad? "I am happy for the guy," I tell Stoner, who is lying at my feet in the kitchen as I measure out his meds.

Stoner has anxiety. Probably why Sammy chose him all those years ago—she figured *it takes one to know one* is as good of a reason to adopt a pet as any. I lower the bowl after mixing in the pet-friendly CBD that I use for Stoner's anxiety.

Sammy and I named him Stoner because all the guy does—now that he's on a perfect dose of meds—is snack, beg for snacks, absorb all the scratches and attention, and sleep.

He's also mastered eating while lying down.

I leave him to eat his breakfast and change clothes back in my room while the coffee I set last night begins to brew. Over a white stringer, I throw on a black hoodie and black joggers, pull a beanie down over my mess of hair, and toe into some kicks.

My friends have had girlfriends off and on since I can remember. It's never really made me bitter or jealous, and it certainly never turned me into a self-absorbed asshole who turns someone else's happiness into my own sadness. Before that night and after that night–that's not who I am.

Or at least I didn't think it was who I was.

But as I shake two scoops of protein into my blender bottle full of water, I'm bitterly thinking of Jamie.

Then as I put Stoner's sweater on–it's the weighted blanket for dogs–I think of Jamie and his girlfriend probably adopting a dog together. "Real fucking cute," I mutter to Stoner like a fucking psycho because the poor dog has no clue he's punched the clock for the day as my emotional support animal. "I have you, Stone-Zone. I don't need to adopt a dog with anyone."

A loose piece of kibble falls from his lip onto the floor, then he lies his head on top of it, huffing out an exhausted sigh. Stoner is a black pit bull-labrador mix, making him the fucking perfect blend of *don't fuck with the muscled dude with the tough-ass dog* and *who wants a wittle chin scritch, who does, you do.* You know?

After loading up my bag for the day, the noise of the keys being plucked sends Stoner into one of the very few bursts of excitement he has. His entire ass shakes as his tail wags with excitement.

He uses his huge dome to nudge open the back door, and he whines impatiently as I lock up. By the time I'm opening the door for him, he's already begun rearing up on his hind legs in anticipation of getting in.

Stray

Riding in the truck seems to be advantageous to both of us—our anxiety seems to go right out the lowered windows. By the time we reach Paradise, Jamie and his girlfriend are still on my mind... just further back. I don't feel as fucking butthurt as I did this morning either, and I credit that to Stoner and fresh air.

Stoner wanders around behind me as I unlock fire exits, flip on lights, start the music, and turn on the neon Paradise sign hanging in the door. The pink, orange, and yellow lights flare against the glass, dropping a small bit of color onto the concrete outside.

Taking a seat behind the entry desk, I shake the mouse to wake up the computer. Jamie–Jamie, who I don't even really care about–pops into my head again.

Followed by my date last week.

I could keep going on dates. Not give up like Sammy said. After all, it's been this long–it's only going to get more difficult. I'm so tired of feeling dejected and nervous around women who aren't related to me.

Maybe I'm thinking of this the wrong way. I mean, fuck, it couldn't hurt to change my viewpoint because waking up pissed off at a guy I barely know all because he's thriving? That is *not* who I wanna be.

Jamie isn't suave–I've been around the guy plenty to know that isn't it. He isn't rich, either–that much we've established. He isn't bigger than me; he isn't more successful.

I unscrew the lid on my canning jar, the smell of peanut butter and chocolate overnight oats making my mouth water. It took me a while to get used to eating at just after four in the morning, but now if I don't eat, I'm a real asshole. The last thing I need is more reasons to be bitter, so I don't skip meals–for everyone's safety. The first spoonful goes down easy and brings a little more life to my tired brain.

Jamie is, and always has been, one thing that hadn't occurred to me until now. Confident. I know his station in life, but anyone else meeting the dude for the first time would probably think he was some entrepreneur of sorts. He talks to everyone easily, smiles, laughs, shakes hands, and doesn't put up a show or front. He's got no ego.

Losing my eye made me the opposite.

I lost confidence but pretended to have more–as a shield to protect my very fucking fragile ego. Stoic and silent became my identity–as a way to fend off any curious people. I never wanted to talk about my eye or that night, so I made myself utterly unapproachable.

And it worked.

But it also led me down this really fucking shitty path of being single still.

I'm not the kind of guy who can just flip a switch. Van and Mally–maybe because of their job or some shit–can just make up their minds about things and move the hell on. Call me immature. Even knowing I need to be confident that I am a fucking catch, the whole fake it til you make it thing just isn't my jam.

I need a baby step.

The oatmeal is finished by the time my crew arrives, looking sleep-deprived themselves.

"Mally, Van, good morning, my dudes." I tip my head at them before tipping my jug of water back, taking down my first set of supplements.

"We'll see if it's good," Van gruffs, smacking his palm to

the center of Mally's chest. "This guy is kind of being a little bitch this morning."

Mally yanks his shoulder back dramatically, his hand going to his collarbone. The man needs a pearl necklace to go with his attitude, seriously. "I'm not being a bitch, Van," he says, holding the last syllable a little longer... again, for dramatic purposes. "I hold people to a certain standard, and when they don't live up to that standard, rightfully, I am upset."

Van rolls his eyes.

Screwing the lid back on my water, I get to my feet and walk with them to the free weight room. "Anyone gonna tell me what mini-drama already took place because honestly, I can't imagine how someone could've already hurt your feelings at four-thirty."

"Ho!" Mally stops in his tracks, causing me to bump my chest into his back. "I didn't get my *feelings hurt*," he clarifies, his blue eyes looking beady already. How does a man have beady eye energy this early? Fucking seriously?

"I'm disappointed," he adds, and though Van is standing behind me, I swear I can hear his eyes roll.

"What happened?" I ask because asking is far less dangerous than not asking, then getting the passive-aggressive cold-shoulder because *"no one even cares I'm mad."* That'd be Mally for you.

Mally adjusts the velcro strap at his wrist, making sure his gloves are secure. Helping him prepare for his set, he sets two seventy-pound dumbbells at Van's feet. Monday means we're working bi's and tri's–it is our ritual for Van to start the first set.

Not just professional athletes are superstitious. When Van starts, we get the best pump, so he always goes first.

"I was getting gas on the way here—"

Van nods to us in the mirror. "There's your problem. Gotta get a Tesla. Electric is better for the Earth, bro."

Mally lets his shoulders droop—yep, you guessed it—dramatically. "Don't act like you care about the Earth. You like it because it goes top speed in like, one second."

My eyes bounce between them as they argue why Van bought an electric car. I'm pretty sure I've heard them bicker about every single topic out there... At least twice.

"Get back to the story; I'd like to get a fucking pump before a bunch of people get here."

Van groans loudly as he begins single-arm isolated bicep curls. Mally turns to me, dragging the hem of his tank along his upper lip. Shoving a tan hand through his beachy hair, he lets loose a sigh so heavy that an onlooker would think the man is disappointed in all of humanity.

"When I paid for my gas, I said *thank you, I hope you have a great day.*"

I roll my bottom lip through my teeth. I can already tell this event is going to be a total non-event and another instance of Malibu being too damn sensitive.

"Okay," I draw out, waiting for the conclusion. Van's groan breaks up the silence.

"The guy didn't say it back. That's all," he says, taking the words from Malibu's mouth. Mally turns to face Van, his blue eyes wide and his hand, again at his collarbone.

"Excuse me, is this your story to tell?" he snarks, using both hands to shove back the unruly blonde hair from his already glistening face.

Stray

"It's not a story, dude. The guy didn't say it back, he didn't say you're welcome, and that got your panties in a twist."

"I think it's a bunch," I correct Van as he lowers the dumbbells to the ground, ending his set.

"Panties in a twist," Van tests, see-sawing his head. "Panties in a bunch," he tests the alternative. "Yeah, I think you're right." Twisting his neck to face Malibu, who is on deck for his set, he says, "you got your panties in a bunch because the gas station attendant didn't tell you to have a good day, too. There, now he knows, and we can move the fuck on to something better."

Mally straddles the bench and grabs his weights, the same that Van used. He's almost as strong but won't admit he'd be better suited ten pounds less. They are in an unending dick measuring contest.

"Well, it's not like you guys have anything else to talk about," Mally grits as he lowers the weights on his first rep.

Working my fingers into my tricep, I clear my throat and let my eyes fall to the front door, which I can see from here.

"I'm thinking of hiring a woman to work here."

Malibu struggles through his rep–though I don't know how much of that is because of my news or because the weight is too much.

"Yeah?" Van asks, his voice faltering from heavy breaths as he does preacher curls on a machine near us.

I nod. "I want to invest in this place. It's... the only thing I'll have when I die. So I figure I'll hire a woman and go after some women clientele."

Van bypasses my depressing comment because that is the way he operates with us. And I have to be honest: I'm glad he ignores the dark shit most of the time. Because it does force me to move on with the conversation, and he never makes me talk about the uncomfortable shit like Mally does. Our only married friend in the group, Batman doesn't always make it to morning lift sessions because of his kids. He'd bypass the comment if he were here, too, but probably because dark and depressing doesn't register for him. The dude loves his fucking life, therefore, is wearing a permanent pair of rose-colored glasses.

Mally grunts as he rises, sweat now dripping freely from his face. Though it's just the three of us in Paradise, it doesn't stop him from tearing his tank over his head and eyeing himself in the mirror.

The man loves to be topless more than a Playboy fucking bunny, I swear.

"You gonna hire a hunny so you can hit on her?" he asks, flexing his bicep in the mirror, studying it like it's the damn Mona Lisa.

"It looks the same as it did ten minutes ago," Van deadpans, causing Mally to flip him the middle finger.

"Maybe if I'm just... more comfortable around women, then dating won't suck so much." *There.* I fucking said it. Admitted a cringe-worthy thing to the boys.

It's not that they aren't here for the deep shit—they are. Hell, Malibu would probably cry like a proud mother if I confided in him.

It's me.

Like everything else wrong in my life, it all traces back to me.

If my life was one of those big ass whiteboards on the wall like they have on those crime shows where they're trying to figure out who killed someone, all the yarn would lead back to me. I am the root of all of my issues, me and my one fucking eye.

Stoner strolls past, his focus on his dog bed on the other side of the gym. It's next to the door, so he's guaranteed attention from the boys on their way out. Just the way that stoned son-of-a-bitch likes it.

"Bro," Mally is panting at my side after jogging to Stoner for a quick *good boy*, his big orange-looking mitt curled around my shoulder. "That's a fucking good idea." He narrows his blue eyes on me, and even though I'm not hiding anything, his expression makes me feel like I'm about to be exposed. "Was this Sammy's idea?"

Not sure why I sigh a bit with relief. "No. I wanna invest in this place. Reach a new demographic. We hardly have any women here." I grab a set of weights from the rack in front of him, Mally still gripping me. He was shorted his pleasant emotional exchange at the gas station this morning, so apparently, I'm his new target.

Starting my own set of curls, I find his eyes in the mirror. "I'd never date anyone who works here. And I'm not hiring some woman so I can fucking prey on her. But it won't hurt to be around more women." I do a couple of reps while he watches me silently. "It's not the women, Mally. It's not that every woman I've dated in eight years is flawed. Life can be a bitch, but it's not pure coincidences."

It only lasts a moment–just a quick flash over his features–but when I see the sad lilt to his lips and the subtle droop of his face down to his shoulder, I remember why I don't talk about how I feel.

Because the pity makes me feel like a massively self-indulgent asshole.

Mally's eyes go to Van's, and they share a conversation with just a look. Before I can call them on what secret shit they have brewing, the bell tied to the front door jingles, and all of us look.

I'm not a big believer in fate. I'm not like rubbing crystals and checking my fucking horoscope. That's the shit I leave to my sister.

But if Jamie walking in at that precise moment wasn't fate or a sign from God or some shit—well, that's *one hell of a coincidence*. With sleepy eyes and fucked up hair, he nods to acknowledge the eyes on him and heads straight to the squat rack, dropping his jug to the floor with a resounding thud. He drops his keys and phone next to it, and the movement illuminates the screen, a photo of the beautiful blonde on the screen.

Yeah, I'm hiring someone to work at Paradise. I need to get comfortable or confident or *whateverthefuck*.

Jamie with the red hair who lives with his mother is a great guy but hell no if I'm going to be jealous of him.

Two hours later, after the boys and I finish our pump, I call Sammy to run things by her. I don't have to, obviously, but the truth is—knowing she approves of shit gives me the confidence to do it.

She's a nurse at the local hospital, but she took today off since she's been working so much lately. Her plans? Netflix and sleep, and not necessarily in that order.

"I hope this is an emergency," she answers through a yawn. "I mean, I don't hope it is, but I hope you aren't interrupting me to ask if I want to work out or some shit."

"What if I don't want to ask you to work out, but it's also not an emergency?" I hedge, giving her a minute to wake up. The grogginess is thick in her voice.

"What do you want then?"

I woke her up; I'm not gonna beat around the bush, or she'll set the bush on fire. "I want to hire a woman to work at Paradise. To expand the clientele base."

"To expand the clientele base," she repeats, dragging it out slowly enough that it makes me nervous. Between her and Malibu, I feel like I'm caught lying to Mom and Dad.

Thank God our parents moved to Hawaii for their golden years, and we only see them twice annually. I couldn't have two more sets of eyes on me, seeing through my bull.

"And," I add as sweat breaks out on the back of my neck. "I think I need to work on my casual comfort level around women that aren't you, Mom, and like, Robin," I say, tossing in Batman's wife for good measure. I'm not around her all that much because she's a busy ass lawyer with two kids—three if you count Batman (and yes, that's how he got his nickname because when you meet a woman named Robin and you roll with a crew obsessed with nicknames, you *one-hundred-percent* do not miss the opportunity to be Batman). Still, birthday parties and random dinners put us in the same place a few times a year, and since I've known her so long, I'm comfortable.

She doesn't even pause. "That's a good idea, Brian," her voice is soft and easy, this time not from sleep.

We leave it there, but with her blessing, I know I'm finally doing something good. It may not be a damn slingshot into a relationship, but at least I'm headed that way. Getting used to being around women and getting over them staring at my eye for a couple of days... will be hard, but it's what I need.

After we hang up, I draft an online ad. I thought I'd get hung up on the wording, but it comes easy.

She has to be a trainer if she's going to work here, so I jot that down. She has to do one-on-one training because I don't have group classes here, so I write that, too. And Paradise is for lifters. The women who come here lift heavy, too, so this woman needs to be able to handle heavy. I add that. Not much beyond that, so I end it there and end up with this:

SEEKING A FEMALE PERSONAL TRAINER FOR INDIVIDUAL HEAVY SESSIONS.
IF QUALIFIED AND INTERESTED, CALL BRAN 555-6792.

Using an online job search portal, I upload my employer information, followed by my ad, and hit post.

Here goes nothing.

4

Elsie

It's irresponsible. It's stupid. It's unlike me.

"Slow shift?" Chris, one of the four employees of Globo-Fitness that works the front desk, asks over the quiet vacuum hum coming from the cardio room. Bringing my gaze from the stack of papers I've been organizing over to him, our eyes meet.

He smiles, and that tingle of delight that I should feel when being smiled at by Chris? It's absent. Like it always is.

I wiggle my palm to indicate the day has just been so-so. Though gyms like these are a dime a dozen–hell, we have five just like Globo-Fitness in a ten-mile radius of our small town alone–we're somehow always pretty busy. Looking good is always important. A lot of people claim they work

Daisy Jane

out just to feel good, but if that were the case, these walls wouldn't be lined with floor-to-ceiling mirrors.

"Kinda. Busier this morning but kinda slow midday." I comb my palm over the desk, sending all the eraser shavings to the floor. After replacing the paper in the printing tray, wiping down my phone, computer keyboard, and mouse with a Clorox wipe, I turn to find Chris has been lingering behind me the entire time.

It shouldn't make me uncomfortable because Chris is harmless. But still. The unmistakable feeling that I'm going to be asked about something I don't want to be is there, bubbling in my belly. Smiling a fake and probably horrendous looking partial smile, I step around him slowly to get to where my purse is stashed in a cubby below the half-moon-shaped desk.

"You going to the mixer tonight?"

There it is. The *thing* I didn't want to be asked.

I guess it's better than *"will you go to the mixer with me?"* but it's still not good. Because I've managed to slip and slide under the radar for so long, and it's been so nice. If no one can corner you and ask you, then no one expects for you to be there. At least not a realistically.

But now, Chris has asked me.

A small group of sweaty, laughing twenty-somethings slip out the front past us. I glance at them, a fake smile on my face, ready to say *thanks for working out at Globo-Fitness, have a great day,* but they're way too cool to talk to the front desk girl, so they ignore me. Turning back to Chris, I expect to see his eyes straying to the parking lot to follow those round buns stuffed into Lululemon a size too small.

Instead, I find his eyes haven't left mine. And if they

have, I can't tell because he's staring at me like he wants to eat me alive, but in a sexy Vampire way. The thing is, though, I watched *Interview with a Vampire* on cable TV a few years ago, and I can safely say I don't want to be eaten alive. Eaten, yes, but eaten alive? No.

I smile awkwardly, but his lips remain tilted up in a slightly devious grin.

"Um, I actually am. My mom's watching Effie for a few extra hours." I smile again, thinking of my daughter and what a sweet soul she is. It hasn't been easy for her watching her Grandma Elaine grow confused, scared, and sometimes angry. But she's handling it like a champ—just like she always does. "Gotta take advantage of that guilt-free mom time," I add, not wanting Chris to initiate any conversation about my life.

The thing is when you're a single mom—no matter who you live with and what kind of situation got you in the position you're in—people are ready to dispense life advice they've decided you absolutely need.

And four years into that? I'm pretty sick of it. And though Chris has never really tried to do that, I admit, my defenses are up.

"Well, I'm glad you're going," he smiles after saying it, giving me a small dip of his head before stepping around me to get to the desk. He slides into the chair, tugs a paperback from under a stack of folders, and spreads it open.

He's reading and I spent my eight hours earning my money, doing stuff that I'm not even sure is my job duty. But I can't risk losing this gig. Not because it's my lifelong dream to say hello and goodbye to people that could give two shits less about me, but because of the insurance.

My mom needs this insurance for her meds. She isn't getting everything she needs, but her meds are covered, and we aren't broke from out-of-pocket pharmacy trips anymore–that's the most important part.

After sliding my purse strap over my shoulder, I lift my palm in an easy goodbye as I walk toward the doors.

"Looking forward to seeing you tonight," Chris says as I pass him on the other side of the desk. My eyes comb over the bright red letters of his paperback. He's reading a thriller of some sort, and I have to admit, I like that he's reading. The other two girls that alternate front desk with us are usually glued to their phones, watching Instagram reels or trying to perfect the latest trending dance on TikTok.

Maybe I'd care about that shit if I wasn't grown up. Having a kid when you're still almost a kid forces you to mature because when it comes between going out with friends or being home for your kid, there really isn't a choice.

She may have been an accident, but Effie is the greatest part of my life. My mom, too. She raised me on her own and loves me with every fiber of her being–and she loves Effie the exact same way. It's funny how you can never run out of love.

I don't have any regrets about what's happened, and I certainly don't wish it was any different–but my life's complexities make it hard to connect to females my age. Our priorities are so different.

Tonight, though, I can be like everybody else and show up at a restaurant, sip drinks and laugh. There doesn't need to be any distinction between ages or whether or not we're parents. Tonight is about drinking with coworkers and having a good time.

And I need that.

* * *

"How long will you be there?" Effie asks as she strokes her fingers through my hair from her spot on the bathroom counter. I'm brushing my teeth–the last thing I do before I go somewhere—and she's watching. Her little fingers connect with my cheek as she sifts her hand through the hair around my face.

"Your hair looks pretty, mama," she says, and I kiss the tip of her nose in thanks as I drop my toothbrush back into the holder.

"Thank you, Effie baby," I reply, hoisting her up to my hip. I carry her into the bedroom and catch our reflection in the closet mirror. Thick blonde curls, messy and chaotic, and a set of piercing blue eyes. She's my dead ringer, and I am a dead ringer for my mom. I always tease Elaine that our DNA is strong because my dad had tan skin, dark eyes, and caramel hair that didn't get passed down, even a little. "I'll be home after you're in bed. But I'll still sneak in and give you a kiss."

She flops on the bed after I lower her to her feet and yanks my phone from the pillow it was on. "Can I play?" she asks, and I tip my head while pursing my lips.

"You know I don't like you using cell phones, Effie."

She grins, her baby toothed-smile so adorable that even if I wanted to bust her for not following the rules, she's too stinkin' cute. "Sorry, mama," she concedes, the blue of her eyes shining brightly along with her grin. Wrapping a tendril of her hair around my finger, I give a gentle tug and watch it spring back.

"It's okay. Now, which shirt should I wear?" I ask her, holding up a black and white checkered flannel with one hand, a long-sleeved black t-shirt with the other.

I wouldn't say my style is grunge because in all reality, I don't have a style. Leggings and shirt with boots. That's what I wear, and it definitely feels like more of a uniform than a stylistic choice.

She wrinkles her nose, making her freckles more visible. I love her freckles. Peppered generously over the bridge of her nose and along her full cheeks, it's another absolutely fucking adorable thing about my daughter.

"Yuck," she says, her eyes crawling over the plaid shirt before bouncing to the long sleeve tee quickly. "They're both boyish."

"Boyish?" I ask, cocking a brow. "Girls can wear anything they want, and so can boys."

She stuffs a tiny fist under her chin to hold up her head as she narrows her eyes at the open closet behind me. She may be four, but she looks so grown up, and debating my outfit with her doesn't help. "I think you should wear the pink shirt," she says, using her free hand to wiggle a finger at the shirt in question.

I don't turn around because I know exactly which shirt she's talking about. The tags are still on it, even. My mom had gotten that shirt for me two years ago, right when her mind started going a little haywire. Black has always been my preferred color–for everything. So when I opened a neon pink v-neck t-shirt on my birthday, I was honestly concerned.

Elaine Francis does not buy things unless she is *certain*

they will get use because use is value, and value is getting the most out of your money. A single mom her whole life, the woman knows how to make money stretch. A trait I'd proudly learned from her and probably the only reason why our household—with one underwhelming income and one income consisting of disability checks—is thriving and not struggling. Honest to God, I couldn't take being broke on top of the other continually unfolding stresses.

But that's when I knew all the things I'd been ignoring—losing her keys, forgetting to turn the stove off, her inability to remember which mailbox was ours—it wasn't *nothing*. In fact, it was something. A big fucking something. And the pink shirt was the moment I realized we had a problem.

"How about I wear the black one but wear pink lipstick?" I offer, and the mention of lipstick has her forgetting all about my drab wardrobe.

"Can I wear some? Pretty please, mama? I won't put it in the washer, I swear."

Yeah, we'd definitely had that happen a time or two. With my black leggings and boots already on, I feed my arms through the long-sleeved shirt and tug it down over my cami. Taking Effie to the bathroom with me, I trace her lips with bright pink lipstick before applying some to my own, fully intending to wipe it off before going to the mixer. Loud lipstick is not me.

Mom is having a good day—I can tell by the way I was greeted when I came home from work earlier—so I feel good about going. On days when she struggles, I call in sick or switch shifts. Karina, my manager at Globo-Fitness, has always been really understanding. The franchise owner extended my insurance plan to my mother because family and whole-body health are so important to him, so I don't know if Karina understands because that's her, or that's the company. Either way, I'm not there just for the insurance but for the understanding and flexibility, too.

I kiss them both goodbye and drive fifteen minutes across town to a small bar-style restaurant called Lines. There used to be train tracks running through the parking lot (also referred to as train *lines*)–that's how long the restaurant has been around. But since the town has grown over the last ten years, the lines have been covered, and the place's name makes much less sense.

But they have good burgers and cold beer with long tables–big enough to fit the entire staff of Globo-Fitness. When I walk in, I hear our group in the back of the restaurant right away. Eyeing the conductor's hat pinned to the wall and momentarily getting transfixed by the model train that chugs along on an elevated track near the ceiling, I smirk to myself about how kitschy this place really is. Effie would love it, but you have to be eighteen to even get in. Even at dinner time.

"Elsie!" a sea of voices cheer my name as I shimmy my way between chair backs and the wall. I slide into the first available seat at our table, which happens to be next to Lacey, a successful and beautiful personal trainer. The seat next to me is open, and I'm relieved to see Chris is already sitting at the other end of the table.

"Got away from the kid tonight, huh?" Lacey asks as soon as I give my drink order to the promptly attentive waitress.

She doesn't mean it negatively, so I don't take it that way. "Yeah, and I kinda need it."

She laughs at that, exposing her bleached and straightened teeth. I vaguely remember seeing her when I first started–though when you start any job, the first few times you meet everyone is kind of fuzzy. At least for me. Let's just say she's had a fucking glow up.

She slides a shot glass at me. It almost looks empty because it's so full, the alcohol aligning perfectly with the top of the glass. "Vodka," she says, nodding toward the tiny glass of trouble.

I toss it back because tonight is about having fun and not worrying about mom, not thinking about the things Jake said to me last week, not trying to solve the future. Tonight is about... *tonight*. Nothing serious.

* * *

Two hours later, I'm drunk. Not buzzed, not tipsy, not "feeling good," but utterly, completely, totally *shitfaced*.

It's irresponsible. It's stupid. It's unlike me.

And it's fucking fun. Because I never cut loose like this. There isn't much opportunity.

"So he says, listen, Elsie, you're a dope chick–"

Lacey sucks in a sharp breath, wincing at my words like they physically wounded her. "Dope chick," she repeats, her nose scrunching up like the words disgust her or that they smell bitter. They are bitter. Or maybe I'm just bitter.

"Oh, just wait," I say, blinking in what feels like unison but definitely isn't; part of Lacey misaligns before realigning as my other eye finally opens. Yeah, I've had too many shots. "That's not even the best part."

"Oh girl," Lacey says, sliding a glass of water into my hand. "Let me hear it."

I'd worn my tangle of curls up in a messy bun tonight but at some point between shot number three and shot number six; it'd come down. Exhaling heartily to blow hair off my face, I realize I'm just blowing straight into Lacey's face by the way she recesses away from me, blinking. That and my hair stays put.

"Okay, so what happened with you and Jake?"

Jake. That's what we're talking about. Okay. Yes. Focus.

I blink again, working hard to make sure my eyes are in it together this time. I think it goes better, but the extra vodka is setting in, and vision is becoming tricky.

"He said to me, I like you so much, girl, but you got too much serious shit in your life." Even through the numbing burn of alcohol, I feel the pain of his admission all over again.

My life is too much for men my age. My life is too much for someone to commit to.

"It's a lot," I continue before Lacey has a chance to respond. I don't even meet her eyes because I don't want to see pity in them, and again, trying to focus on something right now may cause me to puke. "My life. I live with my mom and my daughter. And I want to meet someone. I want to fall in love, you know, like Bridget Jones."

Lacey laughs. "I don't think Bridget Jones was all that happy. I mean, she was off and on with Mr. Darcy until the end."

"I never saw the last one," I admit, "because I do not support Hugh Grant not being part of it."

She nods. "It sucked."

"Okay, so I want my Chandler. I want to find my...." I

pause, trying to think of the male half of any great couple known for a love so paramount that it's part of pop culture. And somehow, the only name I can come up with is "I want my fucking Derek Shepherd, you know?"

Lacey laughs again, and it's then that I risk the chance to meet her gaze. It's moving like I thought it would be, so I turn my eyes back down to my full glass of water. I need to drink it, but like every drunk person on the face of the earth, I'm not doing anything I need to do so that I won't feel like death warmed over tomorrow.

"I don't think you want your Derek Shepherd," she says with a wild laugh, the kind that comes with alcohol and easy conversation. "He died, remember?"

"Oh shit," I say, pressing my fingers to my lips which are, apparently, numb. "I forgot they killed off McDreamy."

She drags a finger across her throat. "So dead."

"Well," I start again, out of options but knowing she gets the point. "I want my soulmate. But I realized when Jake dumped me that I may be too much. I may have too much baggage for that." Finally, I sip the water and have enough energy to raise my arms and stuff my frizzy curls into a bun, looping an elastic around the mess. Tomorrow's problem: detangling that shit.

"And I don't want to sound like I don't like my life. I love my life. I love Effie. And I love my mom; she's literally done everything for me. But I'm seeing now that... my life... is expensive."

Lacey rests her hand on top of mine, and I look up at her. She's still kind of floating around, but I manage a smile. "You mean, it comes at a cost."

I snap and point. "Yes, that."

She clears her throat, and I hear a quiet exchange of words between her and the waitress. A minute later, the woman comes back with some coffee. Lacey takes my hand and wraps it around the mug.

"You sip; I'll talk."

And because I'm drunk and Lacey's always been cool, I do it. And it feels good having someone else hand me the drink. To have someone else take care of me. Even in the smallest of ways, it feels good.

I sip the coffee, hating how bitter it tastes but loving how the smell is even somewhat sobering.

"I heard what you said, all that stuff about your life." Lacey tucks a piece of bleached hair behind her ear, and I realize even her hair is different now. She looks phenomenal, and it's not just being a trainer. Everything about her has improved, starting with her attitude. When I first met her, she was quiet and reserved but not in an introverted kind of way. In an unhappy way. Now she bubbles over at the surface. And her looks? She was a knockout before. But now she's a *polished* knockout.

"You're afraid you won't be able to find a guy... or a man... who wants your life. Who wants to take on everything that is Elsie Francis."

I nod, sip the coffee, then sip the water, and ignore acid churning in my gut from all the booze and greasy fries. "Yes," I say in the simplest of terms because the booze is quickly making the transition from fun drunk to tired drunk.

"Maybe you're looking for the wrong thing. Maybe looking for a man who will open his arms to your life isn't where your focus should be."

Thoroughly confused and moderately concerned I'm

about to be roped into some weird pyramid scheme where I'm propositioned to sell vitamin powders and supplement pills; I sit back and stay quiet. The booze belly makes that easy, too.

She laughs. "Stay with me."

"Okay," I reply, then finish my water.

"What if instead of looking for a guy who will make you feel like he's doing some fucking charity work to love your life, you start seeing men that make you feel powerful. That make you feel in control and strong."

I blink. "I mean..." What is she saying? Even if I was sober, I don't think the sub-text is in English because I'm not getting it. She sees that in my face and leans forward, the ends of her hair dragging through the ring of water left by my glass.

"You choose when you want to see him, you have the power, and you leave knowing he's thinking about you, and it isn't the other way around. He wants you. He is at your beck and call."

"I want to be partners, though," I say because I do want that. I want equality in my forever relationship. I'm not looking to be the woman whose husband's balls are in her hand. I mean, not unless we're in the bedroom.

She pats the top of my hand with hers. "The power you'll feel when you're with a man that gives himself over to you completely will give you the confidence to find the right guy. The guy that wants you and your family and doesn't make you feel like you're too much."

She leans back, away from me, and I'm still confused. "You're not too much, Elsie. *They're not enough.*"

"I never thought of it that way."

"I know," she adds, dipping her chin emphatically. "I can see that. You need to feel how powerful you are and stop letting men make you feel bad about your life."

"Yeah," I say, her last two thoughts settling with power into my brain. She's right. I might be a lot, but maybe I just need to find a man who can handle a lot rather than tell me I'm too much. "I want to feel powerful," I admit, dropping my voice to a private tone. Because even though I'm still not quite sure what we're talking about, part of me knows it's not for other ears.

"Come to my house Thursday after work. Can you swing that?"

I nod, knowing that I have the early shift Thursday and that Mom and Effie have plans to see a late matinee, giving me two hours to make it happen. Even though I'm drunk, I'm also a mom, so I remember those details when agreeing to it.

"Good," she smiles wide with a wink. "Because I really think if you harnessed your power as a female, you'd get some confidence back that Jake clearly took. And with that confidence, I think you'll find everything you're looking for. Men and otherwise."

Well shit. That's quite a thought for her to have. I've never had anyone talk me up or tell me I can do something or be anything outside of mom. But Lacey is, and she's serious about what she's saying. So I agree to meet up with her after work Thursday.

I only hope this isn't a damn pyramid scheme.

5

Bran

I work out until it's very, very hard to feel.

"Dude, all these chicks want to work *here?*" Mally asks, thumbing through the stack of printed responses to my ad. Hastily, I snatch them from his hands because why does this fucking guy need to eat while holding other people's shit?

"Don't get your grubby chocolate donut fingers on my shit, and could you be more cliche?" I ask, my eyes panning down over his crisply pressed blue uniform. Van, who is standing next to him also in full blues, shakes his head.

"He gets food on everything; you know that," Van scoffs, setting down a paper cup of coffee in front of me.

They get donuts and coffee more often than I would if I were a cop. I give them a hard time about it; I have no problem picking low-hanging fruit; jokes about cops and donuts are easy, sure, but damn it, are they fun. Even with the teasing, when they get donuts, they roll through and drop some off to me, and a coffee.

"Seriously though, this is a stack of chicks that want to work at Paradise?" Mally shoves the last of his donut in his mouth and licks the tips of his fingers, thoroughly horrifying both Van and I. Rubbing his probably-sticky hands together, he groans. "I cannot wait for chicks to be here."

Van rolls his eyes. "He's not gonna hire all of them, dipshit."

I rest my hand on the stack of responses. "There's only like, five in here that I'd seriously interview anyway."

"What?" Mally's face drops, his eyebrows giving away his surprise. "You're not bringing more of 'em in?"

I fold my arms across my chest. "Let me get this straight. You envisioned me bringing in one hundred women who are all–if I'm getting this right–fucking knockouts wearing skimpy gym wear," I say slowly, as Malibu nods along with my words. "And then I was going to invite you here, and together we were going to interview them," I use finger quotes around the word interview because I have no clue what the actual fuck he expected.

"I mean, yeah, pretty much."

Van rolls his eyes again, and with the two of them being beat partners, I'd be willing to bet he rolls his eyes a lot. Nudging his glasses up his nose, he says, "Malibu, you're an idiot. This is his place; he doesn't need you to sit in on interviews creeping out all the women."

Malibu shoves a hand through his hair, turning his bright blue eyes to me. "I wouldn't creep them out. I'd impress them." With his fist balled tightly, he flexes his bicep, tightening the navy blue sleeve around his muscle. "See? *Thanks, Paradise.*"

I roll my eye at that. "I don't know how you do it all day, man," I say to Van.

He licks his hand and slaps it against Mally's bicep, connecting with a loud spank. Mally jerks back and holds his arm.

"Dude, not cool. That fucking hurt."

Van turns to me, extending an arm out in the direction of his partner. "See? He's weak. You wouldn't want some weak punk being the poster child of this place. If anything, you'd want me here showing people what hard work looks like."

Behind them, a client comes in through the double doors and only barely gives us a nod. His headphones are on, his jug of water hanging from his hands–the man is ready.

"Alright, actual people are starting to come in, so thanks for the coffee and the show, but you guys need to get the fuck outta here so I can call some of these potentials."

"I'm concerned that you only found a few in that whole stack," Mally adds before dropping his sunglasses down over his eyes.

"I'm concerned that you are both public servants, and I witnessed both of you licking your hands." I flick my eye between the two of them. "That's nasty shit."

"Sorry, DAD," Mally says flippantly as I usher them closer to the door. Once they're on the sidewalk, I thank them for my coffee and donuts and watch their cruiser roll out into traffic, then disappear.

Returning to the desk, I opened the drawer where I'd stashed away the applicants I actually wanted to interview. I love my brothers, but I knew they'd be in here nosing around like always. When we were in high school, they were at my house playing *Grand Theft Auto* when out of nowhere, Malibu started screaming and laughing. When Van, Batman, and I turned around, we saw that Mally had been going through my nightstand and found my spank bank material. I can't remember for sure, but I think it was a women's clothes catalog opened up to the bra page. It was then I knew, even as a teen that if I didn't want them to know something, I'd have to seriously hide it.

Taking a deep breath, I slide my phone from my pocket and enter the first number on the top application. An hour later, I have three interviews set up for tomorrow and two voicemails left for the other candidates.

Even if I hire someone that I don't bond with or grow close to, I'm still growing Paradise, and no matter what happens in my life, investing in my business and myself is always a smart move.

* * *

THE FOLLOWING MORNING, four hours after Paradise opened, I have my first interview scheduled. The Personal Trainer for Individual Heavy Lifting Sessions candidate is named Sara, and she arrives over ten minutes late.

Not a good start.

I selected her for an interview because she has a certification from the National Academy of Sports Medicine and is currently a group fitness instructor at another gym in another town.

She looks fit, but even I know there's more to physically

being in good shape to be a personal trainer. You have to be relatable, personable, kind, and patient.

The way Sara crosses and uncrosses her legs impatiently as I sift through her CV tells me she is not a good fit. But I don't even have to really make that choice because her insensitivity makes it for her.

As I look up at her, CV still in my hands, I open my mouth to speak, but she cuts me off. Talking over someone isn't the greatest thing to do in an interview because it delivers an air of self-importance as well as demonstrates someone's inability to listen. But it's not the actual interruption that seals her fate. It's what she says when she interrupts.

"I'm sorry–before we like, get going here into the thick of it, I have to ask. Where am I supposed to look?" She swivels her head on her neck as if she's looking around me, and it's confusing.

"What do you mean?" Curiously, I glance behind me at the wall in my office–just a big mirrored wall with nothing else on it. So I have no idea what she's talking about.

"You," she laughs at me having turned around, like the idea that there is something worse to stare at in this office is funny to her. Something worse than me existing is comical to her. "Do I look at the patch and your eye or just the good eye?"

"Oh," I say, because what in the actual fuck? Do people seriously think it's okay to talk to other people this way? To disabled people? I don't consider myself disabled. I've said it before, and I'll say it again. But still, this is some fucked up treatment. Does she ask people in wheelchairs if she should ignore their legs?

"Sara, you know what? I appreciate you coming in, but this isn't a good fit." The last thing I'm going to do is sit here and indulge this woman in an interview she doesn't deserve for a job I know she's not going to get.

She nearly bounces to her feet, pushing off the wood armrests of the chair across from my desk. "Cool," she says, then snatches her CV from my hands, and poof, she's gone.

I don't know what offends me more. Her being late, the way she behaved about my eye, or how little she cared that I didn't want to hire her.

I drop my forehead to my desk and close my eye. Overwhelming depression swallows me up right then, so I do what my sister tells me to do when I get this way. Take a deep breath in and exhale a great big FUCK YOU out. It's like a regular exhale but feels better.

I shoot her a text.

Bran: *Interviewing women for the female training position. First applicant asked if she should look at my good eye or my eye and eyepatch.*

Sammy: *What a dumb ass.*

Sammy: *I don't know how you do it, B, but you attract the losers.*

Bran: *Tell me something I don't know.*

Sammy: *You sent her packing, right?*

Bran: *She practically ran out of here when I told her she wasn't a good fit.*

Sammy: *I'm sorry*

Sammy: *When's the next one coming in?*

Bran: *Thirty minutes.*

Sammy: *Eat something, drink water, and sit in the sun for a few minutes. You'll feel better.*

Sammy: *Gotta go; someone's coding. Keep me posted.*

With the last message, I realize there are far worse things to have happened than to be sitting in an interview with an immature, insensitive woman who I will never see again. I need to fucking man up, and Sammy's text message was the reminder I needed.

And because my sister knows me well, I snag an apple from my bag and head out to the sidewalk. Warmth pours over my face, and my black hoodie now feels a little too warm, so I tug it off. I take a deep breath in and send out my frustrations in my exhale. It's one person. One interview. No big deal. The next one will be better because the chances of two back-to-back assholes are slim to none.

The apple leaves my fingers sticky, so after sucking down some fresh air and sunlight, I head back inside.

A few of the mid-morning crew arrive as I'm washing my hands, and they give me their usual *"Braaaan"* followed by fist bumps. I love owning this place. I love being asked questions about how to further develop muscles and knowing how to solve people's physical problems. This place is *my* Paradise. It's the place where my knowledge and passion fuse to create not just a fucking bomb business but a safe place for people struggling. Because we all know when you're feeling blue, taking it out on weights always helps.

Seeing the next interviewee arrive—I know because she's wearing black slacks and a blue silk blouse—I linger around the front desk until she makes it in from her car. The beauty of glass doors is always having eyes on your surroundings.

Something I knew I wanted after that night. To know who is around me. In case.

"Julie?" I ask when she steps in and begins patting down her hair, which was tossed around from the fan over the door.

She nods but doesn't smile, so I don't either.

"Hi, I'm Bran, the owner." I outstretch my hand to her and watch her eyes travel the length of my arm, swirling around each inked design until she meets my eye.

"Hi." Her eyes dart to my eye patch, then back to my good eye. That's what most people do. Look at it once, then try to avoid it like the fucking plague. *That* I can deal with.

"I have another interview right after yours, so why don't we head back to the office to get started."

It's now that I notice she's got a manila folder stashed under her arm. Interesting. The last candidate just carried in her CV, but maybe a folder means more professional. I could certainly vibe with someone more professional than the last chick.

She follows me down the hall and waits quietly behind me when I pause twice to say hi to clients roaming around. Once inside, I usher her to the only seat in front of the desk and close the door quietly. My office suddenly smells like my grandma's couch, and I know I'll have to have the uncomfortable conversation about toning down the perfume if I hire this woman. A small price to pay if she's cool and knows her shit, though.

When I take a seat, I notice her eyes are on me. Not my eye or eye patch but... my body. Usually, they gawk at the muscle until they see my face but this woman... this, what was her name? Julie. She isn't letting the pirate patch steal

Stray

her fun. And even though I'm not attracted to her, her attraction to me sends a little swish of confidence up my spine.

Straightening up against the chair, I open the folder that she's placed on my desk.

"Other interviews today?" I ask, breaking the silence and pulling her eyes from my forearm, where her head was tipped sideways, struggling to read the ornate cursive letters.

She looks at her open folder and up at me. "No, just this one."

I thumb through the multiple pages inside the folder, thinking that she brought a ton of copies, but it's then that I realize... Her CV is... fifteen pages.

"I've never seen a fifteen-page CV," I say with a light chuckle, but my eye moves from the papers to her; she is as serious as a heart attack.

"I have a lot of accomplishments," she says with a regal nod of her head. Her hair is pulled back into a bun, her dark hair looking like night in my dim, poorly lit office. She fingers the smooth edges of the bun and then clasps her hands together in her lap. "They're all relevant."

Beginning to read, I get through the vital details about Julie. Where she lives, where she went to school, her last few jobs, all that. She's worked at a few box gyms in the area, but I don't see any training certifications, so I ask her what she did.

I smooth my hand down my beard, something that sometimes helps with my nerves. I don't really feel nervous, but I don't feel at ease. Whether she is checking me out or not, something about Julie makes me feel... on edge. I clear my throat. "I see you worked at Inspire Fitness, and maybe I'm missing it, but I didn't catch what you did there."

"Security," she says, and when I'm about to nod because female security guards are usually pretty badass, she adds, "unofficially."

Unofficially. The word bounces around my brain for a minute until I turn my eye down to the third page of the CV, where she's listed people I can contact. Skimming the short list, I don't see any people listed for Inspire. Looking back up, I see she's edged forward now, practically out of her chair, her eyes following along with what I was reading.

"Well?" she asks. I want to say, *well, what?* because I haven't even read the remaining twelve pages, she isn't a certified trainer (unless that is ironically the one thing she didn't add to this little book of accomplishments) and I'm pretty sure she just implied that she *cased* Inspire like a crazy person but never really worked there.

Fuck, that uneasy feeling wasn't wrong. Julie isn't going to be the next female trainer here, that's clear.

"Well... what?" I ask, starting to get uncomfortable from the way she's now leaning into my desk.

"Are you going to read my accomplishments?" She blinks. She stares and blinks some more.

"Um, well, I'm seeing here you aren't National Academy of Sports Medicine certified, so—"

"Read my accomplishments." It's not even just a statement; it's a fucking order.

"Julie, I think—"

"Read them." Her words say one thing; her tone says *don't fuck with me.*

I glance at my watch, neon green numbers telling me I have twenty-five minutes until the last interview of the day. I have time, and this woman could be unhinged, so rather than shoo her out, I can indulge her in this massive list of accomplishments and then send her packing... hopefully less agitated than she is now.

"O-kay," I draw out the word as I lower my eye to the papers in my hands. I start to read when she interrupts.

"Read them out loud, so I know that you're reading them."

"No, I'm not doing that." *Because this is an interview, you crazy woman, and in case you didn't know, the interviewee doesn't order the interviewer around.* And the thing is, I was going to read them. Until she got bossy. I may not have confidence, but I have enough backbone to send this chick packing.

She narrows her gaze and then huffs out a little "psh" under her breath. "You know," she says, snatching the papers from my hands. She's lucky she didn't give me a papercut, or I would've kicked her ass out right then. Papercuts are fucking brutal. "I'm a fast learner—which you'd know if you would have read my accomplishments."

I say it before I have the chance to think, which is always a mistake. "Being a fast learner isn't an accomplishment."

Her head swivels back so much that I consider showing the move to Mally since he's got a flair for the dramatics. He'd love that move.

"Excuse me?" The way her brows lift to her hairline is kind of terrifying. With her hair slicked back and the bun not visible from straight on, she reminds me of a pissed-off Steven Segall. I don't want to find out if she's got moves like he does.

"I'm sorry, Julie. I'm looking for someone certified to

Daisy Jane

train." Rising, the international sign for *you need to go*; she matches my movements. Thank God.

"Your loss," she says, stuffing the folder under her armpit again. I just smile because, really, what else is there to do? Awkwardly I follow behind her until we're all the way through the halls and at the glass doors.

"Thanks for your–"

I knew it couldn't be that easy.

"You know," she says, narrowing those eyes on my eye again. "I'm sure people have given you chances to prove you can do things. You should pay it forward." With one more look up and down my body, she stalks off, shoving the glass doors open as she does.

Once I'm back in my office, I close the blinds facing the private training room and lean back in my chair. Maybe hiring a woman to work here was a bad idea, and these candidates are my sign.

At that moment, my phone rings with a text message. Knowing that Sammy is saving lives, I assume it's the boys. Or at least one of them. When I snatch it up and use my thumb to unlock it, I see Malibu's name on the screen.

Mally: *How'd the interview go?*

Bran: *2 out of 3 are done.*

Mally: *Come on, you gotta interview more than 3.*

Mally: *Unless you found her? The golden girl? The one to bring chicks to Paradise?*

Bran: *Hardly*

Mally: *Whaa? Srsly?*

Bran: *Seriously.*

Bran: *The first one asked if she should look at my*

eye patch or my good eye and the second one was just... crazy. And insinuated that I have clearly had help making something of myself and that I should help her, too.

Mally: *Daamn.*

Bran: *This was probably a bad idea.*

Mally: *Gotta sift through poop to get to gold.*

Bran: *You read that in a fortune cookie?*

Mally: *I came up with that on my own.*

Mally: *You like it?*

Bran: *Not really*

Mally: *Don't give up the hunt. Having a chick around Paradise would be legit.*

Bran: *I'm trying to draw in female clients by making sure I have a woman solid enough to deal with men. I'm not trying to make Paradise a pussy palace for you.*

Mally: *But it's a perk*

Bran: *Gotta go. One more today. Really thinking of calling it.*

I type *it's pretty fucking pathetic I can't even get a woman to work near me. I got no chance at meeting a good, normal girl.* But I backspace like crazy before I send it. Because while I don't give a shit if I'm coming off all self-deprecating and negative, I know Mally will care. The sensitive motherfucker. And I don't need him showing up here mid-interview with Van on his heels, trying to give me a midday hug or some shit.

I love him, but right now, I just want to get through this awful fucking day.

Mally: *I don't know how you are meeting all these*

misshaped pieces my man, but I promise your missing piece is out there. Don't quit.

Bran: *Just looking for a strong, capable female trainer. Not my missing piece.*

Mally: *The first step of the journey is knowing what you're looking for, and I know you'll find it. But you won't find it if you quit.*

See—then he pops off with deep and inspirational shit like that, and it's all part of the full-bodied roast that is Malibu. I love the guy, even when he pushes me past my comfort.

Bran: *Gotta go. Thanks, man.*

Mally: *See you at four AM.*

With just a few minutes before the next scheduled interview, I throw my sweatshirt back on and give my armpit a sniff. A little tangy, but it's not like she's going to smell my fucking pits, so I swipe on some more deodorant from my desk stash and call it good.

The thing about owning a gym and being a gym rat is that you gotta be aware of your stank at all times. If I'm not currently sweaty, then I'm coated in dry sweat, and no matter what, there are traces of a workout in my scent irregardless of how I've spent my day. Comes with the territory. It's one of those things I lie to myself about when I get down about being single—I work in a gym and am sweaty as a ballsack all the time, probably better off I'm single.

I wouldn't want to give this place up for anything.

But I'm so fucking lonely that I'd probably become the annoying cologne spritzer at a department store if it meant I'd find a girl.

That's not a good thing to admit.

Straightening up my desk, answering a few emails, earmarking a few pages in the new Rogue catalog–I keep myself busy while I wait.

When I allow myself to look at the clock, it's been ten minutes. The next time I look–after sweeping my office and cleaning the floor-to-ceiling mirror that lines one wall–it's been twenty minutes.

Even if this next person is fucking amazing–we're talking Blake Lively had a baby with Keri Russell, and she was the chick walking into Paradise–I don't know. Being late is something I hate. People who are late are either one of two things: poor planners or complete narcissistic assholes who think their time is worth more than mine. Either way, I'm not interested.

After finger combing my beard, hand-styling my hair, changing into my lifting shoes, checking my wallet to see if I have my social security card (because every few months, I just need to know I have it), I allow myself to look at the clock.

It's now thirty minutes past the start of the interview. She isn't coming.

Being stood up on a date is one thing, but being stood up by someone who you want to hire and pay? Fuck, that hits. And not like a good hit across the ass, either. Kind of slaps me in the balls and sucks the air from my lungs.

Heading out to the main room, despite the fact I've already lifted this morning, I hit the free weights again, music deadening my eardrums because it's so loud. Passing out nods of acknowledgment here and there, I finish my second workout, sweaty and utterly fucking exhausted.

Daisy Jane

That's my habit.

When I'm blue, I work out until it's very, very hard to feel.

I stop by the wing joint on my way home, picking up an order for me and a separate order of plain boneless wings for Stoner. After getting his nighttime CBD dose, he eats and immediately falls asleep. I've been jealous of my dog so often. How sad is that?

After a very hot shower, a fresh pair of sweatpants, and a glass of sweet tea the size of my head, I eat my wings alone at my kitchen table. The only noises in my house are the endless ticking of the clock on the wall and Stoner's breath whistling through his lips, pressed against his food dish.

It's simple and nice. I'm grateful for my gym and my bros, for my dog, and this life I have.

But I go to bed distinctly aware that I am alone.

I need a girl.

6

Elsie

It's code.

"Not that it needs to be said, but I'm going to say it anyway. You, my friend, should not drink Vodka," I tell my reflection in the bathroom mirror. Because not only does drinking vodka make me spill my emotional baggage to work acquaintances at work functions, but it also makes me talk to myself in a mirror. Not good.

My hair—which is frizzy on a good day—is an absolute disaster. One side is smashed flat—all body sucked from it due to my very deep vodka-induced sleep, and the other side put *SideShow Bob* on a damn catwalk, seriously. So much curly disaster that I actually panic for a minute that I won't be able to comb through it.

But I don't have the energy for a mini-meltdown related to hair, and because the mom in me doesn't allow freaking out over non-things (and hair is definitely not a thing to get tantrumy over). I twist the water on and let the shower warm. While the temperature is rising, I slather in some leave-in conditioner that my mom put in my stocking for Christmas last year. It's expensive, so I don't use it often, and truthfully, I'm one to embrace my natural body and curls. But this matted mess is not at all embraceable. It's the opposite of embraceable. It's.... Embraceless.

Deciding to let it settle into the mass of tangle that is my hair, I work at the sink scrubbing off the traces of last night's makeup. We're down to smudged mascara and eye boogers, but those are always the hardest to scrub off. With two makeup-removing wipes and a few cotton swabs, I'm back to being fresh-faced.

"Time to deal with the mop-top," I say aloud to myself because if I'm being honest, I'm still a little drunk. Stripping off my underwear and t-shirt—my standard pajamas—I step into a downpour of warm water and immediately feel sobriety move through me. Something about getting your makeup off and your hair clean is just so life-changing.

While shaving and scrubbing, my mind goes back to Lacey.

"You choose when you want to see him, you have the power, and you leave knowing he's thinking about you, and it isn't the other way around. He wants you. He is at your beck and call."

Having a man want me, having power but being adored for that power—damn. She really did paint a picture of something I didn't know I wanted.

But she didn't say *how* I'd get to feel that power; she didn't elaborate on *what* she does, so as excited as I want to be to meet up with her, I'm equally nervous.

I really don't think I can take another disappointment. With the progression of mom's issues recently, I wake up every day not knowing if Effie and mom are going to be absolutely great or if I'm going to be riddled with IBS at work all day worrying about the two of them.

I can't keep going like this until... I don't want to go down that path. Rinsing out the leave-in conditioner, I turn my thoughts back to Lacey. Because thinking about mom's problems progressing quicker, even more drastically... I just can't. More of Lacey's words filter back into my consciousness, and I'm surprised how much I can remember considering how chummy I got with the booze.

What if instead of looking for a guy who will make you feel like he's doing some fucking charity work to love your life, you start seeing men that make you feel powerful. That make you feel in control and strong.

It drains me to deal with mom, try to raise Effie while working, *and* keep everyone happy and healthy.

Power and control would be... nice.

When I'm out of the shower and fully dressed, I sit on the edge of my bed and send Lacey a text message.

Elsie: *What day this week works for you?*

Lacey: *We said Thursday night. I'll text you my address. Does that still work? Can't wait to see you.*

Effie bounces in the room just as I'm putting my phone in my purse, and I help her feed her wiggly arms through her shirt, let her use me as balance support while she steps into her leggings, and help her spray the detangler before combing her hair. Today isn't one of her usual days to go to preschool, but when I woke up this morning and found mom sleeping on my bedroom floor, I knew we were going to have an *off* day. A day where her mind just can't hold it all together. On these types of days, each time she attempts to remember steps to a crucial task, other parts of her memory fade, leaving her discombobulated and frustrated.

I hate *off* days.

Before texting Lacey, I'd texted Effie's preschool teacher and told her to charge me for an additional day this week, that I needed to drop Effie off. The school—which is private and located on our street (thankfully), is aware of Elaine Francis's *challenges*. And unless they are at max capacity on a certain day, they are very accommodating. I am very lucky.

The week is one I call a *dark week.*

Mom is *off* all week, and when I get home from work on Tuesday afternoon, Effie is outside with the hose running, spraying the dandelions with mom nowhere to be found. Because I love my kid more than life itself, I'm immediately upset because a four-year-old shouldn't ever be left unattended, much less outside. But when I go inside and find mom asleep on the couch, I can't bring myself to be mad at her. Because she's struggling so much, how can you kick someone when they're down?

Wednesday is a bit better—but only because my kid isn't alone outside looking to be kidnapped. Upon returning home from work, I find Effie and Mom inside, watching a movie together. At first, I think we're pulling out of the nosedive that has been this week, but when I focused on the screen, I realized they were watching *Beetlejuice*. And because I don't need my beautiful, precious, wide-eyed daughter running around saying, "*let's turn on the juice and see what shakes loose,*" for the next six months, I had to be the bad cop and shut it off. When I looked at mom, there was zero understanding in her eyes. And it was then I realized we were *still* nosediving.

"Mom," I say, smoothing my hand up her arm as I approach her in the kitchen. She's making meatballs, and something about burying her hands in cold ground meat always puts her in a less irritable mood. I'm glad she has things that bring her comfort, even though she has to live the agony of not knowing *why* she's upset or needs comfort in the first place.

"Hmm," she hums her response, kneading the meat like sore muscles. It's actually kind of therapeutic just watching her.

"I'm going to my co-worker Lacey's house tonight, remember?" I make sure to use a specifically casually dull tone on that last word.

"Yeah," she says, picking up the hunk of meat and dropping it with a slap to the parchment on the counter. Mashing her fingers into the mound, she pulls away the perfect amount and begins rolling it between her palms. "I remember."

"Effie can come with me if you want some quiet time," I say, watching her finish the first meatball and move on to the next.

"Leave her here, Elsie. You can't hold a real conversation with a four-year-old in the room." She turns her eyes to me, brows raised in a pointed expression. "I know that better than most."

Smiling, I nod. "Okay, if you're sure you don't mind being on-shift for a few more hours."

"Just having a drink?" she asks.

The kitchen light is one of those adjustable smart bulbs, and Mom lets Effie set them to cool white, her favorite. It makes our blonde hair nearly white, and from where Mom stands directly beneath the recessed can light, she almost seems to glow. And the moment of mom quietly making meatballs with light all around her, makes my nose burn and my chest tight.

I don't want her memory to be getting worse so fast. I don't want anything to happen to her. I can't bear to see the look on Effie's face when it does; the two of them are like Batman and Robin, for God's sake.

I push aside the bubbling emotion to give her an answer. "Honestly, I don't really know why I'm going. She invited me last week and said she had a job opportunity for me. Maybe"

Mom stops rolling the red meat and squares her shoulders to mine. "Not a pyramid scheme, right?" She winces, and I love seeing the playfulness in her. Especially after a fucking hard week. I fight the lump in my throat and wince right back at her.

"I really hope not. I don't want to meet up with her and have time away from you guys for some shampoo scheme or some crap."

She giggles a little, and so do I.

"Effie's been asking for a pet, you know," Mom says, turning the conversation in a completely different direction. That's one thing the doctor told us about early-onset dementia. The brain is a hugely complex battlefield with massive things going on everywhere at all times. The memory loss she's experiencing isn't the only effect of the disease. Wires get crossed easily and not just in confusing ways, either. This, for instance. The organic flow of conversation isn't always something natural to her anymore.

"I know," I say, going with it because trying to divert back to our original topic can easily cause her distress. And the last few years of my life have been about the opposite; making things as good as possible for mom.

Thus the front desk job. The insurance covers her pre-existing diagnosis, and while the doctors in this network aren't amazing (or even halfway), her meds *are* covered. And the meds are some days the only thing keeping her together, even somewhat.

"Maybe for her fifth birthday. I don't think she's ready to take care of a pet yet, Mom." What I mean is, *I'm* not ready to have another living creature depend on me. Not at all.

Effie zips through, holding an oversized Scar stuffed animal in the air. My daughter always sympathizes with the anti-hero of all Disney movies. Her room is overflowing with posters, stuffed animals, and collectibles of all bad guys. Scar, Gaston, Mother Gothel, Jafar, Maleficent, Sid the toy destroyer, Ursula... if they're not the hero, she loves them. When the obsession began, I asked her why she didn't prefer the princesses or the heroes of those stories. Her response was so sweet and wholesome that I've been feeding her anti-hero addiction ever since. "They aren't bad guys, mama. They don't get enough hugs, and they don't have enough friends. Everyone is happy and good if they get hugs and have friends."

Cute as shit, right? That's my baby.

"Mama's going to her friend Lacey's house for a few hours, okay, Ef?"

She crashes Scar into the stepladder next to my mom before climbing up and nosing around the tray of rolled raw meat. "Okay, have fun!"

I may not be married with my happily ever after, and I may have been dumped for this exact life right here in this kitchen—but the truth is, we're so happy together. Aside from the disease, I have a full, beautiful life. And Jake can go fuck himself because as much as I want a partner, I would never sacrifice this.

After a round of kisses and promises to eat for grandma, take a bath, and only request one regular length story, I make my way to Lacey's house, setting my phone to navigate toward the location pin she sent me earlier.

Holy shitballs.

Lacey's house is... beautiful.

I love my house. It's a cookie-cutter, three-bedroom, two-bathroom place that I grew up in. When I got pregnant at a young age, I decided to continue living there. And seeing Effie have her own childhood firsts in the same place I shared those things with my mom? I'm falling in love with the house all over again.

But Lacey's house is the kind of place that anyone would be jealous of, no matter how emotionally attached you are to your own place. Seriously.

A long lighted walkway leads to her black lacquer door, which bears an ornate gold door knocker in the center. Her lawn is alive and lush, trimmed and edged to perfection—clearly by a professional lawn team. A winding driveway tucks itself into the back of the house, the tail of her SUV barely visible. But damn, even her SUV is new—the temporary paper plates are still on it. Mature olive trees positioned at the corners of the house give a magazine look, and the lights hidden away in the lawn spotlight the beautiful architecture of the colonial-style home.

I'm no real estate agent, but this place looks expensive. And when I step out onto the sidewalk and notice the bullnose edges, I realize I'm in a wealthy neighborhood. And Lacey is a personal trainer at Globo-Fitness.

Seriously?

The video doorbell comes to life as I step onto the porch. Reaching up to knock, the door swings open before I can connect. Lacey is there, smiling, a rush of clean linen and mopped floors flooding my nostrils. I put my arm down sheepishly.

"Hi, I was just about to knock."

She tips her head in the direction of the blue light ring on the doorbell. "My phone notification went off. I saw you were here."

Pulling the door open, she steps back so that I can enter. Stepping inside, I stand awkwardly next to her while she closes the door, turns the deadbolt, and fastens the safety chain. When she faces me, she's all smiles.

"I'm so glad you came."

"Your house, Lacey..." I trail off, my eyes creeping around the interior. The inside of the house is nicer than the outside, and that's saying something. Overstuffed, plush furniture with muted color pillows in different textures, walls painted the color of a fading stormy sky, thick crown molding kissing all the seams of the room, a wall of built-in bookshelves, and holy crap–the kitchen.

The kitchen is larger than the living space and shiny, so shiny I blink a few times. Stainless steel appliances but not just the kind you get at Home Depot–these are industrial, large, and professional. She even has an apron sink–I've only seen those on influencers' social media pages.

"Your house," I say after a few moments of silence where Lacey lets me just… absorb her life. "It's like a rich person's house. An influencer's house. I mean, I'm not trying to be rude. I just… didn't expect it."

Turning on my heel, I find Lacey grinning at me; her long blonde hair now pulled up into a messy wad on the top of her head. She's wearing sweats–casual–but when I focus on the small emblem on the hip of the joggers, I see they're a specific brand. A brand I see at the gym all the time, worn by well-kept housewives. When my eyes leave the $120 pair of joggers on her lower half, I see her top is the same brand.

"That's why I asked you to come. To talk to you about how I got all of this." She loops her arm through mine and walks us to her living space, and we plop down on a cream-colored couch that feels exactly how I'd think a cloud feels.

Smoothing my hands down my curls, I tuck my hair behind my ears, straighten my spine and prepare myself for disappointment. This house has me excited and curious, but now I'm almost sure she's at the top of some pyramid scheme. Maybe she's just working at the gym for the benefits, like me?

"Yeah?" I ask awkwardly because just then, the thought

that she's some black market organ harvester crosses my mind. My eyes go wide as it flits through my brain.

"What?" Lacey suddenly looks concerned, too.

"Uhh," I pale. "I just had this thought that maybe you got this all.... *Illegally.*"

She wrinkles her nose but not with amusement. "Well," she starts, and my stomach free-falls. If it wasn't illegal, she would have immediately said no. Wasted no time in saying it, too. But she didn't say no. She said *well*.

Fuck.

"Look, let me tell you what I do, and I'll let you decide how to feel."

"Okay," I say, noticing the soft slope of her shoulders and the casual crossing of her legs at the ankle. Her body language doesn't scream anything, much less discomfort. I relax into the couch a little and start to listen.

"I am a Personal Trainer for Individual Heavy Lifting Sessions." She pulls her legs onto the couch, sitting cross-legged now, focusing on me more intently.

"Yeah. A PT at Globo." I confirm what I already know, thinking she's using this to lead into the pyramid stuff.

But she shakes her head.

"I'm a personal trainer at Globo-Fitness, yes, but on the side, off the books, I am a Personal Trainer for Individual Heavy Lifting Sessions... for men."

I cock a brow. "I'm confused."

Her lips curl into a lazy but sinister smile. "It's code."

"Code," I repeat moronically because I really have no fucking clue what Lacey is talking about or explaining to me, but my mom senses aren't telling me to bail. The smell of lavender oil being diffused relaxes me, and I can't help but think, *hey, I want a lavender oil diffuser in a massive house, too*. I stay put and hear her out.

She nods. "Yep. It's how my clients find me for *their* needs."

"Find you where?" I ask, thinking I should've probably asked *what needs,* but I have a feeling we're going to get there.

"Online. I post on three different job sites, and that's the code I use for this side business." She waves an arm around the room, indicating her references will be to the entire house. "That side business earned me all this."

"So... what is a heavy lifting whatever trainer code for?"

"A very *personal* kind of trainer. I train my clients to use and discipline muscles they don't work in the gym." Her smile melts away. "And their minds. I help them with their mental strength."

"So..." I think about what she's just said. "You're like a trainer and a life coach?" Something tells me unless you're in a big city like Los Angeles full of lost and overmedicated people, life coaches in Willowdale can't possibly be this loaded. I am still waiting to see what the base of the pyramid is made of, besides people like me.

She jumps up from the couch, and because it's so overstuffed, it's buoyant, and I nearly bounce off too. The parts of me that don't bounce off the sofa are pulled off with Lacey's hand around my wrist.

"Let me show you something. It'll help you understand."

We walk down the hallway, the walls lined with framed photos of flexed muscles taken at creative angles. The photos are so close that individual beads of sweat mirror the camera lens. I stop in front of one and tap the glass.

"These are cool, Lacey."

She beams at the simple compliment, and I realize that she took these photos. Eyeing the off-white mat around the photo, I see LD scribbled directly on it. Her initials.

"You took these?" I ask though it's more of a statement because clearly, she did.

"I did."

Padding down the hall, I take in the assortment of photos, and damn, they're amazing. They look like something in a weight-loss ad or a gym commercial. So professional.

"I bought the camera and took photography classes in my free time."

I nod and smile, thinking about how expensive hobbies are. I'm not broke, but as mom's condition worsens, I realize care costs will increase. And at twenty-two, I'm not neck-deep in savings. Hobbies are not for people like me.

"That's awesome, Lacey."

Still holding my wrist, she leads me further down the hall, holding tight like I'll wander off like a child in an amusement park if she lets go. And maybe I would. This house is *that* nice.

We come to a door—another fancy thing about this house is how tall the doors are. At least nine feet. She opens it and ushers me inside before turning on the lights. When she does, my eyes take a moment to adjust.

It's just a spare bedroom.

Queen-sized bed, lots of untouched amenities like a sleep mask on the nightstand, extra blankets rolled perfectly into a wicker basket in the corner, spare slippers tucked under the white-finished dresser. The bed is covered in shag pillows, all the same muted shades as the living room.

"Nice room," I say because I really don't know why I'm seeing a spare bedroom. Lacey snickers and steps towards the French doors on one wall. I hadn't noticed them before.

"Dang, French doors to a closet in a spare room," I shake my head. "I don't even have double closet doors in my room, and I'm in the master at my house."

With her hand resting on one of the curved handles, she says, "this room has a custom closet. I don't want this in my room because it's work, but I need to keep it somewhere."

Right as I'm envisioning shelves upon shelves brimming with phony hair products or potentially even crappy lipsticks, she pushes open the door, and a motion-sensor light illuminates the massive closet. I can't even focus on the size of the closet, though, because its contents steal my breath.

Rows of black leather, red latex, and nude lace garments span the length of one wall. Each outfit is held secure by a black velvet hanger; I realize that it's not just high-end lingerie. The outfits are all corsets in different styles, a corresponding and matching set of high heels or knee-high boots positioned under each. Above each outfit on a recessed shelf is a faceless mannequin head wearing a unique wig. Some bright colors like magenta and teal, others realistic brown waves, a red shoulder-length bob, and one with a single blonde ponytail.

I could stare at these outfits for hours–there's got to be–I count in my head until I reach twenty, then I stop. My eyes traverse the small room to the other wall, and my jaw splits apart.

On this side of the closet, there are lots of... things.

Stray

Toys, devices, props... My brain can't even process some of the stuff I see, and a lot of it I've never even seen before. I notice a few things that are easy to recognize–a flogger, a whip, multiple sets of handcuffs with varying levels of wrist protection, chokers with rubber balls in the middle–what the hell are those? So much stuff. I swallow, discovering my mouth and throat are dry as dirt.

"You're... a hooker?" I spit out, still facing the wall of things.

"I'm a *female dominant*. I'm hired by men who want to be sexually controlled and get in touch with their own discipline. Learn how capable they are of having restraint and taking orders instead of giving them."

My mouth opens and closes a few times. I blink mindlessly while staring through Lacey, trying to process what the hell she just said because it's not making sense.

"I go by Mistress," she continues, clearly taking my slack-jawed and wide-eyed expression for what it is: utter confusion.

"I think I'm still confused," I admit, turning back to the wall of outfits. The more I stare at them, the more appealing they become. My fingers tingle with the desire to stroke my hand down the slick leather corset. To trace the shiny grommets cinching the rope-like tie that holds the piece together. No matter what it's used for, these outfits... they really are beautiful.

"Clients hire me to take control of them sexually. I tell them what to do and when. They come when I say so. I train them, show them how to test their own limits, show them they can hold back and do more if they can really get control of themselves up here," she taps the side of her head, and for some strange reason, her explanation gives me goosebumps, followed by a serious shiver down my spine.

"I... I can't do that," my response is automatic, and I've said it before; I've really even thought about it. But no. What's there to think about? I can't be a... "what do you call yourself?" I ask, my brain apparently completely detached now because I know she just told me. I think I'm in shock a little.

"Mistress. Some go by Femme, but I don't like that term because it's also the same term to describe a feminine lesbian."

I can't even nod because I'm still so... taken aback. "I thought you sold crappy shampoo in a pyramid scheme."

She balks, cracks up, actual tears streaming down her face, making me laugh right along with her. Her messy bun slides down the side of her head from her arrant laughter, and it makes me move my hands through my hair to make sure it's not frizzing.

When the laughter fades, her blue eyes take mine. "You could do this, Elsie." She presses her lips together, her face growing serious. Goosebumps spread over my arms. "You *need* to do this."

"Need?" I croak, my voice weak and quiet.

She motions to a white tufted leather bench centering the room, and we sit together, facing the wall of outfits.

"It's an incredibly powerful feeling, Elsie, taking a man by his most prized possession–the thing he cares about more than trucks, muscles, or money. Doling out control rather than being desperate to find it for yourself... it is unbelievably powerful."

My gaze flicks back to the garments. A latex bodysuit

with a zipper up the core hangs directly in front of me. Beneath it are knee-high latex boots with a thick platform. Above is a long, pink wig, the ends of the hair curled into half-moons. She speaks again, and I turn to face her when she does.

"Did you know I'm a silent owner of Globo-Fitness?" she asks, sitting up taller as she crosses her legs in front of her. "Being a female dominant started as a thing for power, sure. But it's given me so much, Elsie. Things I don't think I could have found otherwise."

"Like what?" I hear myself ask, but I think I'm only asking to appease her, so she doesn't feel bad for exposing her secrets and vulnerabilities to me, only for me to shut her down. I'm not asking for my own curiosity; certainly not. Because I am not Lacey. I could never do this.

"Confidence."

I laugh a little but immediately stop when her face remains impassive. "You're gorgeous, Lacey. You don't strike me as someone who's ever needed confidence."

She nods like she agrees with that statement. "But," she clarifies, "I was never confident in my capabilities. I grew up hearing I was pretty, but no one ever said, *hey, you can do anything you want as long as you believe in yourself.*" Her gaze floats down to her lap, where her hands tangle together nervously. "It sounds like a speech meant for elementary school kids, but seriously, Elsie, I never heard it. I was always told I needed to meet someone. My mom said my best bet was marrying up." She shakes her head like she needs to physically get away from those words. "All I mean is, I never thought I was meant for more. I never knew I could be more. But being a dominant has shown me I am powerful; its given me the confidence to know I can have what I want—my entire life is up to me."

"All from sexually controlling a man?" I ask, and though it sounds a bit condescending, I don't mean it that way. And her face grows soft, so I know she doesn't take it that way either, thankfully.

"What you do with the men—*for* the men—will make you feel powerful. And that powerful feeling will pour over into other aspects of your personality."

Getting to her feet, she slides open a drawer from behind one of the outfits, a drawer I hadn't even noticed. From it, she pulls a single business card and passes it to me. Printed in the center with nothing else is a single QR code.

Lacey taps her long, french manicured nail over the card. "This will take you to a website where you will have any and all of your questions answered." Analyzing the pixels of ink for a second, I look back up at her.

"Just... think about Els. I heard what you said to me that night at the bar—the shit about Jake and why he broke up with you. I'm telling you, the power you'll feel from doing this will make you an absolute boss in all other aspects of your life. There will never be another Jake."

I think about how my stomach turned on its head about a million times this week during mom's off days. How powerless I felt about her episodes, how aside from calling the doctor's office and asking to be prescribed either a higher dose or more pills—I couldn't do anything to help her.

Feeling confident and powerful in some aspects of my life would be good. Really good.

But I can't do this.

I'm not that girl. I'm a mom. I can't.

Stray

Yet when I leave Lacey's house, not only do I keep the card she gave me, but I also promise her that I'll check it out when I get home.

And when I get home, as much as I tell myself I'm not that girl, I get less than two hours of sleep because that QR code takes me to a site that sucks me in deep all night.

7

Bran

I want everything or nothing.

"What's his name?"

I scratch behind Stoner's ear as he flops down in a pile of cut grass at the park. He did one lap before giving up, and I can't say I'm surprised. I bring him to the dog park four times a week, and the lazy fuck hasn't ever done more than a single lap. Even when he isn't dosed on his anxiety meds, his energy has limits. And that limit is four hundred feet–or *one lap* around the fenced-in park.

"Stoner," I say, leaning back against the bench.

"Oh," the woman says, trying to decide whether I'm a guy who loves weed so much that I named my dog after the act of indulging in it or if my dog is the *actual* stoner. I don't

Stray

clarify because I'm not interested in talking to this dog park woman.

I'm not interested in much when I'm in this headspace.

After two shitty interviews and one no-show yesterday, not engaging with *women* is the only discourse in my brain. The year after that night, I held a worry inside me, keeping it completely to myself for the fear that it would actually be real if I voiced it. But that fear is laughing in my face now.

I may never find someone.

I mean, I could be *fucking* chicks. No doubt. Hinge and Tinder are an untapped ocean of women looking for an itch to be scratched.

But I'm thirty.

I want everything or nothing.

I want a girl in my arms in the morning, not just at night. I want someone to make breakfast for and a person to call when I'm driving home from work–preferably not Malibu. I want to be a dad one day, and I want Stoner to have a friend to play with. I want it all, not some fucked up sliver of it. And I don't want to settle. No one should have to settle.

"Does he want a treat?" the woman at my side asks, wiggling a brown baked good at Stoner. He doesn't even lift his head–an impressive commitment to being a lazy ass.

"That's okay," I reply just as Malibu jogs up. His blonde hair is unruly, and his shirt-sleeve tan is horrendous. But his shit-eating grin is contagious.

"There are so many cool dogs here," he huffs out when he reaches the bench. Sitting down next to me, Mally slaps my thigh, bolting me upright from my lax position. "Okay, I got to pet all of them except the small one with the underbite." He rubs his palms together like he's done with a day of work. "I'm ready to go."

Sometimes I think me and Stoner come to the dog park to let Mally run off his energy, not the other way around.

We trudge back to my truck, and Mally helps Stoner inside because they have each other trained. On the drive to Mally's place, he brings up legitimately the only thing I don't want to talk about.

"So you never texted me, and we didn't talk this morning during the pump sesh. How'd the rest of the interviews go?"

My eye cuts across the cab to him, and I roll it. "Don't even. I know you talked to Sammy."

I'd text my little sister an update only to prevent her from calling me five hundred times that night. And I know she and Mally have an ongoing text chat.

"She didn't," he says, shaking his head. "I swear she didn't."

"Well," I sigh, raking my fingers down my beard as my other hand grips the steering wheel. "If I can't get a woman to work next to me, I don't think I'm ever gonna get one to marry me."

I expect a soft response from Mally because that's how he usually comes back at me when I make comments like that. I'm not hungry for compliments, and I'm definitely not begging to be built up. I'm just being real.

But he's silent for over a minute, so finally, I face him when we pull up to his house.

"The eye?"

"What?" I ask, having heard him correctly but not knowing why he's bringing it up.

"Are you implying that no one wants to work at Paradise

with you because you are missing one of your eyes?" He asks it with absolutely no inflection, and for some reason that makes me nervous.

"It isn't an implication," I defend, unclipping my lap belt so I can turn my body to face him. "It's the truth. The first woman didn't know where to look, and the second one implied that I must've had my hand held to open a business because *I'm missing an eye*. The third didn't even fucking show up."

He shoves a hand through his hair, attempting to smooth it down for some reason. Normally when we're together, his grooming habits are not a concern.

"We're going to get wings. Stay here; I'm running in to swipe on some more deodorant, then we're getting Van." He smooths his palms down his thighs while staring at me with an intensity that has me understanding why he gets all the ladies.

"Jesus, dude, what?"

"We need to talk. We need beer and wings to soften your cranky edge."

"I don't have a cranky edge," I say, realizing this is not my first time taking on defense mode in this conversation. That's not a good sign—if you are the one defending yourself multiple times in one talk, you very well could be on the wrong side of the debate.

He slaps a hand down on my shoulder and pinches my muscle, the way he and Van do to one another all the time. "You are one big cranky edge." He hops into the street, leaving the door wide open as he backpedals toward his house. "I'm leaving this open, so you don't drive off. This talk is important." He points at me and gives me a ridiculous serious beach boy look, which is very similar to an overacting soap star. "I'm serious, bro."

I roll my eye—it always feels like I'm still rolling both—and let my head fall into the headrest.

Mally wants to talk, and we're getting Van. I'm being ganged up on, and not in that "is the camera on?" type of way dudes dream about.

* * *

THIRTY MINUTES, three plastic bibs (yep), forty bucks, and many burps later, the three of us are tucked into a too-small booth, shotgunning wings and slamming beers.

Well, *I'm* slamming beers. Van and Malibu are pacing, but the way they keep staring me down and smiling awkwardly makes me think the pacing isn't for driving purposes but for serious talking purposes.

Bastards.

After I'm halfway through my insanely large order of habanero wings, Malibu clears his throat and pats his chest. Again, I roll my eye.

My head tips as I let loose an exhausted sigh. I'm ready to go on the defense one more time tonight, a speech about not needing more to think about right now practically spilling from my lips. But when my eye meets his face, I see an expression I'm completely unprepared for.

Anger.

The type that's clearly been simmering on the back burner for a while. Christian has only been mad at me once in our lives that I can remember, and it was because I lied to him about continuing therapy after that night. I'd quit because physically going to the office brought me so much damn anxiety–when he found out I'd quit after promising I'd go all year, he laid into me like no one ever has. Not even Sammy.

In fact, that's when he and Sammy grew close. They'd always been friends by association, but when he stood up with tears in his eyes and basically said he'd never speak to me again if I didn't take care of myself–she fell in love. With his friendship, that is.

Sometimes I wish there was more between them because Mally–like Van and Batman–are more brothers than friends.

"I honestly didn't think I'd need to have this talk with you, man," he starts, his voice disentangled from his facetious persona. Awareness jolts through my chest and gut, my heart beats growing heavy from the weight of added nerves. I look at Van, and when I find him intently focused on our friend, his own face heavy with concern, I swallow.

"It's been eight years. And I know trauma doesn't have an expiration date, and I'm cool with that. I'm here if you wanna like, talk about that night or, honestly? I don't even know what you'd want to talk about because you never talk about it."

"There's nothing to talk about," I say, hating how easily the words come because I've said them so many times. Because saying that is a million fucking times easier than saying, *I'm afraid that night ruined my shot at a normal life. I'm afraid that night has made me someone I hate.*

"There is. But you lost the shot to talk about it. At least tonight. Tonight, *I* talk." He smooths a hand down the lower half of his face and then pulls at his neck, letting out a long, controlled exhale. Finally, he laces his fingers together on the table, pushing his wing basket back. Then he looks at me, and my heart nearly stops from his serious demeanor.

"You're Arizona Robbins, dude."

I'm... "Who?"

"You're Dr. Arizona Robbins, dude, and I can tell you from watching her shit unfold, it's going to ruin you if you don't let it go."

If I don't... "What?" He's so serious, but the fucker is making no sense.

Van clears his throat as Mally leans back against the booth, blinking theatrically slow. *What the fuck?*

"Grey's, dude. Come on." Van taps the side of his head, the serpent tattooed down his forearm wiggling as he flexes. "Think about it."

It's been a long time since Sammy and I watched Grey's because apparently, they killed off her favorite character, and *how could they?* But I do remember the name now. Rolling my bottom lip through my teeth, I think about the name again.

"The lesbian doctor with the blonde hair?"

Mally just stares. Van finally nods.

"The leg," I say, offering up the hangup of the female doctor from the hit medical show. She lost her leg in a plane crash and emotionally never fully recovered from the loss, alienating everyone in her life and ultimately costing her both her marriage and her happiness.

I'm not married, but I'm unhappy as hell. Sure I love Sammy and the guys. My parents. Stoner. Paradise.

But you can have love for things and still be profoundly lost.

That's how I feel.

Lost.

"The leg," Mally repeats, and this time his tone is low and caring, making my chest ache. "You gotta know that you're a dope dude. You gotta know you're more than *the one thing* you're missing." He shakes his head and looks to Van, passing the baton.

"We love you, dude. We kept thinking things would change. You'd date a little; we'd be hopeful. But it's time to say it because you aren't doing it."

Malibu leans across the table, fidgeting with the edge of the red plastic basket. "Everything is about missing the eye, and it's turning you into someone scared to live."

I'm not scared is right there on my tongue, but for once, I think about things before I defend myself.

I was considering calling off the hunt for a trainer just because there were a few bad interviews. And honestly, the first girl didn't mean any harm asking where to look. She was just insensitive and fucking stupid. That's everywhere. I can't avoid people. But I let it potentially alter the trajectory of my business.

That shit has to stop. They're right. Being scared that I'm not good enough opens me up to being treated like I'm not.

Jesus, *how did I get to be this guy?*

"My eye is *completely* the leg. I *am* Arizona Robbins." I can't deny it.

Mally sighs and slaps his palm on my thigh, squeezing a bit before releasing. "You totally are. But you have McDreamy vibes underneath the Arizona if you just harness that shit."

I snort. Van laughs heartily, then celebrates completing his beer with a loud belch. Thank God we buy so many fucking chicken wings, or else the owners would probably have kicked us out a long time ago.

"I feel like I'm Karev," Van says, wiggling his glass in the air for the waitress to bring him more. Kind of rude, but like I said, we buy a lot of wings. He nudges his black-framed glasses up his nose.

"You're *so* Karev," Mally says, pawing at the communal French fries Van always buys for our table.

"I'm..." Mally scratches his throat, sticking out his chest as he does. "McSteamy."

Van snorts. "He was the dumbest of all the doctors you know."

Mally shrugs. "Still a doctor."

I take a drink of my beer, and when I set it back down, I find the attention is back on me. "What are you going to do that Arizona *should* have done?"

I scratch my jaw, the grate of my rough beard a soothing noise to my nerves. "Accept who I am *now* and not let what I'm not rule my narrative."

"Not let the missing parts rule your narrative," Van corrects.

"Right, not let the missing eye rule my narrative." He's right. That sounds a lot better. Less whiny bitch, more roll with the punches.

Mally leans in, lowering his voice to Van, but I can obviously still hear him. "Narrative means like story, right?"

Van nods, "yeah." Straightening, they look at me before starting a slow clap, and I kick both of them under the booth in irritation.

Mally grins at me. "Now you have to actually do it."

I nod. "I'm not giving up on finding a female trainer for

Paradise, and earlier today, I made up my mind to quit. So that's progress."

"And you need to start dating," Mally adds, Van seconding it with a clink of their beer glasses.

"That may take some time."

Van shakes his head. "No more wasting time."

And somehow, their frustration and care are making me feel for the first time... like maybe it's not my body that needs to change.

Maybe it's just my mindset.

8

Elsie

Some days, blue is the only color in my world.

"Mama, can I get this?" Effie's little hand curls around my leg, and her strength always surprises me. She shakes me, and I look down at her with my finger to my lips, trying to keep her quiet while we wait in line.

With her other hand, she's holding a tiny stuffed animal. It's a dog with shaggy gray hair and white coloring around one eye and all down his belly. I smile at her as her wide blue eyes look adoringly at the stuffed pup. It's a small price to pay for rewarding my sweet girl, who stands patiently in line at the pharmacy with her mom for an hour.

Yep, I've officially been here for an *hour*. But thankfully, we're next.

After I agree to buy the puppy if she promises to stop

begging Grandma Elaine for an actual puppy, I'm terrified my mom might actually buy a damn dog on an off-day. But without a vehicle, it would be pretty challenging.

"Next," the short man behind the counter calls lifelessly, his dead eyes on mine.

"Picking up for Elaine Francis."

His fingers fly over the keyboard, eyes never leaving the screen. He nods. "It's ready."

Before he steps away toward the trough of bagged pills, I reach over the counter and wrap my hand around his wrist. His eyes flick to mine, and *finally,* the man has an expression.

Salty.

"Ma'am, do not touch me." His jaw snaps together with each word.

I retract my hand like I've touched fire, but don't hold back my words just because I've potentially crossed a weird pharmacy-patient line. Eh, more like a human decency line because I have no right to touch this man. My mom needs help, though.

"Can we get the quantity increased on this one?" I can't remember the name of the complex drug, so instead, I name the other two prescriptions noting that it's not them. He nods his head slowly.

"I know which prescription," he says, annoyed with me. "But no. Your care provider has to increase the dosage." He puts distance between us, probably so I can't grab him again. Smart man.

I fall onto my heels, a disappointed breath slipping free from my chest. I can't quit trying.

"They won't change the dosage without imaging, but our insurance won't cover the imaging because her condition is pre-existing," I explain, but his face doesn't soften in the slightest.

"I don't dose; I just fill," he says, sliding the bag across the counter. He taps the keyboard a few more times; his dead eyes focused on the screen. "Seventy-six—"

"Dollars and fifty-three cents," I finish because this is what it costs every two weeks. Spending less than one hundred and sixty dollars a month on meds is lucky. It doesn't make us broke, which it does to a lot of families less fortunate than us.

But it's also getting to a point where the dosage just is not effective as it once was. What I said about the scan is true—mom's primary care doctor can't increase the dosage until she has brain imaging done to assess the progression of her disease, but the same insurance that so graciously covers the meds for her preexisting condition equally will *not* fund a scan for monitoring a preexisting condition.

Crazy shit, right?

"Okay," I smile, but he barely meets my eyes for the rest of the transaction. Effie waves her puppy over the counter. "And that."

We pay and leave, stopping by the grocery store for some orange juice and pancake mix to take back home. I'm going to work today, but I always get meds and a small amount of groceries before I leave. I take Effie with me to let mom prepare for the day and so me and my girl get some time together before I have to go.

On the days she doesn't have pre-k, I drop Effie with mom and our neighbor, Fanny, who comes over to play cards and keep my mom company on the days she's struggling. I'm grateful for Fanny, giving us her time when she can. I love that some people just are family, without the blood ties.

A few minutes after clocking in at work, the blues find me. It happens when I see Fanny, but it's not Fanny's fault. When I see her, though, every part of me is aware that I'm losing my mom. Effie is losing her grandma.

I hate it.

I fucking hate it.

And all I can do is work here at this place where I'm not making anyone proud just to earn insurance to provide meds that only *kind of* help. Meanwhile, I'm powerless to the actual problem—the disease of early-onset dementia—and my life is too heavy for anyone to step into.

Some days, blue is the only color in my world.

Today is one of those days.

"Els," Karina, my manager, snaps me from my funk. I spin in my chair to find her nose wrinkled, brows dipping on the edges. "Bad news."

I stand from the chair and finger the key on my belt that opens the utility closet. My eyes ask her for confirmation, and she nods reluctantly.

"Where is it?" I ask, trying to keep the disappointment and disgust from my voice. She is my boss, after all, even if we both know cleaning up a stranger's vomit has to be one of the worst things ever.

"Kids play space," she says, shrugging her shoulders. "Where it always is."

After cleaning vomit from a ball pit for two and half hours—*fun*, I know—I return to the front desk, where I am promptly sneezed on by a member who insisted on close-talking when greeting me hello. Like, *I am intimately acquainted with the size of his pores* type of close. After that, the remainder of my shift is spent scanning paper gym applications for the people who don't sign up online. And for everything people do online, apparently, signing up for the gym isn't one of them. Because I have papercuts and a wrist ache, and when I leave, I leave a stack of unscanned papers.

Arriving home, I take a quick shower and then play board games with Effie. We play Trolls Monopoly, Connect Four, and a very suspiciously dealt hand of Go-Fish. After dinner and a popsicle, a bath with way too many bubbles, and several bedtime stories, I put her to bed with a kiss on her forehead.

"Did you have a good day with Grandma Elaine and Fanny?" I wait until the end of the day to ask this when everything has been fun, and we're calm and sleepy, when mom isn't around.

She nods, her blonde curls stretching across the pillow. With her new stuffed dog clutched to her chest, I tuck her in and give her another kiss. "I'm glad. Did you name your doggy?"

"No," she says, her tiny fingers smoothing through the already mangled-looking fur on the new toy. "He's just going to be *dog* for now. I want to save *all* dog names for my real dog. I'll name this one after."

"Effie, we may not get a real dog. Not for a while, at least."

She smiles, her lids drooping with exhaustion from a full, busy, and beautiful day. "I can wait."

Laughing, I give her yet another kiss and take a moment to inhale her smell of fresh shampoo and innocence. "Love you, Effie. Sleep well, okay? Sweet dreams."

"Sweet dreams," she yawns back as I quietly close her door behind me.

Returning to the kitchen, I see that Fanny has gone home, and things are tidied up. Mom is sitting in her recliner, facing the TV, eyes open and unfocused. She hasn't had an awful day, but it was unsteady enough to require Fanny's help.

"We meet again," I say, having been in and out of her hair for the last three hours since coming home.

She smiles but doesn't look my way. "This isn't a mystery; it's a romance," she says of the program playing on the TV. My focus pours over the screen where there are two main characters in time-period garb representative of the 1700s. With her focus only partially on me, I look back at my mom, who has given me so much sage advice over the years. She's in there; no matter what else is in there with her–she's still in there.

"Hey, mom, can I ask you something?"

She hums acknowledgment, so I nab my sliver of opportunity before it's gone. "I've been offered a job–I won't stop working at Globo... this would be... in addition to that. In the evenings, after you and Effie are asleep." I study her profile, but her expression remains impassive, and I don't know if she's fully understanding. But I press on because asking her if she understands me could trigger anger. "Anyway, it's... non-traditional. Really far outside of my comfort zone in a lot of ways."

Mom's head turns slowly, her blue eyes that look like mine and Effie's glossy in the dim TV light. "What would you be doing?"

Chewing the inside of my cheek for a moment while

collecting a sensitive response, I finally decide on "helping men test their limits and find inner strength, I guess." If that's not the most creative workaround, I don't know what is. Hell, maybe I should get a job doing PR or something.

She tips her head to the side, and for a split second, I see my old mom sitting there, listening to me intently like the night I told her I'd gotten pregnant. Even the night Jake broke it off, she'd been completely lucid and herself. Though peppered with drama, I hold those moments close to my chest.

"You've always been good at caring for people, Elsie. In any way, shape, or form. You're a born carer. Helping someone find their best selves–that seems easy for you."

Appreciation and warmth prick at the backs of my eyes, but I smile in the face of my impending tears. Because this is a moment I know I'll remember. I only hope there are more of these ahead.

"Thanks, mom."

For the next few minutes, she talks about what kind of day she's had, what she, Effie, and Fanny did, and then, after bringing her a nice cup of warm water with honey, I help her to her room, give her a kiss and head to my own bedroom.

Sitting on the side of my bed, I hold my phone in my hands for a minute while the image of Lacey's naughty closet flits through my mind.

Can I really wear those things?

Can I really be a dominant female over a man I've never met?

Can I really be in charge of a man's mind and body two hours a week?

Would I really be doing it to help him find some inner

power, the way Lacey framed it all up, or am I really just a glorified hooker?

I think of Lacey's home. I think of those gorgeous photos on the wall. How she said she's now a silent partner of our Globo-Fitness location.

Whether it gives the man power or not, it clearly brought her power and confidence in so many ways. She made it work for her; she didn't work for the job.

I want that power. I want that confidence. I want that personal success of feeling like I own and control some aspect of this chaotic life.

Quickly, I type a text before I can change my mind.

Elsie: *I'm in. Tell me where to go from here.*

Lacey's response is so fast that part of me can't help but take it as a sign that I'm going down the right road. I'm totally one of those annoying people who believes in signs. I can't help it.

Lacey: *I've got a new client for you to meet with on Thursday. Perfect timing. I'll call you tomorrow to iron out the details.*

Lacey: *You're going to be so good at this. And it will bring you so much, Els, trust me.*

Plugging my phone in on the night table by my bed, I set my alarm to prepare for my five AM shift at the gym the next day. Flopping onto the bed, my body, mind, and heart are exhausted from a day of working, then momming, and then worrying about mom's condition.

I really hope Lacey isn't blowing smoke up my ass. I could use a shot of raw female power right about now.

I'm feeling pretty beat.

9

Bran

I don't want to be Arizona. The boys are right.

"You know, with you, they could call it a half-blind date," Batman says proudly, like the joke is even a *tiny* bit original. It's not.

"Dude, I worked a full day at the gym. I'm not picking up an extra shift trying to make you feel funny."

Batman's real name is actually Henry, but when he started dating his now-wife Robin? Well, you don't fucking walk on an organic opportunity to have a badass nickname like Batman. Even if you are just a normal fucking dude named Henry.

He and Robin are the assholes responsible for my blind date tonight, actually. And for some reason, Batman is here

Stray

at my house just thirty minutes before the date. As if I need someone who hasn't dated in years to coach me on anything. I'm not that fucking desperate.

"You guys act like I can't get chicks," I say, feeding my arms into my long-sleeved flannel shirt. Black and white, nothing fancy, goes good with the dark beard and dark eyes– that's what Sammy said. In fact, my sister is who I can thank for my now carefully cultivated style.

Apparently, *meathead* is hot for a minute and then just boring. I'm allowed to wear my joggers, hoodies, and beanies most of the time because of my lifestyle, so long as I wear flannels, jeans, non-lifting shoes (she got me some Vans and sneakers because my Nike Metcons just weren't cutting it) and cologne any other time, I pass the test. According to Sammy, that is.

"We know you can get laid, bro, but I think this whole *Brantervention* is about finding you a serious relationship and not letting you blame your partial eyeball situation anymore."

"Wow," I say, blinking several times at him. "That was insanely accurate and also kind of hurtful." Batman shrugs because he obviously really doesn't care about hurting my feelings.

"Don't care," he says, leaning forward and sucking in some of my personal space through his nose.

"Dude, are you smelling me?"

"Robin told me to say that and make sure you smell good." He rocks back on his feet, giving me a satisfied nod. "You smell sexy hot."

"Dude," I drag out, smoothing my hand through my hair

to adjust the elastic band on my eyepatch. "Don't say shit like that."

He smiles. "So, you ready?"

I shake my head, hating that I'm the group fucking basketcase, but here I am. "Yeah."

"Hey man, you know we give you a bad time because we're assholes, but when it comes down to it, you realize being in a serious relationship will happen as soon as *you're* ready. It's not the ladies that are hung up on the eye; it's you."

I swallow down his words, hating how jagged they tear through my diaphragm as I do. I'm the gatekeeper to my own happiness–that's something I've been battling for years. Because if I accept that truth, then every time I strike out with a woman, it will be because of me. Maybe it will be because of my eye sometimes, but honestly? Probably not.

And avoiding it forever means I'm also avoiding the one thing I'm dying to have.

Kind of a fucked up double-edged sword, but then again, *any* double-edged sword is fucked up.

"If I fall for a dope chick, and we work well together for months, and then she breaks it off because she doesn't wanna marry a guy with one eye–"

"Dude, stop. Just... you have to stop. Stop writing your story before it's happened.

Have you ever felt bad about yourself and then had someone nicknamed after a comic book hero school you with basic wisdom? Talk about a kick in the nuts.

He holds out a closed fist, so I bump it with mine. "Just have a good time and know that you've done enough thinking about your eye for the last eight years. Time to accept it and move forward."

He nudges me with his elbow when I remain silent. "Be McSteamy, don't be Dr. Robbins."

"They told you about that shit?"

Batman's grin is so wide that it personally irritates me. "Duh."

Just then, my phone comes alive in my pocket, and before I even unlock it, I know who it is.

Earlier today, Sammy and Mally decided they were going to start a group text message with me to keep me focused on moving ahead. I told them it wasn't necessary, that the message about being hung up on my own limitations was the reason for my unhappiness—I said I got it a million times. But Sammy's only response?

"Have you been in a serious relationship since that night?"

When the answer was a quick and easy "no," that's when I realized the group text message for moral support was a battle I wasn't going to win.

They were right. I'd been hiding my fears behind poor first impressions. Someone looked at me funny or didn't seem interested? I'd blamed my eye and slunk away, eliminating the possibility of even trying. Because if I tried, I'd be hurt for real, and that paired with my inadequacies over my appearance—I wasn't strong enough to bear it. Cue torturing my muscles to build up that physical wall.

But I don't want to be alone forever, and to work toward that goal, I had to start doing more. Way more.

Enough with the leg, I can hear Arizona's wife Callie

screaming in their apartment, another fight over the appendage, the last straw between them.

I don't want to be Arizona. The boys are right.

Sammy: *I saved the life of a man in cardiac arrest and then immediately went to the next curtain and pulled a TV remote from my patient's ass.*

Sammy: *A two-hour dinner with someone new won't kill you if all that shit doesn't kill me.*

Mally: *Am I missing something? Is he trying to cancel?*

Sammy: *No, I'm just keeping him from trying.*

Bran: *I wasn't going to flake. Batman came by and gave me a guilt trip.*

Sammy: *Because you've wasted eight years hiding behind the eye when in reality, we all get rejected for asinine reasons. You just have to sack up and move on, but you keep blaming that eye for your aloneness because you're scared maybe it's just you they don't want. But you're great, so stop and just go have fun.*

Mally: *Jesus Samantha.*

Mally: *GIF of Samantha from Bewitched wiggling her nose.*

Mally: *Too spot on. This is a build-up text thread. We aren't the stepsisters in Cinderella, but you totally just stepsistered him.*

Sammy: WTF?

Mally: *Tore him apart. The way they tore off her dress.*

Bran: *Wow. Malibu, I didn't know you were capable of making a metaphor that wasn't about your body.*

Mally: *I step out of my box for you, Bran.*

Bran: *Sam, that was pretty harsh.*

Sammy: *This text is to keep you on track. Not to make you feel good. The truth hurts, but it's the only thing keeping you on course.*

Sammy: *Tell me I'm wrong.*

Bran: *You're not wrong.*

Mally: *Damn, I wish I had that sibling mind-share thing you guys have.*

Mally: *It's too late to wish for a baby brother, huh?*

Bran: *You're an idiot.*

Bran: *Gotta go. Have to pick up my date.*

Sammy: *Knock 'em dead. You're a catch. Stop thinking you aren't. It's pissing me off.*

Mally: *^^Samesies.*

I don't know if it's because I'm hopped up on a hefty dose of self-awareness or if it's just because this was written in the cards for tonight, but hot damn. This date is going well.

Like, really fucking well.

Katelyn is her name—and she doesn't go by Kate or any other nickname. That started us off with lots of things to talk about since my guys and I strictly go by insanely ridiculous nicknames. Talk of my friends led to talk of her friends, which easily turned into a discussion of our hobbies and free time. She assumed correctly when she guessed that most of my hobbies involved working out in some form, and I assumed correctly when I guessed that her hobbies were true crime and Wordle—because that's what Sammy likes, too. And she reminds me a ton of Sammy. Not *physically*. I'm not a fucking creep.

But when I told her that my sister is my best friend and

that her personality was similar, it opened even more doors for conversation—this time about family life, values, and upbringing.

I haven't had these kinds of date talks in so fucking long it feels like a breath of fresh air. I mean, it's more fun once you know someone as well as you know yourself and can read them, but still, this process is one I realize now that I really missed.

Because Hinge and Tinder dates didn't give a fuck about anything but what I had between my legs and that I did indeed show up as the muscled, inked man in the profile photo.

This backstory talk feels normal. Normal feels good. Really fucking good.

I tease her about ordering a salad, and she quips back with patriarchal jokes about me ordering a steak and potatoes. We eat, we laugh a lot, and we talk a ton. She of course, looks at my eye a few times but not at all in a way that leads me to believe it's weirding her out. I mean, she knew about it ahead of time anyway.

And when the check is paid, I'm actually excited to see if she asks me inside when I drop her off. I haven't been excited about anything opposite-sex orientated in any serious capacity in ages. Porn doesn't count.

"Oh geez," Katelyn says, peering out the long windows around the restaurant's old wooden door. "It's pouring."

I lean down into the window over the top of her, noticing how fresh and girly she smells. My dick likes that, but right now, it looks like I'll be jogging two blocks in the rain to get my truck, so any hot girl smells are going to have to wait.

"I'll get the truck and come back and grab you when I'm

out front. You don't need to get wet." I smile, taking in her white tank top beneath her open red cardigan.

"Thanks," she smiles back at me, relief in her body language as she settles into a bench seat in the restaurant's waiting area.

It's been a while since I've been able to be the chivalrous guy. I'm kind of excited about that, too.

After jogging carefully in the rain to my truck, I drive it as close to the restaurant as possible, but the front door is packed. I wasn't the only one playing the chivalry card tonight, apparently. Instead, I pull my truck into the back parking lot, which is double the size of the front parking area along the street. Going in through the back door, I realize this is even better because the back door is covered–Katelyn won't have to get her hair wet at all.

I know women hate getting their hair wet.

Shaking off my hair and combing my hand down my beard after I step inside the back door, I cautiously make my way through the restaurant. Sidestepping behind chairs, narrowly avoiding getting an elbow to the nuts from the many arms sawing through meat–I finally make it near the maitre de, and spot Katelyn on her feet lingering near the door.

She's got her phone pressed to her ear as she peers out the front, clearly keeping an eye out for me.

I step up behind her, ready to interrupt her so that she knows we're ready to go, when her conversation stops me.

"Super. Super hot, and we're super compatible. He's like, all buff and sexy."

I can't help but grin at her words. Even though I know I'm hung up on my eye; I also know I am a good-looking guy.

But hearing it? Hearing it is somehow much more validating. I raise my arm, going to grip her shoulder, when she continues, oblivious to my presence looming near.

"But he wears an eyepatch and... I don't know. Call me shallow, but when I envision my life... all of us have all of our eyes, you know?" She giggles.

Her words are... honest. Cruelly honest, but the laugh that follows–short and fleeting, like this whole night is just a funny, meaningless part of her life. It doesn't sit well.

Sweat breaks out along my forehead, and beneath my beard, my skin grows hot and itchy. A wave of anxiety swells in my stomach when I realize not only will she realize I heard what she said, but *I still have to drive her home.*

"Katelyn," I say as I clear my throat, unable to meet her gaze.

She stutters a quick goodbye to the person on the phone and trails behind me silently when I tell her I found a better place for her to get into my truck without getting wet.

I hold open her door and look at my feet as she silently slides into the cab past me. As soon as I'm buckled up and pulling out of the back parking lot, her voice breaks the painful silence.

"I'm so sorry I said that you know, *that way.*"

I don't have anything to say. Because I can and will get over my shortcomings–which means I need to get over shit like this way quicker. I can't let the Katelyns of the world tell me my fucking worth.

I clear my throat. "It's fine. You can't help how you feel."

"No," she starts cautiously. "I can't. But I *can* help how insensitive and rude I am when discussing it. And I can also not discuss it in public."

I shrug and feel incredibly fucking thankful that she lives so close to the restaurant.

In an apartment above a watch repair shop downtown, Katelyn only lives a handful of blocks away, and we're there in under five minutes. My truck idles in front of the little shop, and her apartment glows above.

"Thank you for dinner, Brian. I sincerely hope you find someone. I'm..." she trails off, shaking her head. "I'm sorry again."

"Have a good life, Katelyn," I say because saying have a good night would imply that this ends tonight. We both know it's over tonight, but to save whatever is left of my poor fucking ego, I say life instead of night, to send home the fact that I really don't care to see her ever again.

I keep my face turned forward, my focus on the soft spillage of yellow street light oozing down over an aged car. She says goodnight, and the door clicks closed as gently as possible.

As soon as I get home, I follow Stoner into the backyard and stare up into the endless night sky as he smells around for the perfect spot for his pre-bedtime piss. The universe is fucking huge–look at that sky. Willowdale has plenty of fish in the sea.

Tonight is okay; it's bound to happen.

Despite the pep talk I'm giving myself, I cannot open the group text with Mally and Sammy. I see there are several messages waiting, and as much as I'm down to roll with the shittiness of tonight and not get hung up on the fact she didn't want to see me again because of my eye--I'm not down to talk about it.

Not yet.

Daisy Jane

A red circle rests at the top of my email app, with the number one inside. A new email. Even if it's a targeted ad for protein powder, reading an email right now sounds like a much-needed distraction. Stoner sniffs the same bush he always ends up pissing on, so I click the email app.

From: <private>
Subject: HLT
Date: February 24, 2022
To: Brian Edwards, Owner of Paradise Gym

HI BRIAN,

I'm more than interested in the HLT position, and I think you'll be pleased with my CV, which I can deliver in person at your earliest convenience.

Looking forward to working with you.

Call back at 555-0100.

I READ and reread that email a few times because... *who sent it?* The address has been withheld–which I've personally never seen before–and while there's a phone number, there's no name.

Maybe this person wrote the response quickly, or maybe they don't know their email is set to private? Whoever it is, they may not be the one for the position at my gym, but the fact there is still interest is enough for me tonight.

It's the tiniest little bit of positivity I need to help my mind shut off after that date. I give Stoner his CBD after we come inside, give him an extra treat, take a shower then crash into my bed.

The last thing that crosses my mind before I fall asleep is the confidence in the last sentence of that email. *Looking forward to working with you*, like this nameless woman is so confident in themself that they know I'll hire them.

I like that.

10

Elsie

This man has a sexy as shit voice.

Lacey and I had planned to get together for lunch the day of my first... training session... but my nerves didn't want to wait that long.

I've always been a planner. One to be prepared. When you're a mom, you kind of have to be. Do I have extra socks, bandaids, hand sanitizer, a spare pair of undies, and at least three different snacks? My mind is pretty much two people–one side continually runs through a checklist of *"do I have,"* and the other *does* everything else.

Waiting until just hours before I'm supposed to be a dominant, badass female to decide how I'm going to behave, what I'm supposed to say, and what I'm going to wear? Yeah, *no*. Not happening. Monday morning, as soon as Lacey strolls into Globo, I pass my task off to Chris and trail after her into the office.

"We have to talk. Like, *now*."

Her long blonde hair is styled into gorgeous beachy waves, and her makeup is done to perfection. She always looks beautiful–some may even argue she's prettier without the makeup–but she doesn't normally come to work so fixed up. I step closer to her behind the desk.

"Do you have a client meeting today?" I ask in a private whisper, despite the fact the door to her office is shut and no one with an office is even here yet.

She dances her eyebrows. "I have a lunch date. I've been seeing this guy for a few weeks, and today he wants to see me at lunch."

"Is that like... a big deal, a lunch date?" I have no clue because Jake didn't take me anywhere. Wait, that's not true. I waited in the car when he ran into the check cashing place once. So, yeah.

"Well, we usually just do evenings together since we both are busy."

"Wait–" Suddenly, I have a thought. "Your boyfriend doesn't mind that you... do what you do?"

Her eyes take in my messy curls. Yesterday was my hair wash day, so I have *day two* curls. Not as great as day one or day three, but they don't warrant the stink eye I'm getting. Self-consciously I run my hand over my hair which is down, hanging around one shoulder.

"What?"

"You have a lot of hair." She pauses, and my defenses

prickle up, but before I can say anything, she adds, "I think you'll need a larger wig cap than what I wear. But we can start with one of mine."

"Wig?"

She tips her head to the side. "My boyfriend doesn't mind. He understands its business. Because it *is* business, Elsie. I'm not flirting with these guys. I'm not getting heart eyes and stomach butterflies when I'm working. I'm doing what they *pay me to do* and feeling the way I should– powerful and accomplished." She digs through her purse, which she tossed into her desk chair. Pulling out a small, nude color piece of fabric, she passes it to me. "Save this for Thursday. If you want to wear a wig."

"I'm feeling... overwhelmed," I admit. *It's just a wig cap, Elsie, chill.*

But it's not just the wig cap that's freaking me out. I think I'm only just now realizing that I'm going to be touching a stranger in their most private place, making them do their most private thing.

I don't know if I can do it.

Lacey, who has been staring me down, sticks her finger into my face. "Don't. Don't back out."

"Lacey, I don't know–"

She shakes her head. "Nope. You told me Jake dumped you because of the chaos of your life. You wouldn't trade your life for anything, but you need to feel powerful when you're not super mom and super daughter." She strokes a hand up my arm. "Be powerful for you. Trust me?"

It's funny, even if they aren't your best friend when someone asks you to trust them, you really want to. And I do want to trust Lacey. Because I see her life and know that she wants that for me, too. She stands to earn nothing from my success, and that's how I know there are no ulterior motives. Just a nice person wanting what's best for another person.

"Okay," I say with a sigh. "But I'm a planner. I need to know, like, what to say, what to wear, everything." I force out another sigh, realizing I have no freaking clue what I'm going to do and where I'm going to find the courage to do it.

"First," Lacey says, hooking her purse onto the edge of her chair. She flops down and pulls herself to the open laptop, swiping it awake. A few taps later and her email is loaded up on the screen. "You can see the email that I responded to for you. This is your first client."

"You responded as me?" I ask, knowing how wide my eyes must be based on the instant burning feeling.

She waves a hand down like it's nothing. "For you. Not as you. You'll see." She nods to the screen, so I follow.

From: <private>
Subject: HLT
Date: February 24 2022 4:46 pm
To: Brian Edwards, Owner of Paradise Gym

Hi Brian,

I'm more than interested in the HLT position, and I think you'll be pleased with my CV, which I can deliver in person at your earliest convenience.

Looking forward to working with you.

Call back at 555-0100.

Daisy Jane

From: Brian Edwards, Owner of Paradise Gym
Subject: Re: HLT
Date: February 24, 2022 10:54 pm
To: <private>

Hi there,

Looking forward to meeting with you. Didn't catch a name, but I'll get it when I see you. Come to Paradise, my gym where the position is open, at 8:00 pm this Thursday evening. We'll interview in the office; clients are usually out of here by 7 pm.

Looking forward to meeting with you.

"He said he's looking forward to meeting you *twice*," Lacey grins, looking up at me where I'm hovering over her shoulder, staring at the screen.

I straighten my spine and swallow, but my mouth and throat are dry. Holy shit, I'm doing this. I'm going to this man's gym, and I'm…

"What exactly am I going to *do* Thursday when I go there?"

Lacey braces her sneakered feet against her wood desk and shoves backward like it's her first time in an office chair with wheels. Crossing her legs at the knee, she folds her arms over her chest and narrows her eyes on me.

"Hmm," she hums pensively, "In my experience, it depends on his energy."

"Oh Jesus," I say, draping my hand over my chest, feeling the back of my shirt cling to my suddenly sweaty skin. "I am *so* not ready for this."

Lacey leans forward over her lap. "No matter how ready you are, you feel like that the first few times, no matter what. Trust me."

I nod, then suddenly, every part of me begins wondering if I really need to feel powerful this badly. I mean, I'm a parent. I can't be arrested! Effie can't be with my mom for more than one day. I have to be there to monitor mom's health on a day-to-day basis.

Panic rises up in my chest at the thought that I'm going to do something that would potentially risk my home life. I can't do that.

"You won't get arrested, and he's not going to kill you." She pops her gum like this conversation could be about library books; she's so unconcerned. "Is that what you were worrying about?"

I press a hand to my stomach. "I hadn't even thought about him killing me."

To that, Lacey snorts out a laugh that is so ugly it breaks my nerves and I laugh too a little, lifting the back of my wrist to my mouth to stifle it.

"This is a safe business, and I know that's hard for normal people to believe, but it is."

I point to myself, the person on the verge of being paid to get another human being off, and consider myself the *normal person* in this scenario. "I'm normal?"

She snickers again and this feels like the scary movie equivalent of when the girl runs up the stairs rather than out the door when the killer is after her. Instead of walking away from the laughing blonde and putting this entire thing to bed, I laugh, too.

Because for some strange reason, I believe what Lacey

tells me about all of this. I don't think she'd lie to me. She knows about Effie. She knows some of the troubles I have with mom—though not specifics.

"You're normal, yes." She points to the black font on the laptop screen. "He owns a business, he's having the session *at* the business—those are all big green flags. A lot of guys do this. There's probably security cameras out there, too."

I swallow, processing her words. At a business—one this guy *owns*. My eyes flick to the time stamp on the email reply. Nearly eleven and he was responding to a work email.

"Do you know him?"

She shakes her head. "Nope, like I said. I replied to the ad, thinking this one would be perfect for you. If you flaked, I'd take him of course."

I stare at the email again. The man doesn't say anything obvious or outright. I furrow my brows and let my fingers wander aimlessly over my curls as I stress. "He doesn't give any indicators that he's looking for a Dominant."

Lacey rolls her eyes, her neck still twisted to face where I am behind her in the chair. "Of course he doesn't. That's the whole point of the code, Elsie." She slides back from the desk a bit, so we can easily face one another. "You're not having sex with him unless you want to—I mean, that's not what he's paying you for. But still, it's not something you want to broadcast. It's... legally in a *weird* area."

Those words send a flurry of panic through my veins. Illegalish activity. I'm a mom. I can't do this. I can't–

"They have more to risk than you do. They're almost all wealthy guys with mental hang-ups. Some with small dicks." She shrugs. "They pay you; you do you, then it's over. They set up recurring sessions if they like you, and that's it. They don't... like, text you when it's over, send you flowers, or ask how your commute to work went. It's business. And it will make you feel alive, Elsie. I promise."

Her speech sprinkles goosebumps of exhilaration over my skin.

I know the rational me should be nervous. But there's a part of me–probably the part that really wanted Jake to open-arm my life rather than shove it away– that's excited. I wanted to feel like I held and shared power in a loving relationship. But apparently, I'm too much.

Maybe this is a way to get some part of that feeling without the risk of pain and heartache.

"Let's call him right now; we'll nail down the details for later this week, and based on his voice, I'll give you some... tips," she says, scribbling his phone number onto a Globo-Fitness application.

"Call him?" I press my hands to my suddenly hollowed chest, my eyes wide. Immediately I'm breathing hard and– "oh my God, I'm going to be touching a stranger."

Lacey wants to laugh, and she wants to roll her eyes, so she splits the difference, smirking with a subtle toss of her eyes. "Every gynecologist has a first client, too, Els. After the first time, you'll see, *it's just a job.*"

"But one that makes me feel... powerful," I say, needing to hear the benefits directly tethered to the risks because if I don't remind myself, I will most definitely freak out.

"How will he, you know, pay me?" I ask, realizing that at the base of this gig, it's transactional. I provide the... service... and he pays me. No matter what either of our ulterior motives are, it's a transaction.

"Why do they do it? I mean... if this guy owns a gym, why does he need to pay a woman to get off?"

Lacey closes the laptop and motions for me to sit across from her in the chair opposite the desk. My nerves carry me there, and when I sit, I'm still all fidgety, and my pulse zooms.

"When you post a selfie on your IG stories, why do you do it?"

I wrinkle my nose. I have an Instagram account, but I rarely use it. Especially not to post selfies. I missed that part of my youth by getting knocked up at age eighteen.

"Okay, let me put it this way." Lacey tosses her blonde hair behind her shoulder, being cautious not to disrupt the carefully crafted beach waves. Beach waves are supposed to look natural, yet they always take the most time. This I know from my year-long attempt to have straight hair. "Everybody just wants to feel good. But it's harder for some people to find what makes them feel good. For... a lot of reasons."

I roll my bottom lip through my teeth. "Name some."

Unphased, she leans back and rests her hands on her belly like a true business woman. "Well, I had a submissive once that got too attached to his dates. So he didn't sleep with them for fear of always falling in love. He wanted a dominant to get off, yeah, but he also wanted to control his orgasms. Learn discipline. Thought it would help his attachment issues going forward if he could really *own* his orgasm and realize that coming with someone doesn't mean you love them."

"And you helped him with that?"

She grins so widely that my breath catches. "Absolutely."

Stray

"Okay, what else?"

She hums thoughtfully while studying her fingernails, which, by the way, are perfectly salon manicured. I look down at my torn-up cuticles and shortly trimmed nails.

"Some have small dicks and need me to be dominant in a different way. I show them their control, and once I let them lose it, I show them what they're capable of and how size doesn't matter at all." She looks up from her pink and white nails. "It is all about who you are, not what you've got. I've learned that."

Not satisfied yet, I ask, "what else?"

Thankfully, she doesn't get annoyed but does pull herself back up to her desk. Suddenly it feels like she and I are in an interview. "Men want female Dominants for a lot of reasons. And let's face it. Men can be stupid. I've dommed for men for a couple of months only to find out their reasoning was simply that they wanted to see a woman in a corset, or that they weren't sure if they could come from anyone but their own hand anymore."

I wince. "Death grippers, huh?"

She nods but doesn't linger on it. "Lots of different reasons, just like we choose to become Dominant for different reasons." She points into her chest. "I want the power of men choosing to give me money." Now the white-tipped acrylic is pointed at me. "You want to feel powerful, period."

"I don't even know if it's powerful as much as it is..."

"In control," she adds softly, and then our eyes lock. She sees me far more than I've ever given her credit, and for that I feel bad.

"Thanks for letting me in on this Lacey. I mean, I know it must feel risky."

She nods. "You're the first person I've ever told. But it's because I got a gut feeling about you. I had it before the mixer. But listening to the Jake drama... everything just made sense."

I swallow thickly, acutely aware of the nervous drops of sweat pooling at the waistband of my underwear, having traveled down the hollow of my spine. "And if I don't like it?"

She shrugs. "Then you don't commit to another session."

"Can I leave the session if I don't like it?"

Lacey laughs, and it takes me off guard because our conversation has grown soft and private. "Of course you can. You're the boss, Els, that's the part I don't think you're getting."

"So this guy–Paradise gym guy," I say, because I didn't allow myself to really remember his name. It felt like too much to take in at one time. First the idea that I'm selling some part of myself to a stranger. I'll process that stranger's name when I absolutely have to.

Baby steps.

"You have to give me some ideas on how to behave. I'm clueless."

She lifts her cell phone. "Get yours out, and we'll call."

I nod and follow her directions. Without any double-checking to see if I'm ready, Lacey begins dialing, and I absolutely fucking freak.

"Wait, wait–"

She holds up a hand. "Like a bandaid," she says, holding my phone out to me, the speakerphone activated.

"Did you look at the website I gave you the card for?" she whispers, even though the phone is still ringing. Why am I equal parts hopeful and disappointed at the idea of the call going to voicemail?

"I stayed up almost all night," I admit because if there's anyone who can clearly take the cold honest truth, it's Lacey.

"So you liked it," she grins as the phone rattles through what feels like its millionth ring.

I exhale a controlled and steadying breath. "It was a lot."

"Did it make you wet?" she asks, her tone low, eyebrows dancing.

"Lacey!"

Just then, the ringing stops. Lacey stops, her eyes freezing on mine. My mouth falls open, and like a slow-motion moment of Pamela Anderson running on a beach in the nineties, the Paradise gym owner greets me.

"Hello, this is Bran," the voice tumbles through the phone speaker and falls into my lap, heavy and rough. It feels good. My thighs warm, and my skin pricks with that same heat. Holy shit. This man has a sexy as shit voice.

My cheeks color, and Lacey doesn't let it go. "You like his voice," she overly mouths, and I karate chop my hand through her words, mid-air, focusing on the voice.

"Hi, is this..." Fuck, I didn't think about what I was going to say. Fuck! "The owner of Paradise gym?" Fuck! I should've looked at his name.

He chuckles a little, and my nipples harden. What?! My nipples have only ever hardened at the sound of a breast pump or a crying baby Effie. Seriously. But they're hard now–even though the cup of a molded bra and a thick Globo-Fitness polo shirt. And of course, Lacey has to notice that. She grins, and it's then I swivel my body in the seat, trying to find a moment of privacy from her knowing eyes.

"Yeah, this is Bran. Who's this?"

No name. Lacey hadn't given him a name. Do I want him to have my real name? Am I seriously taking all this time to think through this shit while this Fabio-sounding dude is waiting for me?

"E," I say, sounding way more calm than I actually feel because, let's face it, I don't feel calm whatsoever. I feel... frazzled. But wrapped in that panic and chaos?

Undeniable excitement.

"E," the voice comes back. Bran's voice, I train my brain to know the name of the heat-inducing voice. "Well, E, what can I do for you?"

"I'm the... Heavy Lifting Trainer," I say finally, letting my eyes bounce over to Lacey. Luckily, she's nodding reassuringly, tossing me thumbs up. I'm not typically someone who needs a lot of reinforcement—being a parent and the child of a struggling parent; I'm good with making sound choices and sticking by them.

But when it comes to this uncharted territory and—more honestly—Bran's voice... I need to know that I'm doing good.

A moment passes. "Oh," he says, "was there a problem with my response email? Can you not meet me this Thursday?"

"I can," I say quickly... almost too quickly because it gets a stifled snort from Lacey. I give her death eyes—every woman gives and knows the look—and she presses her wrist to her lips to shut herself up before I kill her. "I just wanted to verify that we're meeting at... your gym," I say, the last two words lingering. I knew this man owned his own business before this call, but somehow it hits differently now that I know what he sounds like.

"Yep," he says, his voice stretching with what I imagine is his body. And after a series of groans and a hushed word passed to someone around him, his focus is back on me. "See you Thursday at eight then."

"Okay," I say lamely, and just as I'm about to hang up, he stops me.

"E?"

My heart falters a bit at my new but very hot nickname. "Yeah?"

"Is this the number where I can reach you?"

"Yeah," I say back. And for some reason, I add, "bye Bran."

My skin ripples with goosebumps and heat when he says, "See you, E."

Lacey lets me borrow several outfits but the toys and devices? I feel weird borrowing things that have been inside other people. Really freaking weird. As the chick who Lysol wipes the pens at the front desk at the gym, I tell her I'll order my own toys.

Except when I'm at home that night, looking on Amazon Prime because fortunately even sex toys come in two days, I start to realize I don't know what to order.

Sure, I went over every single molecule of information when I scanned that QR code and got to Lacey's private website. Her options were neatly listed in a drop-down menu, with each act listed being a separate charge.

She had male chastity, pegging, ass play, prostate

orgasms, nipple stimulation, gagging and choking, blindfolding, orgasm denial and ruin—anything you could or *couldn't* think of, Lacey had it listed as a payable option on her site. Though money was denoted with roses rather than actual dollar amounts.

All in all, two hours of her time where she was fully costumed as Your Mistress, used an array of toys *and* set you up for the next session—one thousand long-stemmed red roses. Which I knew to be, of course, one thousand dollars.

Confused about "setting you up for frustrating success the next time I see you," I make sure Effie and mom are asleep before I get out my phone and call her.

Hopefully she isn't... busy.

"Hey girl," she says, crunching loudly into the speaker. "I'm eating popcorn. What's up?"

"What do you mean when you say setting you up for frustrating success the next time I see you?" I ask, launching right into the topic at hand because I am still way too nervous to do small talk.

"Looking at my website again, I see," she laughs carelessly into the phone and takes another loud bite of popcorn.

"Yeah, I have my Amazon up on my computer, and I'm just figuring out what I'm gonna bring on Thursday."

"Well," she says, crunching some more. "When I make promises to keep them ready until next time, that's usually geared towards my clients who want to be put into chastity."

"Chastity," I repeat, knowing exactly what it is but being completely unable to picture it on a man. I've got a big, nasty metal belt with a padlock at the crotch in mind, and in my vision, it's on a maiden in the 1600s.

"Look it up. I'll wait."

Switching to an Incognito tab in my browser because my mom sometimes uses the computer to look up her soap opera episodes, I type male chastity into the online retailer's search box. The results are plentiful, and my jaw drops.

"It doesn't hurt," Lacey says, somehow aware that I'm already well into the listings. "They like feeling like they belong to us. That their orgasm and power is only unlocked and unleashed around us."

I bite into my bottom lip, the power of the chastity cage worming through my lower half, leaving heat in its wake. The cage is hot. What it stands for–handing their most prized possession to us to keep for *however* long? Even hotter.

And exactly the type of rush I need.

"And do they tell you, or do you tell them, you know, to wear the cage?"

There's rustling on Lacey's end, and I'm pretty sure she didn't just set the popcorn down, but she paused her show. "Elsie, you're the Dominant. You don't ask questions. Ever. For any reason. You make all the choices, and they abide by them." There's a moment of silence between us, then she says, "let me send you a link to some videos. I watched them before I started."

A moment later, a link appears in our text message conversation, and a second after that, the thumbnail for the video loads.

A woman wearing a black corset and long, black coat appears in the photo. Her hand is curled around a hard, pink cock, and the smile on her face is so wide, I find myself smiling too.

"Show up in one of the outfits I let you borrow. Bring

what you're comfortable with bringing. But most of all, the first time is just to establish how bad they're going to have it with you as their Dom."

"How *bad?*"

"How *baad*," she repeats, spreading the word apart sinfully. My flesh warms.

We end the call, and I spend an hour watching several of the videos on the channel Lacey sent to me.

One of the women brings the man to orgasm, through his metal cage, with her gloved finger inside him. Another features a man grinding his erection into nothing but thin air, his wrists bound at his lower back, the woman's lips sealed over one of his nipples.

That's where I stopped.

With two hundred dollars worth of goodies in my shopping cart, I gladly click Buy Now and send Lacey a follow-up text.

Elsie: *I'm ready for Thursday. And I'm excited.*

Lacey: *You got this.*

Elsie: *Wait–how does he pay me?*

Lacey: [IMAGE]

Lacey: *I'll give it to you at Globo tomorrow.*

The image is a business card on Lacey's counter, a QR code in the center. Scanning it from the image of the card alone, a text bubble pops up on my phone screen. "E's Venmo".

I'm not doing it for the money, but knowing a man will put money in that account just to be in my presence?

I raise my middle finger in the air in the privacy of my room. "Fuck you, Jake."

Stray

    I'm doing this for me, because I don't have to wait for men like Jake to make me feel powerful. I'm going to find power on my own. And this man, Bran, wants to help me.

    Finally, the nerves subside and all I feel is excitement.

    I can do this.

11

Bran

I find myself nodding, and swallowing down the sudden rush of drool in my mouth.

"E," I say it again for *at least* the fifth time.

Sammy volleys her head, tucking her dark hair behind her ears before she goes down for the bar. "Cute."

My eye flicks to where the guys are standing; Van is focused on his cell phone screen, Batman spotting Malibu as he benches. Once the weight is reracked, he sits up and waits for the strain to drain from his face before he speaks.

"Like E for easy or something?" he asks, his breath broken. Batman smacks the back of his head. Good man.

"Don't fucking say shit like that. What if he hires her and she's working here in a few days? You'll feel like a prick for calling her easy," Batman says, and the conversation

Stray

interests Van, bringing his gaze to Mally and Batman, then over to me.

"Didn't ask what it's short for?"

I shake my head. "No, why would I? What if it's just E, and it's not short for anything? Who the fuck am I to tell her that her name needs more letters."

"More syllables at least," Mally breathes, lowering himself back down for his next set.

"Bran only has one syllable, idiot," I say, shaking my head. "Since when are we rating people on how many syllables their name is?"

"We aren't," Van says, stuffing his phone into his bag on the ground. "Boo's just hurt because he knows you'll focus more on her and training her, and I met someone, and Batman's married... he's starting to feel like he could be left behind." Van smiles patronizingly at Mally, who immediately reracks the weight and shoots up to his feet, face beet red.

"I did not say that!" he whines, and Jesus, I can't make room for Mally's big emotions right now. Truth is, I'm nervous about meeting E, and I don't give a shit if the E isn't short for anything.

"But you feel it, don't you, buddy?" Van asks, tapping Mally in the chest. His head of blonde hair tips forward.

"Fine, I don't want to be the only guy with nothing to do."

"I'm not gonna like, train her after hours. It's not like I'm getting a girlfriend." I don't understand why Malibu seems to think hiring a female for Paradise will turn into me not wanting to be around the guys.

"Dude, if you hire a hot chick to work here and then

she's all like, *Hey Bran, I got this IKEA bookcase this weekend, can you come build it?* You're one-hundred percent building that bookcase instead of getting wings and beers."

"You made that entire little story up in your head, man. And also, I don't know if E is hot. Or if I'm hiring her." I blink at him.

"He's *worst-casing* it," Van supplies, and since the two of them are partners at work, they know each other's tells. Though, to be fair, Mally is pretty much an open book. He wears it all on his face along with his heart on his sleeve.

"Okay, well, obviously, if she's hot and I hire her, and she buys a table—"

"Bookshelf," Mally corrects, still sulking.

"Okay, if she buys a bookshelf and asks me to build it, I'm definitely going to ditch you fuckers and go build it."

"That's what we want. The baby to leave the nest," Batman says, laying a hand on Mally's shoulder. "Now quit being a bitch and finish your set because Robin needs me home before her Zoom call."

Mally throws his body back down onto the bench, and I turn to face Van.

"We do want that, though, you know? For you to stop worrying and just... go with whatever."

"I'm not hiring a girlfriend; I'm hiring a trainer."

He nods like no shit. "But it's the first step in the right direction. And I'm telling you, with a new mindset, shit will start snowballing. You'll be engaged by Christmas. Not to E, but to someone else."

Snorting out a laugh, I clap him on the back because I needed that.

"I'll get right on it."

He wags a tattooed finger at me. Yes, even his fingers have ink. "You'll see. When you change your mindset, you got no idea what you can have."

Van, my very intense friend, has recently been seeing someone. It's hush-hush, but Mally is basically an unlocked diary, so I'm aware. With his... intensity issues, the idea that Van has a girl gives me hope. Not because he's a bad guy, but because it means he's changed and allowed himself to have what he wants.

"I kinda wish you guys would've told me I was Arizona Robbins a lot sooner."

Van shrugs. "We thought you knew."

* * *

Though I know nothing about this girl, I do find it sexy that she's a personal trainer. Most female trainers I've come into contact with over the years of attending gym expos and sports medicine conferences have been completely fucking badass.

They're fit, but it's not just that.

They handle their shit, and I don't know a better way of putting it.

If you ask them who supplies their car insurance, they know. If you ask them how much their proteins cost at the grocery store cost? They know. Ask them to be on time, and they are. Require they bring something, they do. They have... have their shit together. And maybe that's not all of them, but it's the ones I've met.

I can't deny that the unknown is causing me to build some serious Disney fantasies in my head, too. Like, maybe this chick will end up being more than just a trainer at my gym? Maybe this will end up with some sort of friends-to-more situation?

Because Paradise is a heavy lifting gym, most clients are early risers. That means I can comfortably close up at seven, leaving the few post-work stragglers to finish their final sets before eight.

Tonight is no different, so as long as E is on time, we should be done with this interview and out of here by nine.

I remind myself that just because I'm changing my mindset doesn't mean life will play out like a fairy tale. This chick is coming here for an interview–I don't need to project my desires to fall in love and wife someone up on *her*. That's not fair.

And what I told Van is true. Mally's got his jockstrap twisted. I'm not hiring for this position to date the chick I hire; this is just to grow comfortable.

So the fact that I'm already secretly deep-down in the most private *never talk about your feelings* part of me, having a weird feeling about E... I don't know what to think about that. About how I'm hoping maybe she won't just be the first chick not to care about my eye.

Maybe she won't only be perfect for Paradise.

I also stuff down the fact that I'm having these girly little premonitions because what the fuck? She's a complete fucking stranger.

There's a knock on the glass door.

That complete stranger is here.

I jump to my feet from my spot behind my desk. I've been hiding out in my office, trying to breathe and relax since I'm feeling unusually nervous about this interview. I guess because of the last two, but I don't know. It doesn't quite feel like the same kind of nerves.

When I come around the corner, my heart pulsing at the base of my throat, I'm literally knocked to a stop when I see her.

Face turned toward the parking lot as if she doesn't want to be spotted, E stands front and center, her body positioned between the two doors.

Her feet are... in heels. Black heels. The fucking shiny material that looks like latex or leather or some shit. Her ankles are the only other part of her body I can see because the rest of her? Wrapped in a stone-colored trench coat, cinched tightly at the waist.

She's got blonde hair, and from here, I can tell it's not a wig. The roots are a little darker, but not by much, and the golden locks spill over her shoulders and down her back. Curly hair flies across her face as she turns toward me, a gust of wind providing a few more moments of unknown between us.

She raises a slender hand to her face and pulls the hair down, her eyes immediately meeting my eye. She blinks, and her full pink lips fall apart. I swallow but try to physically hide my jumpy nerves by resuming my pace towards the door. When I get there, I twist the key and look up at her, finding that I need a deep breath and some courage to do so.

She's staring at me already, both of her bright blue eyes tamped down on my dark one. For a split second, as I'm unlocking the bottom twist lock, the tip of her tongue traverses the length of her bottom lip before darting back into her beautiful mouth.

When I pull the door open, my nerves spill out in the form of nervous chatter.

"Hi, E, I'm Bran. I'm the owner of this place. It's uh, it's nice to meet you."

I'm not a nervous talker. Think about it–do the inked guys who live and die by lifting weights usually seem to talk like the Sheldons of the world? No. Even when being blown off, I never get chatty.

That swirl of anxiousness in my gut returns, and I realize... I'm nervous around *this specific* chick. One I don't even know.

"Hi, I'm E," she says, and holy crap, that sexy little voice I heard over the phone earlier this week sounds a million times sexier in person. Like someone wrapping velvet around my aching dick.

What the fuck? Why did my mind go there?

My eye magnetizes to her plump lips, and I watch in what feels like slow motion as she rolls them together. Then I watch her hands–unpainted nails–smooth through her blonde curls until everything is apparently the way she likes it. She checks the tie around her waist, cinching it again.

"To the office?" she asks with a small smile when she finally meets my gaze again.

"Um, yeah." Realizing I was just watching her be a human for the last thirty seconds, I nod and lead the way. Jesus Christ, I need to get it together. I may not have had a serious girl in *years*, but I can't act like a damn virgin. No one wants to work for a man that stares at them like that. "Follow me."

I had planned to usher her ahead of me–the only door open down this hall is the one to my office–but now I don't know if I can handle walking behind her. Holding the door, I discreetly inhale as she passes through, and it's now I notice she's got a large purse slung over her shoulder.

She smells fucking good. Like... girly shit. Clean skin and hair products, maybe some perfume—I don't know what. But it reroutes some of the blood in my body to my dick, which twitches between my thighs. It's been a while since I've had the desire to show him any love, even if it's just with his long-time girlfriend—*my palm.*

E is waking him up.

When I close the door, she stares at the door handle for a moment before lifting her eyes to me. Giving me a pointed look, she looks back to the door handle.

"Push the button," she says, and while I'm confused for a moment, I realize she's talking about the circular built-in lock on my office door.

It clicks when I push it in, locking us in the space that needs no lock. No one's here. I wonder if I should say that, but before I do, she drops her bag on the chair with a heavy thunk.

What do women keep in those fucking things?

Turning to face me, E sifts her fingers down the buttons on the coat—buttons I hadn't even noticed were there. Then she's working that tie like she's a shibari master. Jesus, I'm getting hard just watching this girl undo her coat.

Her coat. I've never had anyone show up for an interview this fucking fancy—wearing a detective trench coat and everything. I mean, it's a little strange for a personal training job interview, but she's quirky, I guess, and I like that.

But once she's freed the waist belt, she opens the coat

and lets it sail slowly and silently to the floor while I'm left to stare at what she's wearing.

There is no pencil skirt and royal blue interview blouse happening here.

My throat works to swallow, but all the blood and liquid in my body have easily rushed south.

I blink, and because I'm nervous, my hand goes to the strap on the side of my head, and I mindlessly adjust my already perfectly placed eye patch.

There's no outfit beneath that coat that begs the question of whether or not she's qualified to train. Hell, the outfit she has on is *not* an interview outfit.

A black corset that ends a little past the top of her thighs–which are bare from tights of any kind–draws my eye to her smooth curves. Her full breasts ache to spill out over the satin material, her waist pulls tight, only to give way to a swell of sexy hips. She tips her chin up as she allows me a moment to take in her body.

I don't know what the fuck she's doing and why she thinks showing me her body will get her the job–but honestly? She's fucking gorgeous. I mean, her body is a goddamn smoke show, sure. But her wide blue eyes, set a little far apart, her plump lips and high cheekbones.... The way freckles are painted over the bridge of her nose and down both of her legs. Her fair skin illuminates under my gaze, and I'm fucking seriously captivated by her.

"Are you a good listener?" she asks, snapping me from where I'd been staring at the smooth slope of her beautiful neck.

"Uh, yeah," I say, my brow finally catching up with the situation by pinching together tightly. "Are you–" I start my question but have no clue what I'm going to ask. Crazy? Confused? The truth is, there's a beautiful young woman in my office half-dressed. I'd be the crazy and confused one to point out that this isn't the place.

Are we still saying YOLO? Because... yolo.

"I am a good listener, yes," she supplies, even though I wasn't going to ask her that. "But I'm here to be listened to, not the other way around, got it?"

I find myself nodding, and swallowing down the sudden rush of drool in my mouth.

"Why are you still on your feet?" She pops a hip, resting her hand on it. The toe of her shiny black heel taps relentlessly against the floor. My floor. In my office. At my gym.

My heart is thudding in my eardrums—*what is fucking happening here?*

"As opposed to...?" I motion my arm back toward my office chair, tucked neatly behind my desk. Her eyes follow my gesture before coming back to me.

She looks right into my eye, not roaming over the patch or looking away like most people do when adjusting to me. She doesn't even seem to notice it. Like I'm the same as her.

She laughs, startling me from her acceptance. "On your knees."

Despite the fact that I'm not slurping a frozen drink, my brain actually freezes. She just told me to... *get on my knees?* I shake my head a little and lift my hands to my temples, holding my brain steady for a moment.

"Wait, I—" but she doesn't let me speak.

"You're Bran; we've established that. Correct?" Her black lashes blink back at me, and I'm momentarily put under some spell. This woman is intoxicating. And I felt it before she revealed the corset. I swear.

"Correct," I agree. "And you're E?"

She presses her bare hand into her chest, and I like that her nails aren't all fancy and fake and shit. "And I'm E," she agrees. "You're hiring me for the Heavy Lifting Trainer position, right?"

I mean, this was just the interview but Jesus Christ, would I be a fool to disagree with her?

"Right," I say, stepping apart as casually as possible, pretending she doesn't realize I'm trying to give my suddenly awake dick a little more space.

"This is your free pass. You didn't know. When I get here for our next session, I expect you to be on your knees and ready for me."

I realize that this is possibly how any episode of *Dateline* could start, but honestly? I don't fucking care.

"But now it's time to obey. Get on your knees."

I drop to my knees, and she steps so close that the toes of her high heels brush my jogger-covered knees. The hard shoes against my body send a rush of lightheadedness through my head, and I have no idea why. I reach out and grip the desk behind her, and she drops one hand to the top of my shoulder.

"Use my thighs instead of the desk," she commands, her voice both quiet and strong like she knows her power and doesn't have to raise her voice.

Unsure, I don't move because touching her feels... wrong. The supremely strange first meeting comes to a record-screeching halt at her request. As if reading my worries, she leans down and takes me by my wrists. Moving me so that my hands are positioned at her hips, she curls her palms into the tops of my hands. The connection is intimate and private, yet... we've only just met.

"Better?" she asks when I sink the tips of my fingers into her warm, bare flesh. Slowly, I tip my head back and find her eyes. She's got her chin to her chest, her impressive cleavage shadowing her beauty. That and the way her full blonde curls curtain her face, she's shadowy. But fucking beautiful.

I'm so confused.

"Yeah," I croak out like a complete idiot because I have no idea what the hell is happening, and yet... I'm *not* stopping things.

My hands are on this fucking gorgeous woman, and she basically put them there. And my heart hasn't raced like this in... I can't even remember if it *ever* has–excitement, nerves, and... happiness surge through me, down my arms, and into my fingers.

I grip her just a bit tighter, and her tongue sweeps across her bottom lip again, like she enjoys my touch but can't or won't admit it.

Then I just stare up at her, holding onto this stranger like she's my lover, and as I do, she places her hands on the tops of my shoulders. "Here's how it will go. I'm hired. We'll meet here every week, at the same time. You'll pay me before I get here, and then when I walk into this office, I want you ready for your training."

Tipping her head to the side, some of the hair guarding her face falls behind her shoulder, revealing the sexy curve of her naked neck. I rub my lips together, every fucking part of my mouth dying to go to that spot. To taste her skin, to feel the rapid pulse in her throat against my lips.

She jars me when she filters a hand through my beard, leaving the other hand on my shoulder.

"You're nervous," she says slowly, her blue eyes so bright—I've never seen eyes like this. She blinks, black lashes fluttering, stirring up my insides. "You seem a little afraid of this, too."

Fuck, I guess I am a little afraid because I don't know what's happening, but I'm pretty sure it would destroy me if someone took it away right now. That's where the fear comes in.

Her hand stops stroking my beard and instead grips my chin. Gently, she lifts my face up just a bit more. "You're lonely but afraid."

Her blue eyes stay tamped down on my exposed eye, and right when I think it's so fucking insane for me to be going along with whatever this is, she names me.

She fucking names me.

The man who can't even get anyone to call him by his real name gets *yet another nickname*.

And this one makes my cock hard.

"Stray. You're my Stray, and that's what I'll call you." Her pouty lips press together as she studies my body now, still gripping my face. Her spare hand kneads the tight lump of muscled shoulder. "Now, my Stray," she starts, and *holy shit*. I know I should have some like, self-respect and shit, and being likened to a lonely animal who belongs nowhere isn't exactly a compliment.

But it's the first time someone's just... called it how they see it. No part of E is pretending I'm anything but what I truly am.

Lost.

Stray

Her eyes come back to my face, and she releases her hold on me, folding her arms under her breasts. "I have three rules."

I'm still holding her hips when she takes one tiny step forward, my nose now less than six inches from her body. Her pussy.

"Wh-what?" I stumble out the question, but I don't even know why. Because even though I can't figure out why this woman is in a corset at my gym calling me a Stray, I know deep down that whatever rules she spits, I'll fucking follow.

Because why wouldn't I? What do I have to lose?

She smirks, and it's the first somewhat playful expression that graces her beautiful face, and my heartbeat echoes its heavy reaction.

"I know you're sexy, but I also know you own this place. So that means I know you're not stupid." Unfolding her arms, she grips my shoulders again, her fingertips send a rush of heat down my spine, making my cock thrum.

"First rule, don't speak until you're spoken to."

Um... "Okay," I hear myself saying. My head is fucking spinning at this entire situation.

"Second rule, don't come until you're told."

Come. *Come.* I don't know why the word comes as a shock, considering she's wearing a corset and very little else.

"Okay," I reply because, um, *obviously*.

"Last rule," she says, drawing it out. My stomach clenches uncomfortably at the thought that this woman may just tell me not to look at her. Maybe whatever thing she's here for, she won't want to do with me looking at her. Experience tells me that anything outside of raw fucking, most women don't want the cyclops looking at them.

But heat forms behind my eye at her response.

"Do not take your eye off me. I want you focused on me at all times." She leans down and presses her lips to my ear, and I feel the small contact between my legs. "No matter how hard it is." She stands back up and takes any semblance of my remaining willpower with her.

"Okay." *What the fuck am I agreeing to? What is actually happening right now?*

"Now, you need to thank me for becoming your trainer." She puts her hands on her hips, trapping mine against her, though I didn't need to be trapped. I don't think I had any intention of moving them.

"Th-thank you," I stutter like a jackass because I cannot get my head around this, but I'm fucking glad my fingers are still wrapped around her.

"Show me you're grateful," she says, curling her hands around mine, lifting them off. "Ankles," she says, and like I've taken this command a thousand times before, I wrap my hands around her ankles and find myself waiting for her to tell me what's next.

Her curls have slipped past her shoulder again, shadowing her face. One blue eye peeking through the golden waves of hair, she nods towards her feet. "You have permission to look down."

I look down at my rough, inked hands gripping her fair, smooth ankles. Her skin shines under the dim light, and I can feel how smooth she is before I even move. Fuck. This is crazy.

"Show your appreciation, starting at my feet, stopping here," she says, and I look up to see her tap the bottom of the corset.

I don't know how she wants me to show my appreciation, but something tells me I don't want her to explain herself again. I get the feeling that... she's in complete control of me *and* this office.

Bending down, I don't miss the sharp intake of breath that leaves her when I press my lips to the top of her foot. My beard grates her skin before my lips touch, but when they do–*fuck me*. Even the top of her foot is fucking velvet.

I kiss the inside of her ankle, then move to her other leg, repeating the first kiss there. Alternating between the two most perfect legs in existence, I pepper chaste kisses up her thighs, my hands following behind my lips. Fuck, her skin is so smooth.

When I'm almost at the end, the tip of my nose nudging the bottom of her corset, I smooth my thumb over her warm skin before I kiss it. I swear I hear a little moan when my lips connect for the last kiss. If I had to look down right now, I'm certain I'd see my dick tenting my fucking joggers like a beacon in the damn night.

But she said the word *come*. So whatever is happening, clearly, the point of this is to make me hard.

I guess?

Placing the heel of her palm against my forehead, she pushes me back, unsealing my lips from her perfect skin. "Next week, we really begin, Stray. Be ready."

Then, on my knees in front of her, I watch her redress in her Carmen San Diego-looking coat, cinching it so tightly at the waist that she sucks in a breath as she does. She slings her bag over her shoulder–and I realize that bag must be full of... things–then makes her way toward the office door.

Pausing, she twists her torso to look back at me, still helplessly and hopelessly on my knees for her.

"Good boy," she rasps, giving me a quick wink of one of her sapphire eyes before the door clicks shut, and I'm left all alone.

What in the fuck just happened?

And when is it going to happen again?

12

Elsie

I was fucking phenomenal.

Holy shit.
Oh my God.
I click the seatbelt into place at my waist, then turn the key in the ignition. My car comes alive, and after a moment of waiting for my windshield to thaw, I pull out of the long, empty parking lot into the bare road.

I wait until I'm a half block away, stopped at a red light, before finally exhaling.

"Holy shit," I breathe, my hands tightening around the steering wheel like I'm moments away from transforming into The Hulk. Only instead of rage and anger turning me into a monster, excitement and power surge through me so rampant that I want to scream and cheer.

Daisy Jane

Lacey was right about this.

I feel *fucking phenomenal*.

Pulse zooming in my ears, my body practically bounces beneath the steering wheel as I replay the last half an hour in my mind.

It had been awkward for about thirty seconds when I was walking up to the double doors. But as soon as he tapped on the glass doors and my eyes were able to really focus on him–holy crap.

I remember Lacey's words about her clients. *They're almost all wealthy guys with mental hang-ups. Some with small dicks.*

When I'd glanced down at the man at my feet, I saw a hint of his package, and yeah, this man definitely isn't one with a small package. Mental hang-ups, though, I can't speak to that. I barely let him talk.

The way I figured going into it–and paired with what I'd seen in my limited online research–if I don't let him speak, it's easier for me to remain in control and guarantee I won't do something stupid like catch feelings.

The red light changes to green, and I pull forward, continuing my short drive home. That man is so handsome. And it's not just the fact that he's a walking protein bar ad, either. Dark hair styled all swoopy and mysterious–seriously, how do some guys do that? Do they look up YouTube tutorials on how to style their hair in an *I don't give a fuck, but I'll make you come on my face* way? And his espresso iris peering at me through those dark lashes. My thighs tighten beneath the wheel at the remembrance. Blinking away the image that has apparently been tattooed on my brain, I force my focus back on myself.

Stray

I was fucking phenomenal.

It was easy to give him the name Stray because he acted just like a stray animal. Scared when I came in, nervous, unsteady on his feet. But hungry for touch. My touch.

I don't know what it says about me as a person who claims to be all for equality and women's rights that a man on his knees at my feet turns me on, but... I guess that's another perk of this "Training" job.

I get to discover things about myself I'd probably never have discovered.

And no one has to know.

I think about texting Lacey when I pull up to the next light, but before I can and without my permission, my thoughts tiptoe back to my Stray.

Goosebumps break out across my neck and cheeks when I remember the way his coarse facial hair felt against my smooth palms. A contrast of my senses to the most extreme degree.

I hadn't expected to be anything but nervous (with a side dose of moderately terrified) at this first meeting. I hadn't expected the client to be hugely handsome, much less to be handsome enough that I wondered for a few seconds if I was about to be abducted and sold into some sort of devious sexual slavery. After all, why does a gorgeous man like my Stray need to pay a woman for anything?

But I can't deny the vast smile that curls my lips as I flick my blinker on toward my street. I wasn't really nervous at all. I'd memorized things from Lacey's website that I never even said. Hell, I didn't even remember half the stuff I'd planned.

As soon as I laid eyes on him, I just... knew what to do.

And I felt so sexy doing it. So... powerful.

Damn was Lacey right. So freaking right. I should really text her and tell her how it went because she's probably concerned I bailed or flaked. I don't text while the car is in motion, though, and since I'm so close to my house, I decided to wait until I'm inside.

But thoughts of my Stray, the way I proudly (and shockingly) owned the situation, the feeling of complete badassery—it all tumbles away without so much as a second thought. Because once I'm parked in my garage, and the door is closing behind me, I see Effie sitting on the steps.

Heavy, tired eyelids droop over equally exhausted blue eyes. Her little head is propped up on her curled fists, elbows resting on her knees. She's only four, but she seems like a middle schooler right now. Not because she looks grown-up but because I know she's going to hit me with a grown-up problem. I can sense it.

Moms sense these things.

I throw open the door, and before I've even swung both legs out, I'm asking her what's wrong. Because Effie goes to bed around 7:45, and it's currently almost nine o'clock.

"Why are you up, Effie girl?" I ask, bumping the door closed with my hip. Fingers nervous on the tie around my waist, I check and double-check no part of my secret outfit is showing. I leave the bag of... goodies... in the car. I'll use it next week, so it may as well stay there.

Effie stands, arms out for a hug. I love that she wants hugs so much. I know there will be a day when waiting for me to come home with a hug in her heart, and a smile on her face will be rare. So I'm a glutton for them right now when she's still just a four-year-old who misses her mama.

But tonight, I suspect it's more than that.

The hairs on the back of my neck rise, replacing the sated goosebumps that formed there when walking to my car at Paradise.

"Gramma," she says through a yawn as I hoist her onto my hip. She grabs at the ends of the belt and begins playing with them.

"Gramma what?" I ask, not letting her know my heart is racing and my mind is going just as fast. I push open the back door as she yawns, my feet moving fast, even in the heels.

"Mom?" I call, then slide Effie onto the kitchen counter. She's so tired she doesn't react with a grin like she usually does. Instead, I press my forehead to hers and use my softest voice.

"Effie girl, where's Gramma?"

She yawns, and I can smell toothpaste on her breath, which means at least the bedtime routine went smoothly. That slows my racing heart just a tick.

"She took the garbage out and didn't come back in."

Fuck. My vision blurs on the edges, and my heart gallops back to full speed, slamming against my ribs. *When* is on my tongue, but she's four and doesn't even have a clock in her room, not yet at least.

"How long have you been waiting for Gramma? How many episodes?" I ask. Since she's been little, I've been a working mom. My mom has always been an amazing babysitter–though she does let Effie watch endless TV. The plus side of that is that every kid's show or cartoon is twenty-two minutes. I use the length of a cartoon to ask Effie about time or to explain to her how long I'll be gone somewhere. Like now.

"One episode?" I ask, smoothing her wild curls back from her sleepy little face. "Two?"

She shrugs and yawns, and it's then that I scoop her up and carry her down the hall to my room.

"Mama's room?" she asks lazily as her eyes pop open when I slide her onto my bed. Tugging my comforter up to her chin, I tuck pillows around her. Her eyes are already closing when I press a quick kiss to her forehead.

"Mama's room tonight. Sleep well, baby." I kiss her again, the smell of baby shampoo and pure sweetness filling my nose.

"Night," she says as I close the door quietly behind me. Tiptoeing to not alert Effie, I wait to break out into a sprint until I'm closing the front door. Sprinting across the lawn in heels and trench coat, I knock anxiously at Fanny's door.

It's late for Fanny because nine o'clock at night is basically two in the morning for older people. I know that, and for that, I am sorry. But if mom were going to go anywhere, I'd think it would be here.

Lights come on in the far distance, I see through the kitchen window on Fanny's porch. A moment later, the outdoor light flickers on, and the sound of chains being unhooked is heard. Fanny's sleep-smashed face fills the crack.

"Elsie? You okay, darlin'?"

"I just got home, and Effie said mom took out the trash and never came back in, but she doesn't remember how long ago, but her teeth are brushed, so I know they did bedtime, and I know mom lets her stay up late so it could've only been like half an hour ago and–"

Fanny kicks open her door and steps onto the porch, hushing me with her finger.

"Slow down, honey. Okay, just slow down." She wraps her robe around herself and catches a residual yawn in her hand. "What was she doing when she got lost?"

"She's not lost," I spit out defensively, but I don't really mean it defensively as much as I do... scared. "I'm scared," I amend because it's not Fanny's fault. She smiles, but it's this sideways, sad smile that makes my stomach sick.

"I know. It'll be okay. Let's go retrace her steps," she says calmly, taking my hand the way I'd take Effie's hand.

Cautiously, we walk down her porch steps and across our two lawns. She doesn't speak, and neither do I–probably because we're both surprised that we're here already. I know I thought I had more time before these types of things started happening.

I mean, I wanted to believe I did. But asking the pharmacist to hook your mom up with more memory pills doesn't exactly scream ignorant to the problem. I was just... so hopeful.

We make it to the side of the house, and thankfully, mom forgot to turn off the house lights. I usually leave her a note to do it because the neighbors on that side have a bedroom near our light, and no one wants to be a bad neighbor.

Fanny peers around the corner first, and the relief that burns through me when she drapes a relieved hand over her chest is nearly overwhelming.

"Elaine?" she calls to my mom, who she clearly sees. Stepping around Fanny, I see the toes of mom's slippers sticking out from behind the recycling can. Getting to her as quickly as possible, I'm double relieved to see she's awake and not hurt. Not that I can see, at least.

"Mom," I say, her eyes snapping to mine once I kneel in front of her. "Why are you out here?"

She looks up at the can, her eyes hazy. Fanny kneels next to me, the smell of Donna Karan's Cashmere making me nauseous. I don't mind the smell of old lady perfume on a normal basis, but after getting off that horrid two-minute rollercoaster where I thought mom was missing (or worse), I can hardly breathe.

Looping one arm through mom's, I stand up and bring her with me. "Come on, let's get inside, okay?"

Mom's mumbling and humming causes a sudden rush of emotion inside of me. "Let's get inside," I say, tears breaking free but both cruelly and thankfully, mom is unaware.

Fanny takes my wrist and slows me down a moment, but mom stays by my side, straightening out her plaid pajama pants as if she's wearing a crepe ball gown.

"I'll make her some tea, get her clothes changed. You get your clothes changed. Take your time, sweetie."

I don't pretend that I can handle this moment on my own. I know I should because Fanny helps me so much, but... I rely on her. I shouldn't, but I do. I emotionally rely on her, and I will again tonight.

"Thank you," I say in a quiet voice.

Mom's humming swipes at my strength, leaving tears in its wake. I'll never get used to watching her deteriorate. I'll never be able to reroute my brain to a place that isn't sad about this.

Instead, I take Fanny up on her offer and sneak to the bathroom for a private moment once we're inside.

I hear the gas burner click to life, then the tea kettle slide across the metal grate. Twisting the lock built into the door handle, I sit on the closed toilet.

She's found. She technically wasn't even lost. She's okay.

I repeat those three sentences to myself for a while, and when they stop holding meaning, I stop, too.

Effie was so brave. My heart tears when I think of how afraid she probably was and how she probably tried to act unafraid. My sweet girl. What am I going to do? I can't stop working–that's how we get the meds we have. Fanny isn't capable of caring for both mom and Effie–and that's not her job anyway.

I'll have to hire help.

I didn't think we were there yet, but it's looking like it's coming soon. We'll be tight on money for a while, but that's okay. Everything I've earned that hasn't gone to this house, our vehicles, or mom's treatment has gone to savings.

Until my recent sexscapade with Amazon, that is. Outside of that, I have a decent savings since mom's house is paid for.

Looking up caretakers will have to wait until tomorrow, though, because I'm exhausted. Before pushing off the porcelain, I toe off my pumps and fan my toes out in the shaggy coral bath mat. Normally I don't wear heels. But tonight, they were part of what made me feel so good.

My eyes flutter closed as a zing of electricity moves through me at the recollection of his soft lips grazing my inner thigh as he kissed me. Kissed me the way I commanded him to.

Standing in front of the mirror, I turn on the sink. Steam fills the air around me as I untie the cinched belt at my waist, then work vertically to free the buttons. My reflection nearly takes my own breath away.

The black corset makes my curves look sexy, my breasts look tantalizing, all pushed up the way they are. My makeup is starting to smear, but otherwise, I look good.

Before the steam swallows the mirror, a small smile curls my lips.

But it isn't just the way I look that has me feeling good.

The way *he* looked at *me*, his fingertips curled into me with hesitation and hope, the feel of his warm skin on mine–*he* made me feel powerful.

I want more of that. Already.

13

Bran

Enough with the leg!

I can't believe I'm doing this. I like, never fucking do this. Ever. Even when I'm sick, I usually drag my ass into Paradise looking like death warmed over.

But this morning, I just... I can't leave my bed. I kept Stoner up all night, too, and he's not keen on waking up either.

The phone rings in my ear, vibrating through my face. My eyelids feel heavy, and my body is a sick combo of anxious and exhausted.

"Dude, you better be in labor because it's three forty in the morning." Mally's grouchy yawn blares through the receiver, so I pull the phone away from my face until he's done. He's a long, dramatic yawner. Surprise, surprise.

Daisy Jane

"I'm in labor," I say, rolling with what he deems the *only* acceptable excuse to have your friend open your gym on your behalf. "Can you open Paradise? If you have a shift, you can take off whenever. Just unlock the doors."

Mally's mood improves. "Uh oh, did you fuck a chick last night?" His voice drops to an annoyingly secretive whisper. "Oh my God, you're still there, and you can't get away," he guesses excitedly.

But I'm Bran–I don't just disappoint myself; I disappoint my friends, too.

"No, I did not fuck some chick last night. I just didn't sleep well. I need a few more hours; then I'll be in."

"Hmm," he says as he loudly stretches and groans.

"Can you or not? I can call Van."

"Dude, don't threaten to call Van. If you wanted to call Van, you would've called Van."

"Can you?"

His sigh is so drawn out that I swear even Stoner wakes up to roll his eyes. "Yes. But I want to be compensated."

"I will bring you food."

"In knowledge," he says. "I want to know why. You have three hours to get your shit together; come into Paradise and tell me."

Glancing at my phone screen, three hours sounds perfect. I know I'm being extremely shitty doing this, but... Mally owes me. For what exactly, I couldn't tell you. The tally is that long.

"Thanks, man. I'll be there in three hours."

"Is the code still the same?" he asks through a yawn, and thank God one of us has our head on straight because I was about to hang up without giving him the only piece of information he actually needs.

"Oh fuck, no. I changed it. It's um," I scratch the side of my jaw, my beard curling around my fingertips. I need to trim it today. And probably get a haircut too. It's been... too long. "Sammy's birthday."

Radio silence.

"Come on, man. I thought she's your bro," I say, happy to squeeze this moment for all it's worth. Mally's been trying to bug me with his friendship with Sammy for ages—this moment feels sweet.

"I know when it is," he huffs, "it's just that... she looks so young, you know? Trying to figure out those year digits."

I snort out a laugh as Stoner nuzzles under my armpit, his nose wet and cool against my blanket-warmed skin.

"Save that high-level sucking up for her, man." I stroke my hand down my beard again. "11-26-94, don't forget the pound at the end."

"Oh, baby, I will never forget the end pound." Mally's grin is audible, and I gotta give him a small chuckle because being sexually witty at half-past three in the morning is pretty impressive.

But then again, my brain is frozen. Stuck in sinking sand with one topic gurgling at my feet, gripping me tight and sucking me in. Down deeper. No hope of survival.

After just one fucking night.

Not even a night. An hour. One fucking hour and I was up all night, tossing and turning. Thinking more than I've thought in years combined.

About her.

E.

"See you this morning then," Mally says, concluding the call.

Stroking down Stoner's back with one hand, I drop my phone onto the nightstand and drape my palm over my chest. My heart thumps beneath me, telling me that I'm alive.

The memory of my lips on her thigh passes through my mind, already familiar to me, and my heart stirs under my palm. The smell of her skin, the soft glow of her blue eyes, the way she stared at me with passion—the beating in my chest intensifies.

Now I'm alive.

I called Mally to open Paradise because I didn't sleep a wink. But because life is cruel, now that sunlight drips into my existence, my eyes are finally heavy, and my mind is trying to slow. I need rest if I'm going to lift and work today. I can't operate on no sleep. I'm thirty. I feel that shit for days if I try to pull all-nighters.

I thought about her all night.

I still have no fucking clue what happened. I played it all back in my mind so many times—she did confirm she knew me, and I recognized her voice from the phone—the call after the job posting correspondence.

Yet... she came in a trench coat—my dick stirs at the memory of that sexy fucking nineties detective vibe she was throwing—that was hot. Scratching the top of my head with one finger, I try to think if I saw in that big ass bag she had.

Maybe her gym stuff was in there?

But... there is literally no fucking way to make sense of what happened.

Then again, what happened that night I lost my eye

Stray

made no sense either, and I've spent the last eight years trying to figure out how to come back from it–trying to solve *myself*.

But maybe that's been the fucking hang-up.

Maybe I gotta stop questioning and wondering and just fucking live. Live or else what? I don't want to die. But the way I've been living up until now, I really haven't been alive.

Roses.

She spoke of roses in terms of money. That's... weird. Swiping my phone from the nightstand, I unlock, and immediately open the internet browser.

After forty seconds of reading a Reddit post archived six years ago, I learn that roses are the standard code used for money in online prostitution.

Prostitution. E isn't a prostitute.

I mean... *is she?*

I don't think so. She's so beautiful–but what the hell kind of argument is that to make on behalf of someone not selling themselves? Just because I feel drawn to her doesn't mean my inner magnet is right.

Locking my phone, I decide to strong-arm my brain into sleep because it's been hours of reliving last night, and I have to stop. And no sooner do my senses release their death grip on awareness than my doorbell rings.

Tipping my phone to see the screen, I see Sammy's face on the fish-eye lens of my doorbell cam. "I know you're looking at the thumbnail on your phone, so answer the door. I'm going to use my key in like thirty seconds so if you don't want me to see what you're doing, answer the freakin' door, Brian Edwards."

Brian Edwards?

Daisy Jane

I got full-named, and I didn't even do anything wrong.

Much to the annoyance of Stoner, I swing my long legs out of bed and pad down the hall towards the front door. As soon as I pull it open, I see my little sister with her key out, moments from barging in on me.

"Why didn't you open the gym today?" she asks before greeting me. Spotting the two brown bags at her feet, I snag them before ushering her into the house.

"Didn't sleep last night." I find her over my shoulder and narrow my eye on her. "I was trying to catch up on sleep *now*."

She hoists herself onto the kitchen counter, bracing the edge. "Toast me a bagel, yeah?"

I tuck into the bags and pull out a few bagels, splitting them with a fork before they go into my multi-racked toaster oven. When everyone in your crew eats like it's their last meal, you buy kitchen appliances that support bulk cooking. Or else Van pouts that he's the last one to get his bagel toasted.

"Why didn't you sleep?" she asks after I hoist myself onto the counter across from her. I have chairs at a dining table. I have barstools. But we always talk best when we sit like this. I guess it's our thing. Before I can answer, she's stacking her questions.

"How was the interview last night?"

I tip my head as I watch all the thoughts filter through her brain, her eyes flicking toward me when she reaches the thought I knew she'd have. "Oh fuck, did you get another little insensitive, uncool, and *highly unrepresentative of the masses* jerk?"

The toaster oven gently whirrs, preventing the room

from an uncomfortable silence. I'm not uncomfortable with my sister, but this topic is slightly triggering.

But that's what I'm working against—not being the sensitive, quiet, triggerable guy. *Enough with the leg!*

"Nope," I say, not sure how honest I want to be. When I look up and see my sister's dark eyes imploring me for answers, the wall I built around last night starts to soften. But because I have no clue what last night even was and who E really even is, I decide to keep it safe. Even though I hate not being honest with Sammy. "Just tired, a lot on my mind trying not to be Arizona Robbins."

Her face softens right as the toaster oven dings. Jumping down, I smother our bagels with butter and jam because cream cheese is great, but butter and jam are where it's at.

Handing her the plate with her food, she yawns, and it teeters in her tired grip. "I'm glad," she says finally. Her yawn is contagious, though, and before we can eat, I'm brewing a pot of coffee so that we can even have a real conversation.

Fifteen minutes later, I'm thoroughly filled in on the hospital drama, not to mention the text messages Mally sent to Sammy this morning after we got off the phone. After we've finished our bagels and an entire pot of coffee, Sammy leaves for her double shift at the hospital. Even though I feel like absolute unrested garbage, the coffee prevents me from getting any sleep.

* * *

DROPPING the brown bag down on the desk, Mally jerks his head up, eyes puffy with unrest.

"Thanks for opening this morning; here's your food."

His blue eyes narrow as he hooks one of his fingers on the side of the bag and tugs it down to peer inside. He looks back up at me, face nearly expressionless. "And what's to drink?"

I raise my arm from below the desk and set down Mally's drink. I went to Starbucks just for this fucking thing because no matter his mood, this damn drink (which, by the way, cost thirteen fucking dollars) always peps him up.

I read the label to him while he tears into an everything bagel, sending poppy seeds and onion flakes directly into the keyboard.

"A venti caramel crunch frappuccino with extra caramel drizzle, extra whipped cream, extra ice, seven pumps added dark caramel sauce, one pump of honey blend, five pumps extra roasted frappuccino coffee, one scoop vanilla powder, banana, heavy cream, double blended."

I need a minute to catch my fucking breath after that. He swipes it from the counter and begins sucking it down, moaning like he's getting head, not drinking the girliest fucking drink on the planet.

"We square?" I ask, volleying a finger between us. "I appreciate you opening up."

He takes another long pull from his frap while shaking his head painfully, his eyes narrowing while watering.

"Dude, drink it slower, and you won't get a brain freeze."

He shakes his head, the drink already halfway gone. "No, man. It's too good. Once I get the taste on my tongue, I'm done for."

"Your future girlfriend will love that."

He tips his head sideways, an expression he picked up

from my sister. Sometimes I swear hanging with Mally is like hanging with Sammy. "Don't change the subject, Bran. I opened up for you; now you need to open up to me."

"Jesus Christ," I exhale, walking around the counter. I nudge him with my elbow until he's on his feet, tossing the huge empty cup into the can under the desk. "There's nothing to tell. I did have an interview. It went fine. I couldn't sleep. That's that."

He reaches in the bag, his tan skin nearly the same color as the kraft paper. He edges towards the door, holding two bagels in one hand, his eyes on me. "Don't think you're off the hook. I have a shift, or else I'd stay here and get to the bottom of this."

"You're at the bottom, man," I say, tipping the keyboard upside down to free it of Mally's snack particles. Apparently the man ate a protein bar, too, because a recognizable clump of cookie dough protein bar topples to the floor along with the seeds. "I was just really tired this morning, that's all."

He puts a hand on his hip, which is holding the door partially open. "And yet this is the first time you couldn't open Paradise."

Pursing my lips together, I stare at him. "Later, dude. Have a good shift."

His blue eyes go all squinty. "If this is about the leg—"

"Dude, I was tired. You need to go. You're starting to piss me off."

He blinks like I've insulted his firstborn. "Is that right?"

"Bye."

One more narrowing of his beady little eyes and his blonde hair and drama are out the door, hoofing it to his truck. Thank God. I can't withstand two inquisitions today. Lying to Sammy was bad enough.

But what could I really tell them? I interviewed and apparently hired a chick that I'm already fucking obsessing over like an absolute loser but don't even know who she is or what she's about?

Uh, yeah. No.

I say hello to a few clients, make a quick pass through the weight room, and head to my office. Closing the door behind me, I twist the lock to engage and flip on the lights.

My eye goes to the spot where she stood. The spot where just being near her and breathing in her intoxicating power made me shaky and heady. Where she had me get on my knees and kiss my way up her legs. The place where I realized that whatever this woman was selling, I was going to fucking buy it. All of it.

Closing my eye, my hand finds the outline of the patch, and I trace it as I remember the way it felt to be near E last night.

It felt so fucking right. Not crazy at all. And I know it's bad math; I know that shit doesn't add up.

But still.

Sliding into my office chair, my hand falls to my lap, where I find my dick rock hard, just at the thought of those thirty minutes.

Whatever is happening can be just between me, E, and my dick. For now, at least.

With that decided, I trace the outline of my hard cock through my joggers, letting my thumb take its time around my head. All of my stress falls away while I stroke myself and think about E.

14

Elsie

From now on, you will refer to me as your Goddess.

The days after a lapse–that's what Fanny and I call them because we really don't know how else to categorize them–mom's always super *up*. Remembers things and wants us to know, busy and energetic–it's almost like, on some level, she's aware of what we've all just gone through, and she can't set aside the mom in her–she wants to make us all better.

Mom's been up and that's given me the opportunity to do some things I should probably have already done.

For one, I leave a message with her primary care doctor, asking the nurse about five hundred times if she was writing my message down. Explaining how she seemed to be progressing and expressing that she needs a scan, I hope to hear back sooner rather than later, but my part is done. I cross it off the mental checklist and move on to the next task.

While Effie is at Kajukenbo class, I pop in my earphones and think about my Stray.

Out of nowhere, I've become some sexual mastermind, and the truth of it is? I like it. And I don't want to stop.

But to continue, I need to do some serious research. Because I'm at a four-year-old's karate class sitting next to a bunch of tired-looking parents in office casual clothes, I realize I'm not in the exact place to watch porn and make a game plan. Instead, I open up my internet browser and type in the word Dominant followed by "female," and am overwhelmed with the results.

Bypassing the inevitable heap of dirty videos, I get down to a forum and click.

Hundreds of users have typed in their personal stories, telling the ether just how they make their *pet* orgasm. Better yet, I see a ton of responses about how they make their pet give their mistress orgasms. I also read posts with other random pieces of information, like how they torture their pet before they come or tease them all week when they're apart.

Shit, a few weeks ago, I wasn't in on this little secret. And now, not only am I aware of the Dominant and Submissive culture, but I'm a card-carrying member.

Damn.

Lacey was so right. I know I've already said that, but she really was. I do feel powerful.

I don't have a login to the site, so instead, I take screenshots of some of the responses–the ones that bring me ideas of my own. In under ten minutes, I swear I have like three sessions worth of things I want to do with... Brian Edwards.

I'd been trying not to remember his name. I guess I'd actually been trying to forget his name. Refer to him as my Stray so that I'd feel detached from him as a person and see him more as a thing.

My thing.

Already, I can see that it will be difficult. Some women have the ability to have fun without getting emotionally attached, but not me. It's why I was so hurt about Jake–granted, I know that was the wrong reason. But I'd invested time into him and got no return back. That was hard to accept.

But with Brian. The way he practically shook with nerves. His dark gaze timid. His other eye–the one covered–hiding a beautiful and tragic story. One that clearly and so sadly marred his soul.

And God, his body. It's not enough that he's ruggedly handsome and completely gorgeous at the same time, but he has the body of a gladiator or something.

Jake was not hot.

Effie's dad (affectionately known as the sperm donor in my head) was not hot.

I don't think I've ever been in the presence of pure, true hotness. Like, seriously. My entire body was humming when his rough hands gripped my hips. I could feel his palms, calloused from earning that expansive chest and solid arms. My lower half seized up in reaction–*in appreciation.*

I'm already thinking about him too much, and it's silly. Really, it is. As a responsible parent and hard-working adult, and general decent member of society, I can recognize that feeling all *chest-fluttery* over a man I know absolutely nothing about is a great way to end up in a ditch.

Putting my focus back on the task at hand, I open Amazon because there is no easier time in the history of humankind like the present to become a badass out-of-the-blue Dominant. Because all of your resources can be delivered to your doorstep in two days, or often less.

How convenient.

Opening a browser tab, I search out the address of Paradise. Just seeing Brian Edwards listed as the business owner sends a wiggle of delight through my limbs. Seriously, *what?*

I don't like this extremely powerful yet highly irrational side of me. She's like Monica Gellar strong, too, because I don't think I could stop this quick-growing addiction if I wanted to.

But I don't even want to.

With his address in my memory, I switch back to Amazon and enter him in as the delivery. After a few more details, a package is heading his way and will arrive by tomorrow morning. God, I love the internet.

I know Lacey said this isn't a relationship where we text each other or anything like that, but since I'm having quite a precarious package sent to Brian at his place of work, it requires at least one text message. And hey, it's work-relationship related. Completely.

My fingers skitter over the digital keyboard on my phone as I draft up a text message, leaving his name as the last thing to enter in case I make a mistake or want to reword things. Not that I need to be putting that level of care into this–I know that. *Type up a quick line and send it, Elsie; he's not your soul mate; he's your client.*

Holy crap, I still can't believe I'm doing this, and I have a client. Me! Elsie Francis.

Glancing up, I see Effie's kajukenbo instructor doing their end-of-class game. He sits cross-legged on the floor and spins a jump rope around him, making the kids run in and jump as it passes. They love it. Squeals and cheers fill the smelly gym air, and I know I'm closing in on my last few moments of peace.

FInishing the text, I decide to try and follow Lacey's advice. I probably shouldn't be texting him in the first place, but since it's important, I keep it simple.

Elsie: *Stray. A package is coming to Paradise. Don't open it until I see you again.*

Closing the text, I think about the things in the forum I just browsed. Female Dominants seem to go by the term Mistress. But something about that title makes me feel like I'm doing something wrong. Like I'm someone's side piece.

Effie runs up to me, her smock already open, exposing her bright pink undershirt. She chose karate as her sport, but she always wants to have a girl shirt underneath because she said it's a boy sport. I tried to explain that karate isn't just for boys, but believing your mom is something you do selectively when you're four.

"Mama, did you see Miss Millie? Did you see?" Effie wraps both of her hands around one of mine and tugs down hard. Looking up, I see Miss Millie–the instructor's counterpart who acts as a helper to all classes–and holy crap.

Her normally fluffy brown hair is overrun with caramel highlights, a sleek a-line bob, and it's all been straightened so sleek, it fucking shines. It's a glow-up she didn't need, but still, it does look phenomenal. Miss Millie passes through the glob of waiting parents, and Effie releases my hand to grab hers.

"Miss Millie," she beams up at the woman who isn't too much older than me. Maybe late twenties? "You look so pretty." Effie reaches up, and Miss Millie leans down, the two of them connecting as Effie feels the ends of Millie's sleek new hairdo.

"Thanks, Effie. Good job in class today; your kicks are getting so good!" Miss Millie smooths her hand over Effie's, releasing it gently from her hair. She's so good with kids that it's almost attractive. I mean, when you date Jake's that you can't even introduce to your kid, the idea of being with someone so innately good with kids becomes something of a sexual turn-on. But... wrong gender here.

We say goodbye to Miss Millie and head out to the car. As I buckle Effie into her booster seat, she twirls her finger in one of my curls. Effie always tells me how much she likes my hair, and I always laugh, replying, I hope so. Because she is a little knock off the ol' mama block, handing her a bottle of water from the cupholder, she grins at me.

"What did I do to earn that smile?" I ask, smoothing my thumb over her soft, pink cheek.

"I like Miss Millie's hair. But I like your hair." She beams. "You're a Goddess."

My chest seems to swell. I know she's just a kid, and right now, everything I do is gold, and I love life for that sheer fact. But still, I can't shrug off the compliment and chalk it up to a kid being a kid.

"A Goddess?" I repeat, taking the Crocs off her feet, so she doesn't kick them off and fling them my way while we're driving. It's happened.

Stray

"A Goddess," she repeats back to me with no clarification as to why. Just a broad, proud smile stretching her face.

"Thank you," I say before closing her door and sliding into the driver's seat. Starting up the car, I connect my phone via Bluetooth and start playing Effie's personal playlist. The first song is something by Justin Timberlake that was jammed into a kids movie and overplayed for years. But it gets her shoulders wiggling, and the sight of her happy face in the rearview is all I need.

Taking my phone from my bag, I send my Stray another text.

Elsie: *And no more E. From now on, you will refer to me as your Goddess.*

There's an alert immediately, but I tuck my phone away. This is the time I'm with my daughter, not cleaning up childcare puke at Globo-Fitness or reminding my mom to take her meds. We're getting ice cream and whatever message that a man I barely even know has sent? It can wait.

But I can't help but think of my Stray when I'm in bed later that night. His beard and dark eye are the last thing in my consciousness before I lose my thoughts to sleep.

15

Bran

In a lust-sick haze

Is it Thursday at eight o'clock yet? That's basically the only thought in my brain since the first night with E.

A few days ago, I got some text messages from her.

First, she told me she was sending me a package and not to open it until I see her again. The way I waited for that Amazon delivery guy was fucking pathetic. As soon as he passed me the small brown box, I went straight to my office and sat it down front and center on my desk.

I tried to imagine all of the things it could be.

Lube? No. Why would she be all mysterious about sending something so plain? Nothing about this chick tells me that lube would make her embarrassed. A woman who shows up in a corset and heels to meet a man she's never met probably has no qualms with buying personal lubrication.

I lift the box but don't shake it, though I realize it probably traveled here in an Amazon truck that bounced it around like a bull rider. Still.

It's heavy, but not overly so. I set it back down and stare at it.

Handcuffs, perhaps? Though I'm not a sexual fucking animal, nor have I really forayed into anything off the beaten path, handcuffs still seem too demure for a top-secret package delivery.

It's got to be something else. I have to think outside the box to know what's inside the box, but I'm struggling.

And now, Thursday morning, as I sip my coffee and stare down at the brown box on my desk, I'm really struggling. I've been dying to know what's inside and whenever I try to talk myself out of caring—*you'll find out Thursday night, Bran, just live your goddamn life*—I think of that second text she sent me.

From now on, you will refer to me as your Goddess.

My Goddess. Fuck, she really is. All that leg and so much blonde hair I could sink my entire hands into it up to the wrists. My dick lifts from my thigh, and I take another drink of scalding caffeine to calm myself.

"Knock, knock," my sister's voice follows a series of quick, closed-knuckle raps against my cracked office door.

"What's up, Sammy?" I ask, leaning forward while sliding under the desk, masking my hard-on from my little sister.

"Just got a lift in with the guys. Why didn't you join us?" She helps herself to my jug of water on the desk, flipping the top as she flops down into the chair in front of me. "Robin came with Batman since the kids are grandma's. We had a nice time." She wipes her forehead with the hem of her t-shirt–a signature Mally move.

I point at the behavior as she's doing it. "You've been hanging out with Mally too much."

She looks at her fingers wrapped in the cotton t-shirt and drops it. "Shit, you're right."

"Start getting all sensitive on me like him, and we'll have problems. I can only have so many touchy-feely people in my life. You know this."

She grins. "This I do know." She drops the jug of water onto the desk after helping herself to a few big drinks. "So, what's up? I haven't seen you in a couple of days. You haven't been texting."

"I text messaged you this morning," I defend, feeling somewhat guilty because even though I did message her this morning, my spare energy has been devoted to thinking.

About my Goddess.

Fucking pathetic. She could be like, a Nazi sympathizer or some shit. But it's new and exciting, and I'm letting myself feel it before it bursts, and I realize she hates dogs and doesn't use her blinker or something.

"A Kermit meme is not a real text."

I shrug because she's right, and I don't feel like defending myself right now.

"You good?" she asks as she both glances at her watch and rises to her feet.

I nod. "I'm good."

"You'd tell me if you weren't?" She takes another drink of my water.

"You know I would." Linking my hands together, I nod toward the door. "The guys still out there?"

She shakes her head as she makes her way toward the door. "No, Van and Mally are on shift today. And Robin said she and Henry are going out of town for the weekend." She wiggles her eyebrows. "Married people code for a weekend of sex."

At that, I laugh because I've heard Batman's horror stories of trying to get fresh with his wife with two kids under their feet. Nearly impossible. And yet when I heard the story, I couldn't help but think... what a good problem to have.

Sure I want to get laid. But to have the reason you're not getting laid be because you have two fucking rad, healthy, dope kids under your feet, wanting your attention, wisdom, love, and time? I always knew I wanted to be a dad, but that simple story of them being so overwhelmed with their kids that even fucking became a scheduled task... it made me realize just how bad I want that.

"Good for them," I laugh. "You working today?"

She nods and sticks out her tongue while her eyes roll back into her skull. "Ugh," she groans, making her most dead, miserable face ever. "Yes, but I wish I wasn't."

"I hear that," I lie because even when I'd rather be doing something else, I'm still always happy to be here at Paradise. I started this place with two sets of free weights from *Play It Again Sports* that I charged to a credit card my parents opened for me. And now I own everything outright–including my location–and I'm doing well. But rubbing that in Sammy's face isn't cool, so I agree. "But it's almost the weekend."

She taps the doorframe and smiles, her dark ponytail swinging behind her. "Thank God. Okay, Bran. Text me later. Love you."

"Love you too, Sam."

I get up and lock the door behind her. I didn't ask about the guys being here so I could go see them—it was the opposite in fact. I love my guys but lying to them isn't easy. Hell, I'm not really lying, but I *am* withholding and we all fucking know, not telling is the same as lying.

Knowing they aren't in the building and that Sammy is gone, too, makes it a lot easier to fall back into my comfortable staring contest with the brown Amazon box. I can think about explaining whatever is happening to the people in my life much later.

Hours later, I've managed to tear myself away from staring at the box long enough to work out my biceps and triceps. I grab a shower in my pristine fucking locker rooms—none of those rust-stained, chipped tile, squeaky pipes type of showers like they have in chain gyms. Paradise is... *paradise*.

One tray of chicken, rice, and steamed broccoli later, I'm brushing my teeth in the bathroom attached to my office with ten minutes to spare when I hear the bells hanging from the door make noise.

I freeze, staring at my reflection, gripping the unrinsed toothbrush. Is that her already? In the time I've owned this place, I've never had someone come to start a workout at nearly eight o'clock. It's gotta be her.

Throttling the instant rush of nerves that surge through me, I wipe my mouth and head toward my office door, so I can meet her in the lobby.

But I don't even make it part of the way because no sooner have I passed my desk than she appears. Wearing that same stone-colored trench coat, cinched tight at the waist. And though I don't think of anything other than how fucking beautiful she looks, I lower to my knees as soon as her blue eyes tamp down on me.

My body remembered our promises before my mind. Letting my chin fall to my chest, I look down at the ground until the toes of her feet come into view.

She's wearing the same black patent heels–I recognize the slightly pointed toe. Her fingers weave through my hair, the tips of her nails grating my scalp, sending heat down my core. My eye closes, and I hear myself exhale roughly. Her touch is changing me... already.

"Stray," her raspy voice makes my cock thicken, and my reaction to shift or change positions to guard it is amazingly not there. I feel myself lift, hardening, becoming visible as she smooths my hair back, using her nails and pads of her fingers.

It feels like fucking heaven. And my cock may be hardening, but my chest is tightening, too. I'm glad my eye is closed because heat stings behind it; the intimacy of these few seconds makes me unexplainably emotional.

"Did you open the box?" she asks, and I swear I shudder when her hand drops away from my head, leaving me hollow. More than anything, I find myself needing her touch again. Wanting to feel her soft fingertips dive into my beard, the supple skin of her inner thigh against my lips, the slope of her ankle draped over my shoulder.

I shake my head, and then she places a curled finger under my chin and forces me to look up at her.

My eye is still closed, but it opens when I feel her doing one of the things I was just hoping she'd do–running her fingers down my beard.

Her blue eyes tamp down on my brown one, fingers still leisurely stroking my face in a way that makes my pulse zoom inexplicably. "Speak, Stray."

I lick my lips. I don't understand why my ears are pounding until I realize... that's my heart. My groin pulses to the same needful beat. "No, Goddess, I didn't."

She pats my head. "Good boy. Now, some things to get squared away before we begin."

The thought flits through that here and now is another opportunity to ask her what in the hell is going on. Does she want to actually work at Paradise? I mean, she didn't show up all week, so I assumed not but... still... *What is happening between us?*

But she bends over my shoulder; her coat still cinched tight. With the heat of her breasts against my back, I groan. I can't help it. Grabbing the ends of my t-shirt, she stands and takes it with her, leaving me shirtless. Nervously, I shove a hand through my disheveled hair, trying to make it presentable. But then, I'm on my knees at her feet... something tells me the way my hair looks doesn't fucking matter.

It's about how we're connecting. It's about how I react to her. It's not really about *me* at all. It's *her* and *us* as a dynamic. And it's fucking bizarre and out of nowhere and.... absolutely freeing.

"Your safe word," she says, her eyes tripping down the ink over my body like Alice down the rabbit hole. Finally, she comes to my waist, and her eyes bounce back to my face. "You like ships?"

I look down at my chest quickly, needing a reminder of the ten-year-old ink covering my chest and core. It's been there so long, I hardly think about it, and it's not like I'm having a million fuckfests where girls tell me how much they like it all over again.

"It's... It means something."

She quirks an eyebrow as a tendril of honey hair slips over her shoulder. I really want to twine that lock around my finger just to feel how soft it is... but I swallow down the urge.

"Yeah?" she asks, studying me so intensely that my face grows warm, my hairline dampening.

I nod. "I've always felt alone." I swallow, almost feeling stupid now to admit the meaning of the art. It's certainly true now but at age twenty, when I got it? To feel how I did then seems silly now, especially since I got the piece *before* that night. The night of the accident. "Like a ship at sea," I finish, telling her the truth despite the pinch of embarrassment in my gut.

For some reason, I want her to know me.

Her lips tighten into a thin line, and a small crease forms vertically between her brows. My heart beats loudly as our gazes idle. "Shore."

"Shore?" My chest still squeezes with uncertainty at this entire thing. But I like the squeeze.

She blinks, her thick lashes hypnotizing me. She's gorgeous; she couldn't be less than beautiful on her worst day. "The shore is safe."

"Oh," I say, "safe word... I get it."

She shakes her head, though, her eyes still intent on me. "No, not because of that. You. You're..." For the first time I've noticed, her gaze darts to the elastic strap tight against my head. Her blue eyes trail over the dark stitching of the leather eyepatch, then snap back to my dark eye. "You're safe now."

My chest goes concave as the words settle. Never felt like I was in danger, but she's right. I do feel safe.

"Okay," I agree, bypassing the clearly emotional attachment she's placed on the safeword, not to mention what she's projecting onto me by using it. The thing is, I don't think she's wrong. But I don't want to think about that now. "I say 'shore' when I... can't handle something?"

She swallows audibly as she nods yes, and her tongue darts across her lip. In a momentary lapse lasting not more than a split second, her mask slips, and I see my Goddess. Whoever she really is—whether that's E or some form of that or not—I see her. Pupils wide with excitement, lips rolling with nerves.

This beautiful woman wants this but is nervous, too. The same way I feel.

And somehow, with a feeling like we're in this—whatever *this* is—together, confidence roars to life inside of me.

"I need to know, please," I say, my voice sounding far more hoarse than intended. But the question is something I just now realized I have to know. I don't like sharing. Not something this beautiful. "Am I the only one?"

A beat passes, and my heart pauses. Then she shoves her hand through my hair, fingers sliding under the elastic band of my patch. She touches it tenderly before releasing it, moving her fingers down my beard and then over the ink along my collarbone.

Her touch is incinerating every part of me that is *man*.

"Am I the only Goddess in your life?" she asks,

surprising me. I don't know if she's asking if she's the only woman holding me by my balls or if she's the only woman I'm seeing romantically, but it doesn't matter which she's asking or why because the answer is the same.

"Yes." My response wastes no time.

She leans down, a shiver running down my spine as her lips graze the bottom of my earlobe. "You're my only pet."

I'm so happy with her response—so fucking relieved—that I can't help the smile that steals my lips. She squeezes my face in her hand, jarring me intentionally only slightly. "My smiling Stray."

Luckily before I can do something stupid and completely emasculating like try to kiss that hand, she pulls her arm back, leaving me unsteady on my knees.

"You won't need your safeword tonight. At least, I hope not." She winks, and my stomach launches to my throat. The sound of a trench coat rubbing against itself nearly makes my mouth water, but my eyes stay on the floor. When it pools at her feet, my dick lifts with excitement, knowing she's quite possibly naked.

Last week it was that fuckin' corset, and holy shit, that was hot. I never thought I was a lingerie guy—probably because I was just in a hurry to get down to it. But there's something to be said for patience.

"Look at me now, Stray. And don't take your eye off me again unless I tell you."

I lick my lips and find my mouth completely dry. At the base of my throat, my pulse hammers, making my mind race. A thick current buzzes between us. My head feels heavy when I tip it up and meet her eyes.

If my mouth was dry before, it's the goddamn Sahara now.

She's not naked. In fact, she's fully clothed.

Looking like she poured herself into it, my Goddess is wearing a sexy black and white pinstriped skirt fitted to show off those mouth-watering curves. Ending just above her knee, the small swell of her calf gives way to kissable ankles. Tonight's heels are those same black ones, shiny as shit with a tiny pointed toe. She looks phenomenal and makes me ache between my legs.

Taking a breath, my eye crawls up her supple slopes to find the swell of her breasts, rising quickly. Covered in a white, sheer blouse, she's bare beneath it, and a tingle works through my temples, my body feeling unsteady.

The raised tip of her *pierced* nipple presses against the sheer white, and my mouth waters to latch onto it. Did not expect pierced nipples, and my cock rages with delight at the discovery. I have to look up at her face, the desire to see her beauty overwhelming. Like I can't breathe if I can't see her. But I'm slow to look up because I know she'll own me with just a few more bats of those beautiful eyes.

And I don't know if I'm ready to be owned. All that shit about loving yourself first–I need to do that.

Lips painted cherry; they shine just like her patent shoes. She smiles at me as she leans over, grabbing the coat. I sincerely hope this hot office worker get up does not get covered by that trench coat because that in itself would be torture.

She fishes around in one of the pockets and returns with two black leather straps hanging from her closed fist. "Stand, Stray." I do.

Heady, a bit dizzy, I blink a few times, and she seems to know when I'm ready to communicate, finally speaking at just the right moment. "Put it on." Holding her hand out, her fingernails flash as she unfolds her palm. A purple rubber ball sitting between the two belt-ended leather straps rests in her hand.

"A gag?" I try to swallow, but my mouth and throat are still so dry. She reaches between us and squeezes the shaft of my dick unexpectedly, releasing me just as fast.

"See? You need it." She taps the purple rubber, and I want to catch her hand, squeeze it and press it to my aching dick, but I don't. Because... that's not what we are. I can already tell. Whatever we are, we're different.

I lift the gag from her palm and buckle it tightly behind my head.

"Until you learn that you don't speak unless spoken to, you wear the gag." She curls a nail under my chin. "Nod now, Stray, tell me you understand." I nod. Precome pools at my slit, and I know it'll be visible through my gray joggers pretty quickly. I swallow, my tongue heavy at the back of my throat from instinctually resisting the gag.

"Now, to make sure we're clear that I make the rules and you follow them, you need this to be memorable. That's how we learn, right? When we remember."

As a man, unless a woman has her mouth on one or Mally has given me a titty twister, I've never been aware of my nipples. My taint? Yes. A single hair on my nuts that's caught in my fly? Yes. But my nipples... not so much.

But they're as hard as fuck, and I'm aware of the room's temperature against them. The precome streams with abundance down my shaft, and I almost can't believe I'm this fucking turned on.

I don't know if it's because I need to plan things or what, but normally a lot of shit needs to be a lock for me to get this turned on. Like, I need to know this woman doesn't throw trash out her vehicle window and that she likes animals. Except now, I don't know anything about her, and I'm finding myself already biting down the orgasm billowing up my thighs.

I'm so fucking turned on.

I nod my head, delayed, but in response to her question nonetheless. Though I know whatever she wants to do to me right now, I'll remember. Fuck yes, I will remember.

She waves her finger over the general area of my desk. "Bend over across your desk, Stray."

Fuck.

The place where I have power during the day is relinquished to her now, but instead of feeling powerless, a rack of weight lifts from my shoulders. I didn't know I'd been carrying it, but breathing comes easier now.

I do as I'm told, my cock hard and angry against the hard surface of my desk. Bracing my hands out in front of me, my saliva pools under the purple rubber where it meets the wood. Her fingers curl under the waistband of my joggers, and my body jerks slightly at the unexpected touch.

"Calm, Stray." She uses her other hand to knead a comforting line down my back, between the swell of my lats. Then both of her hands tug my joggers down, leaving my fitted briefs intact over my cock, making sure they're snug under my ass. From her vantage point, I'm exposed.

I have no fucking clue what to expect, and my mind

clouds with the unknown, my blood pumping through me at light speed.

The deep groan that comes out of me when she slides on finger under the hem of my underwear, her knuckle streaking across my bare ass cheek, makes her pause. Feeling self-conscious at the noise, I begin to clear my throat, wanting to take it back.

Right as my balls are about to crawl up inside me and die of embarrassment—*am I the fucking deep, dirty groan guy?*—I feel her lips in my ear. "Good boy. Your Goddess likes knowing she's good at her job."

Fu-uck. My cock jerks against the table, precome now smearing from my underwear onto the wood. I can feel the slick glide of it, but I don't even care if she sees it. She's turning me into this desperate, leaking fucking mess and... I'm proud.

Then, as my mind whirrs with her impossibly sexy encouragement—removing every single molecule of insecurity and doubt inside of me—a loud slap of hot skin against hot skin eats up the silence of the room.

Then my ass burns.

"Fu-" I gurgle against the gag pressing on my tongue, spit everywhere now. My fingers curl around the edge of the desk, and when I peer up, my knuckles are drained of color. Another hot smack against my bare ass, and holy shit.

"Good boy, Stray," she says so fucking softly that I can barely hear it over my jagged breaths and errant heartbeat.

She spanks me again, this time leaving her palm over the molten skin to soften the blow. But even the sting of her whack feels fucking good.

Finally, something really feels fucking good. My cock

feels harder than it's ever been like it's more wood than the desk it's trapped against.

Her hand comes down on my ass again, and this time, she says, "You're beautiful, Stray, but just because you're built like a God doesn't mean you're in charge." She hits me again, two hard whacks back-to-back, my chest sliding forward against the desk. Gripping the edge tighter, my eye closes as she spanks me again. "Your Goddess is in charge, don't forget that."

I'm slippery against the desk when she spanks me again, and I realize it's because I'm all sweat and spit, and if she pulled my underwear down, I'd add some more liquid to the mix. Because I've been leaking like crazy. With each spank, a new rush of liquid eagerness slips free. The urge to reach down and grab myself against the desk and stroke is overwhelming.

But that's not how this is going to go.

And I'm more than fine with that.

Her nipples grate against my bare, sweaty back as she leans over me, her palm cupping my slapped cheek. Red lips pressed against the back of my ear, she whispers. "Don't come."

And before I can wrap my head around those two words, she reaches around my waist, slipping her hand into my briefs. I suck in a large, rough breath at the touch, and when her lithe fingers curl around my rock-hard shaft, I moan so rough and broken that a second wave of humiliation washes over me.

She's going to think I've never been fucking touched with noises like that. But just like before, she coo's "good boy" into my ear. And then, with the perfect amount of pressure, she strokes me from root to tip, just once. Then, as random and quick as it started, her hand leaves my cock, reappearing with a swat on my bare ass one more time.

I bite down on the ball, the hinges of my jaw burning from exhaustion. Heat spears my groin, and a burning fullness tingles in my balls. Oh my God, when she told me not to come I really didn't think it would happen. I've never had launch issues. But on the last spank, she leaves her hand on my ass.

The sensual curl of her fingertips into me, the excessive amounts of precome making my cock slide against the desk in my sticky briefs... The absence of her stroke, the hot sizzle of my burning flesh covered by her small, warm hand.

My abs tighten, my core buckles down, and my thighs flex, and as hard as I try, I can't stave it off.

I'm the Stray, but she sniffs out the impending explosion and sifts her other hand through the back of my hair, tugging it as she degrades me for not following her directions. Her touch at the back of my neck is soft, contrasting.

"Bad Stray. I told you not to come."

Without my permission and against everything I logically want to do—*follow her orders*—my shaft tightens and my ass clenches, the first rope of come so powerful it passes through the nylon of my briefs, spilling out onto the wood. I turn my head and focus on my hands as my cock throbs and twitches, a week's worth of come and desire sticky against my groin, wet on the desktop.

Panting, embarrassed from actually coming and having the urge to cover myself and finger the strap of my eyepatch for comfort, I try to stand, but a rigid hand falls across my lower back.

Daisy Jane

"Stay. Bad boys don't get to move."

Fuck, everything she says is like, the hottest fucking possible thing. Where did this chick learn this? Before I can go down a rabbit hole that I probably don't want to go down, she's making her way around to the front of the desk.

"On your elbows, look at me."

Slowly, I slide onto my elbows and hold my head up just enough to face her. When she crouches to be eye level with the desk surface, my core tightens, my pulse picks up. I've never had a woman bring such a fucking range of emotions out of me. I don't know how to feel about that.

I peer down into the private space between my body and the desk, just as she looks, too. She's surely seeing just what I see–the angry and still swollen head of my cock pushed tight to the now nearly translucent nylon fabric of my tight briefs. The slit of my cockhead is visible through the come-soaked fabric, and across the desk is evidence of what a bad listener I am.

Puddles and streaks of thick, white cream, she reaches out and swipes through a mass of come, holding it between our faces.

"You didn't listen." Her voice is both soft and controlling. My cock twitches his approval. "Bad Stray. I guess spanking isn't your form of discipline."

Reaching for her coat from the chair, I watch as she feeds her arms through, works each button patiently, and cinches the tie at the waist. Rolling her lips together, even in my drunk post-nut state, I can see her cheeks are pink, and her expression is lustful.

Maybe she enjoys getting guys off? Maybe that's her deal? I mean, it can't be *me* that she's all hazy-eyed over.

She digs a card from her pocket and slips it under two of my fingers, still curled tight to the desk like we're in an earthquake. Eyeing the card, I look back at her, still unable to speak from the gag in my mouth.

"Half a dozen roses. The card will take you straight to my account." She tilts her head to the side, eyes going to the swell of my still exposed bare ass. The noise of approval she makes in the back of her throat is quiet, but I catch it nonetheless.

"The box," she says, of the Amazon package I'd been staring at all day. "When I'm gone, get acquainted with what's inside. I expect a photo tonight, and I'll let you know what's required throughout the week."

My mind reels. I'm not sure what I expected but daily or even midweek contact between... *sessions?* What are we doing? How do I classify the last thirty minutes? Either way, I didn't think we'd be in contact.

But I find myself nodding like a fool, looking like a complete asshole with my load blown all over my desk and spit soaking the side of my beard. But I'm not letting a single moment of confusion wedge between us.

Whatever this is, it's too good to lose.

She rests her hand on the doorknob, her chin drifting to the top of her shoulder. God, her blue eyes are so fucking intoxicating. I certainly feel drunk.

"Goodbye, Stray. Don't forget, a photo of you and your gift or the punishment for not listening will be far worse." Then she winks and is gone.

And I'm left in a lust-sick haze, Lysol wiping my mess off my desk, a smile as wide as the sea on my lips.

16

Elsie

The Goddess to the Stray.

When I get home from Paradise, I'm more than freaking grateful to find Effie conked out in her own bed and Mom happily playing online Scrabble with Fanny. They say it's less pressure to play on their phones instead of in person. And I'm sure it's because both of them cheat.

But I'm grateful for the thesaurus right now because after saying hello, all I want is the privacy of my bathroom and a hot shower.

"Come tell me how your work thing went after your shower?" Mom calls as I have one foot in the hallway.

"Um," I stumble through options in my head but settle on, "sure, yeah, sounds good. Give me ten." In the shower, I'll think about what I'm going to tell her.

After I think about... *him*.

Turning the water on, I sit on the closed toilet, checking the door lock no less than five times to make sure I have privacy. Effie may be passed out from a busy day, but I also know how easily four-year-olds can find reasons to get out of bed, too. With my phone in my hands, I open up Instagram and start typing his name in the search bar.

I shouldn't do this.

Lacey *said* I shouldn't do this.

But how can I *not* do this? My Stray... and holy shit, how natural did it feel assuming the role of his Goddess? I'd be baffled by it if I weren't so busy basking in it and how good it feels to be *her*. The Goddess to the Stray.

I pull my legs together at just the internal mention of our names. With my focus back on the screen, too many Brian Edwards flood the screen. One is listed as Brian Edwards, with the profile name as "Bran." The circle portrait is small, so I bring the screen closer to my face. It's him. The patch over one of his eyes gave him away; his ropy arm slung over a tired-looking but beautiful dog. He's shirtless, and my mouth waters at the memory of him shirtless over his desk.

Guiltily, I click the profile. Butterflies swarm my ribs, and I find I'm anxiously dragging my now bare foot against the coral shag rug.

The screen fills with squares of my Stray, noted as Bran, not Brian. I wonder about that for all of two seconds before my gaze gravitates toward a photo on the bottom left of the screen. Eagerly, I tap, and it enlarges before me.

Stray, sunshine illuminating the edges of his body, a vast range of mountains and sky his backdrop. One arm is extended to the sunset, his face in the widest grin I've ever seen. It makes me grin, too, as the steam from the shower drifts around the small space.

What would make Stray, this smiling, gorgeous, strong, fit, powerful, happy human, need to pay a woman to... well, do anything? I can't wrap my head around it.

I lock my phone and set it on the counter before standing to strip from my naughty teacher outfit. I didn't borrow this from Lacey–this is actually one of my interview outfits. Of course, I wear a bra and camisole under the blouse normally but still. It worked tonight.

Lacey warned me to not get lost in this man. It's business. He's a client. And this is why. Because rather than checking my Venmo to make sure my Stray has paid me, I'm searching his Instagram profile, wondering what he's going through to need someone like me.

I shouldn't be wondering *anything* about him.

In the shower, though, my hand falls between my legs, and my fingers dip into my aching pussy, finding myself still wet and swollen from earlier.

My eyes close as water saturates my dense curls, dropping heavily down my face. Tipping my head back, the stream rains on my skin, and I exhale at the scalding water temperature.

Anything not to feel the heat between my legs.

I wash my hair and force my hands to stay above my waist, knowing that relief from this sexual tension would only heighten my already growing interest in my Stray. By the end of the shower, I've convinced myself to stay strong. Business is business. This is fun and new, and that's the reason I'm feeling attracted to him. That's all.

Stray

When I'm out and in my pajamas, wet hair dripping down my back, I notice a text on my phone.

It's him. And the way my belly twists and weaves with excitement and nerves is alarming, but I blow past those signs to pull back and open the message as fast as humanly possible.

My pussy flutters, sending me back onto my mattress, my knees pulled together tight. My breath takes a moment to show up, and when it does, it's heavy and hot.

The message has no text, only a photo.

My Stray's engorged and pink cock, veiny and angry, trapped beneath a stainless steel chastity cage. The cage I had sent to Paradise.

At the open peak of the cage, a dark dash peaks his cockhead, liquid glistening over it. My chest hollows as the memory of him in my palm rushes back. I'll never forget the noises he made as he tried to hold back but couldn't, coming from that final spank to his perfect ass.

Never thought I'd care about a guy's ass, honestly. I guess that was because I'd never seen my Stray's smooth, shapely, muscular cheeks because I wanted to tear his underwear off him completely. I just... thought that would be too much for our first real session.

I bite my lip and fight the urge to cave into the pulsing in my clit. To slide my fingers under my panties and touch myself to that picture. Because as much as Stray's locked-up cock leaking for me makes me want to straddle my pillow and ride with his name on my lips, I can't.

This is business.

I send him a quick text back.

Elsie: *15" silver chain. Sturdy but pretty. Buy one and carry it with you.*

Bran: *Yes, Goddess.*

His immediate response back has me envisioning him all wrapped up in his sheets, alone in his dark bedroom, nothing but the glow of our message against his handsome face. I want to believe he's somewhere thinking about me, wondering about me–the same way I am for him.

But I lock my phone and head to the living room, trying hard to put it behind me. It's just work. It doesn't matter that I'm totally drawn to this guy who I barely know but in some ways already know better than all the men I've ever met.

"How was your night?" I ask as I settle into the couch adjacent to where mom still rests in her chair. My hair drips onto my forearms, making me shudder.

She looks up from her book, noticing the still-running tv, before turning to me.

"Oh, how was your night, sweetheart?" she asks, bypassing my comment as if I only crept into her consciousness just now. That's okay; at least she's not confused.

"Good," I nod, giving her a genuine smile. She returns it, and instead of soaking in the happy, simple moment, *sadness bitch slaps me.*

I want her to be *her*, not this new version. And I know she can't help it. And I know it's selfish to be thinking of myself and not her, but I just wish she was the old her so much that sometimes it overwhelms everything else.

But before I can indulge myself in tears, mom's eyebrows go up. "Oh, we got a goldfish today."

"A goldfish," I repeat. "Why didn't you tell me after

Stray

work?" I don't remember her mentioning it. And how did they get it without a car? "Did Fanny take you?"

She nods proudly as if she's aware of her work-around, though I know she isn't. Mom doesn't know she doesn't drive because of her memory. She thinks something's wrong with her car. The truth is, I sold her car a few months back and put the money into her bank account for meds and groceries.

She isn't going to drive again. It needed to go, and we couldn't afford tags and insurance on a driveway ornament.

"Well, does Effie know she has to feed it?"

Mom rolls her eyes, and even though I want to get frustrated because I don't want to clean the bowl and I know I'll have to, I don't let myself do anything but smile.

"What did Effie name it?" I can't wait to hear the response because my daughter is insanely random in a hilarious type of way.

Mom wiggles her eyebrows. "We bought it but didn't tell her. It's a surprise for when you're off work. Thought we could give it to her together." She shrugs like it isn't insanely sweet and a really good memory to make before we can no longer make sweet memories. "That was Fanny's idea."

I'll have to remember to thank Fanny. She knows what she's doing, and I love her for it.

"Tomorrow," I say, knowing I'll be off a bit early. "I get off around noon. We can give it to her after preschool."

Mom smiles and turns back to the tv, still holding the book but not looking at it. She detaches more easily when she gets tired, and I can see now I'm losing her.

I get up, pushing the blanket off my legs. When I turn to go to my room, planning to tell her goodnight from the hall, she stops me.

"How was the experimental job you told me about?"

I did tell her I was going to an experimental job, but I can't believe she remembered. And I really can't believe she's remembering it now. Half of a smile pulls one side of my mouth.

"It was good. Really good."

She nods. "You're good at making people feel comfortable. You always have been."

I open my mouth to respond but then... I don't know what to say. Being good at making people feel comfortable is an intimate compliment.

I wonder if my Stray felt comfortable with me?

I'd been nervous going in there, but at the sight of him, I became his Goddess, like I'd disappoint him and deepen his pain if I couldn't be the powerful, cock-clenching woman he needed.

"Thanks, mom," I say as she turns towards the tv, blocking me out of her sight. I head down the hall, dragging the tips of my fingers against the bumpy texture of the wall.

Maybe I gave him comfort, and that's exactly what he was looking for. And he gave me confidence and power, and that's how I needed to feel with him... powerful.

I smile as I slide into bed, grabbing my phone to take a quick peek at that photo again... just one more time before I fall asleep.

17

Bran

I woulda paid her double.

Sammy pops her gum, and it irritates me.

"Don't do that. It's gross."

She makes several punctuated blinks while her head swivels back on her neck. Great, now I'm going to get it from her.

"Sorry–I'm just tired," I admit because again, I didn't sleep. Stoner rolls onto his back, huffing out a tired lungful. Sammy reaches down, scratching behind his ear. Once again, I think my dog has saved me from an angry woman.

"Why are you so tired lately?" She baby talks to Stoner, but the question is for me. The whole talking to the dog like a baby thing isn't helping my early morning irritation. But I don't need to get griped on right now—I don't think I have the mental space for anything else.

All I can think about is E... and I know I shouldn't think of her, and I definitely shouldn't be calling her E. She told me to forget I ever knew it—or just as much.

I can't even explain how wild my head is right now. I can't pin down this feeling to hold it, tear it apart, figure it out. I'm just... riding this unstoppable rushing wave of affection for this gorgeous girl I barely know.

She put me in a vulnerable position. Physically, yes, but there were moments when I felt extremely bare emotionally, too. But she met those sharp edges with softness, comfort. I've never felt so... *taken care of,* as fucking weird as that sounds. Like in her heart, all she desires is to make me writhe but hold me tight while I do. And God, do I want that.

She didn't focus on what's missing from me. She focused on what I am, how she sees me.

Maybe it's for the money. I mean, apparently, this is her job. She had me pay her. Six hundred dollars, by the fuckin' way.

I didn't even hesitate.

I woulda paid her double.

My cock was so hard for her, lying against that table. And I'm painfully stiff for her now, locked in this fucking monstrous, evil contraption.

It doesn't feel like it's about the money. God, do I know how stupid I sound. I'm every fucking fool on the documentary following a woman who cons so many men that she's a millionaire.

That fleeting thought makes me angry at myself—E isn't

that person. I just... can't believe she is. But she *is* a paid *something*, and not because she has nothing better to do.

There's a reason. And maybe if we keep seeing each other, I'll get to find out.

"Why are we here, anyway?" Sammy nods to the shop behind us. We're sitting out front of a small cafe, waiting for my watch to be fixed. At least, that's what Sammy thinks. I ordered a silver necklace here for my Goddess, and I'm picking it up. I bought her coffee and a doughnut next door while we waited for the shop to open. But still, she's grouchy.

"Picking up my watch. Let's not forget, you wanted to come with me." It's true. She'd called me this morning after she got off work, and I'd already been at Paradise for a few hours. I told her I was headed out on a breakfast run, and she insisted on coming, despite the fact she yawned through the entire conversation.

"Yeah, yeah," she said through another wide yawn. I nudged her coffee toward her, and she finished the last of it.

The Italian man appeared in the window, giving me a nod.

"I'll be back," I told her, and ten minutes later, I had the chain stowed away in my pocket, cinched inside a black velvet pouch. My watch got a new battery and cleaned—I enjoy it on my wrist openly several times, feeling like quite the actor.

I can't wait to get this necklace to my Goddess.

After dropping Sammy off at her car in the parking lot, I head back to my office in Paradise, locking the door. I don't have plans to be up to no good, but now that my Goddess and I have been in this space together, being here gets me hard. Like, I walk through the doorway, and my dick is steel. It takes me a few minutes to calm the fuck down.

Today, I'm not in a rush.

I lock the door and get comfortable at my desk. With both hands holding my phone, I hold them out over my stilted from growing dick. I flex my groin, making my cock press against the warm steel.

I text her.

Bran: *734 Newbury Way.*

With everything that had been going on with E and before that, the real focus had been finding a female trainer for Paradise. Shit, I still have to do that.

But why? I wanted to stay focused on Paradise, yeah, but if I'm honest, it was to help me learn to be comfortable around women for long periods of time.

Kind of a selfish reason to create a job position and hire someone now that I think about it.

But because my mind had been a mess the last two weeks, I'd completely forgotten what was starting today. I realized last night late when I was going over my appointments for the day, looking for a time to go necklace shopping.

Then I saw it.

Office remodel.

I forgot I was getting heated floors put in my office and having the whole thing repainted. I had Mally and Van to blame because after their stupid asses had swum laps out back in December, they came into the office to stand in front of the big heater vent and complained endlessly that their feet were ice.

They seriously wouldn't shut the fuck up about it.

Now ten grand later, I'm getting heated floors out of

spite. I will not let those dumbasses get on my nerves even if it costs… ten grand.

Three dots hold me in suspense as they wiggle and writhe around on the screen, taking my guts with them.

Then.

Goddess: *Stray, why are you giving me the address to a white house with blue shutters and pink flowers with a black truck in the driveway?*

My dick pulses in the metal, angry and desperate to get hard for this sweet, smart ass girl.

Bran: *Did you just look up my house on Google Maps?*

Goddess: *So it's your house.*

Goddess: *Goddesses and dog houses don't mix.*

Bran: *Damn, you type fast.*

Bran: *Office at Paradise is being remodeled.*

It only just then occurs to me that she may not feel safe coming to my house… and what's worse is that she may have a *reason* not to feel safe coming to my house.

My grip on the phone increases as I grind my teeth in frustration. I don't fucking like that.

Bran: *If it's a safety thing, I understand. I respect that completely. I don't want you doing anything you aren't comfortable with.*

But I can't leave it there.

Bran: *Just so you know, I'd never hurt you. I'd get hurt for you.*

Bold but oddly true. I know, I know, insert split screen of idiot man in the documentary here.

I'll take my chances.

Goddess: *Okay*

Bran: *What's your name, Goddess?*

I don't know why I ask. I know the rules. I know this isn't my business. Fuck. I wish there was an unsend option for text messages. But the three dots that had been rippling across the screen halt, then disappear as she presumably reads my message.

Goddess: *If I answer your question, do I get to ask you a question?*

My hand comes down across my eyepatch, the tips of my fingers traveling the length of the dark elastic attached. I don't want to talk about my eye or that night or what's under the patch or anything else that I usually get asked.

She hasn't given me any reason to think she cares about my eye, but then again, I'm paying her for affection, aren't I? Realizing exactly why personal questions have no place in this, I send a text, wishing I'd never have asked her name in the first place because I don't want to answer questions about myself.

Bran: *I'm sorry I asked. It was an overstep. I know that.*
Bran: *Until the office is done, it's my house or a hotel.*
Goddess: *I'll see you Thursday at eight, at your house.*
Bran: *Thank you, Goddess.*
Goddess: *You'll make it up to me, pet.*

The construction foreman taps on the door, and I call for him to come on in as I stuff my phone into my pocket. Glad for the cage right about now because without it, I'd be sporting an awkward boner.

Shaking the foreman's hand, he explains that the job should only take two weeks. Since I worked some construction when I was younger, I know that two weeks can easily be six, but I'm not impatient. Packing up my laptop and some paperwork, I grab a few other things and leave the space.

Deciding to work from the entry desk for a while, I send a few emails and text back to Malibu, who has been trying to get wings with Van and me tonight. I agree to go because there are two more days until I see my Goddess. And I need to seriously reroute my brain because, between the cage and thoughts of her having a reason to be nervous about coming to my house, I think I'll actually go insane.

Bran: *Wings tonight sound good.*

Mally: *Good. They have a new flavor. It will blow your mind.*

I roll my eye. The idea that a wing flavor could blow my mind was completely realistic just a few weeks ago. But now? The only thing that can blow my mind is somewhere in this town, and I won't see her for two days.

Gonna be a long forty-eight hours.

18

Elsie

I said sit, Stray.

He wanted to know my name. And then I'd asked him—both playfully and strategically, I thought—if a response would earn me a question in return.

I'd planned on asking him just one single word. *Why?*

Why are you doing this thing with me when you're... *you?* What demons are you hiding? I mean it would've been a loaded question, but I can't understand why this man wants a Dominant.

His capable physique, handsome features, broody style—I really just don't know why.

But he lost interest and diverted from the question.

I guess he didn't want to know my name that bad.

And it's my own stupid fault for getting bummed at that

because Lacey told me not to do the very freaking thing I'm doing. She said–*these guys have hang-ups; this is business, don't catch feelings.*

Instead of listening to the experienced person, I decided to do everything my way.

And here I am, feeling bummed that my Stray doesn't care to know my name, dying to know why he's doing this and what is keeping him from bending the world over his desk because he looks capable of it.

I try my best to shake off the feelings of disappointment and inadequacy during the two days between our texting and our meeting.

Surprising Effie with the goldfish Fanny and mom got her was a good diversion. She'd already dumped an entire can of fish food in the bowl less than one day later, but still, watching her attempt to care for a pet was pretty stinking cute.

And she'd named him… Fuzz. When I asked her why she named a goldfish Fuzz, she rolled her little eyes at me.

"He's orange, but lightish orange, more like a peach than an orange."

I followed that logic so far.

"Peaches have fuzz, so I'm calling him Fuzz."

I grinned at her explanation, and though the store had sold them a female goldfish, its gender would never be an issue without another one in the tank.

I'd been asked out on a coffee date by a gym member, and while I politely declined, it did feel nice to clearly be seen as more than the polo shirt holding the mop.

Still, I thought about my Stray for those two days. More than I wanted to. More than I should have.

And now, as I pull on some of the borrowed clothes from Lacey, my turkey sandwich and barbecue chips I ate for dinner jumping around my stomach—I'm nervous.

I'm the Dominant. *He* pays *me*.

If anyone should be nervous, it should be him. Though the thought does nothing for my nerves as I cinch my coat around tonight's rather ballsy outfit and sneak quietly out the door. Mom, Effie, and I spent most of the day together, and I've already said my goodnights to my little girl. They're cuddled up on the couch watching *Encanto*, and slipping out is the best for all of us right now.

Mom's doing good today, and I don't want to do anything to jostle that.

Driving to Stray's house, I have a fleeting moment of utter and sheer panic.

What if this guy locks me in his basement and keeps me captive forever? But before I can sufficiently picture it and freak out, I laugh at myself. Because even though what I am doing is a little stupid on my part, the truth is, I wouldn't have met with him at all if I was seriously worried about that. And I certainly wouldn't meet with him *twice* if I thought this was all just a long con to murder me.

Having looked up his house—which is adorable, by the way—on Google right when he sent it to me, I know just how to get there. The funny thing is, I'm so insanely attracted to this stranger both physically and emotionally—which I know is insane—but it's even more comical when I realize he's been so close to me this whole time, yet our paths haven't crossed until now.

I mean, it makes sense. He owns a gym, and I work at a different gym. I take care of Effie and mom and don't have a lot of time to go out or even take walks around the neighborhood. And he is a business owner and by the looks of it, definitely a bit older than me. He probably had a full life, and it occurs to me as I pull up outside of his place that maybe that's why he does this thing with me.

Maybe he doesn't have time to date, and so he pays for sexual gratification, using the Dominant and Submissive relationship to rid himself of any responsibility or decision making. From what I've seen, he has a dick—a freaking nice one from what I've seen—and it needs servicing. Maybe that's what I am.

A dick servicer to fit into his busy life.

I put my car in park and glance at my bag of goodies on the passenger seat. Why hadn't I thought of this before? He's just too busy. This is how he gets that last piece of his needs met. No emotional attachment, no frills, just dick-hardening excitement and orgasms.

I want to believe that's why. But something in my gut tells me I'm still not quite there on his reasoning. And I am so irritated with myself that I care.

I'm pretty sure if he didn't even want to know my name that bad that he isn't sitting around thinking of his Goddess and all the reasons why she does what she does.

Clearing the jumble from my head, I peer out the passenger window and stare at his cute, quaint, and quiet-looking little white house. The shutters are painted blue, the cement steps leading to the matching lacquer door are clean, and a vibrant green banana plant rests in a cerulean pot near the door. Everything is neat; the grass is trimmed and edged, his pickup in the driveway glistens like it's never missed a wax, and in the corner of the yard near the fence is a planter box full of vegetables.

Fuck.

The hopeless romantic in me gets pussy flutters at his neat and perfect little home. Time to think with my brain and not my dreamin' ovaries.

Getting out of the car, I close the door quietly because even though it's only eight, something about this neighborhood tells me it's full of people already in bed. At the very least, they're in their pajamas.

When I make it to the porch, the tall door swings open before I can knock.

My Stray stands there, his lips a thin line, his eye on mine. We just stare at one another for a moment, and I don't even know what he's wearing, but still, my pussy flutters, and my chest tightens.

Teakwood and amber drift toward me, curling under my nose, pulling me towards him. He steps back, allowing me into his house, and as I step past him, I suck in a lungful of his heady, masculine scent.

He didn't smell like this before, I'd remember.

"Goddess," he says, and the word almost knocks me back because I'm still adjusting to the nipple-hardening timbre of his voice and the fact that this handsome piece of art is referring to *me* as Goddess.

But he's not attracted to a bumbling blonde in disbelief. He's attracted to the woman who takes his needs and squeezes them, doling out relief when she sees fit. I don't know why that shocks me.

That's why I'm here, after all.

"Stray," I dip my head and acknowledge him for less than a second before turning my attention to his home.

The lights are off–like he doesn't really want me to see his private space. My stomach drops, but I force my chin up. So he doesn't want me to see his house–big deal. I'm not here for that anyway. I shouldn't read into it because there's nothing to read.

This is business.

Lacey would be so annoyed with me right now. Something she'd said comes back to me as I turn in the entryway, my eyes going back to my pet.

What if instead of looking for a guy who will make you feel like he's doing some fucking charity work to love your life, you start seeing men that make you feel powerful. That makes you feel in control and strong.

That's right. My part in this business isn't just the money he puts into my Venmo. It's the power I depart with that I'm here to grab. The strength and power of being a Dominant– seeing my choices and commands unfold before my eyes, everything in my complete power.

That's why I'm here, and I can't forget it.

I pass him my purse, loaded with goodies. The top is zipped, but I don't miss that his eye flicks to the metal teeth. He wants to know what I've brought, and he will find out. But not so easily.

"Take me to your room, Stray," I say, turning toward the long, dark hallway. And as he steps past me, I follow but only make it a few steps before I hear a loud grunt and sigh behind me. Startled, I jump back towards the wall, my palms gripping the flat surface.

I must've gasped, too, because my Stray turns on a light

from a doorway a few steps ahead, a soft glow illuminating the bit of hall between us. He smiles–a genuine reaction, and it's so adorable. No, it's *hot*. Wait, it's freaking pulse-zippingly sexy. I lick my lips and follow his eye, his gaze guiding me to the source of the grunt and sigh.

Five feet behind us stands a dog.

Its shiny black coat is partially covered by... a sweater. A blue and white sweater with... "Snoopy is his favorite," my Stray says just as I'm tipping my head to study the cartoon woven into the little sweater.

My lips curl into a small smile, and I raise a hand to the dog.

I just waved at a dog.

"He doesn't know how to wave," my Stray deadpans, making my smile grow. Then he smiles, too, and my belly gets all warm and fuzzy like it does after the first shot of alcohol. "But that's what you heard. Or should I say who."

I look back to the dog, who looks... almost annoyed.

"Is he mad?" I ask, kneeling to get the dog to come to me. Because hello, a cute dog wearing a Snoopy sweater with grouchy old man energy? Obviously, I'm going to try and pet him.

"He's not mad; he's *lazy*. He sleeps in my bed, and..." he rakes a large hand up the back of his head, smiling again. So many smiles tonight. My romantic heart and tingling lady parts almost can't take it. I'm not here for that. "Well, he's irked that there's someone else here."

I look at the black dog in his Snoopy sweater, and now that he's said it... the dog does look kind of irked. When my gaze goes back to my pet, he shrugs. "He's got anxiety. He likes routine."

Me too, I think to myself, but I stop myself because not only is that too personal, it doesn't even feel true anymore. I'd stuck to routine a lot the last few years because it was easier to raise a child and navigate mom's mental deterioration when I had a schedule to live by.

But by definition, becoming a Dominant following a random drunk bar conversation after being dumped is not at all routine-like.

It's sporadic, random, and chaotic.

That's me now, at least a part of me, and I cannot deny that I like it. And Lacey was right—I like the feeling of power and control, too.

I want to ask the dog's name. But when he finally comes to me, I force myself to overlook the silver name bone dangling from his blue collar. I don't need to know this detail. Nope. Not why I'm here.

After a chaste behind-the-ear scratch, I rise and ignore the adorable and very grouchy-looking dog, who honestly seemed to just let me scratch him to appease me.

I like this dog and his lax, sassy attitude.

"Here," Stray nods to the doorframe where the light pours out. "This is my room."

Raising his muscled arm, I watch the image of a topless mermaid entwined in rope flex and almost appear to swim as his muscles torque beneath the inked skin. Adjusting his eyepatch, he drops his hand away quickly when he sees me looking. Almost like he forgot for a moment I was there.

Not the biggest ego booster, but okay.

I'm here for a job. And let's not forget, he didn't care enough to know my name.

Right. This is work.

When he closes the bedroom door behind me and turns on the lights, we both notice we are practically nose to nose. His breath is surprisingly–not minty like he'd just brushed to prepare for our session. Not boozy like he'd needed to calm his nerves for our session, either.

"Did you just eat..." I trail off as I lean towards him, sniffing where my nose hovers above his broad chest. Which, by the way, is covered by a black hoodie. Didn't know I was a hoodie girl, but I think not knowing I would make a great Dominant will top the list of things I learned about myself this year.

"Cherries," he says, and the color of almost ripe cherry floods his normally russet cheeks. "I have a tree in my yard. I was picking them before you got here. Popped a few."

"You pick cherries at eight o'clock at night?"

He shoves a hand through his dark hair, which falls in styled waves naturally once he drops his arm back down. Of course, he's effortlessly handsome. Because the universe couldn't drop this confidence-building situation into my lap without making it tricky, right?

I push past him as he answers, and he follows, setting my bag of tricks down onto the neatly made bed.

"I go to work early, so it's the only time. And if I don't pick them, my neighbors ravage the tree over the fence. Pick me dry."

Like small talk usually does, it makes me sad. Because I know he's only obliging me. I asked, so he answered. There isn't some unspoken mutual interest, and the more I hype myself on this being a romance in the making, the more this endeavor loses its purpose.

If I don't get power from this–I leave this feeling more

powerless than before—it will have all been for nothing. And I can't have that. I need the reins on some part of my life—it's the only thing getting me to my feet each time I'm bucked off the horse.

Reminding myself why I'm here, I untie the waist of my coat and let the jacket fall to the carpeted floor below.

Then, I look at my pet. My wild, wandering creature. My Stray. My lost, beautiful ship at sea.

"Stray, give me my necklace." I open my palm and tap it. His eye is on my open hand—not my outfit—when he digs in his jogger pocket. Pulling out a small, black velvet pouch, my pulse zips when I see the store name printed over it.

Sinatra's.

He got me a nice necklace. I mean, it's not mine to keep. Just to use throughout this whole... thing. But still, I'm a little shocked. And he's watching me. He must be. Because he says quietly, "I didn't want to turn your neck green with something cheap."

"Front pocket of my bag," I instruct, swallowing down the shaky nerves that strangle my vocal cords.

He does as he's told and, without another command, places the key in my palm. He watches me intensely as I remove the silver chain from the pouch and slip the key on. Grabbing gloves from my bag, I turn my back to him, sweeping my long hair over my shoulder to give him access to my bare neck.

"Put it on me."

He does, and I swear he makes... noises... as his fingertips and knuckles graze my skin. Noises of frustration and need— but that's not because the skin on my neck is fucking beautiful and enticing. It's a neck, not a tit.

It's because he's locked up. He's been locked up for a handful of days now. The picture of his cock behind the steel cage dances behind my eyes, but I spin to face him, not needing a mental image. The real thing is right here.

"Get naked and sit on your bed, legs off the edge." Then I fold my arms across my chest like a pissed-off school teacher and watch. Wait and watch as he does exactly as I said.

He doesn't argue. He doesn't barter. He just... does what I say. Easily. And quickly.

And I'm already starting to feel good. Distancing myself from overthinking about him and our dynamic, I snap on the black latex gloves I'd packed. Reaching into my open bag, I grab the massage oil I packed and flip the cap open with a click. By the time my gloved hands are slick and shiny, I see my pet is completely naked in front of me.

The only thing he wears is his eyepatch.

"I said sit, Stray."

Nodding, he sits on the edge of his bed. Taking a few steps back–toward what appears to be a massive closet with two closed French doors–I run my hands down the edges of my body, starting at my breasts, ending at my hips.

Tonight, I'm wearing a patent leather corset and a tiny red leather mini skirt. My lipstick matches the skirt, and my toenails do, too. But my feet are covered by thigh-high fishnets, as well as a pair of red-bottomed high heels I borrowed from Lacey.

"Tell me, pet, do you like your Goddess's outfit?" I smear my gloved hands over the corset, knowing how hot it looks to see oil smeared across leather. Lacey told me to do it. And I'd tried it ahead of time, not wanting to work out the kinks in front of my... *client*.

He swallows, his bent legs spreading further. My eyes fall to the shiny silver between his meaty thighs, and my mouth puckers a little at the glistening slit that peers at me through the opening.

"I think you know how I feel about your outfit, Goddess," he rasps. Smoothing his palms over his naked thighs, my pet rolls his bottom lip through his teeth, and I'm painfully aware of how much he wants this. Wants *me*.

"Are you leaking for me, or are you leaking because you've been locked up?" I hear the very sexy questions topple out of me and try very hard not to clap a hand over my mouth and wince. I'm the hot mama saying these things. And yet, it feels like an out-of-body experience.

He clears his throat, and his dark eye pierces me, nearly deflating my confidence as his Dominant. With just one heavy look, I want to be the one locked up with him at the helm.

"You are the reason I've been a faucet." His fingers curl around his naked knees. "Not just now. Since I put it on, seeing you again, Goddess, is all I've thought about."

The heat swirling in my chest drops to my groin, a rush of warmth spreading through my pussy. Somehow, this talk of leaking is feeling incredibly romantic.

His uncovered eye studies my lubed, latexed hands. "I don't know why you're wearing those, but it's not helping the cause." He nods forward to the heavy metaled cock hanging between his spread thighs.

I look at it. A trail of precome strings between his cockhead and the carpet. My pussy clenches, and I do my very best to hide how much that turns me on.

Approaching him slowly, I climb into his lap; my face pointed directly at his. The steel cage connects with my tailbone beneath my mini skirt, and warmth spreads through me. Who knew the feel of metal would get me going.

Rocking up on my knees, so my throat aligns with his neck, I grip his shoulders.

"Suck it, Stray."

His hands cup my ass over the red mini skirt, and without question, he leans into me until his warm lips are pressed against the slope of my throat.

My eyes close tightly, and I can feel the tiny silver key lift from my skin as he sucks it and part of the silver necklace into his mouth. His beard grates my skin erotically.

Rocking myself gently against him–and his locked up cock– he groans against my throat. I only catch the noise because his mouth adjusts a few times as he suckles the metal key.

"You're locked up because I told you not to come, do you remember? Do you remember how you came on yourself, on your desk, after I told you not to?"

With only a tiny bit of guidance from Lacey, I'd planned out tonight's session pretty well. I knew physically what I'd do with my Stray. But because I'd spent so much time thinking about him, I didn't give the required amount of thought to what I'd say tonight.

When it comes down to it, what I say is just as powerful as what I do, if not more so. With my oiled-up hands, I drag them over the mountainous curves of his chest, stopping when they're pressed to his pecs. Thumbs and forefingers aligned; I command him to suck harder as I twist and pinch his nipples.

He groans against my throat, and the vibration of his deep voice moves through my chest, my own nipples hardening. Releasing one of his nipples, I keep pinching and twisting the other one, loving how his body immediately responds to my touch. Reaching behind me, I use my free gloved, oiled hand to stroke across the swollen, stretched skin of his balls.

This time, the groan that breaks past his lips is loud and attacking, and he doesn't try to stifle it.

"*Fu-ck*," the word comes out harsh against my throat as the wet key drops down against my collarbone. "Goddess... I..." His words escape him as one of my fingers slips to the sensitive stretch of skin between his ass and balls. Stroking with pressure, I massage it, my other fingertips still grazing his swollen sac as I do.

"Spread your legs further, Stray," I command. His dark eye hovers on my corseted breasts, and it floors me to have his hungry gaze on me as I'm touching him so privately. I mean... that's sex, right? Having fuck me eyes on you while you're fondling someone's naked, private bits.

But it feels like so much more than that with my Stray.

His knees widen, and my gloved fingers grip the metal cage. His spine straightens, and he groans in reaction. As I jostle the cage, he smashes his lips to my throat, and the grate of his barbed beard against my hot, needy flesh sends *want* through me.

I'm here to get him off, but holy crap, I'm so wet right now. And when I curl my fingers into a strip of exposed skin pushing through the cage, dying to escape, it makes me feel high.

And I use that endorphin rush, that mental high, to take this session to the next level. I slide off his lap, and wetness gushes past my lips when I see his face.

The tip of his nose is pink from friction, his lips are swollen from sucking the key to his cage, and his dark eye is stormy. His Adam's apple dips heavily as he swallows, stroking his palms down his broad thighs.

With my eyes on him, I hook my thumbs inside my panty straps and tug them down, still not giving him a single peek at my bare pussy. Keeping the skirt on, I watch him stare at the wet, crumpled panties on his carpeted floor.

Slowly, I straddle myself over him again and take my time lowering myself completely.

My lubricated pussy connects with his shaved groin with a quiet little squelch, and he lets out the sexiest, neediest hum in response.

"Goddess," is all he says after the noise finishes its departure from his parted lips. I replace one hand over his nipple and reach back to his balls with the other.

In a pat your head, rub your tummy type of way, I clutch and release his very big sac while dragging the side of my thumb over his hardened nipple. His head tips back, but I reprimand him.

"Suck the key, Stray, suck the key and don't come."

His mountainous thighs tremble beneath me. His voice is broken but sexy. "I don't know if I can," he admits, and his admission stirs up my insides. "Feeling you wet against me…" he trails off, only to come back to his sentence after looking down at our laps. "I'm close."

Breaking character slightly, I giggle. "You won't come from just feeling me. You need contact. Friction."

He smoothes a hand up my spine, and my breasts ache for more of his touch. Thank God I've got the corset on, or he'd know just how much I like this.

"I always have before," he admits, "needed friction, I mean." He swallows, and the sound of his saliva traveling through his body may as well be moans and grunts because it awakens me in ways I've never been woken to. Wrapping his palms over my shoulders, he pulls me down so that my wet lips smear against his shaved groin. We both groan a little.

"But tonight," he trails off, voluntarily stretching his neck to bring his mouth to the key. He sucks it in, taking some of my skin with him, and I gasp. Remembering I'm in control, I let him mouth the key for a moment longer—mostly just because I like it too—then place my oiled gloved hand on his forehead, and push him back.

"Strays don't call the shots," I tell him, sliding off his lap. His eye hovers on the shimmering slickness my eager pussy left behind.

"Fu-ck," he says, transfixed by the arousal I've left on him. Then I look to where he continues to leak freely and understand his primal attraction to seeing a woman ready to be fucked.

Seeing him ready to fuck makes my legs ache to be spread, my back itch to be thrown against a mattress, and my stomach clench in anticipation of what would probably be the best orgasm I've ever had.

All at just the sight of his leaking, locked cock.

I did come here to gain power, to give pleasure... it's not the Goddess's job to make herself come. That will have to be on my own time. And as I survey the locked, muscled, sexy man at my mercy, I know that time will come the moment I get home.

I dig through my bag until I find the blindfold, and before he can eye it, I slip it down over his head. I also grabbed another thing that I packed and have never used–I didn't want to borrow any devices or toys from Lacey, so the handcuffs are brand new. Took them out of the package just a few days ago.

Falling to my knees between his spread ones, I use one gloved hand to reach up, still wanting to flick his nipple. He growls something fierce.

"Stray, put your hands behind your back."

He does.

Standing again, with a loud metallic clink, I close the cuffs around his wrists. Straddling his lap, I lean forward and force the key against his closed lips. He opens, realizing he needs to suck again, and does.

Once the key is in his mouth, lips sealed around the chain, I rock my wet pussy against his cage and talk to him.

"Stray, I hope you've been a good boy all week." He sucks the key harder at the mention of *good boy*, and I realize that he likes the praising term. "Were you a good boy?" I ask, throwing him another pun-intended bone. He jerks his hips up toward me, nodding only slightly to keep his mouth on the key.

"Do you think that your Goddess should reward your good behavior?"

He spits the key out, and I stifle a laugh but don't bother hiding my smile–he can't see me anyway. "Yes, Goddess. Please. Please let me come before I do anyway."

It burns me up that he is so close to the edge. It makes me feel like an *actual* Goddess, not just a pretender. I know if he hadn't been in that cage the last few days and if he weren't battling whatever it is he is battling, he wouldn't be on the brink of blowing from simply feeling an aroused woman's genitals.

Look at him. He's probably back-stroked through hoards of women at some point.

Maybe he's heartbroken? Maybe that's the reason why we're doing this?

The beard burn growing across my neck is the sensation I need to be pulled from my thoughts. I'm not supposed to be figuring him out. I'm not supposed to be wondering.

Make him come, take your power, and leave Elsie!

I rock my hips into his, my body breaking out in goosebumps as I imagine both of his hands kneading my ass underneath the leather skirt. I cuffed him because feeling his hands on me... it was too good. Without the cuffs, I'd probably give him permission because his hands feel so good that I probably couldn't bring myself to make him stop.

Reaching behind me, I adjust his locked-up package so that it's resting against my seam, pushed forward just slightly. The little lock of the cage juts against his groin, but he doesn't complain. I let my body slide back in his lap, giving his junk more room. Then slowly but surely, my body begins rolling, my slit pushing against his very red and very engorged balls.

Didn't know I had a thing for big, swollen, full balls, but here I am, biting the corner of my mouth as I nudge them forward with my bare pussy. He curses at the third pass, and though he can't see me, I wrap my hand around the sticky key at my neck, fingering the jagged edges.

My orgasm builds as the steel cage slides between my lips, nudging my clit.

"If you don't come for the next minute, Stray, I'll let you watch me come."

Then I really begin riding and grinding against his locked dick. My eyes want to close because the friction on my clit is so intense, so good, but I have to watch him.

His muscles flex—especially the ones running the length of his arms. Still cuffed behind his back, his muscles go ropy and tight when my cunt smears against the cage, and they relax when I swivel my hips away from the contact.

His inked chest rises and falls quickly, and I can see his pulse hammering at the base of his throat. I'd love to reach out, place my palm over his heart and feel the way my body makes his heart erratic—but that's too intimate. That's not us.

He is my Stray. I am his Goddess. We don't do that.

So I ride him, bumping his cage every few seconds to find friction that fits us both. And as I'm about to tell him he only has to last thirty more seconds, his neck fills with strain. His jaw clenches.

"*Fuckfuckfuck*," he growls, the depth of his voice jolting me every time I hear it. So deep and delicious. "If you don't stop moving, I'm going... I'm gonna..." his erratic breathing intensifies, and I look down in time to see the first rope rocket from the wide slit of his cock. His hips jerk, his white teeth bare down on his bottom lip.

"Fuck, *fuuuu*," he lets the exclamation hang as spurt after spurt of thick, hot come soars into the space between us, dropping back down on the cage, on his groin... *on me*.

I drag my fingertips through his come and feel the undeniable flutter and pulse of an impending orgasm hit me.

"Oh my God," I sigh out, my thighs quivering around his rock-hard ones as my pussy flexes and pulses, orgasming from the experience of making him tip over the edge. And having his come on me. I smear the blob of come around on my inner thigh as I ride out my orgasm almost motionlessly–because I don't want him to know.

I feel like I'm cheating or that I stole something. I'm not here to get off, so as my open, hungry sex clenches tightly at the sight of him covered in his come from me, I don't say a word until I catch my breath.

"You didn't make it a minute, Stray," I chastise playfully, feeling a bit guilty because... *neither did I.*

Though every part of me wants to gather up all the extra moments surrounding my orgasm, I know I can't. Because if I linger, he'll wonder why. You only linger in the moment if you come; everyone knows that.

Sliding off his lap, I pull a towel from the bag and begin cleaning up our successful session.

"If you take the cuffs off, I could do that," he says, somewhat quietly. I glance at him, kind of loving that he can't see me, and take in the beads of sweat on his forehead and the way his chest still isn't steady.

"I'm a *good* Goddess. Like a *good* fairy godmother. I'll let you enjoy the moment, Stray, but you'll owe me."

"Oh yeah?" he asks. His tree trunk-like neck fills with strain as he struggles to keep his head up, facing me. I don't know why since he's blindfolded.

"Yeah. Even though you couldn't last a minute, I'll clean you up, and your punishment is keeping the cage on."

"I thought my punishment was not getting to see you come."

I'm glad his eyes are covered because I smile. I liked that response. But it's all part of the dynamic.

"That, too," I add, swiping the terry cloth over the last of his come. I tell him to remove the blindfold, and he does.

I know they say comparison is the thief of joy, and I teach that to Effie often. But as I think of the dribbles Jake produced when I'd give him a lotioned-up handjob in the backseat of his Acura TL (plot twist: it was his mom's car), I can't help thinking how very wrong that statement is now.

Comparison is bringing me more joy than ever because if I have to compare my Stray to Jake, I traded a pencil for a beer can, a foot for a yard, a stream for a waterfall.

It's almost unfair to Jake to be compared to a man like my Stray. It's not even apples and oranges. It's like comparing artificial sweeteners to raw sugar cane. One is the thing you're telling yourself is the real thing; the other is the real thing. No denying.

Before I uncuff him, I slip into my coat and tie it up. Though he hadn't a damn clue, I knew I'd shared that intense orgasm with him, and letting him see so much of my bare body after the orgasm felt... too intimate. Dumb, I know. But because I was already beyond interested and intrigued, the smart thing to do is protect myself.

Even though I don't know much about my Stray, each morsel I discover keeps me hot on his trail, eager to consume every single crumb I can.

With the cuffs, blindfold, and towel stuffed back into my bag, I lift it up on my shoulder as he pulls his athletic pants over his meaty, built thighs. I try not to watch, but something about watching him get dressed is paralyzing. I've never been so interested in watching someone do mundane things until Stray.

But I force myself to concentrate very hard on my keys, which I'd dug out of my bag just as a distraction.

But when he hears them, his head jerks up, abandoning the tie at the top of his pants he'd been working on.

"It's that time, huh?" he asks, sounding almost... *bummed*. But then again, I'd just stimulated his nipples and teased him until he came. Of course, he wants me to stay. He's a man.

"Yep," I said, knowing that one deviant act per night as his Dominant is all we can take.

Or, all *I* can take at least.

"Next week?" he asks hopefully as he slides one ropy arm through the sleeve of his black hoodie.

I nodded. "Can you be a good boy until then?"

He strokes a hand down his beard, and I notice he has a small phrase inked over his palm. In ebony ink, each letter carefully printed, I eye the passage.

Just keep swimming.

He smiles, his dark eye glistening happily. He looks relaxed and sated, and it should bring me pleasure to know that I am the reason for that. Instead, I wonder why he isn't relaxed and happy all the time.

"Don't have much of a choice, do I, Goddess?" His voice drops low on my name, making my flesh ripple with heat. The same hand that stroked his beard drops to his crotch, where he palms his metal-contained cock. "This makes it hard to be a bad boy."

Like I was born to be his Dominant, his Goddess, like I'd

rehearsed a script with all of this in it, and this moment was a play, unfolding perfectly, I add, "Actually, it makes it hard to get hard." I step towards him, patting his chest. I could've been patting a piece of wood; he's so firm.

"See you next week."

Turning on my heel, bag thrown over my shoulder, I walk out. Stoner is lying on his side, his snores echoing off the narrow hallway walls. He doesn't stir as I walk past him and make my way to the front door. I want to turn around and eye the place one more time, to soak in the details of my Stray, but I know not only is it dark, but it is a bad idea, anyway.

I walk out, the smell of coconut oil still stuck in my nose. As I drive home, I create and chant a mantra to keep myself focused.

This is just business. This is just business.

* * *

Though it was well past nine when I got home, I knew the nighttime routine had gone horribly wrong. Because when I stepped into the house, ready to hang up my Dominant hat and slide into some mom pajamas, I stopped in my tracks, the door bumping my butt.

"No! No!! No!" Effie's tiny voice pierced my high, sending me to the proverbial floor with a maddening thud. My heart and stomach dropped, too, because hearing your child cry with such pain is agonizing.

Running to the sound of her voice, I find Effie standing between mom's legs; her balled-up fists slamming into mom's chest. In her recliner, mom's arms are holding Effie's hips as she lets her granddaughter wail and cry.

Letting my bag hit the ground with a thud, I drop to my knees between the two of them and stroke some sweat and tear-soaked hair from my daughter's face.

"What's going on? Why are you upset?"

A clear trail of snot streams between her nose and top lip, and I used the sleeve of my coat to wipe it away. Mom's instinct is to get rid of the snot by any means necessary.

Steadying herself with a deep breath–something my mom taught her that I find amazing–she turns to me, her bottom lip quivering.

"Fuzz is a goner."

I have to bite the inside of my cheek. Leave it to kids to deliver death news in a funny way. Turning to face my mother, I find her doing the same thing.

"I didn't know she'd fed him," mom admits, and then our silly few seconds of enjoying Effie's antics disappear. "I couldn't remember if I'd fed him, either," she adds, and that sentence holds all the things I need to know.

She overfed the fish–probably fed him all day–and he ate until he couldn't.

I stoke a hand down Effie's wild curls. "We'll get a new fish, okay?" I don't want a new fish, but I'd buy a swarm of bees if it took that painful look from her face. "Let's get some rest now, okay?"

I smile softly at mom, whose awareness is clearly deteriorating. I'm lucky she kept it together as long as she did–I got home just in time.

Watching Fuzz swirl around the toilet bowl as the sink

water warms, all of my high from my night as Stray's Dominant seemed to get flushed, too.

I'd made him explode with the subtlest of touches, which made me feel so good that I'd come, too.

My reflection held a power I couldn't see during the day. But I couldn't even find it now, after our session like I had last time. I wash my face and braid my hair, change out of Lacey's corset into one of mom's old Fleetwood Mac t's and some boxers, then head to my room.

I half expect to find Effie in my bed, curled up with her puffy eyes and pink cheeks. But she isn't there, so I tiptoe to her room and leave a kiss on her forehead before coming back to my room.

Laying out my work slacks and polo for the next day at work, I focus on everything I need to do to make the following day successful. I try very hard not to think about my Stray as I dig through my ankle socks, eventually tossing a white pair on top of my laid-out clothes.

When my feet spread through the cool sheets, I reach over to plug my phone in and see that I have an unread text message.

Bran: *Thank you, Goddess.*

I fall asleep with a smile on my face and thoughts of our session in my brain, grateful to be able to feel good amidst the chaos of my real life.

19

Bran

I love you, but I don't want your dick.

"Well, well, well, look what Stoner dragged in."

I love Mally. I do. But sometimes, his voice feels like a screwdriver being twisted through my brain. I'm not even hungover, just... processing. And when I'm processing something, everything externally overstimulates me to the point of instant irritation.

Case in point.

Malibu opened for me at Paradise again this morning. And though he did me a solid, his voice now makes me wish I'd lost hearing in one ear instead.

Stoner, who saves his four minutes of energy for Malibu every day, struts around the desk and goes to his hind legs, Mally taking his paws.

"Hi baby boy, I missed you. Yes, I did. Did I miss you? I missed you. I missed you," he coos to my dog, the two of them pressing their noses together. If I had both eyes, now would be my time to roll them.

"He isn't a baby; he's a fucking dog." I slide my prepped meals into the small fridge I keep under the desk and crumple the empty bag I brought them in.

"He's too cute, aren't you? Aren't you just way too cute?" Mally's blue eyes turn pissy the moment he peels his gaze from Stoner. "You can't be rude to me, bro. I woke up at 3:45 in the morning for you."

He's right. And my confusion is what's making me snippy, not Mally. I've had to stomach him baby-talking my dog for years. It always bugs me, but never enough to get pissy.

"Sorry. And thank you for opening." Paradise is the one thing I can rely on in my life to bring me fulfillment—a sense of purpose. And this is the second time I've not been able to peel myself from my bed and come to work, all because my brain couldn't slow down.

I'd gotten two hours of sleep last night, if that, and that was being generous.

But I couldn't stop thinking about my Goddess.

Never knew being deprived of senses would be something I liked. After all, losing half of my vision has been the sole source of my life paralysis for the last eight years. But with my hands at my back and my vision darkened, everything she did to me became so goddamn heightened.

Like a fucking skyscraper.

Her whimpers, the exhales she tried to control and hide.

Her orgasm.

Stray

I knew she came when I did. I didn't need to see her to know. I didn't need to be inside of her to know, either.

I knew because of the way her fingertips drove into me hard for a few seconds, by the way her hips swiveled with urgency during that time. The way her thighs quivered around me and how flushed her body was when I finally got a look at her.

I knew.

And as soon as she left, I wished she hadn't. All of me wanted her to stay, and not just because the key to my cock hung from her neck. Though I had to admit, seeing my freedom at her throat, accessible *only* to her—fucking hot.

I kept my hand on my cock all night after she left, not because of the cage. Touching it brought me some illogical feeling of closeness to her. Every time I tried to push her from my mind, the memory of that silver key contrasting with her velvety skin came flooding back, and I'd fall down the rabbit hole of my Goddess all over again.

"You feelin' okay?" Mally asks, unknowingly reaching his hand down into said rabbit hole to fish me out. I have a feeling my bros will be doing a lot of fishing until things with my Goddess and I are over.

"Not sleeping great," I admit unhappily because that part is true. I'm not sleeping well. The fact that I'm not sleeping well because some gorgeous woman has my manhood hanging by a silver chain, and I want more of her in ways I shouldn't, can be my little secret. At least for now.

He reaches up, pressing the back of his palm to my forehead like a concerned mother. I swat his hand away, which prompts him to get his phone out, holding it up to me.

"I'm texting Sammy and telling her you're being weird."

I don't want Sammy up my ass thinking I'm going through a hard time. I already hate how much she tries to hook me up with people and how much she worries about me being lonely. I'm her older brother. There should be no worrying on her end.

"Don't," I say, my voice serious. But Mally is Mally and unafraid to ruffle feathers the same way he's unafraid of being soft and tender. If you like one quality, you gotta love them all because that's how Mally is.

"I most certainly will," he huffs, his eyes narrowing on me. "Why aren't you sleeping well?"

Fuck. It's either come clean to some degree or have him tattle on me to Sammy. Both options annoy me, but the former is the least painful. If I feel overstimulated by Mally's inquisition, Sammy's would break me.

With one hand steadied in front of me, I slow his questions.

"Fine, just chill." I swallow, acutely aware of the elastic holding the patch to my eye. I fiddle with it when I'm feeling anxious or depressed, but sometimes when I'm really frazzled, all I can feel is that elastic string pressing into my temple. Mally studies me but doesn't take his thumb from its comfortable spot hovering above the on-screen keyboard. "I met a girl."

* * *

Forty-five minutes later, Van, Mally, and Batman are circled around the bench where I'm doing chest presses.

Telling Mally I met a girl was probably a mistake.

Because now Sammy not only knows that I haven't been sleeping well, she now too knows I met a girl. As soon as I'd said those four words to Mally, he fired off a text to the group, and one to my sister, spreading the *"fucking bomb ass news,"* his words not mine.

The guys came in for a morning pump and have been harassing me about the mystery girl since.

They've even given her a temporary nickname.

Callie.

You know, because I'm Arizona Robbins and her love is Callie. I know, a nickname is problematic for a myriad of reasons, the glaring one being that the two same-sex-oriented doctors don't even *stay together*, but I let it go.

Because the more you fight their creativity, the more it sticks. That's why eight years later, I'm still Bran. When they first discovered the hilarity of calling me Bran because it's Brian without an eye—*who I am*—I railed against it. Threw a twenty-two-year-old version of a tantrum.

So, of course, the nickname stuck like fucking Gorilla Glue.

I let them call my Goddess by the name Callie temporarily. And what else can I do? Suggest her actual nickname? I don't even know her real name, much less what she goes by to close friends—and telling them that I call her Goddess? Yeah, that's never gonna happen. I may be losing my marbles as I become infatuated with her, but I'm not a complete fucking moron.

"So you're really not going to tell us anything? Like, where Callie works or what she does or what her favorite color is or who her favorite actor is or where she grew up and how many siblings she has and if she likes Stoner or not?" Mally asks, hovering above me as I lock the bar into place overhead.

Van rolls his eyes as Batman's head pings between the two of them.

"Do you honestly think she wouldn't like Stoner?" Van quips, locking the extra weight he added to my bar. At least one of them is focused on the pump.

Batman snorts. "If she doesn't like Stoner, we don't like her."

I adjust my grip on the bar, remaining silent to prepare mentally for the next lift.

"Right? Stoner is so cool." Mally's gaze drifts into the distance, and I swear, if possible, his pupils would be shooting fucking cartoon hearts. A grin jostles his contemplative gaze. "Where is that cute son of a gun anyway?" And because Mally has golden retriever energy, he also has golden retriever focus, too. He disappears from above, undoubtedly looking for my lazy pup.

Van spots me as I lift, and when I'm through with my eight reps, he leans over me, resting his big forearms on the bar.

"This is one of the girls you interviewed to work here, isn't it?"

Turning my head upright for a moment, I glance around the gym space. I don't see Mally, and Batman is now engrossed in a phone call, presumably with his wife, Robin.

"Yeah," I reply, "I mean, who else would it be?"

He nods knowingly. "She still gonna work here then or not?"

His question is pretty simple, one that should've crossed

my mind by now. But it hasn't. I scratch at the side of my jaw, trying to figure out an answer to give him.

"I guess not," I admit, feeling a bit sad at the thought. But then, she was never going to be a trainer at Paradise, so I have no reason to be sad. Fuck, this nameless chick is making me feel all sorts of things, and it fucking terrifies me how much I love it. Even the unending nerves I love.

He nods, thinking. "You gonna actually hire someone still?" He curls his hands around the bar as we change positions. "Tens on each side," he directs. Unclipping, I slide a ten plate on each end of the bar, then secure the clips again. He lowers the bar to his chest with the first rep, powering it back up with ease. Silently, I stand behind him as an ornament more than a spotter because Van is fucking strong and rarely needs it.

When he's done, he sits up, using the hemline of his Willowdale PD t-shirt to wipe sweat from his forehead. We both look at Batman, who is still deep into a conversation with his wife. Across the gym from us, near the front doors, Mally cradles Stoner like an infant, wiggling his nose into the dog's as he sways and probably baby talks. I can't hear him, but his mouth is moving, so he's probably making an idiot out of himself.

Knowing we aren't checking our friends' location for the hell of it, I blink at Van, whose torso is twisted on the bench so he can see me.

"What?" I ask, wanting to get this conversation over with. Not trying to be a prick, but I'm grouchy when I'm processing. Overstimulation has never been a friend to my brain.

"If you don't hire someone to train here, Sammy and Mally will catch on."

I consider what he's saying and know he's right. And I'm not looking at stacking lies here. It's too much work.

"Well, I'll tell them she's one of the candidates then."

Van nods, but his face tells me the answer isn't what he was looking for.

"What?" I ask again, wishing he'd just lay back down and finish his fucking pump. Sometimes Paradise feels more like a hair salon than a damn gym.

"Nothing, it's just... I mean, if you like her and she likes you—which it sounds like she clearly does—maybe her working here still isn't a bad idea. Double up on the fun."

Double up on the fun? This coming from the man who I'm ninety-nine percent sure is stalking a girl—Mally isn't great at keeping secrets.

"Then when she decides she doesn't want a cyclops as a long-term boyfriend and dumps me, she's the first face I see when I come to work every day?" I lift my gallon jug to my lips, stopping before I drink. "Double on the pain, not fun."

Van rolls his eyes, and I hope to fuck one day they get stuck up there. I'm tired of having eyes rolled at my concerns.

"But if it works and you guys stay together, then you get to work together, too. Win, win."

He leans back against the vinyl bench, adjusting his chest to align with the bar. Hands on grips, Van's dark eyes pin me to the floor, and it's like I'm the one with a weight on my chest I can't lift.

"You can win, you know." He bangs out a couple of reps, saving his breath for me when he brings the bar above him the fifth time. "You may not believe this, but I just recently learned that we're usually the ones keeping ourselves from happiness."

I quirk a brow at him because as long as I've known Van, he's been as single as I have, and he's got both eyes. Not all imperfections are visible, though, and I know that.

"You keepin' yourself from happiness, too, sensei?"

He grins as he pumps the last few reps, locking the bar on the rack above him when he's done. "As a matter of fact, I am. But I'm working on that now."

He rocks up from the bench, getting to his feet with a small hop. Slapping his freakishly large hand to my shoulder blade, he squeezes. "Let's get happy together."

I blink. "I love you, but I don't want your dick."

He rolls his eyes–see, wouldn't it be nice if they got fucking stuck so he'd quit that shit?--but we're men, so we can't let a comment about someone not wanting our dick to go by. It is written in our DNA to outwardly project that everyone wants our dick.

My DNA has a gap in it, obviously, since I haven't thought anyone really wanted me since that night. Van, however, is getting along just fine.

"I think if you knew what he could do, you'd feel different." He slaps my back, and we drink from our jugs as Mally saunters back to us, black dog hair sticking to his white stringer.

"God, I love that guy," he says, a stupid grin on his face. Van looks at his watch.

"We need to get out of here. Shift starts in two hours, and you owe me donuts."

The stereotype is true: cops like donuts. The stereotype that cops are overweight: not true in their case.

We bump knuckles and say goodbye, and around noon, Sammy strolls in. I should've known Malibu would've spilled his guts to her already, but I thought I had more time. As she crosses the parking lot in seafoam-colored scrubs with her dark hair in a messy knot on her head, I go over my story.

I did meet a girl. She is one of the interview candidates. We're just testing the waters to see what's between us before we make a move on any choices.

That sounds good, I think to myself. I smile at her through the pristine glass, happy with my speech. When she sees my smile, her eyes pinch down in that pissed-off way that only sisters can pull off, the kind of gaze that terrifies you and causes you to immediately rethink everything you've done for the last few days, to see where you went wrong.

Stick to what you told Van, I assure myself, tipping my wide shoulders back with confidence as she flings open one of the glass doors.

"Why in the fuck am I hearing about you seeing someone from Christian?" His name is a slurred, angry jumble.

"Samantha, this is my business. Tone down the language," I say, full-naming her the way she full-named Mally while giving her a cautionary pump of my palms. At that precise moment, Jamie, newly *relationshipped up* and in the middle of a bulk, strode through with another guy.

Another reason I can't hate Jamie–the guy brings me new members consistently. He slapped the guy with him on the back, barking out a laugh, followed with, "that's what I fuckin' thought."

Stray

The doors swoosh shut behind them as Jamie lifts a hand in a silent goodbye.

Sammy pushes her sunglasses to the top of her head and cocks a brow at me. "Language isn't the problem here, clearly."

Fucking Jamie.

Sighing, I lead her into a small office used for consults for privacy and close the door.

"Okay, listen, I did just start seeing a girl, but I've only seen her a few times." The trench coat and corset flash through my mind, then that tight skirt and see-through blouse, and then I see my Goddess in that corset and red mini skirt from last night. "Three times," I clarify.

Sammy crosses her legs at the knee and rests her hand in her lap; the details I've given her clearly not even close to being good enough. I'm the older sibling, but a lot of the time, Sammy feels like my mom. And no one feels comfortable under the angry stare-down of their mother.

"And you told Christian but not me?"

I wince. "I can't handle you calling him Christian. It's weird."

She wrinkles her nose. "It is kind of weird." I know I'm not in that much trouble, and I'm grateful she's giving me a little relief. I don't like upsetting Sammy. Hell, I don't like telling partial truths to anyone because I don't like receiving partial truths, either.

But this thing happening between my Goddess and I doesn't have a name, and we haven't given it any definition or boundaries. I mean, maybe we have but fuck, I don't even know how or what got it started, what she's thinking... what's going on, really. I mean, I'm paying her to control me, and I like it; that much is clear. But how do you tell your little sister that you met a woman that you're basically enamored with, but you don't know her name or what she wants in life and that you're paying her to torture your cock, so you don't have to think or feel or make choices but that you're actually feeling and growing but still you don't know what's happening between you and her?

Yeah.

No.

I'll be honest with Sammy–and the guys for that matter–*when I know what it is*. Until then, I'll protect it like glass because, in a way... that's what we have. Something beautiful but breakable, and I need to protect it until I know if we're trying to shatter or trying to be shatterproof.

"Listen, I didn't tell Mally first and exclude you. You know it wasn't like that. I called him to open because I didn't sleep well—"

She twists her lips to the side, cupping a hand to her mouth to catch the invisible vomit that my words bring.

"Take it easy–I wasn't up all night laying pipe."

Her disgust morphs into humor. "If you call sex with a woman laying pipe, I'll tell you right now, Arizona Robbins, the leg is the last of your worries."

"I'm trying to keep it clean for you since you're my sister." I fold my arms across my chest, irritated that I can't even explain shit to her without being razzed. "Okay, fine. I didn't stay up all night fucking. Better?"

She winces. "I get it. There's no way to word it that prevents me from, at least for a split second, seeing an image I don't want to see."

"Anyway," I say, cutting through the bullshit. "Van kind of guessed it was one of the girls interviewing for the job here at Paradise because I'm too pathetic to have met one on my own obviously."

Her expression grows gentle, but her eyes are sad for me, and I hate that. I hate that she barged in here after probably a fifteen-hour shift at the hospital because my well-being is always a priority for her. It should be the other way around.

"You aren't pathetic at all. You have one singular issue, and it's crippling you." She smirks.

"Yeah, but that singular issue is a missing eye," I deadpan.

She shakes her head, strands of dark hair falling out of her greasy bun. "It's not. That's where you're fucked up." She leans forward, sliding her purse strap up her shoulder like she's just about done with me and this conversation. That's probably for the best. "It's your head." She taps her own. "You're hung up on the fact that you aren't who you used to be. And the one eye is keeping you from fully seeing... Seeing how fucking amazing you are *now*."

She rises but halts in the doorway, gripping the white wood. Her eyes, which match the color of mine, bore into me.

"Mally opened because I couldn't sleep. I had a lot on my mind." I swallow, not avoiding my sister's intense gaze. This is why we're solid. We don't avoid each other. "I like her a lot, but I don't know where her head is at, so I'm not going to talk about it yet. I'm just... I'm not ready. I'm gonna see where things go. But I promise, Sam, you'll be the first to know when things change. Okay?"

249

Daisy Jane

"Okay," she says, adding, "and I better be the first to meet her, too."

"If we get that far."

"*When* you get that far."

20

Elsie

It's Cinderella immediately falling in love with Prince Charming levels of ridiculousness.

The last couple of days have been... exhausting.

I have a day off from Globo after switching days with someone to accommodate... something. I don't even know. If someone asks me to switch shifts and it doesn't screw too much with my Effie time, I always do. Storing up good karma and whatnot.

But because of working the earliest shift one day and the latest shift the next, around Tuesday I was feeling like a huge, loosely tied but overstuffed bag of ass.

This morning is my day to sleep in. I mean, I'm not talking noon type of shit, either. Just... wake up naturally. I haven't done that in over four years. My eyelids have never fluttered open, my arms have never leisurely explored the cool sheets while I stretched my back, and I have never rolled over and decided to sleep in.

I've never had the chance.

This morning was my chance.

And yet I awoke earlier than my alarm would normally go off and in a much less pleasant way than the alarm. If something is worse than the loud Apple radar noise reverberating in your skull, that thing must be pretty freaking bad because phone alarms are quite possibly the worst noise.

Well, second worst now.

Effie's piercing scream was the cause of my eyes shooting open in immediate panic. I was out of my bed and tearing down the hall so quickly, I hadn't even realized she wasn't in her room. My *mom brain* just sent me there, and when I slammed the door against the wall as I flew inside, seeing her empty bed threw a new kind of panic inside of me.

Soul-stealing, gut-wrenching panic. Then her sharp cry came again, and I realized she was in the house... sounded like the kitchen.

Redirecting my energy, I flew to the kitchen to find Effie in a crumpled ball on the floor, rocking while clutching her knee to her chest. Tears swam down her little cheeks, and her blonde curly hair stuck up straight everywhere like it always did in the morning.

"Effie, baby girl, what happened?" I ask, my voice as calm as it can after waking up thirty seconds ago thinking someone was being kidnapped or worse. I take a breath, pressing my palm to my chest as I study her leg draped across my thighs. She points to a red knot protruding from her knee.

"Gramma wanted me to cook breakfast this morning. I

promised I was gonna," she sniffles, and I wipe under her nose with the hem of my oversized sleep t-shirt. With my other hand, I rub down her back, soothing her.

"Can I push a little and see if it's serious?" I ask, and she nods bravely.

"It's broke, I know it."

"Knees are hard to break, and kids are really durable," I tell her, remembering when my mother said those same words to me when I fell off my scooter and got gravel under my skin. I was horrified, but after mom did the very thing I'm doing with Effie now, I felt cured. Sure, my knee ached for weeks, but when your mom is calm, the world makes sense.

I grin at her. "Maybe we can use some of the special bandaids."

She frowns, blonde brows pull tight for a moment before she claps, her whole body wiggling with delight. "The Iron Man ones!"

I smile. "Yep. I'll sit you at the table; then I'll go get them, okay?" I ask, smoothing my thumb down the bridge of her nose, booping the tip.

She agrees, and after I scoop her up and deposit her on a chair at the dining room table, I grab the bandages from the hall bathroom and return.

Effie's got the remote in her hand and is fidgeting with the buttons, her tongue out and her eyes focused. As I'm unpackaging a too-large bandage with Iron Man's body soaring through the sky illustrated on the front of it, the TV comes alive, cartoons flooding my brain.

"Turn it down, yeah? Grandma's still sleeping."

"Yeah," Effie says, punching the down arrow on the aged remote. The same one we had when I was a kid. It's universal. Mom loves the damn thing even though new TV remotes have far fewer buttons and are easier to use. At this stage with her dementia, I don't want to change anything because not only did I read online that changes to routine will create chaos, but it can also lead to inexplicable emotional distress.

We don't need any more of that since it seems she's tapping into a secret reserve of it more and more frequently these days.

Sticking the bandage over the pink skin, I smooth down the edges while pushing around the knot gently with my thumbs. "How's it feel?"

Forgetting about her knee because cartoons, she winces when she realizes I'm pushing on it.

"Ouch," she says with a sucked-in breath. Again, I stifle a grin because we've all been there. Getting special treatment all day from mom and grandma because of an injury? Who wouldn't want it?

"I'll get you some peas, and you can watch cartoons while I make breakfast, okay?" I smooth her curls back from her face, and she nods absent-mindedly, having given her focus over to SpongeBob. As I walk back to the kitchen, I remember what she'd said. Getting through the chaos of an injury as a parent allows your brain to do this magnificent thing where it shuts down any and all other noise. But now that I know it was a counter-climb gone wrong and it was her knee that got hurt and not her skull, her words confuse me.

Sticking my head over the edge of the couch, where Effie has moved, I ask her about her comment.

"Grandma wanted you to make her breakfast?"

Effie's eyes are glazed over with Bikini Bottom. I nudge her shoulder, and her blue eyes flick to mine. "What?"

"Grandma asked you to make her breakfast. That's what you said. Did she?"

She nods. "Yeah. Yesterday she said you can get up early and make blueberry pancakes because they're my favorite."

I straighten and am very grateful for Bikini Bottom because Effie's eyes go back to the screen where SpongeBob talks to his squirrel friend.

Blueberry pancakes were what I made for mom when I was a kid and wanted to do something special for her.

It's possible; I think to myself as I pace back to the kitchen, that she just wanted to share the tradition with Effie. Maybe she didn't think Effie was me. Maybe she wasn't terribly confused. And maybe she was kidding. Because if she wasn't being playful, then she directed a four-year-old to use the freaking stove.

And my mom... the one that raised me and didn't let me use adult scissors until I was in junior high school... she wouldn't do that.

Dementia is so heavy. No one tells you what it weighs. How fatigued your body grows from shouldering its weight without breaks. Some days it may feel lighter, but other days–when you're adjusting to the idea that this is a normal weight for you to carry now–it's so incredibly heavy I feel like I can't even move. I can't even take a step.

But moms don't have the choice to give up.

Moms don't get to quit. We don't get to vanish beneath a stack of blankets and dodge the sun, hide from our responsibilities, or push the weight off onto someone else.

Moms know–it's us. Everyone depends on *us*.

Right then, as I'm folding fresh blueberries into pancake

mix, wiping away stray tears so no one can catch me, I think of Jake.

I didn't love Jake. We were only together for six months, and six months is really not that long. Not at all.

And I only think of him because I have no one else to think about. He was the last one to hold my hand and hold a place in my life.

This life that is so overwhelming and heavy, dark and sometimes impossible to lift.

He didn't want it. It was too much.

All in all, I didn't want Jake to be my husband. But I know now that there was a reason I stayed with Jake, despite the signs to break it off obviously and clearly being there as early as one month in.

I wanted a partner, though. I always have.

I loved being raised by my mom. She showed me what a strong, independent woman really is. I never had a dad around pitching in with child support and weekends away. She did it all on her own, and because of her, I didn't have to do the same thing even though I'd put myself in that exact position.

Effie's sperm donor–I wouldn't pay him the honor of calling him anything more than that considering he's never even seen her–hightailed it to whereverthefuck as soon as I told him I'd gotten pregnant.

Since then, it was just me, mom, and Effie.

But I knew I wanted more. I wanted a partner to shoulder life with me. A man who would make decisions with me, who would want to take on some of my life, and I would take on some of his, too. An equal.

I wanted an equal, and I wanted Effie to see that you can

be a strong woman despite not wearing a power suit and holding a law degree. And you can measure your successes on more than careers—you can measure your success by the love in your life.

I couldn't show her that, not yet. Right now, I'm struggling not to fill these pancakes with salt from my tears. I don't have the energy or time to spare to date and find a partner, to find an equal. And if guys like Jake were representative of men my age—I wouldn't be able to show my daughter love for a while.

I'd have to be okay with that.

Thirty minutes later, Effie and I had eaten a gross amount of pancakes because eating my feelings was something I'd been known to do here and there. I mean, I didn't seek out a junk food binge, but if something awful or traumatic happened and a plate of fries just happened to be there? I wouldn't say no.

Mom got up and came out in her pajamas and bathrobe, hair a sleepy mess, and decided to join us. She was herself. She sipped her coffee the same slow way, and she cut her pancakes how she always did, taking care to dip each bite into syrup from a small dish rather than drowning her food in them like the rest of us. She laughed; she stood behind Effie and braided her hair as Effie licked the rest of the syrup from her plate. She even agreed to go to the park with us— that's what Effie chose to do this morning on my day off.

Throwing on jeans and a tank top, sliding my feet into a pair of old Nike sneakers, I got Effie dressed in something similar, and we waited on the porch for mom to get ready. I hate that she couldn't even take time to put on a little makeup without me worrying that she'd forgotten. But thankfully, she came out after a handful of minutes, and we started the short walk there.

After making a fool out of myself on the monkey bars and chapping the backs of my thighs on a plastic slide way too small for me, I decided to tag out and rest on the bench. Mom and Effie were busy on the swings, giving me a moment to myself.

I don't know if it was the fresh air or the fact that mom is doing okay today. Something shifted in me, and before I could course correct and tell myself to stop, I took my phone from my pocket and typed out a one-word text message.

Then I hit send.

And I'm surprised to see that not only is his *read receipt* on, but he reads my message instantly, responding just as quickly.

The message I sent was simple. My name. He'd asked me, and I hadn't pressed him to answer because I'd been too busy trying to barter. But a huge part of me–the part of me that reminisced about Jake in the kitchen this morning–wanted him to know even if he gave me nothing back.

Maybe Lacey was right. Maybe he's flawed, maybe he's cut deep, and I just can't see it, and maybe I am nothing more than a temporary, disposable human Bandaid.

Still, I can't deny that I'm attracted to what we do. And part of that is him, despite the fact that I don't know much.

He doesn't know much about me either, but now with that text I just sent, he knows more.

Elsie: *Elsie.*

Stray: *E for Elsie.*

Stray: *I know you saw my name in our email. But no*

one calls me that, so I guess I'm really telling you my true name by telling you my nickname.

I smiled at that message, not because it was funny or anything but because it was so honest. I loved reading it because it helped me better understand him and his thought process.

He wrote again, quickly.

Stray: *When I lost my eye, my brothers decided it would be cute if my name lost the i, too.*

I read his message once, then again. Despite the callousness of the nickname given the situation, I can't help that a giggle slips past my lips. I trap it with the back of my wrist, though no one is around to chastise me for laughing at something mean. Habit I guess. I swallow the rest of the giggle and type back to him.

Elsie: *Bran?*

Stray: *Yep. They all call me Bran. Even my sister.*

It feels natural and easy, and it almost feels strange to leave it, so I keep typing.

Elsie: *You have a lot of siblings?*

Stray: *One sister.*

Stray: *Ah, I just reread my message.*

Stray: *My brothers aren't my actual brothers. But I trust them as much as I trust Sammy. Been friends since we were just kids.*

Elsie: *Sammy?*

Stray: *Oh fuck, that's my sister. Sorry, I'm conversationally challenged, even over text message.*

Elsie: *You are not conversationally challenged, trust me.*

Stray: *How do you know? In the three times we've been together, conversation wasn't on either of our minds.*

Elsie: *You don't look like the type of man to be challenged by anything. Not easily, at least.*

It's the truth. He really comes off as the strongest man in the world—the strong silent type. But it feels like an overstep, so my fingers scatter across the screen, doing damage control as Lacey's words about not getting interested somehow come back to mind.

Dots bounce around the screen, filling me with a really foolish hope that I have no business owning. Quickly, I end the conversation. Always good to go out on a high note, right?

Elsie: *See you in a few days, Stray. Be a good boy.*

I hold up my arm where the necklace is wrapped three times around my wrist, turning it into a bracelet. The key slides down the inside of my forearm, the sun reminding me it's metal with a glint and shock of heat after a moment.

Bran. I edit his contact message from Stray to Bran. It feels too personal; it feels like I haven't earned that. But I lie to myself and say it's in case someone sees the contact in my phone. If Effie ever got it, how could I explain Stray? She couldn't even read that word, I don't think, but still, I tell myself it's because of that, knowing just how big of a liar I really am.

Lacey crooks her finger at me. Glancing at the monitor on the desk—the one filled with security camera footage from all around the gym—I turn back to her. "It's gotta be quick, though. Chris won't be on for another fifteen minutes."

Lacey rolls her eyes. She only kept this job for the health

insurance; this much she told me when she'd contacted me last night about taking another client.

She has rheumatoid arthritis from her years as a gymnast and now needs injections to manage the long-term pain. Her wrists have been hurting her so much lately, that she needs to pass off a client. She said she only has one client at a time since these are business relationships but still intense relationships nonetheless. Managing more than one at any level of decency would be difficult, at best.

But she thought she'd ask me. I said no, so I can't imagine why she's calling me into her office at Globo-Fitness, not more than twelve hours after that exact conversation.

She doesn't bother sitting or guiding me to a seat like she's done in the past. She closes the door quietly, turning to me with wide eyes.

"The client offered double."

I shake my head staunchly, not entertaining this at all. I don't have anything against the woman who would do this–take care of two men in this personal way–but the truth is I don't want to branch out.

Being taller than her makes it extra uncomfortable to say no; I feel like a mother scolding her child. I mean, I know just what that feels like, and it's awkwardly similar.

At nearly five foot seven, I didn't consider myself tall until now.

Lacey rocks on her feet, shrugging. "Fine. I figured," she huffs, all of her excitement and hope from just a second ago completely gone now. "Had to check." She pushes straightened hair from her face, smiling like she really doesn't mind that I'm saying no again and her indifference is a relief.

"Well, so?" she bats her eyes, waiting like I went on a

date with the high school quarterback.

"So... what?"

She rolls her eyes playfully, swatting my arm. "How's it going with the guy who owns Paradise?" She wiggles her brows at me mischievously, and I hate that I blush.

"Good," I say, trying very hard to keep my face impassive and careless. But the heat sears up my neck and colors my cheeks. Sweat dampens my armpits instantly. "It's good." Then I add an ever so casual shrug.

Her eyebrows fall into a flat line, and her ips turn down, unimpressed. "Don't even lie to me."

I rub the back of my neck, finding it damp with nervous sweat. Gross. "I like him," I admit, wishing that I didn't say it but honestly caught too off guard. I hadn't really expected Lacey to care beyond the initial setup. Or beyond getting her stuff back from me.

"I'll bring your stuff back next week."

She pops her gum. "You don't have to." Then she folds her arms across her chest, studying me in a way that makes eye contact very difficult. "Did you buy your own stuff? Like lingerie and stuff?" Her voice is so midline and emotionless that my stomach lurches.

"I will," I tell her, though I hadn't thought about buying anything else because I still hadn't gotten to use all my purchases on Bran yet. We'd only seen each other three times. We needed a lot more time. "I haven't yet, but I will."

"If you do, that means you're committed to this."

I nod so quickly it even surprises me. "I am."

"Elsie," she says my name in a warning tone like I'm about to do something stupid, and she's saying, *hey, you know this is stupid, right*. And I hate that it feels kind of fitting.

"What?" I play dumb but half-hearted at best.

"Take it from me." She unfolds her arms, resting her hands on my shoulders, but it's kind of funny since she's still slightly looking up at me. Her eyes deepen with a seriousness I've never seen on her taking over. "I fell in love with my first client." She swallows, the movie of their meet-cute clearing playing in her mind. Then her eyes suddenly snap to mine. "All it did was take me away from time I could've spent feeling empowered."

It's then I see that Lacey has her own pain, her own multi-flavored box of trauma to cause her to seek emotional and physical control.

The way that she says all these men have a pain or a fatal flaw, maybe she just feels that way because that's her: rejection and unhealed pain.

"You're taken now though, Lacey. It's easy to say you'd do it differently when you're on the other side."

She nods, but her palms stay planted on me, and her eyes remain intent... and kind of crazy. "I know. You're right. But I'm telling you that these feelings of control are what you're going to grow from. The lust will take away from that."

"What if it could be more than lust?" I foolishly, embarrassingly, and cringingly ask. Because I know he has a dog who has anxiety. He has an adorable house with a garden and a cherry tree. He has a dip in his past that must shackle him to some untrue, unsavory, and terrifying things. But he works hard—his body proves that—but his business, too. It's thriving. Best friends. A sister.

But it's insane. It's Cinderella immediately falling in love with Prince Charming levels of ridiculousness because we don't even know each other.

Even so. Watching him come on his desk, body writhing for me. My bones ache to feel that electricity again. My body thrums to feel his hand wrapping my throat while he fucks me silly.

I shake my head, hoping the thoughts fly out. Lacey is dangerously close to being psychic for how easily she reads my mind.

"It's not. I'm just... I don't know. Really drawn to his energy."

She studies me like she wasn't expecting that response. "Keep it Dom/Sub. I'm telling you." Her soft smile and tilt of her head made me feel a little crazy.

But then, maybe it *is* crazy. And maybe I'm fine with it.

Back at the front desk, Chris had clocked in and was organizing a new batch of paper resumes turned in online.

"Hey," he nods at me casually.

"Hi." I sit next to him, my head falling back against the chair as I zone out, replaying that conversation in my mind. Is it crazy to stay the course? Go after that lost ship at sea, knowing nothing about where it's headed?

"Have coffee with me," Chris says. "I know that was a weird way to ask but I feel like, God, I don't know. I like your energy Elsie, and I'd like to get to know you."

Lacey walks by with her sunglasses covering her eyes. She smiles and falls into the arms of her boyfriend, who is waiting outside. She's happy now. She has the relationship I'm looking for. So maybe she's right. After all, she has been right about a ton of freaking shit so far.

I turn to Chris and give a conciliatory smile. "Okay, I'll go out with you."

21

Bran

One step closer to McSteamy.

Stoner must be hanging around Van too much because I swear he just rolled his eyes at me. I don't blame him. After all these years together, for me to be waking up with a smile on my face is a bit... vexing. I'd be annoyed by it, too.

Truth, I'm kind of annoyed with myself. A couple of weird, boundary-less sexual encounters and some text messages have me fucking giddy. And indulgent. I'm never fucking indulgent. Not with cheat days, not with spending money, and never, ever with my heart.

Sounds like I'm a softie, and I hate that, too. But I won't deny that all the failed dates and awkward eye contact over the years have made me jaded and protective because of that. Unfortunately, it has everyone in my life concerned about me. Afraid they'll be the ones with their single friend living in the apartment above the garage. That they'll be the ones to have an Uncle Bran for their kids because I never found a family of my own.

Or maybe they're concerned out of genuine love because they've watched me recess deeper into myself over the last eight years. And eight years is a fucking long time.

Feels like an entire lifetime some days.

My hope that things with Elsie and I become more is so strangling that I decide to throw Sammy a bone of relief. I text her to meet me for donuts at the shop near Paradise. I know Mally and Van will be coming by this afternoon because they're working the night shift this week. I'll keep their mouths full and their brains focused on rings of sugar.

Works like a charm. Then they won't butt their noses in my shit until I'm ready. Sharing with Sammy is different. It's like... I don't know, telling a safe. Or a wall. She just absorbs, it becomes part of her, but she is incapable of sharing; it goes against something written into her DNA, I swear.

Mally and Van aren't trying to be disloyal–the way they solve problems is together. Hell, they work together all day. So when they share with each other, I know it's coming from a good place. Don't care. Still don't want to deal with it, good place or not.

After assuring Stoner I'd never do anything as disgusting as waking up grinning again, I feed him, take him on the world's laziest walk (to the edge of our lawn and then back), then I get ready for the day.

I run down my mental to-do list. Check on office contractors. Meet Sammy for donuts after opening at Paradise. Maybe... texting Elsie and seeing what she's up to.

She didn't leave the text open-ended, but I want to talk to her. Even if it's just a few characters on a screen, and if she doesn't want to talk to me, I'll know. But I gotta fuckin' try.

I'm no Arizona Robbins.

I'm fucking McSteamy.

Wait. He dies.

I'm Bran, and I'm gonna try my damndest to appreciate what I have and move on from my past.

* * *

IN BASKETBALL SHORTS AND A STRINGER, hoodie slung over my shoulder; I head into the donut shop. I've already opened Paradise, Stoner is asleep under the entry desk, and a few people are lifting. Construction on my office is halfway, the heating for the floors installed, and the actual flooring is going down.

I'm ready for them to be out of my fucking space.

Sammy must be just paces behind me but probably just came off a long night shift and had her head down the whole way in. She slips into the booth across from me, her dark hair in a frayed braid over her shoulder. With bags lining her eyes, she nods.

"Get me coffee. The smallest because I'm gonna crash after this."

I nod. "The usual?" Her donut order has never changed.

I bring back two glazed donuts and a small coffee, sliding it to her. She smiles, exhaustion wrinkling the corners of her eyes. "Thanks." She mauls the freshly baked donut on the first bite, the still-warm dough collapsing with a shatter of glaze against her hand. She licks it off, and I am thoroughly fucking grossed out.

"I hope your hands are clean, you animal."

She takes a large swig of the hot coffee, unphased by its temperature. My sister is kind of terrifying in that way that both makes you *actually* terrified but also strangely proud. Like yeah, my sister could fuck you up... but she could fuck me up, too.

"So why did you want to buy me sugar and insult me?" She finishes off the first donut with an impressive three bites. A boy behind the counter appears, sliding my order of two dozen donuts onto the table, two pink boxes stacked neatly between us. She nods, mouth full.

"Dumb and Dumber coming by?"

I nod. The guys aren't the only ones who can dole out nicknames. Sammy and I are known to have a few for them, too.

"Yep," I nod, knowing that Mally and Van will put down at least one dozen. The rest I leave on the edge of the entry desk. They're usually gone within an hour.

"So why did you want to see me?" She pops the lid off her little coffee, and billows of steam aggressively knock her in the face as she brings the cup to her lips. She takes a drink, and I wince. That must fucking burn? She somehow slams the paper cup down. "Well?"

Nervousness swims inside me. And then I realize something as I find myself smiling at Sammy with that same sick smile that made Stoner roll his eyes; it's not nervousness. It's happiness.

God, I'm fucking corny.

I think she's just about ready to vomit up those donuts

from the look on her face. But the door opens behind her, and my attention is seriously diverted.

It's Elsie.

She's wearing a coat; all zipped up, her curls stowed away beneath the down material. The tip of her nose is pink, and her smile is wide, long enough to reach out to me and wrap around me. My chest buzzes with an electrical current that can only be felt by another person. Hot, frenzied, exciting. It sends a ripple of energy down my limbs, making me shift in the booth.

Stepping in behind her is... some guy.

He's probably her age, looking much younger than my thirty years. He's smiling, and fuck what he looks like, he's *with* her, and he's smiling. Nothing else matters. Fabio or some asshole–it doesn't matter who; he has what I want.

The vision in my good eye clouds over as my temples pulse to the fucked up drumming of my thoughts, each one thudding down louder and harder than the last.

She is seeing someone else.
She is seeing someone.
She's happy out with someone.
They're in daylight together.
They aren't a secret.
She's with him.

I can feel Sammy's eyes boring into me, but hollowness overwhelms my chest, so maybe that's what I feel. The immediate emptiness. The sudden draining of happiness.

For some reason beyond me, though we were mid-conversation and I was just giving her shit a second earlier, Sammy doesn't say a word as I outright stare–jaw unhinged– as Elsie is ushered to the counter by some guy.

My hand falls to my lap, the edges of my fingers tracing the cool steel caging my cock. A thick knot appears like magic in my throat. Everything behind my ribs feels warm and fuzzy, and not in a TV Christmas special type of way.

You fucking idiot.

You're paying her for whatever it is you two are doing. She has no real affection or loyalty to you. The thoughts crash into me hard and fast, and I slap a palm to the table unexpectedly, needing to physically center myself. Sammy's eyes dart to my hand, and I look back at Elsie just in time to see her looking at me.

Eyes wide, jaw parted and moving. Moving like she's thinking partially aloud and as confused as me. But then her gaze snaps forward. The side of her neck is flush.

I give my attention back to Sammy immediately because she's here. She showed up for me after a long day at work. I'll give her the truth because she's earned it. She deserves it, and me, for that matter.

"That girl I was seeing. Or... had seen a couple of times," I say, keeping my voice private.

Sammy nods, licking the last of the glaze from the pad of her thumb. "Callie, they told me her nickname."

I nod. "I saw her out with someone else. She told me she was only seeing me." I shrug, realizing then just how fucking hurt I am, no matter the arrangement between us. It just... fucking hurts. And it fucking sucks.

The cage bobs heavily between my spread thighs as I adjust in my seat, using Sammy's body to block as much of Elsie and the guy she's with from my view. It only helps a little, but a little is better than none. The sight of them burns my nerves. Makes my chest ache.

I want this fucking cage off.

Sammy taps my hand with hers in a brief show of physical affection. "I'm sorry, Bran. But that's a *her* issue, not *you*. Don't stop looking. You aren't this big fucking legless lesbian you think you are."

I snort unexpectedly at that, and I needed that laugh very fucking badly. When it fizzles, I nod. "I know. I'm forging ahead with Operation: One Eye is Good Enough."

She winks. "There you go."

I hold up two crossed fingers, being playful to mask the crushing disappointment in my chest. "One step closer to McSteamy."

When I get back to Paradise, I send Elsie a text message, canceling our session for tomorrow. Then I lock my phone and put it away, meeting the guys for a late-day pump. Invest in the people that invest in me.

And keep moving on.

22

Elsie

I've never even kissed him, and just the thought of it drives me wild.

The pink icing drips into a blob on the white napkin. Pinching the corner, I spin it to find a view that doesn't make me sick. But from every angle, the donut makes me want to vomit.

"Want me to get you something else?" Chris asks, oblivious to the icing mustache he's rocking. I tap my lip to tell him, and I imagine if it were Bran. I'd want to kiss the icing off.

I've never even kissed him, and just the thought of it drives me wild.

I shake my head. "No, I just don't normally eat this early. I kind of forgot about that when I said yes."

Chris laughs, smoothing the paper napkin between his hands. "I kind of sprung it on you to go today."

Truthfully, I'm grateful we came. I'm glad Chris asked me again. Because he said it himself–he is feeling my vibe. He *likes* me. And Bran, this guy that my heart is so invested in, was on a breakfast date.

And who gets breakfast this early? Someone working the night shift or two people that have been boning all night. I know what Bran does, and Paradise closes by eight at night. That only leaves the other option. He was dressed casually, too.

I swallow the puck of stomach acid that seems to be playing hockey in my throat. It doesn't go down easily.

"Thanks for asking me again. I'm sorry I couldn't the first time. No childcare." My eyes drift towards the large window next to me and go to the spot where I last saw Bran. He and the woman stood out front of the door, they shared a hug, he pressed a kiss to her temple, and they parted ways.

And I can't stop looking at that same spot. Like they're going to teleport back and redo it differently or something.

Not gonna happen. I focus on Chris for the next ten minutes, reminding myself often that he likes me. He wants to be here with me. I realize having to remind yourself that while on a date doesn't exactly paint the most romantic of situations.

Back at Globo, I'm barely holding back completely ridiculous tears when my phone vibrates. I don't know if I hope it's Bran or not. What did he think when he saw me? Probably what I was thinking. *You lied. You're with someone else.* Or maybe he didn't care at all? The fact that he's texting me right now, though, gives me hope. If he didn't care, he wouldn't text.

Bran: *Canceling tomorrow's session.*

I pop into Lacey's office at some point after I've sufficiently spun out in a bathroom stall and paced the private length of the hallway between the janitorial closet and the child care center.

He's canceling. And while for a split second I consider the fact that he could be canceling because he saw me with someone, I come back down to planet Earth. Because look at him. Like he needs to care about some girl he pays to make him orgasm.

He's canceling, I'm sure, because he doesn't want to see me out in public and have me go all wide-eyed and pearl-clutching. I should've just acted like I hadn't seen him.

This is the problem with jumping into a Dominant/Submissive relationship without having any conversations about it. Our expectations clearly need to be calibrated.

"What's up?" Lacey asks as she slides the guide onto the top of a scale. She steps off and scribbles the number onto a clipboard dangling from the wall.

I close the door and keep my palm fanned out against it for privacy. "I need you to take over with my client. I can't do it anymore."

Her face doesn't drop, and she doesn't pop off a desperate "what, why?" that I partially expected. Instead, she pinches her gaze on me, making my stomach flutter nervously.

"Why?"

"It felt good at first like you said." I tuck some of my unusually wild curls behind my ear. "I felt powerful. I felt...

things I really didn't think could come out of a Dominant/Submissive relationship." I force myself to quit being a baby and meet her gaze, even if I get teary over three stupid sessions. A lot happened at and in between those meetings, and Lacey's gentle eyes tell me she gets it.

"I want that relationship. I wanna feel that power. But... something happened, and now I feel like it's dipping my bucket, you know?"

She wrinkles her nose, giving me a quick, playful smile. "You say that to your kid?"

I nod. "Yeah. But it applies to adults. My bucket was running over, but now... it's not."

Reaching behind me, I unclasp the necklace at the back of my neck.

I'd put it back around my neck during the days I worked because my Globo polo covered it. And I loved the cool metal key against my skin. I loved running my fingers along the ribbed edges, thinking of him locked up... waiting for me to bring him release.

"You'll need this. I have him in chastity." I drop the keyed necklace in her palm to find her eyes have gone full moon on me. "What?"

She shakes her head, her smile layered with shock and pride. "You really went for it. I kind of thought you'd be a corset-wearing and whip-using kind of Dom." She shrugs. "Most are in the beginning." She rolls the key in her palm before plucking the chain with her other fingers, inspecting it. "But you went and locked up his dick and got yourself a nice necklace to show who's in charge."

I hadn't thought of the necklace that way, but hearing it made sense. When I'd been looking up Dominant and

Submissive sex roles on the internet, I'd seen a variety of collaring ceremonies. I didn't deep dive on that, though, because it seems collaring went with other roles, like daddy and little, and I knew I didn't want any other roles for us but dom and sub.

Limiting ourselves to a certain kink or fetish would've done just that... limit us. As Dom and Sub, we could be anything. And once I met Bran, I shamelessly knew that *we* could be *everything*.

"It was probably too much for me in the first place," I lie because I just want to get out of here. Sliding my hand down the door to catch the handle, I pull it open and step into the hall, stealing any privacy we had. "I'll text his address, the date, and time. Okay?"

She peers left then right down the long, empty hall. "Okay."

Then I do that very thing just moments later from around the corner.

But I think he *wants* his session; he just doesn't want it to be complicated. I get that. And I'll give him what he wants.

I delete our session from my calendar for tomorrow so my phone doesn't taunt me with any cruel ghost reminders.

23

Bran

"Don't run after her if you can't keep up."

"If you don't quit, you're going in, and I don't care how much you whine at the door; you won't be able to come back out." With my hands on my hips, I warn Stoner, who refuses to look at me. His head turned with confidence and arrogance, and I drop my arms to my sides.

"Fine. Don't look at me. But I know you can hear me."

Crouching back down at the edge of the raised beds, I lean over to yank the last few carrots from the soil. I had a good crop and looked forward to picking them in the next few days. Then I'd turned back to see that Stoner had consumed over half of the freshly plucked vegetables.

The familiar grunt followed by a metallic clank tells me the little thief has flopped down behind me, ready to sleep off his organic snack. Fucker. Even asleep, he's basically my therapy dog. A service animal of sorts. Because despite being aware of his instant deep snores, I still talk to him.

"If I had known you wanted the carrots, I could have given you the carrots." I drag the back of my wrist along the dampness on my forehead. "You didn't mention carrots at all. You never said *I would actually like less eggplant and more carrot.*" I toss a crooked, short carrot into the pile. Because they aren't perfect doesn't mean they won't be great, goddamn it. "I didn't know carrots were a thing on your radar. You're saying, *eggplant, eggplant, eggplant,* and all of the sudden, I catch you sneaking carrots."

I can't really get into how crazy I am for projecting my bullshit onto a sleeping dog because someone walks up from behind me.

"Bran?" her voice is not as soft as Elsie's and much more nasally. I don't like it. Rising to my feet, I turn to face this woman who is on my front lawn at nearly eight at night.

"That's me," I say, folding my arms over my chest, knowing full well my soil-coated hands are imprinting filth on my white stringer.

Silver glints at her neck as the dying sunlight flickers against her. My eye is pulled to the flash of light, and then I see. The key. The necklace I bought Elsie. My Goddess.

This woman is wearing it. Who the fuck is this woman?

"Can you come inside?" I ask gruffly, and she notices I've seen the key because she nods quietly, nervously, and trails after me into the entryway.

I close the door behind us and jump straight into it.

"Where's Elsie?" My hands are at my hips in a way that makes me feel like Sammy. I'm forcing my spine to stay straight, though every inch of me wants to lean forward, dip down into her space and suck up all her knowledge of Elsie and whatever the fuck is going on.

But my hampered aggression and clear strain does not phase this woman. She meets my stance, putting her own hands on her hips.

"How do you know her name is Elsie?" Her eyes are the color of an April sky, blue and clear as hell. But she narrows them on me with heat in a way that makes me reactively irritated. I'm not the bad guy here, but I'm getting vibes like she will tear my head off. Then–

"What?" I ask before I can realize that I had to work to get Elsie's name from her. And that, I know now from this woman's comment that that was abnormal. Like she told me, but shouldn't have, or normally doesn't.

"I told her when she became your Dom that she shouldn't use her real name. She told me that she wouldn't, and she hadn't when I checked in on her." She shakes her head all slow like she's making a point that I don't quite catch. "So, how did you know her name is Elsie?"

I swallow, which is a feat in itself, considering how dizzy I've suddenly become. Reaching out, I casually brace a palm against the foyer wall, like it isn't the only thing keeping me up.

"A Dominant?" My brain isn't the only thing on spin cycle. Now my stomach is swirling angrily, too. A Dominant? As in... Dominant and Submissive?

The blonde's hands fall away from her hips as she leans back, finding the wall opposite me with her butt. She backs up against it, resting her body while she studies me. *Studies* is the only way I can describe it. Her eyes crawl over every ragged inch of me, all the while her neon pink bottom lip is pinned beneath her glaring white teeth.

"Oh Jesus," she exhales, tipping her head forward slightly as she gives it a shake of disapproval. "You guys caught feelings, huh?" She stands up straight, still backed to the wall. "I warned her not to. And see?" she waves a palm amidst the vacancy between us. "I was right. Because she's not here, and *I* am." She hoists her bag up higher on her shoulder, and it's just now I realize she even had a bag. My stomach freefalls when I finally register that she's wearing an ankle-length fur coat. How did I not notice that when she walked up? I spotted the key right away, that's why.

"She got in too deep and sent me." She says, more to herself than to me, I think.

"I canceled on her for today," I admit to this stranger, for reasons unknown even to me.

She pops her gum, and it grates on my nerves. "Then why are you asking where she is?"

I don't have a smart answer to that. I don't even have a *good* answer to that. So I don't say anything. She takes off the necklace, handing it to me before giving a resigned smirk or sad smile, I'm not sure which. "Don't run after her if you can't keep up."

Then she's gone.

I lock the door behind her until I hear two loud, angry barks.

"Fuck," I grit out, swinging the door open to find a disgruntled Stoner nosing his way past my calves. "Sorry, dude." Then, though he doesn't understand, I am not a monster and will not let my main man's emotions dangle like that. "I didn't lock you out because of the carrots. It was an accident. I was thinking about *her*."

But I canceled, and someone else showed up because that's how businesses operate.

Whatever we had, it ended as weirdly and abruptly and as illogically as it began. And so, before I hop in the shower, I use that key to set myself free, stashing the device in my bedside drawer.

My Goddess may be gone, but it doesn't feel like time to move on.

24

Elsie

I couldn't resist you

Though mom's having a lucid day, and I should just be grateful, I'm not.

I'm cross. Grouchy as fuck. Salty. Call it what you want, but every part of me is sore and sensitive, and everything that everyone says or does wears against that rawness in me. Effie, of course, excluded.

"This is the third one in two weeks," I say as I empty the water-filled plastic bag into the fishbowl. The new Fuzz plops in with a small splash. "Just let Effie feed it. Because I think the two of you are both overfeeding, which would make the dumb fish like quadruple fed."

Mom waves a hand like I'm basically speaking gibberish and takes a sip of her coffee. It's infuriating sometimes how flippant she can be about things I care about, about the things only I can take care of.

But I can't say that because rubbing her nose in what is happening to her would be cruel. I dispose of the empty bag and wash my hands, taking a few calming breaths as I do. When I turn back, mom is smiling to herself as she reads the funnies in the paper. She never read comics before, and somehow this is one of those weird changes that really affect me. She snorts at something Garfield is doing, and I need a fucking minute.

The world spins beneath me as I pad down the hall. "Gonna lay down for an hour or so, okay?" I call back, not knowing or caring at the moment if she heard me. She's got her coffee, pastry, paper, and all the doors are locked. I have the car keys, and Fanny is out front, watering her lawn.

Falling against the back of my door as it closes, I slide into a puddle on the floor, holding my head in my hands.

My mind is racing so hard I can feel it in my temples, pulsing beneath my thumbs–chaos storms inside of me.

She can't remember she's overfeeding the fish.

It's better she's enjoying the funnies in the paper than staring blankly at a fucking wall.

Calm down.

Then my phone rings, startling me from the mini-breakdown I was just toeing into. I answer it quickly, without checking the caller ID, just to make the loud ringing quit. Effie is in preschool, and it could be the school.

"Hello?" I answer, my voice sounding like I'm on the brink of tears. There's heat behind my eyes, but I blink it away.

"Hey." The voice is both rough and soft and collapses my shoulders even further. *It's him.*

Bran.

And the subtle casual greeting of *"hey"* as opposed to a more stifled, cool "hello" makes my toes tingle. Hope is building, and I'm so down right now that I let it build.

"Bran?" I ask because I really don't know what else to say. And I want him to know I recognize that voice. Like an earthquake between my legs, I feel his timbre inside me when he speaks. I *know* that depth.

"Yeah, it's Bran."

Silence drops between us, spreading out quickly, taking hold of everything in its grasp. We stay that way–choked by the quiet–for what feels like a few minutes. But it doesn't feel like we're struggling or at a loss for words. It's almost like we're staring through the phone. Everything I experience with this man is so... real and intense, despite the fact that it's all been through a phone, through a cage, *actual* contact minimal.

"Why are you paying me?" I have the courage to ask the question that's been bouncing around my brain since the donut shop the other morning. If I'm honest, I've been wondering since I saw him.

He remains quiet, leaving me feeling compelled to clarify. "Look, you know you're a panty creamer. I didn't need to see you with *her* to know you can easily get women. So why are you paying me to get you off once a week?"

There. I finally said it. If he is protecting some twisty chasm of pain and trauma inside of him, then I've pushed and overstepped. But how can I know what's safe to ask when I don't know what's what at all?

Stray

"First of all," he grumbles, and even though I have no clue what he's going to say, the grumble makes my pussy flutter. Seriously. He could say, *first of all, I'm a murderer,* but it would be too late. My pussy has already and is currently all aflutter over that deep, growling voice. "That was my sister." He waits for a beat like maybe I'll remember. I do remember, but he fills the silence before I can. "Sammy, my younger sister Sammy."

"Your only sibling," I feel compelled to say, so he knows I *did* remember. It's important to me that he knows I remembered everything he's said to me.

"Yep."

"What's second? You said, first of all. So that means there's more." Please, if there is a God in heaven, let this man give me more.

"I was trying to hire a personal trainer for individual heavy lifting sessions."

This time, we both grab that silence. I know I do, gripping the phone so tight it strains against my ear as my eyes widen.

Lacey said it was code. That *everyone* knew what it was code for and that anyone looking to seriously hire someone would know *not* to use that specific site and those specific terms.

I don't have balls to crawl up inside me and shrivel, so I guess the equivalent would be my ovaries. My ovaries implode, and my ego withers away like a thirsty vine in the summer sun. I'm done. Put a fork in me. Seriously.

I went into a real job interview in a trench coat and a fucking corset! I spanked him! My hand flies to my face, covering it from the truth. But you can't hide from that shit. Not ever.

"You... You..." I trail off, wiggling and writhing uncomfortably in my spot on the floor. This information is so uncomfortable that I can't even sit with it. I leap to my feet and start pacing my room. "I... I was wearing a–"

"A corset and high heels and a silver trench coat," he finishes my sentence, supplying nothing but accurate details of my wardrobe that first night. Weeks back.

"And..." My mind doesn't race; it spins like a drunk top on a fucking seesaw. "You thought I was there for an interview like that?"

"Uh..." he trails off too, and just like that–in the thick of what I would deem my most cringeworthy and uncomfortable, embarrassing moments–we both laugh. Not hysterical, nothing to make us cry and hold our sides, but enough organic laughter to slice through the tension.

"It spun me out a little," he says eventually. "And I was like, wait a second." Then he pauses, chuckling softly again; even his laugh bears belly-scraping depth. "But then, I don't know."

"You *do* know," I say. I can feel his truth right at the surface, waiting for him to pluck.

"Beautiful woman in a hot outfit? How could I say no to that?"

"A woman would never say yes to a stranger under those twisted, confusing circumstances."

"You knew my name. You responded to the name in the email, so I knew it was the same person who'd applied. I just didn't know why you were doing.. Well, all the stuff you did."

"But," I supply, feeling his hesitancy through the ether.

"But I've been lonely for so long. And you came to me. You wanted me. You weren't going to laugh or slip out without a word. You were there on purpose, for me, looking like a goddamn movie star." He swallows, and the thick noise puts goosebumps down my back. "I couldn't resist you, Elsie."

My feet stop, but my head keeps going, spinning a wide berth on my shoulders. Did he just tell me I'm beautiful?

"I put you over your desk."

"I know."

"I gagged and spanked you."

"Oh, *I remember.*"

"I made you come on the desk, in your pants."

He sighs, and my entire body incinerates with the dark and dirty undertones in it. "Trust me, I know."

"And you thought I wanted to be a personal trainer?" I'm confused. I'm embarrassed. I'm turned on. I'm interested.

"I didn't know what to think. But that first night after you left Paradise, you were all I could think about. Then when I saw you again, I was fucking desperate for more of you. Even if it was in this backward, confusing, paid dynamic."

More silence as we both sort through our mental filing cabinets of new information.

"Why are you a Dominant?" His question is easy and expected. Yet I'm not prepared to answer, and instead of taking a moment to stall and formulate one I can not be embarrassed about, I hand him my truth.

"You're my first. At my day job, I work with Lacey, the woman who presumably showed up at your house. I just got dumped and... in my real life..." I choose my words carefully so as not to puncture those I love. They are not to be blamed. "I feel powerless a lot. Lacey told me this was a good way to feel powerful. And I just... I went for it. I needed something, you know?"

"I cannot see how a woman like you could ever feel powerless." He bypasses my question with a supremely sweet compliment. I ignore the flush it brings to my cheeks and am glad this is a phone call.

"Well, that's why I did it. And Lacey was right. The night we met in the office at Paradise, I left there... vibrating," I explain honestly, getting a little high just remembering how freaking good I felt that night. "I was so happy. So up."

He makes a soft hum, acknowledging my words, somehow like he knows I'm not done.

"You made me feel that way. And every time I've been with you, I feel like I matter."

"You don't matter in your real life?" His voice fills with a sadness so heavy it could sink us both. Like he understands feeling like you don't matter. I hate that he knows.

"I do. I matter a ton. But..." I finally sink onto the edge of the bed, relaxing some as the conversation unfolds. "I felt like I mattered to you, and the people in my life can't always make me feel that way. Or like, they aren't aware that I *need to know* I matter." I snort, hearing my own words. "That sounds really stupid and immature and selfish."

"No, it doesn't." His response is quick. My heartbeat gains momentum. "Elsie, can I say something?"

I nod first, forgetting we're on the phone because I'm in such a daze over this man. I'm literally dreaming of him as we speak. It's... scary. But exciting. "Okay," I reply, a little breathless.

"I want to keep seeing you if you're not with *him*."

Him. There it is. The reason he called off our session. The reason I pushed Bran out of my head as if the possibility of this beautiful person taking a serious interest in me, was so unbelievable that I was more eager to believe he just didn't want to see me any more than necessary.

I need this Dominant thing more than I realized.

It felt like a very good time to be honest and make sure my words were both clear and just right.

"I haven't lied to you, Bran. You are the first and the only man I've had as a Submissive." I swallow thickly, finding my voice growing sparse.

"Are you seeing anyone... casually, as just you, Elsie?"

Those words hit my pulse like adrenaline, and I'm smiling but definitely trying to hide that I'm smiling when I answer.

"No."

He hums his approval, and all of the tension and nerves inside of me pull tight at the sound. I want him. "Would you consider getting to know me through text message and on the phone six days of the week?"

My brow dips as I finger the edges of my bedspread. "You still want me to be your Dominant every week?"

"Fuck yes," he retorts, like this is his final answer, no life-lines needed.

"And then you want to talk to me the rest of the week... like..." my tongue feels thick in my mouth as I prepare to say the word. "Dating?"

I hope he can read the subtext; I'm worried it will be too

much, too soon, and he'll scare away. That I'll scare him away the more he gets to know me.

The moments tick by without an answer, and my sanity slowly unravels until he finally responds.

"Definitely. I just... I can't believe someone dumped *you*."

"As easy to believe as you having trouble meeting someone."

We sit there with the outsider's perspective of one another, silently digesting. Mom stirs in the kitchen, and I think I hear something drop.

"I have to go but in our sessions, we're Dominant and Submissive. Not Elsie and Bran, okay?" If this talking thing doesn't work out with Bran, I'd like to continue building my Dominant experience. As crazy as it came to me, I think I could really enjoy it. When Bran realizes that my life is complicated and prickly, I want to have kept our professional boundaries intact. For both of our sakes. So I can be ready to find another client and so he can feel safe while we're together as Goddess and Stray. If his emotions become tangled in that dynamic, he loses some of his safety. Because even though I know now that he didn't seek me out to fill any voids, I realize now that his confidence needs repairing. I want to do that for him.

It's best this way.

Caution is smart. It isn't as sexy as *all in*, but it's smart. And I need to be smart when it comes to a man as all-engrossing, addicting, and beautiful as Bran Edwards.

"Okay," he agrees easily, and I'm relieved. "The Goddess and her Stray," he says, his voice dipping into a darkness I've never heard. Chills run through my body at the idea of having that voice poured directly into my ear, a shortcut to my veins. What his beard would feel like against my shoulder as he spoke to me, lips touching me.

I'm wiggling on the bed as I say goodbye, hear his goodbye, then reluctantly end the call.

I'm terrified of the potential role reversal because I like being his Goddess, but this man makes me want to throw myself at his feet and beg for a taste of him.

25

Bran

My clothes are off in less time than it would take to spell my name.

"It's without a doubt the girl," Mally says around his bite of wings. He licks the orange sauce from his fingers, grossing me out. Turning to find solace in my sister's face, I only find her doing the exact same thing.

"You guys are disgusting. Your hands touch everything. You're putting the world in your mouth when you lick your fingers."

Batman does one of those point-snap-finger waggles at me. "Yes, that! I say that to my kids. Well, Robin does."

Van sucks the meat off of a wing and drops the bones in the styrofoam tray split open in front of him. "You've got dad lectures down, you hear that?" he bumps my arm with his elbow, rolling his fingertips on a wet nap.

Sammy rolls her eyes and pulls a finger out of her mouth with a pop. "I washed my hands right before they brought my wings, Bran."

Mally's about to say agree mindlessly with her, his mouth open and everything, but he stops, turning to face Sammy with a ripple in his brow. "You did?"

She winces away from him as she makes quick work of another wing. "You're making Bran smug and satisfied with your bad hygiene."

He stares at his fingers for a minute, holding a habanero wing hostage. "Fuck it; I'm halfway." Then returns to his nasty finger-sucking. "Anyway," he says, mouth full. Jesus, he may be a good guy, but I now realize, he has bad manners. "You're *diverting* the focus."

Van bats his eyes at Mally. "You're still using the word-a-day calendar I got you."

He nods proudly. "I am."

"You needed a calendar to teach you the word divert?" Sammy drops her last wing in the basket, calling the battle against the honey barbecue boneless wings. She made a valiant effort but stopped shy with just three left.

Mally shrugs. "You don't need an English degree to put handcuffs on people." He slides closer to her in the booth, wiggling his eyebrows at her before leaning in. "Come over and find out."

"Dude." Van doesn't have any siblings, but even he knows they're off-limits. And anyway, Mally flirts with everyone. I can't even hate–the bastard is charismatic and giving and kind. And only moderately child-like and annoying. For guys our age, that's a catch. Still, he can flirt with everyone *except my sister.*

"Not cool, man." I shake my head.

Sammy rolls her eyes. "I don't need a white knight, but thanks. And you're right, Malibu. He is all puffy stickers and streamers because of a girl." Sammy winks, and even though I hadn't really filled the guys in on the rollercoaster that Elsie and I had ridden the way that I did with Sammy (mostly because she happened to be there as it launched), I also hadn't mentioned any of the good progress. Like deciding to be in contact daily, which by the way, has been goddamn fucking fantastic.

I forgot how much I liked having a girlfriend. And even though we haven't given ourselves any labels, having someone to text in the morning and check on throughout the day fills my soul. I'd told Sammy we'd worked through our problem, that thinking she was with someone else was just a miscommunication, and Sammy accepted it.

As my sister, I worried she might forever see Elsie as a deviant since I had actually thought she'd lied to me. But luckily, she only continued her positive support, and I was happy.

Even now, when she was spilling the beans to the guys, I wasn't trying to hold it as close to my vest as before. Because now, we had some defined edges to us.

Elsie and I had agreed to just talk to each other for now. Only date one another and see how it goes. That was shareable information.

"They're exclusive," Sammy adds, grabbing Mally's nearly full beer. As if remembering the finger-licking conversation moments ago, she returns it without any stolen drinks and then makes quick work of mine.

Van slaps my thigh beneath the table. "Good for you, man." His dark beard hides most of his face like mine does, but I can still read the unmistakable pure happiness in his expression.

Mally's mouth opens, and I'm grateful to Robin right now because Batman is engrossed in his phone, unable to be present. Normally I'd bitch that if he was gonna be with us, then he had to be *with* us. But now, I'd love for Mally to get a text to engross him.

I stop him with a shake of my head, and it works. His mouth snaps closed as a pout settles over him. The man loves pouting as much as tearing off his fucking shirt after one set at the gym.

"Not sharing anything yet. We're only seeing one another, that's all."

That *is* all. For now. And that's all I told Sammy too. The rest... whatever happens now that we've agreed to see each other... needs to be for just us. For both of our sakes.

Mally nudges my basket. "You're not eating. You seein' your girl tonight?"

"So what if I am?"

He grins, his lips rimmed with dayglo orange. "You're gonna have to take a shit now."

Sammy gags on her mouthful of my beer; it's hers now. I love my sister, but no way in hell am I drinking backwash. Though... I'd drink after Elsie. Any fucking day. Warmth creeps up the back of my neck at that delicious thought.

I shake my head, unwilling to discuss bathroom habits at

the dinner table. Granted, the dinner table in question *does* bear a sheen of mysterious sticky substance, the corresponding booth is overstuffed inside torn vinyl, and the food we're eating is being done so out of clamshell containers and plastic baskets. So, yeah, I probably *could*, but I don't want to.

"See, that's why you're not eating."

I take a dramatic bite of a chicken wing. The truth is, I hadn't thought about having a noisy digestive system for our meeting tonight. Meeting? Appointment? Session? I don't know what to call it.

I *am* nervous to see her tonight, though.

We've been talking a ton since we had that life-changing phone call last week. How fucking lame is it that a girl agreeing to want to "see" me via phone call is life-changing?

But it is. And I may have a big dick with balls to match, but I can eat humble pie when it's served to me. Big junk and all. Because the exchange between her and I was real, and it's the first dose of *real* I've had in ages.

Random hookups do not count as real. Filling a rubber while my head is torqued away from any signs of humanity and life as a stranger writhes beneath me is not real. It's... saccharine. A knock-off of the real thing. Connection without actual connection. Release without giving up anything but come.

Talking to Elsie puts my head in the clouds in a good way. Pulls me from my self-indulgent bullshit and makes me see ahead instead of behind. I've been thinking about the past for too long. It's time to look forward. And she seems to be willing to look forward *with* me, even though I can only do it with partial vision.

I fend off a few more stupid comments from my people,

including my sister. She teases, but the bright sound of her jabs gives away her complete happiness. She'd really worried about me, and I hope deep in my gut that this would be the connection to relieve her of her worry–that Elsie and I could be more than Goddess and Stray.

Van and Mally head to get ice cream after wings because they are disgusting bottomless pits, Sammy gets a ride home from Batman, and by the time I get home, I have just enough time to take a shower and get dressed before eight.

Stoner had been asleep all evening–shocker–but his head perked up as soon as the doorbell rang.

"For me, not for you. When is it ever for you?" I shake my head at him as he tucks away his snout under his thigh, curling back to sleep.

It would be nice for Sammy and the boys to stop worrying about me, yeah. But it'd be nice to stop talking to a dog like a human diary. Perks everywhere.

I unlock the door, feeling my heart pulse in my throat as I slide apart the chain lock. She isn't my girl–not yet, but fuck, it feels like she should be. My eye meets hers, bright and shining, the way Sammy's voice sounded earlier. Puffing my chest out, I tip my head in a greeting nod. "Hi."

Her cheeks flush, but as if she has allowed herself a few seconds to be Elsie, and she remembers why she was here, she pushes her chin up and rolls her shoulders back.

"Hello, Stray."

I swallow, and watch the silver-gray trench coat move past me in a blur. Just the sight of her dirty, old-time detective getup makes me hard.

Now that I'd taken myself out of chastity, my cock had

been as hard as the metal it had been behind. All fucking week.

I woke up with morning wood that could support a fucking building. I was hard at Paradise, just staring at the vacant, upturned office, remembering our times there. I could do this all day-long; story short: I was hard all the fucking time.

But the thing I'd started to realize about myself is not that I was the one holding me back but that I'd also been held by some depression, too. Wind never wove itself between my bare toes as I stood on the edge of life, ready to give up. I'd never been that dark, not even right after the night. I hadn't, however, done normal things, healthy things for a man my age.

I jerked off, yeah, but only when it was absolutely necessary. Only when the pain and fullness couldn't be ignored, when I'd leaked into my briefs for days on end, the pressure of existing alone at the peak of me, ready to eject. Ready to pull the ripcord on loneliness. Those would be the times I'd do it just to be done, taking a few seconds of pleasure as my come pulsed out of me in long, tearing rips. But then clarity. It settled over coitus; it swallowed those moments of relieving exhale and replaced all of it with a cloud.

The cloud of sadness and loneliness that had been so dense, I didn't even know it was there. I'd been looking through that cloud for so long; that's what I thought life looked like.

It lifted after that phone call with Elsie.

And now that I know what things can feel like, look like... *be*... I'm chasing it. Like Strays do, I'm chasing instinct, desperate to sink my teeth into and hold the feeling in my mouth and hands and heart forever.

She has that bag over her shoulder—the one she'd brought with her before. She peers at me over her shoulder as the dark hallway swallows her up. I hear my bedroom door open, moonlight whispering across the hall floor from my open window. I make my feet move toward her. I've been nervous all day, yet I hadn't thought about *this*.

What my Goddess was going to *do* to me. I'd thought about Elsie instead, and now I realize I should've prepared for this more. Because I promised her that we're dominant and submissive when we're together on these nights, hearts be damned.

"Come, Stray," she commands, and I go to her, ready to come.

She closes the door but hesitates, hand still on the doorknob. Whispering as if it's the indicator she's breaking roles or characters, she leans towards me. "Is it okay to close the door, or will Stoner get mad?"

I can smell her shampoo with how close she is. Or maybe it's her body lotion. Or maybe that's just her—all floral and sexy and shit. About now, I kind of wish the cage was still on because my dick is turning to stone already.

"He's okay," I say, trying to ignore the swell of appreciation behind my ribs. Being considerate of my dog is really not that big of a deal, but it's the reach of her care that I love. How she clearly cares about things important to the people she cares about.

I'm one of them, and I'm a junkie for more.

Standing with just a foot between us, her eyes hold my eye as she releases the tie at her waist, letting the notorious silver coat drop to the floor. My heart rate kicks up a notch, my mouth falls open, and I find myself tracing the elastic on the side of my head nervously. I've seen her... *Dom gear*. But now that we've agreed to try more outside of this night? Looking at her feels like something I need permission to do.

"Can I look at you, Goddess?" I ask, my mouth saying Goddess, my brain saying, Elsie.

She pinches my chin over my beard and forces my eye to her chest. "Look at me, Stray, look at everything that will belong to you if you can be a good boy."

Holy shit.

The corset, the school teacher outfit–those outfits could've been a nun's robe compared to now. Haphazardly with neither reason nor rhyme nor clear intention, black leather straps maze over her naked body. Silver grommets attach leather to leather, the body harness smashing, pulling, lifting her everywhere. My mouth goes dry at the sight of her naked breasts peeking through the ambitious outfit. More than a palmful, they're full, skin fair, and supple. I rub my lips together, wanting to seal my lips around one of her nipples.

Her nipples. I must stand there and stare at them for a healthy twenty seconds. Areolas, the color of natural peanut butter ombreing to milk chocolate, they call to me just as much as a damn Reese's cup. At the center, her nipples are hard nubs with silver bars driven through. The cage would be put to the test right now because my semi just went full fucking fledged.

Her fingers, which I forgot were fed through my beard gripping my face, tug me lower. "Keep looking at your owner, Stray."

The fucking confidence she has being a Dominant makes my head whir. Knowing that she isn't some experienced sex worker, I'm her first Sub... it makes it that much hotter.

Red fabric gobbles up her lean legs and ends with a band of lace on her thighs. I want to reach out and snap the fabric and pull her into me as she winces from the sting. My eye has made it to her black, shiny pumps when she reaches out, without warning, and cups my cock.

The unrelenting ridge of my erection must feel good to her, too, because a tiny moan escapes her lips as she feels me. Her swallow is loud as she tips my face upright, still cupping my groin.

"Tell me, Stray, did your Goddess give you permission to come out of your cage?"

I don't know why I feel brave. Maybe the unexpected metal piercings, maybe it is the voluptuous curve of her side boob or the smell of her skin. But I suddenly want to be punished by my Goddess. *Need* to be a bad boy.

"Strays don't belong in cages. Strays run free."

Another smile, this time one I am fortunate enough to see. She takes her hand off me, and I feel the absence everywhere.

"I'll let you run free." She steps away, and I feel that distance, too. "Until I decide you've had enough freedom." She continues to put space between us, and the further she gets, the more of her body I see. Everything is soft and smooth where it needs to be, hard and erotic everywhere else. Fucking perfect.

Her curls have been tamed, ironed free of their body, and her hair is pulled back into a sleek ponytail. It is sexy as hell, but I like those vivacious natural curls, too.

I don't think there is a hairstyle, outfit, or despicable thing my Goddess could do that I wouldn't like.

"Now get naked."

I hesitate, if only for a moment, but in that second, she leaps. "Was there a word you didn't understand?" She taps an invisible watch, banding her wrist. "Now," she overly enunciates the word. Heat flares inside me from the raw excitement that her attitude and wit bring. And I never thought sex and orgasms could be partnered with the things she makes me feel but... thank God I was wrong. About so many things.

"Get naked," she finishes, equally over-enunciating the last two words of her command. Because that's clearly what she was—my commander.

Two things men can be very quick about if needed: coming and taking steps leading to coming. My clothes are off in less time than it would take to spell my name.

Her lashes flutter as her eyes center on my cock, heavy and eager between my legs. I stroke myself once, just to see if her face changes while she watches. I notice a heavy breath leave her body while a flush eats up her cheeks, the tip of her tongue tracing the wide curve of her bottom lip.

But like a good Goddess, she shifts her energy back to our session. Digging through her bag, she must locate what she needs because a sinister smile spreads over her face.

"Come, Stray. Stand here." She points to a spot right next to her, and takes her bag off the bed, to the ground, and lowers to her knees. My cock weeps at the sight of all that beauty at my feet. Using my palm, I smother the capped head of my dick to smear away the excess precome.

I went to her.

"Keep your eye ahead," she says, and then I hear the leather of her bag. My pulse skyrockets with anticipation. She taps my ankle. "Lift this one, then the other."

I do as she asks, feeling her loop something around each foot as I lift. Then she shimmies whatever it was up my legs, the backs of her knuckles grazing me as she does. Just the backs of her knuckles, but her touch leaves a trail of fire in its wake—my entire body burns to be touched by her. To be teased by her. To have her at the helm of me *entirely*.

She fastens, adjusts, then rises. "Look at me, Stray."

My eye moves down to find hers, bright and excited. I love that she can be my Dominant Goddess, my keeper, and my ruler but also holds happiness within those confines. Or maybe I just love her eyes.

Our gazes idle while her hands work between us. I smell rubber or something that reminds me a lot of what it smells like when you put a spatula on the bottom rack of your dishwasher. She's belted me along with the thigh straps and I have no idea what is happening. I'm not even eager to look. I am more eager to see what she's doing with whatever she is putting on me.

She smacks something, her smiling eyes still on my hungry one, and it makes my body want to surge forward with the momentum.

"Look down."

I do.

My mouth goes dry. I attempt a swallow. My ass tightens in nervous anticipation. Around my hips and thighs is a leather harness, closely matching the one she's wearing on her naked body. The only difference? Hers holds only her body, and mine doesn't hold my body at all.

Standing out between our bodies, fixed to my harness, is a long, thick dildo. Black and shiny, made with veins of strain and everything. Below the fake cock is my own, just as long and proud.

Her fingertips outline the most ominous wave inked into my skin, the one turning the ship on its side. "Lie on your back on the bed."

I do as I'm told, breaking one rule out of necessity. "Goddess," I lift my head, watching her pull two items out of her bag while she hovers above me on the bed.

"Yes?"

I swallow, not at all ashamed of what I am about to admit. Because it is a testament to her beauty. And that fucking fire body of hers. "If you ride this," I grip the rubber cock, "and I have to watch, I'll come."

She smiles like she knew I was going to say that. "You think you're lucky enough to watch me come?" One of the items she'd gotten out of the bag was dangling in front of me–the cuffs. Without being told, I sit up and bring my wrists together at my lower back.

The ends of her ponytail are hypnotizing as she shakes her head no.

"In front of you, Stray."

I do as she says, and the second item? A rope. With my fists bound by metal at my belly, the rope burns my skin delightfully as she loops it around the link between my wrists. Kneeing her way up my body, she looks down at me with her hands resting atop my headboard.

What a fucking view. The underside of those glorious tits, those wide blue eyes.

"Turn your head, Stray." I take in the sight one more

time, committing it to my desperate memory before doing as she tells me. I hear the rope hit the wall, the distinct gnawing noise of the rough fibers grating the espresso wood. I don't need to look down to know that goosebumps rise from my flesh. Excitement can't be hidden, even in tattoos.

Her warmth leaves my face as her knees shimmy down my body like a dirty fire escape.

"Stray, look at your Goddess."

Again, I do as she commands because I want to. I want to be pleased by her but *fuck me*; I want to please her, too.

She tugs the loose end of the rope, yanking my hands up in the direction of the headboard. I look down at my cuffed, roped wrists hovering above my belly. A dirty pulley system of sorts. I like it.

"Now jerk off."

I blink, and her face remains motionless. She blinks back. She taps her invisible wristwatch again, and my lips curl into a smile at her sass. "Now," she drags out the word, and I enjoy how her mouth turns into a perfect little circle as she makes her way through the letters. What would it feel like to slide between those pretty pink lips and feel that sassy throat tighten around my fat shaft?

I move my hands to my cock and grip it, sticky and rock-hard.

She shakes her head disapprovingly, and I release myself instantly to please her.

"You said–"

She doesn't have to interrupt me with words. Tipping her head forward, she locks her eyes on the fake cock strapped to and pointing up from my groin. "Jerk off *that* cock."

I blink down at my dick, erect and pink, veiny and hungry.

"The fake one?"

She nods.

"The one that *isn't* dying to come?" I smile, and I think it is the first time I've smiled at her because her face softens almost indescribably. Like she's seen a shooting star, but it happens so fast that she doesn't have time to point it out. That's how my smile is, too. It disappears after a moment, then she nods.

"Yep, that's the one." Then she folds her arms over her bare breasts, stealing them from my view. But since I'll apparently be jacking off a strap-on, maybe it's for the best.

From between her crossed legs, she produces a bottle of lube. The crack of the cap flipping back makes my cock pulse and bob against the dildo, and she side-eyes it with a smirk. When I think she's going to put lube in my hand after she fully lubricates herself, instead, she drops the bottle and holds her hands out.

"Hands," she says simply. Releasing the strap-on, I hold my hands out. She repositions herself onto her knees, leaning forward to reach my hands. She closes her hands around one of mine, shaking and rubbing to transfer the lube. We both ignore the way my cock responds to the intimate touch. She repeats this on my other hand, then hands down orders, effectively ending the tender moment.

Maybe it wasn't tender to her, but it felt that way to me.

Moving to a spot between my legs, she nudges my thighs apart so she can sit cross-legged. My spine jolts when she wraps her palms around my cock. Jerking my head from the pillows, I growl like a wanderer staring down his future.

It was clear she'd grabbed her tits since they glistened from streaks of smeared lube. Her nipples stare back at me, the milk chocolatey peaks summiting her lush breasts. With her ponytail up, there was no denying how much she enjoyed it, the sides of her neck ruddy and flushed.

My cock bucks and bobs, my ass pulls together as the crumbs of an orgasm gather inside me, starting to form something more. Something too big to be held in.

"Continue," she breathes, holding her slick hands along my thighs, hovering.

I want to be her good boy, so I do as I'm told—the Stray eager to please.

Stacking my fists, I'm surprised at how fucking good it feels when I drag my palms along the slick cock.

I'm not bisexual. I never have been. Nothing wrong with it, but I just don't get hard from men. I can admit when a man is handsome, and with that said, I've been around the guys showering, and if Van or Mally don't stand me up, I don't think any man could. Those annoying fuckers are, by all standards, *built*.

But when my fists pick up the pace, pumping the strap-on jutting up from my groin, my own cock twitches in horny delight.

Horny delight, I said it.

"How does it feel?" Her voice is smoky and raspy. I imagine hearing that voice whisper my name while pumping deep between those prodigious thighs.

"Strangely hot." I don't even consider putting up a front. This woman bought a cage with my dick in mind. Seems like we're past shyness. And being real and truthful is so easy with her.

"Good." I blink and catch the tail end of a smile as she turns her gaze down toward the action beneath her. The ends of her ponytail sweep across her shoulder, and I don't even get to focus on the sexy way she flings it back, exposing the slender curve of her neck—because she wraps and stacks her fists around *my* cock.

My cock.

Not the strap-on, where I'm currently pumping like I only discovered masturbation a month ago. Shit, when did I start really getting fucking into it? The down pillow clouds my hearing as my head drops back. Biceps starting to burn, wrists going numb, I pump that strap-on like it's actually going to blow if I keep it up.

I'm going to fucking blow if I keep it up.

No, if *she* keeps it up.

Twisting her palms, her hands work my length in opposite directions, making my inner thighs tremble. The bed seems to vibrate in the room—her working hard on me, me working hard on the fake cock.

"Hold on, Stray." That same smokey tone that was hot before, is now murderous, threatening to shove me off the edge with ease.

Stupidly, I lift my head and pop my eye open. Her ponytail sways to the rhythm of our aching bodies, her delicate hands do dirty work, pumping hard up my throbbing erection. Precome bubbles out my slit, making a break for it, sliding down the purple-rimmed cap of my cockhead.

Fu-uck. I feel like I've never come before in my entire life. I feel like I'm on the brink of exploding, losing my hearing, not being able to inhale or exhale, see or think.

I try to swallow, but my mouth has been open in aching delight for so long, everything is a desert.

My hands are foolishly still jacking like I'm going to win Olympic fucking gold. Her hands are working much slower than mine, but with her twisting technique—not to mention the way she runs the pad of her thumb over my slit and down the seam of my balls every so often—*I'm close.*

"I."

Yep. That's all I can say. *I.*

I. I. I.

The Goddess knows my breathlessness is my pathetic surrender. My cease-fire. I can't do battle with her anymore. She's won. She's making me insane, but the good insane, like a happy Tom Cruise jumping on a couch about love type of crazy.

She *owns* me.

My ears fill with the fast grinding of rope against the headboard as she uses her pulley system to steal my hands off the dildo.

She pulls them just far enough back so that they're unable to grab at anything worth grabbing. My neck is straining so hard, my vision is pinching in, but I can't take my eye off the erotic movie I'm screening.

"*Wha?*" I can't even finish the word.

'*I*' and '*wha*' are my contributions to this. *Great, Bran.*

Blood rushes through my ears. With a dirty grin that I fucking adore, she bites her plush bottom lip, her gaze fixed on my cock. But then she wraps her hands around the strap-on, not moving them.

"Do you want me to move my hands?"

The impending orgasm that's currently burning up my

tailbone and vibrating in my groin is taking all of my blood and energy. My brain struggles to understand. "Yeah," I finally groan because I want her hands all over me. I want her pumping me, catching my load in her palm, then smearing it up and down my still throbbing cock. I want her mouth on mine and–

"Say it." She rolls her lips together. "Say it now, Stray. *Now*."

"Move them," I pant it; honestly I do. I'm no better than Stoner staring at his post-CBD rawhide. "*Move your hands*."

Fuck, at least it's full words and a sentence. Better than *I* and *wha*.

This time, my Goddess follows my commands, but instead of moving her hands back to the real flesh and blood, the dripping cock bobbing and throbbing in front of her, she pumps *the strap-on* instead.

Then she twists her talented hands on it, the way she did me. My jaw burns and my neck locks up from the continual strain, but I ignore it because how the fuck could I look away now?

Her hands stop. "Say it."

"*Move them*." It comes fast and easy this time, and I know that's foreboding in itself.

She pumps the dildo once. "Say it."

"Move them."

Again, she jacks off the rubber dick bobbing in the harness on my body.

She tells me to say it, and now I understand the game. She wants me so fucking needy, hungry, *begging* her to come. The control that I thought I had from getting to tell her what to do... *damn she's good*.

Sweat glistens along my body as my hips lift from the bed to meet her pumps. I moan and groan, *move, move, move, move,* as she does repeatedly. Clenching my ass, thrusting my hips, watching her hands so goddamn close to my cock working another dick?

Agony. Heaven. Maddening. Erotic.

My requests grow space as my breathing becomes more frantic. When I don't say it right away, she pulls the rope, jerking my arms up higher, pain searing down my arms.

Perfect pain. Beautiful pain.

"*Move, move, move,*" I pant out again, and as my eye moves to her face, just for a moment, she does the same thing. Right at the same time. Our heated gazes idle, the room thick with undiscovered feelings.

She pumps the strap-on again, the corners of her lips curling into the sexiest, cutest fucking smile I've ever seen in my whole life. With two eyes or with one.

That's when it happens.

My orgasm says *fuck you* to this entire game and rockets up my cock, releasing a long, thick stream of come. Whipping angrily from my slit, I come in abundant ropes that sling up my groin and belly, landing with a heavy thud. My hands are numb, but my fingers are moving, itching to touch myself, to stroke as the last of my orgasm bubbles from my tip, beading down my shaft.

Outside of wet dreams, I've never orgasmed without touch. And she just made me come from being so fucking sexy.

"Lie back."

I'm still panting, my head a fucking top it's spinning so hard, my chest heaving to breathe, neck burning for relief.

Dropping my head back, the chaos and spinning of that orgasm begin to subside. Beneath my beard, my skin is hot. I'm sweaty everywhere, come now sliding down my sides, bleeding into my bed.

Gently, she releases my wrists. Then with her knees bracketing my torso, she shimmies up my body and uncuffs me, releasing the rope from the bed too. My come clings to her thighs, and how she doesn't even acknowledge it fucking *wrecks* my head. God, I want this girl so fucking bad. Because it takes a strong fucking woman to plan and execute so much badassery.

I love that.

I want to give myself to her. I am her pet, her Stray. I'd do anything to please her. Just like a fucking dog.

She slides off me and disappears. She doesn't know my space well–she's never even used the bathroom here. But she comes back with a bath towel, warm and damp on one end. Smoothing the terry cloth over my heated, sticky body, my eye closes.

Her voice is gentle when she speaks, all smoke and rasp gone now. "How did that feel?"

A tremor rumbles down my spine, reverberating through my legs. They shake a little before I stretch through the feeling. "Fuck," I sigh because there isn't a word for how that felt. There isn't a word for how I feel now. There isn't a simple way to describe the complexities of what's going on inside me mostly because I don't even understand it yet.

I just know I want this girl. I fucking want this girl.

It's not the intense nut talking, either.

She cleans me up carefully and thoroughly–I had no idea that aftercare was something to be delivered to men. I've been jerked onto my belly before and left to penguin-jog to the bathroom before come got on the carpet. But my Goddess took care of me in all ways.

She taps a finger on my hip bone. "Lift."

She shimmies off the harness, but she holds a silent palm out when I attempt to sit up. I lie back.

Swiping the towel down her thighs, she then wrings her hands in it, cleaning herself up last. The harness shifts against her skin, revealing red marks where the leather has rubbed. I want to smooth those little burned parts of flesh with my mouth and tongue, with my fingers. I peer down to see my dick stirring.

Once she's dropped the strap-on and lube back into her bag of tricks (the one that makes me fucking hard just at the sight), she perches her hands on her hips and tips her head to one shoulder.

"Where's the cage, Stray?"

I lift my head and nod toward the dresser, my body heavy with relief, still pulsing with the need to touch her. Have a conversation with her. To feel her on me. Anything that includes her.

She retrieves the cage. "And my necklace and key?"

My eye moves around the room as my brain struggles to wake the fuck up. Where did I put it? "Dresser," I say, back to no longer being able to make sentences. Because even if I'm getting locked the fuck up, that means she's going to do it. Her hands are going to be on me, and if that's what's left for this session and nothing else, I fucking want it. I want it bad.

She retrieves the key and positions herself between my

legs again, in the same spot. She's snuck something else up with her from that bag, but I didn't notice until now.

With a click, gentle mechanical vibrations fill the room. She smiles, and while that toothy, gorgeous smile and the sound of the vibrator should just make my dick hard (*they do*), my ribs seem to shrink. This girl does shit to me, shit I've never felt before.

My eyes trail down her body, rediscovering her beauty. Her words from our phone call bounce around my brain. I make her feel powerful. I make her feel *up*, she said.

"Goddess," I start before she can do whatever she has up her nonexistent but highly sexy sleeve. "You said I make you feel powerful."

She blinks. "Yes."

"How?" I don't mean to sound like a compliment grab, and I don't love how it sounds. Still, I need to know.

She wastes no time in responding. If she were contriving and plucking perfect words and thoughts, trying to build a great answer, I'd think she was lying. But she replies on the heels of my question.

"You're handsome." She wrinkles her nose with a shake of her head like her response underwhelmed her. "You're beautiful. Built. And I'm making you tremble. I'm making you lose control." She shrugs like it's so fucking easy. Simple, even. "How could that not make me feel powerful?"

"Just because I pay you doesn't mean you have to lie to me."

Fuck.

My auto-defense response, the one I'd built up over the years to protect myself from being the joke, fires off without my permission, my brain and mouth in cahoots strictly out of habit. "I'm sorry," I say, not adding Goddess, because I'm sorry I said that to Elsie, too. "That wasn't fair."

I expect that even though I've apologized, that cruel and degrading sentence will drive us apart and ruin what we have going on. Because it was *cheap*, insinuating she's just a paid service doing a job. I need some reprogramming, and STAT, because I know that's not who she is.

"I'm not used to... compliments," I finally finish, wishing I could rewind and do over the last thirty seconds of my existence.

Then my heart, like the Grinch discovering it's better to be cool than to be a fucking prick, expands a few sizes. Because she smiles, unphased and unaffected. The vibrator flicks back on, and I hadn't noticed she turned it off. My focus was just... on us.

"You asked, and I answered."

I nod. "Okay."

She tucks the vibrating wand between her lips, eyes fluttering closed at the immediately seductive contact. Fuck, I've never seen a woman masturbate in real life, and after less than five seconds, I'm fucking hooked.

Kneeing closer to me, she breathes heavily as the vibrator works her pussy and her hands work... the cage. My cock is hard, so she warns me before delivering a gentle(ish) slap to my balls, making my spine curl. It softens my cock, too, just enough for her to slip me into the cage with tender but needed force.

"You slapped my sac to get me to fit in there, didn't you?" I ask with laughter and excitement in my veins, my balls a little terrified.

She wiggles her eyebrows at me. "Tuck pillows behind

your head so you can see me, then put your head on your hands."

While I do as I'm told, she gets comfortable between my spread thighs, draping hers over mine in two intersecting v's. She raises the wand up so we can both see it, sticky from her body. She's wet, the wand is soaked, and my cock swells under the metal of the cage. Then she lowers it, pressing it to the hot strip of skin between my ass and balls.

My legs jerk, but hers press down on top of mine, preventing me from moving.

I own a lifting gym and squat 285 pounds. But her lean little legs hold me down like a metal fucking mousetrap, and I add that to the fucking fast-growing list of things I like about this girl.

"You know you're gorgeous." I have the urge to make sure she knows.

With my hands interlocked behind my head, I watch her torture me with the wand, which warms and pulses through my lower half. If I wasn't caged, I'd be a bobbing mess right now.

"Stray, I can make you come again, all locked like a good, dirty boy. But you have to do what I say. I am your Goddess, aren't I?"

Yep. I'm hypnotized. Intoxicated. Drunk off her. However you want to say it, I'm about one blown load away from tattooing her name across my fucking heart.

"You are my Goddess." You are *so* my fucking Goddess.

"Now, repeat after me, and I'll make you come." Slowly, she nudges the wand up, connecting with my balls just barely. The slight sensation, the trembling it sends through my fiery skin—I swear it's hotter than if she were sucking my dick.

The anticipation is king. She is queen.

"I am fucking perfect." She moves the wand and pets the exposed strips of skin through the cage, making my shaft twitch angrily.

"You are fucking perfect."

The wand flicks off; the room hums with how much I fucking want her.

"Stray. Say it."

I swallow, my eye meeting hers. "I'm not. You are." It sounds childish, and it seems like an easy thing, being able to say I'm perfect if it earns me attention from her in the form of coming.

But getting those words off my tongue feels like eating glass.

"Stray." Her fingers stroke slowly over the pebbled skin of my swollen nut sack, then smack. She smacks my nuts again. I wince. "Say it."

"I can't."

"You are the reason women spend an hour picking the right outfit. You're the name they carve in the tree. You are the guy they have dreams about." She flicks the vibrator back on and holds it to my taint. It feels so good. I want to come. I could come. *I could.*

I can't say that, though. I tell her that again.

The wand goes off. She leans over the bed and opens her hand, dropping the toy directly into her bag. "Then you don't come." From the spot next to her, she takes *her* necklace and fastens it easily behind her neck.

There are things I should say, or maybe not. I don't

know. The night screeches to a halt as she lifts herself off the bed and picks up her coat from the floor.

"Don't you want to take that off? Your skin," I sit up and get to my feet, making my way to her in just a few steps. With my hand at her collarbone, I slip my fingers beneath the straining leather and slide them against the heated strip of skin beneath. "You're red. I don't want it to hurt you."

Her eyes tamp down on me, studying me. At least I feel studied. Actually, that's not true. Under her gaze, in her presence, with her holding my leash... I feel *solved*.

"It's okay," she says, and she sounds like Elsie now, instead of my Goddess.

I watch her beautiful naked body disappear from my sight as she feeds one arm through her coat and then the other. She closes and cinches it, looking up at my face.

"Thank you."

"Thank you for tonight. It was fucking amazing." I swallow, courage coming to me now, now that I don't have to think or talk about myself. "You are fucking amazing."

She rocks to her toes, and my heart jolts when her palms press to my pecs. *She's going to kiss me*, I think, but then her lips dance against the bottom of my ear lobe.

"*You* are fucking amazing." She pulls back, hoisting her bag up over her shoulder. "When I'm done with you, you'll know it."

Something tells me this strong woman in front of me is right. And confidence is something I need.

I don't like the part about her being done with me, though.

Before I can say something I shouldn't and ask her to stay for a snack or tell her how fucking beautiful she is for no reason other than I cannot stop thinking it—she slips out my bedroom door. Moments later, her car comes to life.

I look down at the metal swinging from my groin as I walk to the kitchen. Everything with her has been so.... different. A Dominant and Submissive. I'm caged. I came... touch-free.

I like different.

I want to *embrace the different*... forfuckingever if I can.

26

Elsie

No matter what I'm doing–building him up, touching him, laughing with him–I always feel empowered.

Bran: *If you say any other movie than Die Hard, I'm going to seriously have to rethink us.*

Elsie: *Die Hard?! That's not a Christmas movie.*

Bran: *Oh, it most certainly is.*

Bran: *Fine. What's your choice, then?*

Bran: *Don't say Home Alone. Please. It's good and everything, but it's not the end-all-be-all of Christmas movies.*

Bran: *Although the mom is Home Alone is pretty hot.*

Elsie: **scoffs**

Elsie: *Of course, it's not. I'm not that basic.*

Elsie: *You think the mom in Home Alone is hot?*

Elsie: *Her haircut is the shape of a mushroom.*

Bran: *I think you're forgetting; a lot of good things have the shape of a mushroom*

Bran: *And anyway, under those shoulder pads, I bet she's all sweetness.*

Elsie: *Okay, MOVING BACK TO THE MOVIE.*

Elsie: *Clearly, the best Christmas movie of all time is the family holiday classic...*

Elsie: *JINGLE ALL THE WAY*

Bran: *Goddamn.*

Bran: *Beautiful with good taste to boot. I'd say lock me up; I'm yours, but, well. Points to crotch*

Bran: *I forgot about that one. Good shit.*

Elsie: *So, so funny. I love Arnold.*

Bran: *Yeah?*

Elsie: *Oh yeah. *Fans self**

Bran: *You like the muscle guys, huh?*

Elsie: **crickets chirping**

Bran: *??*

Elsie: *I like you, dumbass.*

Elsie: *Say that in Red Forman's voice, and it will be funny, not mean.*

Elsie: *I didn't mean it mean.*

Bran: *I don't think you could ever be mean.*

Elsie: *Everyone can be mean.*

Bran: *Not me.*

Elsie: *You were mean two days ago.*

Bran: *When you were at my house?*

Elsie: *Yep.*

Bran: *I was mean?*

Bran: *I'm sorry*

Bran: *What did I do?*

Bran: *I would never be mean to you*

Elsie: *You weren't mean to me*

Bran: *Who was I mean to? It was just you and me.*

Bran: *Stoner?*

Bran: *Trust me, you do not want to listen to Stoner licking his asshole while you're trying to do... anything. Much less dick-related stuff.*

Elsie: *LOL*

Elsie: *Not Stoner.*

Bran: *I know I'm a man but hell. I'm really confused.*

Elsie: *You were mean to yourself, Bran.*

Elsie: *You didn't let yourself come again.*

Elsie: *That's the consequence of being mean; that isn't the mean part.*

Elsie: *The mean part is that you can't say something good about yourself. I think it's because you really don't see it.*

Bran: *Pun intended? Yes or no.*

Elsie: **Palms forehead**

Elsie: *I'm sorry, poor wording choice.*

Elsie: *You're mean to yourself, Bran because you don't realize you're worth being good to.*

Bran: *Well, fuck. That got deep.*

Elsie: *Do you think I'm right?*

Bran: *Baby. I will never say you're wrong. You got my cock in a cage, and you have the key.*

Elsie: *LOL*

Elsie: *I don't want to be right because your most precious organ is in my hands. I don't care about being right, actually. I just want you to see it, so you can start seeing yourself how I see you.*
Bran: *With two eyes?*
Elsie: *The total package.*
Elsie: *Gotta get to work.*
Elsie: *Thanks for the morning text. I enjoyed talking.*
Elsie: *I'll text you tonight after work, okay?*
Bran: *You better. Have a good day.*

LYING on my back in the center of my bed, I drop my phone to my chest and grin like a fool at the ceiling above. Since we'd decided to start texting on the six days a week we didn't see one another, I've been a damn grinning idiot.

I expected a few texts here and there. What are you doing, how's it going, that type of stuff. I mean, I hoped it would graduate into more, but I was wrong. Bran jumped in full force, asking me about my favorite foods, if I like socks or bare feet, do I have seasonal allergies, what's my favorite color to wear, all sorts of things discovering my personality.

It's been so fucking great.

This morning, I woke up to a string of texts asking me to choose my favorite movie for every holiday of the year.

Getting to know Bran makes me feel like the rosy-cheeked heroine on a WB series. I can't stop smiling. I can't stop the effervescence brimming from me.

This isn't Goddess and Stray. It's Bran and Elsie. And I love it.

I just... I haven't mentioned my family. It's not because they don't mean the world to me and I don't love them with all my heart—they do, and I do. And it isn't because I'm embarrassed–I'm not.

It's just... Jake said I was a lot. And I know, as stupid as Jake is, that I am. *I am a lot.*

My mom and her dementia, an extremely active four-year-old, and *I* manage all of that. And work. It is a lot. I can't deny it.

Bran is working through his own shit. Helping him do it feels like summiting Everest. It feels like breaking the tape at the finish line of a race. I feel good, high, happy, and accomplished. Most of all, no matter what I'm doing–building him up, touching him, laughing with him–I always feel empowered. Strong. Good.

I don't want that to end.

And I know I should tell him more about me but... I don't know. As much as I like him–and *gah*, I really do–we've still only known each other for a few weeks. I'm still his Goddess, too, and though we now realize we stumbled into those roles haphazardly–we still have them. We've agreed; in fact, we still want to be those people one night a week.

I want to honor those roles, too. So I justify my choice to withhold those details of me, telling myself it's to keep things neat, keep things good and tidy, as they should be.

The worst lie you tell is the one you tell yourself.

I'm afraid that if I let him in, Bran will see me the way Jake did, and I can't face that. Not yet.

There, the truth.

It's bitter, so I swing my legs out of bed and stalk down the hall, looking to chase one bitter with another.

"Coffee?" I ask through a yawn, pressing the back of my wrist to my gaping mouth.

My mom is standing in the kitchen in her bathrobe, wiggling her fingers through Effie's messy curls. Holding her stuffed Ursula in her lap, she's sleepily watching the tv across two rooms. "We're out," she deadpans, eyes flicking to mine in faux-horror.

"Out?" I swallow. "Of coffee?"

Mom nods solemnly. "What could be worse, right?"

I don't have to be at work for another two hours, and my giddiness from the conversation with Bran is still flowing in my veins. "Quick breakfast at Flip's?"

Effie launches herself toward me, and I crouch to catch her.

"Yes! Yes! Yes, yes, yes!" she wails happily, writhing with excitement in my arms.

Flip's is short for Flip-Flapjack's, a breakfast place in town. It serves breakfast only, and it's open all day. The inviting atmosphere makes it pretty packed, and today I'm sure will be no exception. Effie loves Flip's because you get to write on the table, which is covered with disposable kraft paper, a bucket of markers, and crayons in the center. Understandably as a four-year-old that feels the need to tag everything more than a graffiti artist, it's her favorite part.

We spend the next fifteen minutes getting dressed to go. Actually, we spent four minutes putting on clothes and eleven minutes looking for one of Effie's *SpongeBob SquarePants* slide sandals which, believe it or not, was ultimately in the first place I told her to look. The back patio.

After too many games of Tic-Tac-Toe, a lot of practicing 3D cubes, and writing our own names, we order way too many pancakes. The other reason the restaurant is called Flip-Flapjack's is because their menu boasts an impressive seventeen different flapjack recipes.

Since Effie is four and everything is about chocolate, she selects chocolate chip flapjacks with whipped cream and, surprise-surprise, hot fudge on top. Breakfast of champs, I know. Mother of the year, I also know.

Mom gets whole wheat with flax, hemp hearts, and bananas, and I decide to try something new. There's a "hot cake" on the menu called "Henry Hot Cake," named after... *Henry Cavill*. It's got protein in it because clearly Henry is muscley and glorious. It's vanilla protein made with coconut flour, drizzled in a glaze. When our food is delivered, we inhale it. Mom and I probably drink an entire pot of coffee together, and when I have just a few minutes left before I need to go to work, I drop Effie and mom back at home, then head in.

A really, really good morning. With mom–her brain seems to be okay right now–and with Effie–who hasn't said "RIP Fuzz" in at least two days, which has been nice. With Bran, too. Guilt eats the pancakes in my gut because I know I should tell Bran about my life. I know I should give him more than "I hate three-quarters sleeves, and I think Taco Bell is amazing." The fear that I'd scare him off–even though I know if he scared off that easily he wouldn't be worth it– still chokes me. Keeps everything locked up tight inside of me.

* * *

Stray

THE NEXT FEW days are so, so good. Mom struggles a bit one day, but Fanny is there to keep her going, bringing over bingo cards and a DVD of the pre-recorded game.

Effie is Effie, my bubbly, beautiful, curious girl. We practice riding her bike (with training wheels), and she rides easily without falling for the first time. In pre-school, she writes her name almost legibly, and it hits me how fast she's growing up. She was just a newborn, and I was just a teen mom, and now we're here, hanging her hand-written crayon name up on the fridge.

The front desk at the gym is even pleasurable, too. I talk some new members into signing up for the Globo-Fitness Bootcamp with Lacey; Quinten and Cordelia come by again; I chat with Chris over a book he's reading, making sure he knows it's strictly friendly, and no one pukes in childcare. *Winning*.

Bran and I talk over text messages every free moment, and sometimes when we aren't even free. I'd kept my phone at my hip during movie night, not wanting mom or Effie to notice I was texting.

Though mom's condition hasn't changed, and I was still fighting to get her the scan she needs, things seem better lately. Easier to cope with and handle.

The power I feel from being the Goddess to the Stray– it's changing me. For the better.

And the idea of giving up the man who gave me that power is painful to think about.

So I don't.

27

Bran

Somehow, it doesn't feel like that's the truth.

Bran: Why was six afraid of seven?
    Elsie: Because seven eight nine.
Bran: Damn.
Elsie: Yeah, I was eight once too.
Bran: DAMN. Sizzlin' with those comebacks.
Elsie: *smirks*
Bran: Okay, I got one you won't know the answer to.
Elsie: Try me.
Bran: What's the best thing about Switzerland?
Elsie: Umm.
    Bran: No, don't Google it. You either know or you don't.

Elsie: Okay, I don't know the answer. I give up. What is the best thing about Switzerland?

Bran: I don't know.

Bran: But the flag is a big plus.

Bran: [IMAGE OF SWITZERLAND'S FLAG]

Elsie: OMG.

Elsie: I choked on my drink.

Elsie: That's funny.

Bran: I thought so, too.

Elsie: Where'd you hear that?

Bran: Didn't hear it. Read it.

Elsie: Where?

Bran: In a book of jokes.

Elsie: You have a book of jokes?

Bran: I got it for Christmas from my buddy. He's a joker and one year decided it was hard to bear the burden of being the group's funny guy, so he got us all joke books so we could be funny, too. To lighten his load.

Elsie: Is he hilarious?

Bran: He's an idiot, and we laugh at his idiocracy, which makes him believe he's legendary levels of funny.

Bran: The joke book is funny though

Bran: But I'd never admit it to his dumb ass

Elsie: Oh yeah? So you're telling me I know a secret?

Bran: Hmm.

Bran: I guess you do.

Bran: Does that mean I get to know a secret about you?

Elsie: Girl code says I don't tell secrets.

Bran: That code works on yourself?

Elsie: I'm going to make it work in this case.

Bran: I will of course, respect the girl code.

Bran: My sister would castrate me if I didn't protect and honor women in all facets of life, even when they're trying to keep secrets from me.

Elsie: I think it's cool that you're close with your sister.

Elsie: Hey, I gotta go; something came up. Talk again soon.

Bran: Talk again soon.

"Dude, look at yourself right now." Mally's voice sweeps over my shoulder, then his hands follow, gripping me. He shoves me to face the wall of mirrors in the lifting room at Paradise. From behind me, he pushes his fingertips into my cheeks, resting his chin on my shoulder.

"Look at this smile right now, bro. Seriously. Fucking adorable." I jerk away from his grandmotherly behavior and turn to face him. "Van," he calls to Van, who's re-racking dumbbells a few feet from us. "Look at how cute and happy Bran looks."

Van's heavy arm pump was taxing, evidence slipping down his temple in heavy beads of sweat. He glances at me before rolling his eyes at Mally.

"Leave him alone, Boo," Van quips, dipping his hands into a bucket of ground chalk. I grin because whenever Van breaks down Malibu's nickname to the last two letters, I always imagine it being the nickname a twenty-two-year -old gives her girlfriend. *Boo.*

My amusement is unnoticed because Malibu is out for blood. In the form of gossip, of course.

"It's going good, huh?"

"*It's going good, huh?*" Van mimics Mally's frat boy tone. "Leave him alone, man."

Malibu narrows his blue eyes at Van, folding his arms over his chest in a pout. "Fine, but if you were asking, I wouldn't stop you."

Van smacks his palms together, a cloud of chalk appearing like a magician about to pull a rabbit from a hat. "Do you hear yourself? It's not about what I can do versus what you can do. It's about recognizing that Bran isn't there yet, bro. He doesn't want to talk about it, not yet."

Mally turns to me, looking bruised but curious. Squeezing his shoulder, I nod.

"He's right, man. I don't want to talk about it yet, okay?"

Malibu flings his bulky arms down and stalks off, muttering under his breath how no one ever tells him anything. He may have missed the point, but at least he gave it a wide berth.

Van's eyes flick to me as he reaches for another set of dumbbells, the seventy-pounders. "I'm still teaching him. Don't forget; he's a latchkey kid who's also kind of an idiot."

"But a good cop," I add.

Van nods. "A good cop." He does exactly *two* reps before meeting my eyes again. "Not as good as The Bodfather, though."

"Of course not."

* * *

LATER THAT AFTERNOON, Sammy comes by my house. She had the day off and spent it, in her words, "without pants, watching murder shows, eating shit from a take-out box, and sleeping." It's not my idea of a fun day off, but Sammy seems satisfied, sliding onto my couch looking restful and sated.

"I heard you're zipping your lips about your girl," she says, twirling a piece of her long dark hair around her finger. She studies the ends that stick out and begins picking at them with her other hand.

I love my sister. She's arguably always been my very best friend. But I'm not ready to share about my girl with anyone. It feels like sharing would pop this fucking blissful bubble we're in. I slap my hand on her thigh and give it a squeeze. "I promise you, Sam, you'll be the first human diary I turn to when I'm ready to spill."

She rolls her eyes but grins. "I better be."

From my feet, I grab a canvas sack and hand it to her. "Now go get your cherries; I have plans tonight."

Her head twists, and her eyes widen. "Oh really?"

"Yes, really. And she's coming over here, so I want to vacuum and do some shit before then. And I still have to trim my beard," I pull a hand down my beard, then trace the elastic of my eyepatch. "And shower. I just need some time."

Sammy waves her hands in surrender. "Fine, I'll get my cherries and go. Geez."

When she's at the sliding door, ready to ravage my backyard fruit tree, she stops and turns to me. "See, though, do you see? It's not you. It's always been them. It's what we've been trying to tell you."

I nod, blinking back the warmth behind my eye. "I know," I say, and for the first fucking time, *I actually believe it.*

Before, I always figured they were trying to make me feel good because they love me. It's like when an ugly person asks how they look; you don't tell them you look ugly; you think that they look great because that's the kind thing to do. I thought I was their kind thing to do.

But I believe it now. Because Elsie doesn't seem to give a fuck about my eye. When she's my Goddess, she doesn't let me come if I don't see my worth. That's... fuck.

I raise a palm and wave her off. "Alright, go pick your cherries and hit the road." I love my sister, but equally, it's time for her to get the fuck out. I watch as Stoner trails after her, his black fur soaking up all the remnants of the sun. An hour later, she's gone, and I start to prepare for the session with my Goddess.

* * *

WITH MY GOOD eye sealed over the peephole on my front door, my dick thrums at the silver swish of the trench coat in the fisheye lens. I pull open the door right as she makes her way up the steps.

"Hi," I greet her, my heart a goddamn stampede. I've never even had a horse gallop heartbeat over a girl, and now she's trampling me. And I fucking love it.

"Hi," she smiles, and I love how slowly she lets her eyes creep over my body, taking in as much as she can. Her blues follow the edges of my ink, explore the carved ridges of my muscles, and end up on my crotch for a hot second before coming to my face.

"Hi again," I greet, teasing.

"Hello," she says, dragging out the last letter playfully. "You are a handsome, delicious man, do you know that?"

I shake my head, feeling flush eat up my cheeks like a

schoolgirl, and turn so she can't see it, pulling the door open. "Get in here, baby."

Baby. It's not the first time I've used that term for her. Over text, I've dropped it a few times. She's never pointed it out or asked me to stop. But this is the first time I've said it in person. She stills with one foot in, her cerulean eyes wide and piercing.

Oh no. She looks... almost shocked? Is it not appropriate in person? Does it not feel natural to her? Because it feels natural to me. It feels right. It would feel better to whisper it over her shoulder in the morning with my arm around her waist, my hand between her thighs. But this feels like the steps to getting there. Unless... I'm off base.

But I don't have the guts to ask, and she recovers with a smile, leaving me curious about that entire interaction. I shift gears immediately, though, because Elsie trails down the hall, stopping to give Stoner a few behind-the-ear scratches, then walks straight into my bedroom.

Her trench coat has my mind racing. My mouth is watering. Last week, she had on a leather strappy fucking thing that made me writhe. This week?

After closing the door behind me, I turn to face her, stuffing my hands in the pockets of my joggers. I recently learned from Elsie that women love gray sweats. It's like their safe-for-work porn. It just so happens that between depression and owning a gym, I also don't own anything but sweats. She didn't touch on the bit about depression but said instead that they were hot on me.

"I like your hair." It's down, back to being curly and full. "You look gorgeous." Pretty didn't feel like it hit. Beautiful wasn't big enough. Gorgeous won out.

She smirks a little. "Thank you, Stray." The powerful enunciation of the S is a subtle reminder that she isn't here to be Elsie. She's here to be my Goddess. Which reminds me, we have a few housekeeping things to take care of if we're Goddess and Stray.

"Listen, before we get started, I have to bring something up." I rake a big palm up the back of my neck and down over my head, pulling at the ends of my hair as I do. "You said not to pay you anymore. But... even though we're like, getting to know each other outside of this, I feel like if I'm taking you from your life a couple of hours a week, you're coming here with this stuff... I should compensate you."

Worried that this, like the comment about being paid to tell me things I want to hear, could create a divide, I step closer, nervous.

But Elsie is unphased. Her lips form a disapproving frown. "No." Then she tugs at the belt around her trench, unknotting it. Her coat opens like clouds parting to reveal the sun. "Now get naked and sit on the bed."

Well, that's that.

Once on the bed, she sheds the coat in front of me. Holy shit.

Red lace and straps, a garter belt hooked to fishnet thigh highs. She looks like something out of *Pretty Woman*, and I mean that in a mouth-watering way. The silver barbells in her nipples poke through the cherry-red lace. Her belly is exposed, and I love that she carries just the tiniest bit of softness low on her belly.

Fuck, is there anything about her that I don't like? That doesn't make me hard?

Then I think, if she were to be an influencer, I'd have a

problem with that. Women live lives just for Instagram photos, sucking in, sticking out a leg, and making everyone miserable until getting the right shot. Selling things to people who can't afford them, peddling a lifestyle that doesn't exist.

Yeah, that's one thing I couldn't get past.

"Goddess. What do you do?"

She toes out of her black patent heels, and I notice when she does, the undersides are red, like her lingerie. Fuck, how is the bottom of a shoe making me hard(er)? I've got it bad.

Dropping her bag on the edge of the mattress out of arm's reach and eye's view from me, she digs inside, clearly looking for something. I watch the key to my cage dangle from her milky white, velvety neck, and I reach between my legs, giving my balls a short tug. I need some fucking relief, even if it's pseudo like that just was.

Finally, she finds what she's looking for.

"What do you mean?" she asks, positioning herself between my legs. This has become a familiar position to us, and I like it. I get the full fucking view. I mean, I'd obviously rather be looking up at her tits while she writhes on my tongue, but one-eyed beggars know better than to be choosers.

"What do you do for your day job?"

She tosses me something shiny and metal, and I reach out to catch it before it lands on my chest.

"Cuff up," she says when I open my fingers to reveal the handcuffs I'd already worn. *"Baby."*

My eye jerks to her, where I find a tender expression battling for control of her stoic face. She looks back down to her bag, then from it, pulls out lube and that little vibrating wand she used last week.

I glare at the wand since it was the last thing to tease me before I was caged.

"How about this?" She leans over my thigh, lowering the bag to the floor. I slip the cuffs on, and she reaches forward to tighten them. I don't need her to, but it's cute as fuck. She lightly knees my sac as does it.

Swiping her finger over the opening of my cage, she holds it up as if she were checking the weather. When I look, she smears the finger over my groin, leaving precome in its wake.

"Already a greedy boy." She squirts the lube into her palm, letting the bottle drop to the mattress after she clicks it shut. "That's why I'm going to make you earn the answer to your question."

She grips my kneecaps, the dark hair greasy from the lube on her hands. Even that feels good. "Knees up."

Vulnerable, I pull my knees up, exposing everything to her. Man, is this how women feel during sex? Because I do feel pretty open and exposed.

"You get ten questions. All to help you answer your first question."

"So like, twenty questions, the game, only ten instead?"

She nods.

"I think I should get the same amount of questions."

She slides her fingers under my sac, dragging her nails up the bumpy seam, smoothing the pads of them over my taint. "You won't last that long, answer or not."

I swallow thickly. "No?"

Here we go. Back to *dick feel so good, me no talk good* mode.

I gasp slightly when her fingers circle my ass, hips lifting from the bed in reaction. "No. No to the question of if you will last more than ten questions and no to you lifting off the mattress." She smoothes her hand up my groin, tracing the ribs of my chastity cage.

Settling between me, she continues. "Have you ever played the hot and cold game?"

"The kid one? Like, close is hot, far is cold?"

She nods, honey gold curls wild as she shakes her head to fall behind her shoulders.

"Yeah."

Lifting the wand in the air, she smiles at me. Everything inside of me is molten, and despite the raw heat roaring inside me like fire, my nipples harden as if I'm cold. With her other finger at my ass, she pushes a tip in, reminding me to stay put.

"The warmer you are with your questions, the deeper this goes."

"Warm is supposed to be getting close; warm is the good one," I stumble, staring at the vibrator that looks at least a foot long. Maybe it's two feet. Fuck. Is this what women go through when they see big dicks like mine?

For a moment, the Goddess pauses; I think becoming Elsie. "It's six inches, and likely only four will go inside you."

"Four?!" I jerk my head up, and she laughs.

"If you're good at the game."

I let my head fall back. I've never stuck anything up my ass. But I'm not against it. I really am not against doing or trying anything when it comes to her. I need crackers to go with that cheese, I know, but it's true.

I don't waste any of the limited time we have by arguing or asking questions. She's usually only here an hour, not

Stray

much more. I hand over my trust to make the most of the time, our time together too.

The toy fires up and wiggles against my ass.

"Ask, Stray."

I close my eye, so I don't have to stare at my white ceiling or be enticed to look down and watch the show. If I see her down there, well, I don't feel good about my lasting time. Let's just say that.

"Do you work from home?"

The wand moves in slightly, barely breaching my opening, introducing me to a slight burn. I can take it. "No," she says after.

I swallow, wiggling in the cuffs to take pressure off the spot they'd been resting on. "Do you work here in town?"

My thighs fall apart despite the fact that my ass is clenching. Retracting it, she smoothes the blunt capped head of the toy around the puckered skin of my hole, then slides it in again. My ass takes it much better. "Yes," she answers.

The vibrator sends intermittent ripples of uncured pleasure through my cock and balls, down my thighs, too. I stay focused, knowing that she probably really won't tell me what her day job is if I don't win this game. And goddamnit, I like that about her, too.

This town is smallish. We have restaurants, churches, one department store, a grocery store, a couple of gyms, and a movie theater, though to be fair, I don't even know if that's open anymore. Eliminating the movie theater and churches because, well, *come on*, I'm left still unsure.

"Does it involve food in any capacity, whether it's selling or preparing?" It feels like a cheat because it's two questions that potentially widdle away the grocery store and restaurant idea.

Surprisingly, I'm happy *and* irritated when she jerks back on the wand, hollowing me. The lubed broad end of the toy is back to teasing my hole. "No," she says, sounding as frustrated as my cock feels.

Thinking I'm being funny because she knows what I do, I smirk from under my closed eye. "You work anywhere related to health and fitness?" I expect her to smack my balls, which by the way, I'm beginning to like, but instead, the pressure between my cheeks builds as she thrusts the wand deeper into my ass. Deeper than it was last time. So deep. I groan, and I know I'm leaking right now because... holy shit, this fucking feels phenomenal. It feels like my entire groin is in the back of her throat, and she's gargling me. All of me.

"Fu-uck, that's good."

"Yes," she answers. "You're hot. So hot, Bra–*Stray*."

Goosebumps rise up on my arms, and my groin coils tight, my cock weeping. My chest thumps at her words. She was going to call me Bran. Hot is part of the game, I tell myself.

I want more of that fucking wand, more of Elsie and her life, so I go for broke, hoping I'm right.

"F-Fitness? You, you work in fitness?" I pant out, my knees pulling up slightly. God, I'm five seconds from bearing down on this like a woman on Jon Hamm's lap. She is making me someone I don't recognize. I'm becoming someone I don't recognize. I fucking love it. It's what I needed.

"Oh fuck. *Ohfuckohfuckohfuck*." I'm groaning and writhing, her answer "yes" a soundtrack to my quickly building and on-the-way orgasm. The wand explores and kneads parts of me I honestly had no fucking clue existed. Again, no ass play. Not until now.

Spinning it slowly, the sinful burning is gone, only an untouchable pressure and pleasure deep inside of me now. My cock struggles to grow beneath the cage, pounding with the need to thicken, grow fat and long, and fuck her silly. Her hand connects with my bare, lubed-coated ass, and I know then that the wand is deep inside me. I can feel it deep, too, pressing against something achy and tender.

"Fuck, baby, fuck, *fuck*."

"Ask another question." The smokey, seductive tone is back. Lord help me.

"Gym," I spit out, "you work at a gym." I don't know if it's a question or a statement. Sweat beads along the curve of my upper lip. On top of our chaotic meeting, she works in a gym of all things? *What the...* my head gets dizzy from the irony of this information. Another fate flag is waving in front of my face. Thank God I still have one eye to see it.

She spins the wand as she tilts it, the end of it putting pressure directly on the most sensitive spot inside me. Then the wand really begins humming, my ass vibrating as she turns the intensity up.

"Yes." She says, her voice torn open for me to pick through. She wanted to call me Bran. She works at a gym. I *own* a fucking gym.

"*Ohmygod.*" I can't control my thoughts. They bounce around my brain, never sticking. Inside the cage, my dick weeps to get hard. "*Fuckfuckfuck!*" I chant because something is happening, everything is going white-hot, my working eye temporarily clouds, and my toes roll into the bottoms of my feet. "Oh, oh, *oh*," I groan so fucking loud that I hear Stoner give a single protective bark from outside the bedroom door.

Then it happens. I'd say again–she made me come hands-free last time. But this time isn't exactly the same thing. Being ruined and coming is a whole lot different than having a vibrator cranked up your ass and *blowing*.

But that's what I do because it feels so good, and she's here. She's with me. We're together in this thing.

Like having your finger over the end of a hose, my hip-thrusting jostles the metal cage, and as come pulses from my slit in rhythmic waves, it goes everywhere.

On my chest.

On the bed.

Back onto her forearms.

When I've essentially painted a three-foot perimeter around us and am sensitive and spent, she slips the toy out of me. Quickly, she scrambles over my leg and off the bed, coming up to where my arms are behind my head. She unlocks the cuffs, smoothing her fingers over the red, sensitive skin. The same way I touched under her body harness.

She only does it for a moment, turning away from me to drop the stuff back into her bag. But it's not about how long she does it. It's that she wanted to touch me. She found a reason to touch me. And not my cock. Tender, fucking sweet touches.

I may have been one-night-standing it for years, but I've seen *The Notebook*. I've read Julia Quinn novels–Sammy tricked me, I'd like to say.

Those are tender touches, and I won't talk myself out of

it like I have talked myself out of everything since the night of the accident.

I know it's real when I feel it.

She goes to my bathroom, and I sit up in my bed, resting my back against pillows propped up on my headboard. When she returns, she has a warm towel. The mattress barely dips as she sits next to me, the red lace grazing my thigh. Slowly, eyes on her own hands, she cleans me up.

It's quiet. It's slow. It's soft. Unspoken words hang between us like gray storm clouds full of rain. We're falling into each other quickly, and from the way she won't meet my eyes, I'm pretty sure she doesn't want to talk about it.

"Are you a trainer? At the gym you work at?"

Her eyes flick to my face for a split second before she begins to wipe the sheets next to me. "No." She resumes her serious come cleaning.

"What do you do at the gym you work at?"

"Don't," she says, and immediately her face has changed. Stonelike, impassive, like nothing I can say now will matter.

I don't understand. "We talk about this kind of stuff over text. Our real lives."

"Don't, okay. Please?"

My brow dips. "I own a gym, Elsie. If you don't like where you work or don't like what you do there, you can work for me. With me. Do whatever the fuck you want." I mean that. I want that, in fact. "I mean hell; it's the reason we met in the first place. I was looking to hire someone."

Jerking off the bed, she tosses the towel in the hamper and picks up her coat. Fuck, this isn't good. I stand up, pulling on my sweats so I can walk her out. My body is sticky with remnants of dried come and lube, but I'd walk out in public looking like the inside of a grade schooler's sock if it meant figuring out Elsie.

Shoving her arms into her coat, she doesn't bother cinching it or buttoning it. It swings open, giving me sexy peeks at that fucking hot body of her in that red lace. She swings her bag over her shoulder and pulls open my bedroom door, stopping, just like last time.

"I don't work at a gym because I love fitness, Bran, okay? I do it because they offered insurance that didn't turn away pre-existing conditions."

The same as before, she walks out. I trail after her, and so does Stoner. She turns once on the porch and gives me a partial smile, and it feels forced. "Talk to you later."

"Drive safe, Elsie." I follow her down, off the porch, partially to her car. "I'm sorry," I say, having no idea why I'm apologizing, but it feels absolutely vital that I do. We were having a good time. She was the most perfect Goddess ever.

"Bye."

That's all I get. She doesn't even meet my eye. Just tosses the bag into the passenger seat, red lingerie still visible from her open coat, and drives into the night.

Well, fuck. I scratch my head. That happened fast.

My gut twists. Pre-existing conditions? I send her a text.

Bran: *Pre-existing conditions? Elsie, are you okay?*

Elsie: *I'm fine.*

Somehow, it doesn't feel like that's the truth.

28

Elsie

I'm choosing to ignore the flashing "TOO LATE" sign in my brain.

"Pop in here for a minute," Lacey says from the hallway, bracing herself in her doorway. I nod, turning to Chris.

"Cover me for a couple of minutes?"

He looks up from his split open book, nodding. "Sure."

I nod to a few clients as I round the entry desk. Once I'm at the end of the hall, I knock on Lacey's door, unsure if she's still alone.

"Come in," she says when she sees me peeking around the corner. "Close the door."

I do, and I don't want to talk about what I'm almost ninety-nine percent sure she wants to talk about: Bran. How it's going with our sessions and how we're doing with one another. The other night was... weird.

He asked about my job—I honestly didn't think he'd guess it. Like, what the fuck? And I even gave him fewer questions, less opportunity! His kind and receptive response to knowing I work in a gym was to offer me a job. With me, he'd even clarified.

He's so sweet. I fucking like him so much. I love how he toggles from playful to tender so easily. But he likes me back.

Yes, it's a BUT. Because he's growing, accepting himself. I can't come barreling in with my collective early-onset dementia, four-year-old who kills fish, and, in a couple of years, a quickly growing pile of medical bills I'm destined to face once mom needs round-the-clock treatment.

He's on the cusp of being free from his self-doubt. I want better for him than all my bullshit.

I need to get through it on my own, anyway. Mom raised me on her own; I can take care of her. I can and will do this, and I'm proud to, but I won't make someone else give up their freedom with me.

"How's it going with your guy?" She pops her gum, and why is that so annoying? The noise wiggles under my skin, burrowing it right in my FUCKING QUIT center. I rub my temples. Effie had a nightmare last night.

She said she was scared someone would break in, and grandma and I couldn't protect her. I'm pretty sure it was a ruse to ask for another pet. I'm tired; I don't want to face the inquisition right now.

"I can't talk about this right now, Lace, honestly." I fall into the chair across from her desk, and she sits on its arm, peering down at me.

Stray

"Why not?" Pop. Smack.

Fuck it. I don't have the energy to be coy. Through a yawn, I tell her a simple version of the truth. "I messed up. Caught feelings. He did, too, I think. But I'm worried my life is too complicated."

"Do you still feel powerful when you're his Dominant? Is that aspect still working?"

I nod. "I do. And it really, honestly feels like there's more there, too." I feel like the Dominant and Submissive roles are the gorgeous flower of our story, soaking up the sun and tangling in the breeze. But there's more to us. Stem. Roots. I just don't want him to get stuck with my thorns.

"So?"

I narrow my eyes and prod at her, trying to poke holes in her singular response. "So? Aren't you the one who said not to do this exact thing I'm doing?"

Pop. Pop. Smack. She shrugs. "Yeah, but you already did. And he's fucking hot as shit. If you guys have a connection, why the hell wouldn't you go for it?"

I blink. Well shit. In under thirty seconds, Lacey the Mistress just poked holes in my entire reasoning.

"You know my mom has early-onset dementia. We have a lot of complications, and bad days. It's stressful, and it's only getting worse. Not to mention the medical costs that are coming, in prescriptions and visits and long-term care." I swallow; the way my life sounds makes my eyes warm, but not sentimentally.

"And Effie. I have Effie. I'm raising a human being. I can't just like... wear a bikini on a boat and sleepover for funsies." I stand up, feeling flustered and overwhelmed by hearing about my own life. Holy shit. "I'm a grown-up."

"We all are. You know what being a grown-up is about? Taking risks when the benefit will be great." She smiles at me like I'm a moron. Maybe I am. "Sounds like the risk of overwhelming him with general life items is worth the two of you ending up together."

"General life items?"

"I'm not trying to downplay your shit, Els. But everyone has their shit." On my lead, we walk toward the office door because I told Chris just a few minutes. "My dad is in prison. I want to have a baby, but I can't, and my RA is a bitch. I don't talk to my mom, and I'm two classes shy of having a bachelor's degree." She pulls open the door, passing me a final *'figure it out, you moron'* smile. "See? We all have things."

* * *

THE REST of my shift at Globo is spent in a daze, staring at the cover art of Chris's book while he reads. It's slow, Thursday's are usually slow because the Friday mentality means letting yourself off the hook for absolutely arbitrary reasons under the guise you've earned it simply by existing and performing your minimal obligations. It starts a day early.

Once I'm home, Effie practically mauls me on her first stop in the "I Want a Dog" tour. She follows me to my bedroom, sits on the toilet while I shower, and even sits on the counter while I cook, begging. Using the argument that because she can now climb onto the counter on her own, she can take care of a dog, *she begs.* She promises things she's incapable of, she resorts to crying, and finally, two hours after I've been home, she gets mad.

Stray

"But I said I'll take care of it!" She slams her foot down, hand on hip. Her curls are in a bun because she painted at preschool today. She's adorable, even when she's a turd.

"No dog, Ef. We have enough to handle here already." She doesn't know I'm managing grandma day-to-day, working, raising her, and trying to find some sliver of self in it all. To her, it is a dog, and she wants one.

"That's not fair! Fanny said we have a good yard for a dog!"

"Effie girl, Fanny doesn't live here. She doesn't have to take care of the dog. I do. Okay? And I don't have time. I really don't."

She slides from the counter and stomps off. "Not fair. Not fair. Not fair."

I slide the lid on my pressure cooker and set the dial. "Dinner in twenty," I call to my mom, who so carefully managed to ignore the entire dog conversation from her spot on the recliner, some reality show littering the TV screen.

"Alrighty," she calls, sounding actually oblivious. I talked to her twice while at work, Fanny once, too. She isn't having a bad day, but by the time five and six o'clock rolls around, she does grow a bit... fuzzy.

I head to Effie's room and take a seat on her bed, where she is dramatically face down, her little legs flailing.

"Grandma sometimes forgets things, you know?"

She sits up, not expecting this conversation. Even though she's four, kids are fucking smart. Acutely aware of things we swear they're oblivious to. She faces me, the tip of her nose like a cherry.

Bran's handsome smile floods my mind, the tingle of his

beard against my skin, the smell of his sweat and his bedsheets.

"Yeah." She rubs a curled knuckle to her eye. "Sometimes she can't remember good."

I nod. "That's right. So mama has to help her remember things, like taking her medicine and stuff. And even though you don't see me doing a lot of things like that, when you're not around, mama is doing a lot to make sure grandma is okay. That she doesn't forget something important and get lost or hurt. You know?"

She nods. "Okay."

"But one day, I promise, we will get a dog, okay? Until then, can we be happy anyway?"

She blinks. "Yeah."

I kiss her forehead. "Thank you, Ef. I love you."

"Love you too, mama."

She jumps down and bolts to the corner of her room housing too many Barbies and drops to her knees, immediately over her meltdown. I wish it were that easy for adults.

I sneak to my room after checking my pressure cooker to make sure I still have time.

When I take out my phone, I have a text from Bran waiting. My chest gets tight, my heart fluttering excitedly. But for what? Lacey could be right, but I really care about Bran. And while "everyone has their stuff" works in theory, actually dumping said stuff on someone else? Not quite as simple.

Bran: *Can you tell me more about what you said to me?*

We've been texting all week, close to normal, the elephant in the text being the fact that I wouldn't elaborate on my need for Globo's medical insurance. I waste no time texting back, seeing how the message has sat unread for two hours already.

Elsie: *I'm happy to get to know you, and you me. But I can't get into some details, okay?*

Bran: *Can't or won't?*

Elsie: *I don't know.*

Bran: *Why?*

Elsie: *Can you drop it? We can't keep going if you can't drop it. Seriously. I like you, but I don't want to talk about some things, okay?*

Lacey apparently had one thing wrong. She said those men that hired mistresses and dominants did so because they had a deep-rooted, fatal flaw, a void to fill, a mommy issue to unpack. But now I'm the elusive, miserable clamshell–an unexpected twist.

Bran: *I don't want to lose you, so okay.*

Elsie: [GIF OF SEAGULLS IN FINDING NEMO SAYING "MINE, MINE, MINE"]

After I send it, I realize it was a stupid choice. I just got through planning out how I couldn't be his, how we couldn't be real. Holding down the message to unsend, I realize there is no unsend. The rippling dots of an incoming message appear, and then his response is there in blue.

Bran: *God, I love that movie. Can't wait to have a kid one day and show them.*

Oh, Jesus. Nothing has ever made me want to puke more than the wave of guilt washing over me reading that.

That sentence is another reminder that I'm no good for him. I'm not telling him about a HUGE part of my life.

HUGE.

And I'm beginning to think my own twisted, backward, protective logic is... well, stupid.

If the roles were reversed, I wouldn't have been hurt at first. Because we were Dominant and Submissive, nothing more.

But the night I agreed to talk to him, to build something around our arrangement–I should've told him. I should've. But I was scared. I didn't know where this was going, and honestly, I just wanted happiness. I didn't want to pull my complications into a world where all I knew was power and pleasure.

I'm still scared of so much.

It's too late now. We've gotten to know one another. I didn't *fall* for him, and I'm not currently *falling* for him. I'm waving from the bottom of the fucking Bran Edwards well. Hi everybody, I'm down here, I fell down here that first night, I think.

Elsie: *Gotta have dinner. See you tonight.*

Bran: **winds clock forward**

Elsie: *See you soon.*

I close my phone, tears of guilt sprouting from my eyes. I should have just told him. I should have. Now I'm just an asshole.

But that only seals me to my fate. I cannot drag him into this hard, emotional journey ahead. There's no point in prolonging this thing if it can never be more, and it's best to end it before we're both supremely attached.

I'm choosing to ignore the flashing "TOO LATE" sign in my brain.

texting back, seeing how the message has sat unread for two hours already.

Elsie: *I'm happy to get to know you, and you me. But I can't get into some details, okay?*

Bran: *Can't or won't?*

Elsie: *I don't know.*

Bran: *Why?*

Elsie: *Can you drop it? We can't keep going if you can't drop it. Seriously. I like you, but I don't want to talk about some things, okay?*

Lacey apparently had one thing wrong. She said those men that hired mistresses and dominants did so because they had a deep-rooted, fatal flaw, a void to fill, a mommy issue to unpack. But now I'm the elusive, miserable clamshell–an unexpected twist.

Bran: *I don't want to lose you, so okay.*

Elsie: [GIF OF SEAGULLS IN FINDING NEMO SAYING "MINE, MINE, MINE"]

After I send it, I realize it was a stupid choice. I just got through planning out how I couldn't be his, how we couldn't be real. Holding down the message to unsend, I realize there is no unsend. The rippling dots of an incoming message appear, and then his response is there in blue.

Bran: *God, I love that movie. Can't wait to have a kid one day and show them.*

Oh, Jesus. Nothing has ever made me want to puke more than the wave of guilt washing over me reading that.

That sentence is another reminder that I'm no good for him. I'm not telling him about a HUGE part of my life.

HUGE.

And I'm beginning to think my own twisted, backward, protective logic is... well, stupid.

If the roles were reversed, I wouldn't have been hurt at first. Because we were Dominant and Submissive, nothing more.

But the night I agreed to talk to him, to build something around our arrangement–I should've told him. I should've. But I was scared. I didn't know where this was going, and honestly, I just wanted happiness. I didn't want to pull my complications into a world where all I knew was power and pleasure.

I'm still scared of so much.

It's too late now. We've gotten to know one another. I didn't *fall* for him, and I'm not currently *falling* for him. I'm waving from the bottom of the fucking Bran Edwards well. Hi everybody, I'm down here, I fell down here that first night, I think.

Elsie: *Gotta have dinner. See you tonight.*

Bran: **winds clock forward**

Elsie: *See you soon.*

I close my phone, tears of guilt sprouting from my eyes. I should have just told him. I should have. Now I'm just an asshole.

But that only seals me to my fate. I cannot drag him into this hard, emotional journey ahead. There's no point in prolonging this thing if it can never be more, and it's best to end it before we're both supremely attached.

I'm choosing to ignore the flashing "TOO LATE" sign in my brain.

Stray

I'll have to end it. It's what makes the most sense. And after tonight, I will.

29

Bran

That's it. Next time we meet, I'm going for it. I'm asking her to be mine.

I'm on my way to Paradise, happy as a goddamn clam when police lights glare in my rearview. Veering to the side of the road, I shift to park and wait.

I wasn't speeding; I didn't roll a stop.

What I did do, however, was ignore several text messages in our group thread. Not because I was trying to be a dick or anything but hell, I've been thinking about Elsie so much lately.

Mally rolls up on the passenger side of my truck, eyebrows to heaven, hands on his hips. I peer back into my side mirror but don't see Van. He slides into the seat without my permission.

"Don't look for Van. He's not here. And he's not the one you're ignoring." Mally folds his arms over his uniform and vested chest. "Rude."

Adjusting my eye patch, I roll my good eye and sigh. "I'm trying to figure shit out, man. I'm not trying to ignore you."

He studies me skeptically, his blonde hair lifting with the breeze of his open door. "Fine," he finally decides. "But if I talk to Sammy and find out you're withholding from me?" He blows out an ominous whistle. "I'm gonna kick your ass."

I pat his shoulder and give him a nudge out of the cab. "Right. Got it."

He slides his aviators on and leaves, and I'm left wondering how many hours of body cam footage Mally must have to explain to the Chief. And... still, I'm thinking about Elsie. That wasn't a lie. I've been totally fucking preoccupied.

I don't like that for some reason, she won't share with me. Maybe she can't? I don't know. And really, that's what makes me pace my hallway, clenching a stress ball like it will shit out the answers if I grip it hard enough.

I don't know.

The unknown is exciting if you're eighteen with a hard-on for life and a penchant for excitement. The unknown at age thirty? Irritable bowel and lack of sleep–that's what you get for it.

I fell for this girl.

I'm okay with that. It's not the fall that kills you; it's the abrupt stop at the end. Now that's what I'm not okay with—falling, after everything I've been through–falling so far down for so long, then *crashing*. Turning into a million, smashed, fragile, unrepairable pieces and being so far down, no one can fix me. Not even myself.

I want to think I know Elsie. And I want to know she won't hurt me.

But that goddamn unknown. What pre-existing condition does she have? She said it wasn't her in question, but who the hell else could it be? She works at Globo-Fitness, which sent me for a fucking ride when she told me that. She said in her real life, she often felt powerless. Is she sick? Is she struggling with something?

I need to know. Because I want to be with her, help her through whatever the fuck it is that's happening.

She's given me things I'm embarrassed to admit I needed.

Confidence.

Should I have let my eye turn me into a self-conscious recluse for so long? Should I have let all those one-night stands and bad dates sour me to love? No. And I hate that as a grown-ass man, I needed someone to show me that. But I did.

My bros and Sammy had been trying to show me that for years. But having Elsie–beautiful, smart, funny, intoxicating Elsie–see me for *me*, see the good before the bad... like I said, I Grinched out. My heart grew. And as it grew, she became a part of it.

Her existence in my life is crucial to my beating heart, as much as my aorta, as much as the valves and arteries. She keeps my blood moving; she keeps my heart pumping happily... She gives me a reason to see the future.

I know our last meeting wasn't fucking unicorns and rainbows and that she got irritated with me for pushing her.

The thing is, she shares so much with me in our texts. I feel like I've known her for half of my life. To shut down on one specific topic... something's not right. I think I know her well enough to know she isn't keeping me from it to hurt me.

She'd never hurt me...

She's keeping it from me to protect something or someone, maybe even herself. And I know the only way she'll let me in is if we're real—*a couple*. Eat meals together, grocery shop, sleepover.

If we end our Dominant/Submissive relationship, she can still be my Goddess. Hell, she'll always be my Goddess now. No matter what. But we can transition to *more*.

I want more. For the first time in a long time, I need more.

And I think she does, too. So I guess it's time to take a risk and tell her exactly what I want.

Time to make her mine for real.

But as self-aware as I am now that I've had my balls slapped and my orgasm ruined, and I'm officially more addicted to her than before—the old Bran is still inside me, too. I'm a little... nervous. So I do what I always do.

I call Sammy.

"Yo," she answers, loud clanking in the background. "What's up?"

I stretch my legs over my desk at Paradise, my office having just been completed a few days ago. It feels good to have it done, but I have to admit, I hate that I can't see or feel my first meeting with Elsie here anymore. The room is too different.

Then again, my dick is locked up, so maybe it's best that

memory isn't prancing in front of me, giving me a hard-on. After all, I am on the phone with my sister.

"Hey, you working?"

She snorts but then shouts away from the receiver to some poor soul nearby. "That's mine, thank you very much." She huffs loudly, returning her focus to me. "Some people are so rude. I swear."

"You working?" I ask again because she sounds distracted.

"When am I not, Bran?"

"On your days off," I deadpan.

"Har, har. What's up?"

"Can you talk?"

Beeping and paper tearing sounds off on her side of the call, and then I realize she's in the cafeteria. "Sorry, just getting some food," she confirms. "You talk while I eat."

"What are you eating?" I ask, partially because she wants me to keep her accountable and on track now that she's been lifting at Paradise. And partially because I'm hungry as fuck and just want to know. And maybe part of it is nerves... building the courage to say this to her.

"Clam chowder."

I wince. Clam chowder from a hospital cafeteria sounds like food poisoning in the making, but I never tell my sister shit like that. I know better, or rather, *she does*.

"Now talk."

My feet fall from the desk with a thud as I sit up straight in my chair. Smoothing my hand through my hair, then down my beard, I launch into it.

"I want to ask the girl I'm seeing to be serious. To like, really be my girl. But the last time we were together, she mentioned something about her life that concerned me but then closed down. Couldn't tell me more."

"Mmm," she grunts acknowledgment through a mouth of chowder.

"And I don't know if she doesn't want to tell me because she's protecting someone or something..." I scratch at the side of my jaw, choosing the right words to sound honest without sounding like a little bitch. "Or if she doesn't want to share any of the really gritty shit because she just doesn't want what I want. I mean, I know she likes me, Sam. I may not be fucking churning through relationships, but I know she likes me. There are these moments where I think she really fucking likes me too..." the sentence dies mid-air as Sammy sucks down a drink of something—probably diet soda—and her swallows come loud through the receiver. But it buys me time.

Time to remember how my Submissive name went forgotten, how in the throes of our intense and passionate session–she'd called me Bran. That meant something because she takes the role of Dominant very fucking seriously.

God, I liked that, too.

"Listen," she says against the light clink of a spork being dropped. "I don't know this girl. I don't know what's going on in her life because, like I said, I don't know her. But I'm a woman. Let me tell you when I shut down."

"Okay," I say, straightening even further in my chair because posture helps me focus.

"One, when I'm really, really hurt. Like someone said some mean ass shit that I can't recover from right away." She takes another drink, and I wait. "Or something so painful happened that it'll take me some time to get on my feet. In those situations, the wall comes up because I'm raw from the hurt."

I scratch at the side of my jaw, considering her words. "I don't think Elsie's hurt. I mean, I don't know. What are the other reasons?"

"Okay, the next reason I will ice you out is fear, and I'd say this is probably responsible for eighty-five percent of my ice-outs." She gulps more soda. "If I'm scared of losing something good–a job promotion, the good vibe between a guy and me, the last maple bacon donut at the shop–I'm a clam. Instantly. Because I don't want to talk about my fears because then they're too real. I don't like feeling scared and vulnerable."

"That sounds like the likely culprit. I can feel her hesitation, you know? And it sounds like there is some sort of fairly serious stress in her life. I just don't know what."

"Fear and stress go hand in hand." She gulps again, then, like the lady she is, belches. "I think you should talk to her about everything."

"Obviously I will... I want to ask her for more, and I guess I was just looking for a thumbs up or thumbs down."

"Brian, I will never red-light you. If you feel something for this girl, you're an absolute fucking moron if you let being scared hold you back. No offense, but it's held you back for so long already that it's already kind of cringe."

"Gee, thanks. What a way to build my confidence before I ask this girl to be my serious fucking girlfriend and then ask her to bare her soul to me." I shake my head and roll my eye.

"Tough love works better than that mushy crap," she

adds, adding another belch, too. "You need the pain. The pain will make you do the right thing."

Pricks of heat rise on the back of my neck. My sister would undoubtedly vomit up her clam chowder if she knew just how fucking right she was. Because I do need the pain. I like the pain Elsie gives me it makes the pleasure immeasurably good.

"Thanks," I say, appreciative of her even though she's moderately rude and has bad manners. "Love ya, kid. Talk soon."

"Good luck. And hey, remember, even though you're my brother and your sexual existence is repulsive to me, you know any woman would be fucking stupid and backward not to want you. Okay?"

"Yeah, yeah," I say, waving off the sentiment, not letting her know the way her words drop heat and hope into my chest. "Have a good shift. Don't get stuck with a dirty needle."

"Bye, Bran," she says irritatedly before hanging up.

Setting my phone on my desk, I rest my elbows on my knees, leaning forward with my head in my hands. If I don't ask her to be my girl now, the tension could grow. She could keep building that wall. And I don't want that.

One of my hands slips from its spot cradling my temple and goes to my crotch. Giving the cage a jiggle, emotion and need roar to life inside me in a swell larger than the one inked on my chest.

No one has made me feel so much.

That's it. Tonight, I'm going for it. I'm asking her to be mine.

30

Elsie

It's you, Elsie.

The worst thing about being snippy and bitchy is how you feel after. I honestly don't know how bullies function as human beings after they've bullied.

I feel awful after refusing Bran's sweet question a few days ago. He's kept our natural flow of conversation going through text messages, not passive-aggressively punishing me or being angry with me for anything.

It made me want him more.

But everything about him does that to me. Makes me want him. Puts a want so deep inside me that it's part of my marrow—wanting him will be unshakeable for the rest of my life, no matter what happens between us now. I'll always want him.

I just can't have him.

But I *can* make up for my behavior. I can give him a session unlike any other—one to go out on a bang with. Or, I guess, a pop. I know it's not where we're headed—I think we could be something—but that would just be disastrous for both of us. I'll feel so much emptier if I tell him about everything and it doesn't work with us in the long term. Or if it's too much, but he's such a good guy that he forces himself to stay, and our pain triggers more of his trauma.

I care about him too much.

Before I head to Bran's for what I know is our last session, I plate up some grilled chicken breasts and salad, complete with corn on the cob for mom and Effie. Sometimes I think someone in the Universe is watching because mom has had good days lately. A string of them, longer than she's had for a long time.

Deciding I needed to end things with my Stray has been hard. Harder than I thought, considering our paths have been tangled for just over a month. But it's hurt, and I've been trying to hide that hurt since mom doesn't even know about him. And like the Universe saw me dog-paddling with just my nose above water, instead of throwing me a weight, she threw me a buoy.

I needed the buoy of mom's alertness this week. I needed to feel like the three of us were like how we used to be—just us girls, happy and healthy.

Thanks, Universe. I will never use another Ziploc bag again.

"Have fun tonight, sweetie," mom says to me as I cut Effie's chicken. When I'm done, I sit next to them and take my first bite. I know it's good because Effie is chewing through it like it's her last meal. But to me, it's flavorless.

"Thanks."

I told mom that I was going to a friend's tonight. Now that I'd decided things were ending, there's no point in keeping up the false pretense that seeing Bran is some second job or charitable event.

I bathe Effie, put her in her neon yellow *SpongeBob SquarePants* pajamas, comb her curls, and put her favorite Hulk slippers on her little feet. We read *Goodnight Moon*, she asks me why books pretend that animals can talk when we all know they can't, she reminds me that she so graciously let me off the hook for getting a dog while not-so-subtly reminding me she wants a dog, then asked me why I've been wearing lipstick.

Thursdays, when I see Bran, I wear lipstick. When I went to Paradise that first night, I felt like slathering on lipstick was like a shield of armor. It made me someone different so that real me, Elsie, couldn't be hurt. He didn't like me and didn't want to be with me? That's fine; that wasn't me anyway; that was the role I was playing.

Yet the more time I spent around Bran, the more I realized... I wasn't playing a role. There is a Goddess inside me–that's part of me. And if I hadn't sat next to Lacey at the mixer that night, and if Jake hadn't dumped me, I'd never know just how much I love being a Dominant. How much I love being his Goddess.

"To feel fancy," I explain to her, and that's good enough because she nods, giving up the curiosity.

Heading to Bran's tonight, I drive with the windows down. I need the cool, fresh air to keep my senses sharp. I'm coming to blow him away because that's what he deserves for his softness and kindness, but I *am* ending it.

The wind slapping my eyes keeps me from crying, too.

Tonight's outfit is... *different* from my usual. I'd been wearing corsets, fishnets, and sheer blouses to show off my piercings and tease him... classic seductress stuff. I smooth my hand down the pleat-front khaki pants I got off Amazon.

Tonight's outfit is more to show him that I've been listening. That I've *seen* him, and even though we're not a forever– I saw him and loved every bit... even the goofy stuff.

It's probably dumb, but it's too late now.

I park my car, checking the knot of silk scarf at my chin. I tighten it, patting the top of my head to make sure it didn't slip back. I had to get dressed in the garage tonight before I left because this outfit would gather more giggles and garner more questions than my tits at my chin in a corset.

Grabbing my bag from the passenger seat, I get out of my car and take a long, deep breath. *This is the last time. Make it happy, not sad. Bran was a season, and seasons end.*

I don't even believe myself, but I want this to be good for him, so I practice my smile as I make my way toward his front door. I fidget with the tie on my trench coat as I wait at the door.

He opens the door in just boxer briefs, his dark hair wet and stringy–a sexy mess. Beads of water glisten on his chest, tattoos shiny from the moisture. "Hi," he smiles–God, does his smile make me *feel the feels*. It makes me mushy and warm and tingly; it makes me think about hunting Easter eggs with Effie that he's playfully hidden for us; it makes me dream of being pinned to the mattress by the sheer force of his hips as he fucks me like crazy all while telling me *I'm the one, I'm his Goddess.*

Whoa. Take a breath, Elsie.

Suddenly, I'm rethinking my outfit.

"Baby..." the skin-warming nickname hits differently now, knowing I don't get to hear it after tonight. "You look..." He steps back, gripping the edge of his door, his eye roaming quizzically up and down my frame. When his dark eye finally makes it to my face again, he notices the silk scarf wrapped around my head.

I bite the inside of my cheek. "Scarf's for my neck; I just tied it around my hair so the wig wouldn't fall off on the drive over. You know, because I had my windows down." The words topple out of my mouth, stacking onto each other disastrously. Jesus, I'm nervous.

He flashes that grin as I step up toward the door. "Get in here and explain."

In the entryway, I wait for him to lock the door, and I give a curious Stoner a few head scratches, too. After he's done, Bran turns to face me, hand pulling at his beard, a deliciously controlled smirk lifting his lips.

Quickly, I work out the tied scarf under my chin and shimmy it down my head until it's wrapped behind my neck. Nervously and quite regretfully, I finger comb the plastic-feeling wig, roll my lips together, and go for the tie on my coat.

Once it's unbuttoned, I slide out of it and hang it on the rack behind the door. I noticed it the first night I was here, but I've never used it. I like the way my coat looks hanging in his house. *Take a mental picture, Elsie, because this is it. Don't back out now. For his sake.*

I smooth my hands down the coat, suck in a breath, then spin on my heel to face him.

He blinks, and the smile that takes over his face makes my eyes go warm and wet. I blink a few times, then wipe my eyes under the guise of fixing my makeup. He's so busy taking in my getup that he doesn't notice luckily. Though he hasn't said a word yet, I know he likes it. I can feel it, and my heart swells like a freaking balloon at how rewarding it feels to make him *this* happy.

I'm making the right choice. He deserves this, a life filled with just this after what he's been through, losing his eye.

"Baby," he says, shaking his head, eye raking over me in a way that makes me clench my thighs and itch to fan myself. "I fucking love it. It's super fucking weird, I'm not gonna lie, but *god damn.*" He steps back, his tongue darting across his bottom lip as he eats me up again, for the third time. Pride and power surge through me, and I feel a lot like I do when I have his orgasm in my clutches and he's looking to me for reassurance.

"Do you, uh, know who I'm dressed as? Like, I know it's weird, but it's not just an 80's mom costume. I'm someone *specific.*"

He looks up at me, and a dense fog over silence rolls between us. After he steps toward me, he finally responds. "You're the mom from *Home Alone*. I know exactly who you are."

I'm breathless at his intensity, at the secret subtext of everything firing off between us in this dark, small entryway. Burning spreads through my jaw when he takes it in his hand, bringing his lips down low, nearly touching mine.

"I said I thought she was hot. I said it two weeks ago.

And now you're here, with my cock in a cage, dressed as her, and goddamnit, it's weird. It's weird and new and exciting, and I love it." His lips, wide and soft, press to mine lightly, just for a second, before he steps back and turns, heading down the hallway.

I press my fingertips to my lips in the corny, stereotypical way women do in soap operas after their hero has kissed them. But it's a reaction; I can't help it. I want to seal that subtle, sweet kiss into my soul forever. Nothing will ever feel as good; no kiss will ever be that right.

He's never kissed me. We've never kissed. And it was the shortest, lightest, most perfect kiss of my entire life.

I follow him down the hall, walking slowly to use the time to my benefit. I need to recover from that and stick to the plan now more than ever.

Closing the door behind me, I drop the necklace and key on the nightstand. I've incorporated cage removal into our session tonight, and once he figures out why, he'll be hurt. He will, but a little hurt now is better than *a lot* of hurt later.

"Stray," I start, dropping my bag of toys next to his nightstand. "Use the key to remove yourself."

I fluff the horrendous red bowl cut wig I'm wearing, and he smiles at me as I do. I'm letting him out because I'm selfish. And I'm a glutton for pain. Because I want to touch his cock, feel his orgasm pulsing in my hands, stroke him, and watch his face as I do. I want my skin all over his skin. I want to steal as much intimacy from him as I can while I can.

Once he's unlocked himself, he drops the cage and the necklace into the nightstand drawer, where it was the first time he took it off.

"How was it in the cage, Stray?"

He reaches for himself, but I shake my head. "Hands on your thighs."

His grin slides off his face, and the only thing left is heat. His cock comes to life, thickening against his thigh for the first time in a week. "*Hard.*"

I shake my head. "The opposite."

He swallows, the tattoo of a triton on his neck going along for the dip. "I don't normally jerk off a crazy amount, just normalish. But since being in this thing, it's all I can fucking think about."

I nod, stuffing my hands in the large bucket pockets of my 1980's shoulder-pad-clad sierra colored blazer. "Tell me about it."

His palms skate the length of his meaty thighs, and a surge of wetness makes my pussy tingle. The crown of his cock grows pinker as his erection gains momentum. He's so hot. Straddling that thick, perfect cock would feel so good. My insides clench at the thought. My body begs for his intrusion, my pussy growing wetter by the moment.

"It's not the cage. I take it back. It's you." He looks at me now, straight in the eyes, nowhere else. No game, no costume, no roles. Brian looking at Elsie. My bones vibrate inside me.

"*It's you, Elsie.*" His voice is so soft, the knot in my throat rough and heavy.

"Goddess," I correct because I need to shield myself from the intimacy of my real name. Of knowing, seeing, and wanting me. It feels too good. "Goddess, and if you call me anything else, you'll be back in the cage. Got it?" I lean forward as he reassures me that he understands and slap his swollen balls with more force than I did last week. "Got it?"

"Got it," he grimaces, his eye meeting my face. He isn't angry. He looks more turned on, more needful than before.

"It's you. I can't stop thinking of you, and because of that, all I wanna do is jerk off."

I know it's a dangerous game, but I ask anyway because I love to torture myself. "Why?"

"Because you're gorgeous," he answers quickly, simply, like I asked him if the sky is up. If the sun is yellow. If we need air to live. "You're strong and funny," he eyes my costume. "Really fucking funny. But thoughtful too. And fuck..." he lets his head drop forward, hanging it between his shoulders for a second before lifting it up again. His fingertips are curled into his knees, and his beautiful cock is bobbing between his spread legs, almost completely hard now.

"Ruin me now, Goddess," he says, finding my eyes. His is glassy, skin ruddy. "I need you to ruin me now, *please*."

Wanting to be as close to him as possible without irrevocably fusing us–which it often felt like we were, I concoct a new plan. With his dick aimed my way, begging for my touch, I decide tonight I'm going to give him something we'll *both* fucking love.

Because I want to taste him, and I'm going to.

Falling to my knees between his open legs, I run my hands up his thighs and enjoy the way precome beads on the tip of his cockhead at my touch. "Every minute you don't come earns you more of your Goddess. Got it?"

He nods.

"Speak, Stray. Let me hear you say it."

"Got it," he barks out.

"Now, don't come."

With that—and because I'm so horny I'm about to combust—I kiss him.

My lips seal over the smooth, capped head of his cock, and my tongue hungrily laps at the moisture. My body hums with delight at the salty, musky taste of him. Wetness slides down my thighs beneath the ridiculous mom pants.

Hands still riding his thighs, my lips kiss all over his head. *He moans*, fucking me upside down on Sunday, *He. Moans*. Deep, panty-drenching, soul-stirring, dream-making, future-planning moans that almost wreck me. Almost, for a split second, it makes me wonder if maybe he and I could work. Maybe Jake was a one-off, and that a man like Bran can handle his own shit *and* mine. That we could help each other with it all.

With a pop, I release his cock, and he growls now, sounding like a starved stray, desperate and foaming at the mouth to feast. Clenching, my pussy flutters at the noise, my flesh pebbles, sweat grows under the wig.

"Well done, Stray."

His eye is foggy, hazy, drunken, and lost, like that one kiss to his dick made him lose the ability to think or speak. All he can do is sit there with his erection hot and hard between us, wanting, wanting, wanting, and *waiting*.

Tugging the wig off, I shake my blonde curls free. I promise more Goddess with each minute, and my plan is to shed this get up and be completely bare and nude for him. To use me as his canvas. Selfishly, I want his orgasm dripping from my skin, burning into me, reminding me that I *know* the feeling of equal ownership no matter what.

Leaning forward, I suck his crown into my mouth, tracing the hard edge of him with the tip of my tongue. This time, he doesn't groan but instead, keeping his hand on my head, he tangles his fingertips in my curls, smoothing through them softly. My eyes flutter closed as more salty precome hits my tongue. I count off in my mind until we're at a minute of him affectionately stroking my hair while I binge on the head of him, swirling my tongue and suckling slowly.

I lean back. Sweat peppers his bare chest. Breathing heavily, he grips his knees so hard that his nail beds are white. He's thrumming between us, leaking as much as I'm soaking.

Shaking my shoulder, I shimmy out of the mom-blazer. I'm wearing a cream-colored blouse underneath, but no bra. Tucking the fabric in at the waist of the mom jeans at my back, it pulls taut against my tits. The expression on his face hardens as he tips his head back to take a breath, the masculine ridge of his throat bobbing as he takes in air.

"Fuck, your tits are so goddamn perfect."

I have to look away from his face. His words, his crawling timbre, it's too much. Kneeing in closer, this time, I place my hands on top of his on his thighs. No more stroking my hair. It feels too good.

Sealing my lips around him, I use the tip of my tongue to stroke the sensitive skin behind his head, even nibbling it a little at one point. His spine goes concave as I begin to work my lips lengthwise down his shaft. His dick is fiery and stony, contrasting erotically with my swollen, eager lips.

A low hum comes from somewhere in the room, and I continue working his length with my mouth, thinking it's probably his phone on vibrate or something. Then it sounds again. Did the wand turn on on its own? Sometimes the cheap shit off Amazon has a life of its own if the batteries start to go dead. Maybe it's that?

It hums, and neither of us can ignore it on the sixth pass. I jerk up off of him, a string of saliva and precome dripping from his peak to the floor. *My phone.* That's my phone vibrating.

I look up at him, and he nods like he suspects it was that. "I'm not going anywhere."

Spinning on my knees, I dig through my bag until I reach the compartment near the very bottom. My heart races, my temples pound–mom almost never calls me when I'm not at home. Only once that I can remember, right after I'd started working at Globo, and Effie had to come home from her Montessori *pre*-pre-k program because she had a fever and we were out of Tylenol. That is literally it.

I answer before my brain can process pertinent pieces of information like who's calling. "Hello? Mom?" I cup my hand to the phone as if that's going to prevent noise from traveling as if I've invented a way to defy the proven science of sound.

On the other end, in the background, as clear as day, I hear the noise that sets every single mother on edge: the ragged, piercing, painful cries of my daughter.

"Effie, what's wrong with Effie?" I'm trying for the sake of the situation to stay calm, but with each strangled cry that comes from my baby, my guts twist, and my instincts claw at me to yell, shout, solve, help.

"Elsie, it's Fanny."

I look at my phone screen and then slam it back to my ear. It is Fanny, but she's calling from my house. "What's wrong with Effie? Is Effie okay? Is she okay?"

Bran's hand curls down over my shoulder, fingertips sinking into me with comfort and awareness. I want to put my hand on his, and suck up his warmth and strength to get through whatever this is.

But I don't.

Bran doesn't know about mom's dementia; he doesn't know about my daughter. There was a reason for that. To keep business as business. Lines have gotten too blurred already. Panic and anger and confusion storm inside of me as Fanny explains, her voice smooth and calm.

"Effie is completely fine. She is not hurt; she is not sick. She is panicked and upset."

Why doesn't relief flood me? Why don't I feel better?

Mom. "Mom," I say aloud, not even to Fanny but to myself.

"Listen, Elsie. Effie got out of bed to get a glass of water. She couldn't reach the glass and went to find Elaine."

My heart sinks. A tingle of sickness ripples through my lips, saliva pooling under my tongue as stomach acid burns the back of my nose. "Oh my God," the words fall out, quiet but raw, giving away my fear and pain in just one second.

"Now wait. Okay, Elsie? Wait a second. She could be fine. It's just... *we can't find her.*"

"How... You... Did Effie...?" I can't put together a single fucking sentence.

"Effie is a smart girl, our sweet, smart girl. She came over and got me for help. She did the right thing." Her voice drops to a private tone. "I've looked everywhere, Elsie. I didn't want to worry you. But... It's been an hour."

"*An hour?!*" I leap up and spin, not knowing what to do

with all this powerless energy pooling inside me. She must've wandered off the moment I left. Oh my God.

"If we call the police, they could help us find her...." She lowers her volume again. "But it could scare Effie and Elaine, too, for that matter."

"I'll, uh, I'll be home in ten minutes. I'm coming now." I drop the phone in my bag without hitting end. Mom's been gone for an hour. She left my precious baby home alone with an unlocked door at night. I feel sick. I'm going to be sick.

But when his large hands turn me to face him, and I see the concern weathering his forehead, the sickness slides back down.

"I have to go." Tears spill over my lashes, rolling hot down my face. "I have to go."

"Slow down. What's wrong? Who's Effie?"

I step back from him and shake my head, tears coming fast and hard now. "I can't tell you. We're... we're Dominant and Submissive. We agreed—" I'm sobbing now, ugly face and all– "you promised, when we're Goddess and Stray, that's all we are. I can't tell you this. You can't know about this."

You don't deserve to ride this downhill coaster. You deserve nothing but good. Things I don't say.

"We are more than Dominant and Submissive, Elsie. We are Goddess and Stray, but we are Bran and Elsie. It's all the same, and it's so much more than some two-hour a week predetermined roleplay. I know it, and you know it. And I don't know why you're fighting it, but we'll deal with that later. Right now, who the fuck is Effie, and what the fuck is going on?" He smooths his wide thumbs over my burning cheeks, taking the tears as fast as they come. "What's wrong?"

My lips tremble; the words are there. *My mom is losing her mind, and tonight she wandered off, and I have a daughter who she left at home alone and...* I can't. "I need to get home now. I have an emergency at home. I have to go."

He jerks open a drawer and yanks out clothes he doesn't even bother looking at. "I'm driving you. You are not fucking driving while you're this upset. No goddamn way Elsie. You can shut me out later after we get you where you need to be."

I don't say anything. He loops his arm through mine, leading me quickly through the hallway, the entire time his thumb strokes my arm. He whistles once and snaps twice, and a moment later, a groggy-looking Stoner is shoving through the doggy door to the garage.

It's a blur as it happens, but Bran buckles me in the passenger seat and opens the back door for Stoner to hop in. Moments later, we're driving down the dark streets, periodic bursts of light raking through the cab from aging streetlamps we pass. He holds my hand tight over the center console of his truck, and once, he lifts it to his lips, pressing a soothing kiss to my knuckles.

The tears don't stop, though. Because mom is missing and Effie had to first-hand witness the demise of her grandmother.

I'm losing mom. It's happening. I don't even mean physically, either.

"Here," I say, before the GPS he entered from my direction alerts him to his destination.

"It says four more houses–"

Stray

"Stop, Bran." Immediately, he pulls over and throws the truck in park.

"I have to go. Please. *Please.* I have to go." And I can't give him more because my life needs me.

The truck headlights float over the asphalt as I run full sprint towards my house, my oversized pleated pants slowing me down some. Stupid outfit. Stupid idea. Selfish me for getting in outfits and playing games when I needed to be here, handling this, taking care of the people I love.

I reach the sidewalk and double over, the sickness that Bran stifled at his place washing back to me with more force than before. Hands to my knees, my eyes relentlessly water as I empty the contents of my stomach into the gutter.

Calm, I tell myself as I jog towards the house, panting, wiping my mouth on the cream blouse sleeve. Pushing open the front door, I go straight to the kitchen, where Effie is wrapped in a blanket on the counter, sipping from a mug.

Fanny is there, standing at the edge of the counter, phone book spread apart in front of her.

Lifting Effie from the counter, I smother her in kisses—on her forehead, on the top of her head, all over her cheeks. She whimpers gently into the nape of my neck as I cradle her there, so fucking thankful that this call wasn't about her.

Fanny doesn't give a moment's attention to the love-assault because she's a mother, too. Finally, I lower Effie back to the counter. On the surface of her hot cocoa are two large marshmallows, which she prods with the tip of her tongue as cocoa dribbles down the side of the mug.

Normally, I'd tell her to get a spoon to eat the marshmallows. Or tell her not to do that. I would do something; that's the point. But I can't.

"Did you call the police?" I ask calmly, not trying to hide anything from Effie but also not wanting to worry her again. "You did a wonderful job calming her down." I wrap my arms around Fanny, and we hug. She smells like cinnamon and drug store body lotion and safety.

"I'm always here for you girls," she says, softening her voice for Effie, but she remains unphased because she's still chasing the sugar bombs in her drink. I stroke my thumb down her cheek.

"You did so good, Effie girl. Going to Fanny's was the right thing to do. I am so, so proud of you. So proud." Tears coat my cheeks, and Effie tips her head, considering my emotion.

"I don't want Gramma to get lost again," she says finally, after holding her mug idle for a moment. Rubbing down her arm, soothing her, I make a promise I know I'm going to make good on. I have to.

"You won't be alone with Gramma anymore. Don't worry, Ef. This won't happen again." I swallow down the sob of guilt wracking my lungs. "I'm sorry this happened. It's my fault."

Fanny reaches out, and we form an emotionally codependent triangle when she takes me by the shoulder. "This is not your fault. She's on meds from a doctor; she was good today. You wouldn't have left if she wasn't good."

I shake my head, unbelieving of it. "Oh my God, I should have known she could go bad quickly after so many good days. This is my fault, Fanny, and you're not gonna convince me it isn't. Now, I'm going to change clothes, grab a flashlight, and head East. Can you stay here with Effie?" I cup

Effie's ears, earmuffs protecting her from the sourest bit. "In case I find mom, and she's..."

Fanny doesn't make me finish the sentence.

"I called my son to come to help. He already went up the street. You go down toward the park."

I nod. "Thank you." With another kiss to Effie's head and hug to Fanny, I run down the hall and change hurriedly into yoga pants and a hoodie, shoving my feet into sneakers and running back out of the house. With the flashlight from my nightstand, I flick it on, pointing it down the nearly dark street.

I have to find her. She has to be okay.

31

Bran

The singular word which meant nothing to me moments ago is now life-changing.

Jerking forward, I squint at the shadowy figure in the street ahead. A tiny light flickers on, and the person turns, shining it down toward me. Spinning back immediately, the figure runs the opposite way. A street light illuminates the person for a moment as she sprints beneath it, down the road, and the swish of gold curls has me out of my truck, jogging towards Elsie.

She told me to go. She begged.

But how could I go? How could I just flip my truck around and drive back to my place and get in my bed and go to sleep? How can I exist with any normalcy or peace knowing my girl is twisted, in pain, going through something?

I can't.

She veers off the road before I can even put a dent in the distance between us. Moments later, the vast night sky reverberates a wail, loud and heart-stopping.

I pick up my pace, not knowing if what I'm doing is right or wrong, only knowing that I can't fucking stop. Apparently, I am the Stray, running from the rules in the night. She really chose the perfect name for me.

As I'm coming up to the house neighboring the address Elsie gave me in the truck, I see her. My girl. Curls strewn about, the lazy night breeze picking up strands and dropping them. Her arm is around a woman, and I can't see her face, but she has the same wild tendrils of honey hair.

On the phone at my house, she'd asked whoever had called her if it was about her mom or someone she at the very least called mom. The matching hair gave it away.

Her mom was in trouble or... something. My stomach churns as I stop in my tracks and watch. They hobble together, staying in the road I think to absorb any and all street and moonlight that they can. When they're directly in front of her home—the house numbers glow from a rectangular box near the front door—their heads swing to the door as it rushes open. My gaze follows, too.

A little girl wearing Spongebob SquarePants pajamas gallops out, her arms wide, face twisted in an emotional flurry. "Gramma!" she cries. "Gramma, *Gramma!*"

Elsie lowers to her knees in a crouch, and another woman appears in the doorway of the home, then rushes to meet the others in the street.

Daisy Jane

I can't hear what they're saying, so like the creep in the shadows that I'm currently being; I step forward quietly.

"Come on, let's get you inside, okay, Elaine?" The other woman studies Elsie's mom. She turns to Elsie and in a quieter voice, says, "she looks okay. Where was she?"

"The Edwins' porch. I.. I don't know. She's not saying much. She's...." Elsie shakes her head, fresh tears wetting her cheeks. "I think she's okay."

"I'll take her in." The woman takes Elsie's mom inside and Elsie, still crouching, takes the hands of the little girl in the SpongeBob jammies.

The little girl's hair is... blonde and saturated with ringlets and waves, just like Elsie's. The little girl... *looks like Elsie.*

"Gramma's going to be okay, Effie girl, okay?" She wiggles the girl's hands, and my heart flutters when she lifts the tiny palms to her mouth and places kisses on them. "I promise, Mama will be here from now on. Okay?"

Mama.

Mama.

Mama.

The singular word which meant nothing to me moments ago is now life-changing.

"Head inside, okay? I'm gonna walk back down to The Edwins' house where Gramma was hanging out, and make sure she didn't leave anything, alright?"

The little girl nods, turning into a lightning bolt as she veers through the lawn up the path into the open front door. It slams shut, and for a second, Elsie stays there.

She doesn't do anything but put her hands on her hips and tip her head back to drink in the night.

My feet take me to her, not listening to the part of me that says *don't*. *She asked you to not butt in, so walk away. She doesn't want this.*

"Elsie," her name is so delicate and beautiful, and when she turns to see me—it's there. A flash of warmth before her brows pull together, and she instinctively wraps her arms around herself.

"What are you doing here?"

She doesn't back up—she even meets me halfway, and when we come within a foot of each other, we're positioned perfectly under a street light. Flickering, but still, at least I can see her face.

I stare into her eyes, so many things going on in my mind. So many questions. Why didn't she tell me? Why didn't she tell me? Why didn't she tell me? Okay, maybe just one.

"You're..." my voice breaks on the first word, and I can't hold back the emotion. Her walls may be up, but mine aren't. She broke them down, and now she's going to need to swim because I cannot hold back the flood. Not anymore. "You're a *mama*."

My eyes fill with tears. My girl, this woman I like *so hard* is a mama. She has a baby girl. I find myself squeezing at my chest, the news and pain and emotion of all it tightening so much I can hardly breathe. I rub my sternum. "You're a mama." A tear breaks free, and her bottom lip starts to tremble.

"Elsie, I don't know why you didn't tell me about your daughter. I don't know, is it..." My hand lifts and my fingers go to my eyepatch but quickly, deliberately, almost offensively, she swats my hand away from my face.

"Shut up, Bran. You know I don't even see that. You know it doesn't matter."

Her words are heavy and sharp, and I believe them because of it. Because it's so out of her character to be so stern and serious.

"Okay. I don't know why you won't let me, but Elsie, I want more with you. I was gonna tell you that tonight. I swear. I was going to tell you I want to start some real shit with you. Because I fucking like you a lot, and I think you feel the same way."

I take her hand from where she's holding herself, stroking her own arm as she takes in my words. Her eyes close as I weave our fingers together, bringing our joined hands to my mouth to kiss her inner wrist. She shudders, and I continue to lose the battle with my tears.

"You didn't just go along with me showing up that night at Paradise because I was wearing a corset, Bran. You went along with giving yourself to a stranger because there's something broken inside you. Something that needed mending." She swallows, and our roles reverse as the pad of her thumb drags over the top of my hand slowly.

"I don't know if it's because of losing your eye, I don't know what, but... my life is heavy. Really heavy, Bran. Like, some days are like walking in quicksand. And things aren't going to get better. They're only going to get worse."

I open my mouth to do battle, to fight the things that can be argued against—to say that I can and will do everything with her. That I'd follow her to the edge of the Earth and jump if it meant we were together.

She shakes her head, and like we're the Stray and the Goddess, I obey and listen.

"I think whatever it is you were battling when we met, I think you're better." She releases my hand and tenderly strokes my beard, her fingertips tracing my lips. My chest burns. My eye waters.

"You're right. I like you, Bran. I like you a lot. But my road is dark, and yours is light, and something tells me you're finding the light for the first time in a while."

"Because of you," I add, a glutton for her touch; I lean into it, trapping her hand to my face with my shoulder. "I've worked through my shit because of you, baby. I wouldn't just fucking say that. You brought the light." I swallow hard and stare into her wide blue eyes, brimming with sadness and fear. "But you'll take the light with you if you go."

The front door opens, and the little girl is on the porch. "Mama! Mama! We need help!" This time, the call is casual, and it hits me again that my girl has a little girl. Fuck. She's even stronger and more amazing than I even knew.

"We need food! Gramma's hungry! Fanny can't cook! I want a weiner! Or mac n cheese! Ma-maw!" The girl's voice grows desperate, and she stomps her Hulk-covered foot to the doormat.

Elsie takes her hand back. "I gotta go get my mom bathed. Feed everyone. I'll... I don't know, Bran. I'm sorry. I gotta go."

The blonde curls are the last thing I see before the door seals shut.

For once in my life, my mind goes blank. My body takes over, putting me behind the wheel, driving me across town, then back to Elsie's. I quietly deposit the bags on the porch, firing off a simple text.

Bran: *Porch.*

Daisy Jane

I don't stay to watch her pull in the bags of food I picked up from a local restaurant. I got a spread of things, not knowing what they wanted but knowing the beautiful little girl belonging to the woman I'm falling for wanted mac n cheese, or a hotdog, so you better believe I put both in there.

Stoner passes out as soon as we're back, having snarfed some fries from the bag I got just for him. Me? I don't sleep a goddamn wink the entire night.

32

Elsie

He's been different since he met you. Happy, floating, really.

Despite the massive energy crash once the adrenaline peters out, I don't get a wink of sleep the entire night.

When I wake up, Effie and I make pancakes. Because she's four, she doesn't seem to be phased by last night's incident. Her main concern is now back to getting a dog and adding sprinkles to the pancake batter.

Fanny and I gave mom a sleeping pill last night to get some deep sleep. She's still asleep, but as I pour the last of the batter, there's a knock at the door.

I want it to be Bran. I want so bad for it to be Bran. But last night, I turned him down. He told me he wanted more, that he could handle me–*us*–but I turned him down. And he met my rejection and confusion with love, leaving two huge bags of food on my porch.

He found out about Effie. He must've been so hurt. I would've been if the roles were reversed. But he gave me the benefit of the doubt. One I hadn't earned and certainly didn't deserve because clearly he could handle it.

It didn't even make him question what he and I have together, either.

I hide my tears in my sip of coffee as I remember his. His beautiful, emotional tears at the discovery that I'm a mama.

You're a mama. The way it sounded was so untaxing like he wasn't pained by not knowing. Maybe he even sounded a little happy.

"Morning, sweetie pie," Fanny says, pressing a kiss on Effie's head. She's swinging her legs under the table, taking huge bites of pancake, her blue eyes glued on Squidward and his current slew of challenges. Fanny slides into a seat at the table, but not before turning her chair to face me, where I'm at the stove, scrambling eggs for mom.

"How are you, darlin'?"

I shake my head, not even bothering with the tears anymore. They're not for Bran, but they're for the fear of *what if* of last night and for the pain of knowing one day, we will be on the other side of that *what if* because she's progressing.

"I'm not ready for it to progress." I wipe the snot from my nose with a paper towel. "I'm just sad, but I'm okay. I have to be okay."

Filling a mug for Fanny, I pass it to her, along with the cream I keep in the fridge, especially for her. When a woman like Fanny does as many favors for you as she does, the least you can do is stock your house with their amenities.

"Who left all that food last night, Els?"

I look up, finding Fanny's expression soft, pliable, willing, and ready to take whatever of my troubles she can, even if it's just through listening.

Sighing, I sift the spatula through the goldenrod mixture, the smell of eggs nauseating me with how worked up I still feel. "His name is Bran. He owns Paradise, one of the weight-lifting gyms in town. We met under strange circumstances, but we've been seeing each other for over a month and.... I really like him. I blew him off, though, because he's had his own self-admitted traumas and... I know mom's getting worse."

"Think he can't handle more?"

I snort at that because when I think of Bran, I think about a man who can handle anything. Physically, he's strong and big, swollen with muscles and power oozing from his every pore. And then I think of him—his words so tender and real. *I want to start some real shit with you.* He'd said that after seeing me hobble up the street with my dirty, confused mom. He'd said that after seeing my daughter screaming for food on the front porch.

He'd meant it, that's why.

It's then, staring at Fanny's gentle smile, that I realize what an absolute idiot, martyr, protective, scared human I am.

I told myself it was for Bran, but he cried when he found out I'm a mama. He begged to be part of my life. One month or one year makes no difference to me because I feel it from him. He wants me, he said it. Then he showed his care by leaving food for my entire family on the porch, knowing I was stressed and upset.

And I know then that I had made a mistake.

And it will be messy. Sloppy. Tearful. Hard. But if he's still willing to hold my hand through this chaos of life, I'm willing to put my hand in his and give him my trust. Because he's shown me I have no reason not to.

"I'm falling for him," I tell Fanny, mostly just to say it out loud and test the words. But the grin that swallows my face as I say the words and the excited flurry that zips through my gut is the way I know... I mean those words with every part of me.

"I know you are, sweetheart." She smiles into her coffee, a loud commercial for slime blaring in the background.

"Yeah? How's that?"

"Because you'd be a fool not to fall in love with any man who gives you the effervescent glow you've had the last few weeks. If it's the sex, then it's the sex. But whatever it is, he's a keeper. You've never seemed happier than you have lately."

I blush at Fanny's mention of sex. "Actually," I trace the edge of the mug, staring down at the last drink of caffeine. "We haven't had sex."

Fanny slaps the counter. "*Welll,* shit. If that man is making you feel that good, and he hasn't even tickled you with the pickle, you're set for life."

"Fanny!" Abandoning my mug, I press my palms to my cheeks, finding them fiery from her words.

But God, she's right. I'm so into him, and we haven't even technically consummated things. I mean, I've made him orgasm, but outside of that... we've never been Bran and Elsie in the intimate setting.

"Well, am I wrong?"

I shake my head, looking down quickly at my yoga pants and hoodie from last night. "Fanny, can you watch Effie?" I look at my watch. "Mom usually sleeps until ten when she's on the Ambien. I'll be home by then."

She winks. "Go get your guy."

I never understood how moments like these played out in movies. A wink and a go get 'em? When does that actually happen in real life?

But it's happening now, and I'll take all the cheesy movie moments if it means I get Bran back. I'll be a walking cliche if I have to. Whatever it takes to get the one good thing I was so desperate to shove away.

* * *

THIRTY MINUTES LATER, I'm pulling up to Paradise in Fanny's station wagon because my car is still at Bran's house. He drove me—we'd held hands across the console the entire way—which meant I had no car.

I should be more nervous than I am, but I'm tired. I'm exhausted. And honestly, I'm excited to tell Bran that he was right. That I do care about him. That I'm an idiot and a half who was just... scared to show someone their life only to be told, the same way Jake told me, that I'm too much. That it's all too much.

Pulling open the glass doors, a woman pops up from under the desk as the bell jingles loudly. I recognize her, her dark hair so much like Bran's. It's his younger sister. Sammy.

The thing is, she doesn't know who *I* am. Now the nerves grow because I know that Bran and Sammy are best friends. And I broke his heart last night, sending him away from me when he wanted to be there for me the most. If he's filled her in, she probably hates me by now.

"Hey, girl, what's up? You looking to sign up? You're looking a little lost."

It's that moment that I decide fuck it. Because if it works out between Bran and me, the way I handle this situation is crucial to our foundation.

I shake my head, smoothing my clammy palms down my thighs. I went with jeans, sneakers, and a tank top. Nothing fancy. But it was clean, and I wanted to get to him as soon as possible. My hair, down and still sort of damp from the shower, traps heat against my neck as my nerves grow.

Outstretching my hand to her, I smile. "Hi, my name is Elsie Francis. I've been... kind of... seeing your brother for the last five and half weeks."

Her eyes are colored like Bran's eye, with shades of gingerbread and caramel close to her pupil. She looks down at my hand and then accepts easily, shaking it. "Hi Elsie, I'm Sammy, but you already know that it seems."

"I do. I, um, saw you in the donut shop with Bran a couple of weeks back. After I freaked out and thought you were his beautiful girlfriend, he told me that you were in fact his sister." I swallow, "his best friend, actually."

She shifts weight on her feet, eyes studying me. I don't know if she's angry, but if she and Bran share expressions, she seems... relieved. I stay quiet, my eyes flitting back to the hall where his office is. Is he here? The yellow construction tape and orange safety cones are gone, and I wonder if the remodel is over? He didn't tell me. He'd been sharing so much about his business with me the last few weeks but not knowing the renovation is done hollows me a little, like I already don't know as much about him as I want to.

"We're very close. He saved my life eight years ago."

She blinks and doesn't say more, and as much as I want to dive into those words and rip them apart, find out all the specifics... I know that has to come from Bran. She knows it too because she changes the subject.

"He's not here, though." She glances at the watch on her wrist; at the same time, a burly blonde beachy-looking guy saunters out of the main lifting room, up to the desk adjacent to me.

"Still hasn't texted you back?" the beach-man asks, shoving a tanned hand through his mess of blonde hair. He leans over the desk, and I can smell the fatigue and strain of his workout. I try to control the wrinkle in my nose to not be rude. It is a gym, after all.

Sammy swats him, her palm connecting with his wide bicep with a smack. "You stink, Mally, so step back. She doesn't want to smell you."

His blonde eyebrow lifts as his gaze drops to my feet, only to climb up the length of my body. Sammy smacks him again, and this time, he cups his hand to the spot like he's been wounded.

"Hey, that hurt," he drags out, rubbing his massive arm. Hard to believe a bullet would even hurt this guy. No one looks like this guy or Bran at Globo-Fitness.

She rolls her eyes and turns her focus back to me. "He called me to open because he wanted to sleep. Said he didn't sleep much last night." She twists her lips to the side, chewing at the inside of her cheek. "But something tells me you probably knew that?"

The burly blonde man slides closer to me, and my instinct is to edge away. Not because he's intimidating, but... he really freaking smells like an armpit.

"Yeah," I say ruefully, wishing I would go back in time and knock some fucking sense into myself and see that Bran wanted all of me, not just the Goddess. My eyes fill with tears when I see him in my memory, emotional but holding his heart out, open to me. *You're a mama*; he'd said, his own eyes wet at the discovery. Not once did he say, *you should've told me*. Not once did he step away from me, like Jake, and say, never mind, it's too much.

He stepped closer, and somehow I was stupid enough to step back.

Knowing one of the most important people in his life is in front of me, I put it all on the table. Not before asking for the dude next to me for some privacy.

"Can you excuse us for a minute?" I smile at him, and the dejected, hurt, and shocked look on his face has me looking over my shoulder because, geez. I only asked for privacy, and he looks seriously butthurt.

Sammy claps a hand over mine atop the desk. "Don't worry; his feelings are always hurt." She nods at the man. "Mally, get lost. You know I'll tell you later." She grins sheepishly at me. "Honestly, I probably will. And if I don't, he'll annoy Bran so much that he'll eventually spill it just to get Mally off his back."

"Mally," I repeat. "Do his parents like ducks a lot?" Maybe Mally is short for Mallard? I don't know, seems like a stretch, but then again, Mally is a strange name.

She laughs, but less at what I've said and more like at the

man who stalks off in a pout after swiping a meal container from the fridge under the desk.

"Mally is short for Malibu. We've been calling him that since puberty. Doesn't he just remind you of a guy rollerblading on the boardwalk at a beach somewhere?"

I glance over my shoulder and find Mally's blue eyes pinched on me from back at the shoulder press machine. He startles, noticing us catching him staring like a creeper, and turns away.

"Lord, that man is nosey," Sammy huffs. "Anyway, his real name is Christian, but I'm going to go out on a limb here since you've been seeing my brother and say you know we don't use real names in this group."

"Group?"

She explains, her messy top knot sliding to the side of her head as she speaks with animation. "Bran's got a tight-knit group of friends. I'm the tag-along sister, so his best friends are mine, too, by default." She counts on her fingers, one name per. "Mally–who you just met–is a police officer, Van– we call him the Bodfather because even his muscles have muscles, Batman–his real name is Henry, but we started calling him Batman when he started dating a super badass woman named Robin. They're married now, kids and all that. And you know, Bran's name is Brian, but... well, yeah."

I snort. "I like that. That's awesome."

She nods. "But I don't think you came here to talk to me about how those dips got nicknames."

I shake my head. "No, not really."

"I don't expect you to tell me anything, and honestly, I know I gotta hear it from my brother first. To be fair to him. But whatever happened between you two, I just want you to know my brother cares about you. More than he's ever cared about anyone. I'm not guilting you. You gotta do you, girl. I get that. But if you don't feel the same way—"

"I do," I cut her off because I can't bear the idea that anyone doubts how I feel about Bran, least of all his sister and best friend. "I... I really care about him. I just... I got scared. My life is messy, and I didn't want to involve him."

She nods like she knows exactly what I mean. And maybe she does? I certainly hope I get to learn her backstory. Maybe one day we'll be like sisters, too.

If I didn't lose him already.

"Everyone has messes. Don't be afraid of letting him see your mess because I know my brother. He will roll up his sleeves and dig into it with you, hip to hip, elbow to elbow until he physically can't anymore."

I smile at that because it's clearly the truth. It's his character to help, care, give.

"I thought I was protecting him," I admit, realizing how much I want to say this to him. How much I need to say this to him.

"Before you, he didn't think he could find anyone because of his eye. He thought that's all anyone ever saw because that's all he ever saw. What was missing." She bites at the inside of her cheek again, controlling her words like she doesn't want to say too much because still, neither of us knows if this is the beginning and end or if this is just the beginning.

I hope the latter.

"He's been different since you met you. Happy, floating, really."

"I need to talk to him. I fucked up. I need him to know that I made a mistake."

She nods. "He's at home. Asleep." Smoothing her hand down mine, which seems out of character for everything I know about sassy Sammy and smiles. "Good luck. But don't fuck with his heart if you're not sure. I'm a nurse. I know how to kill you without it showin' up on a blood test."

The blonde man slides next to me, unable to stay away. "She isn't kidding."

She winks, breaking the icy tension of her "playful" threat. "I'm kind of kidding."

"Thanks, and I really hope I see you again soon," I say, wanting to get the fuck out of there and find him. Get to him and grovel.

I smile at Malibu. "Nice to meet you, Malibu."

"You, too." Then before I walk out, he adds, "so you're her? The girl Bran's been shacking up with?" *Smack.* Sammy hits him again. "*Spending time with,* I mean." He rubs his arm, eyes still on me. "You're the girl?"

I nod. "I hope so."

33

Bran

I can be the one who pulls the thread. I can and will unravel you.

"You sleep all day, so I'm pretty sure it won't kill you to go outside for an hour." Stoner rolls over on the kitchen floor, watching me out of one eye as I drink my protein shake. He does that a lot, keeps just one eye on me when he's halfway between sleep and awake. I'm beginning to wonder now if he isn't just taunting me. He may be a stoner, but he's smart as shit too.

After I dropping the food off at Elsie's house last night, I went home and paced. I didn't even try to lie down and sleep because I knew that I couldn't.

I couldn't stop seeing that little girl, her neon pajamas and wild hair, her bare feet, and shiny blue eyes. My girl has a girl. I went from wanting Elsie to be mine to feeling like I can't exist without her or the life she has that I don't know about. Whatever the darkness is—why her mom got lost or whatever is happening—I don't care. I want to be there with her. I want to be walking down that road with a flashlight, too.

But she doesn't want that. And the cruel fact of life is that if someone doesn't want to do something, you can't force them. I know it well enough since my entire crew has been trying to get me to hang up my Arizona Robbins coat for years. But I had to come to that conclusion on my own.

Elsie does, too.

If she wants to go on with life alone because it's less scary than trusting someone to stay with you as you do battle, then I can't change her mind.

I can only hope she does change it.

Because I want her.

She's a mama. "She's a mama," I tell Stoner, though I've already told him a trillion times. I can't believe it. And she seems to live there with her mom and daughter, with no man around. Where is Effie's dad? Effie. That's her name. I heard Elsie say it a few times. I want to know so much more about Elsie now, yet she's pushed me away.

I shouldn't have gone over there last night after she told me to stay back. I shouldn't have.

"Alright, you're sitting on the porch for Vitamin D, and then you can come back inside." I toe into my running shoes and unlock the deadbolt, giving Stone a whistle and two snaps. Reluctantly, he shuffles over and barely breaches the front door threshold before releasing a deep, closed mouth grunt.

With my foot, I nudge him out. "Outside is good, Stone Zone. Trust me. You need fresh air."

Dramatically–shit, this dog could belong to Mally–he flops down, hiding all but the W on my welcome doormat. I pop in my AirPods and take off down the road, the cool morning air stinging my senses, jolting the heaviness from them.

I like to lift, but nothing clears your head like a long run.

I'm only two blocks from my house when the music in my AirPods stops; Siri comes on to tell me I have one new text message.

Stopping, I pull my phone out and see... it's from Elsie.

Elsie: *Can we talk?*

My pulse, zipping from exercise, pounds in my ears as I write back as fast as possible.

Bran: *When?*

I turn around, sprinting back toward the house while clutching my phone.

Elsie: *As soon as possible. I really need to see you. Talk to you.*

Bran: *Meet me at the park near your house in 20?*

Elsie: *Thank you, Bran. I'll see you then.*

I jump in the world's fastest shower and pull on some clothes, thoughts of this meeting pinging around my brain like a rubber ball in a box. They're everywhere, and I can't latch onto any of them. Maybe it's my brain's way of protecting my heart. Because one thought that bounces through I wish I could catch and get warm and fuzzies from? The one where she shows up and says, *I want you,* and *I'm sorry.*

But it was only twelve hours ago that she rejected me. So I guess it's good that thought is fleeting. I don't want to get my hopes up. Uncapped, open-ended hope is my greatest source of heartache. When you expect nothing, however, you cannot be disappointed.

I pat Stoner on the head, lock up, and keep that fact in my mind as I head toward the park near her house, this time driving her car so she can have it back. I'll walk home. Sadly, I'll probably need the quiet and alone time after this meeting, so the walking may come in handy.

I park her car at her house and walk to the park. She's already there, golden hair down in gentle curls. She's got her legs crossed at the ankle, jeans covering her slender legs, those perfect tits covered by a hoodie.

"Hi," I say, approaching from behind. She stumbles a bit as she slides off of the picnic bench and scrambles to her feet to greet me.

"Hi," her usual soft voice has been replaced with a higher pitch as she worries at her bottom lip, rolling it under her teeth over and over. "Sit?" She waves an arm over the picnic table, and we slide in without another word about it.

"First, I just want to say... I'm sorry."

I want to reach for her hand, hold it between mine and comfort her, but I don't know where this speech is going. If this is a follow-up "sorry it didn't work, and I just want to make sure I'm not the bad guy" speech, it's best if I keep my hands to myself. And if it is that talk, I don't blame her. She didn't mean for us to fall; neither of us did.

I stay silent, which urges her to continue.

"I thought I was protecting you by keeping my life separate." Her blue eyes glitter with tears, but she keeps her focus on me, her words flowing more steadily with each sentence. "Lacey told me that the men who hire Dominants usually have this chasm of pain in them that they're trying to fill. So I stayed back from the start, telling myself we were just business." She tucks her curls behind her ears –her entire focus is on this. Us.

"But I knew that I liked you right away because..." she rolls her lips together, going pink in the cheeks. "I thought about you so much after that first time we met at Paradise. And not just sexually."

"Just?" I wink.

She grins, but I can tell she's set on this speech, and banter will have to wait. "And even after I knew we met in a ridiculous, haphazard, backward, and unconventional way– and that you truly weren't trying to hire a Dominant–I still wanted to protect you."

"Why did you think I need protecting?"

She studies me for a pensive moment, and I can see the answer is right on her lips, but she's nervous to say it.

"Tell me why you wanted to protect me."

She sighs, worrying her hands together atop the green lacquer table. "I got the impression you didn't see yourself the way I did. But the more time we spent together, the more you seemed to prove me wrong. And the better you got, the less I wanted to share because I thought, he's happy, he's gaining acceptance with himself, why do I want to throw a wrench in the mix for him? Why would I drag anyone into my mess if I didn't have to?"

"Even if I was hung up on my eye still, it doesn't mean that I wouldn't want to have you and your troubles in my life." I smile at her, the first smile I've given her since yesterday before everything went down. Smiling at her awakens the dormant parts of my heart. Like I'm meant to smile at her across a table for the rest of my life.

"There's a second reason," she adds. I shift, the hard wood beneath my ass making me uncomfortable.

"My last boyfriend broke up with me because he said my life was too much. Too complicated." She wipes a tear from her eye before it can roll down her cheek, and I want to wipe it for her, but more than that, I want to steal away the reason for the tears in the first place. Anyone can wipe a cheek, but only a man falling in love can stop the tears in the first place.

"I love my life. I don't harbor resentment toward anyone who doesn't want to be a part of it. But it was then I realized... my life could be why men don't want to be with me, and I worried that if you saw my real shit, the hardness, everything outside of the Goddess role... you'd leave. And I knew if you left me because of my life that you weren't worth having, anyway, but I couldn't bring myself to tell you because I didn't want to lose you." She snorts a humorless laugh. "Guess that turned out really well, huh?

I smile at her but try to control the hope branching out inside me like a vine on crack. Because she's explaining doesn't necessarily mean she's going to want me back. Maybe this is just how mature people break up?

"I realized this morning that you have only ever given me signs of wanting all of me, my mess included. And I kept pushing you away, thinking I was protecting you, but... I was hurting us both in the process." She swallows, wiping at her cheeks again as her tears finally slow down. I hate seeing her cry. I'd rather get a fucking tooth pulled with no meds, seriously.

"I'm sorry, Bran and... I was wrong about us. I want you. I want you to know me, know my troubles too. That is... if you still want me. If you want *us*."

Us.

The word means so much more now that I know she's a mama.

"Can I ask some questions now?"

She looks nervous like she was hopeful I'd jump out there and just agree to whatever. *Hell, baby, I want to do that. I want to open-arms take you back, and kiss you until my lips are numb. But the us she mentioned... it's more now, and I need to know about it.*

"Yeah," she answers quickly, "of course you can."

I swallow the image of the curly-haired little girl bouncing around in my brain. "Your daughter, you have a daughter," I say, realizing that's not a question at all, but Elsie easily reads the subtextual question within.

"Effie is my daughter. I got pregnant a month after I turned eighteen. It was unplanned and unexpected, and the guy who knocked me up went into the military to escape his responsibilities, and neither of us has looked each other up since." Her nervous energy works in my favor; the floodgates remain open. "My mom was a single mom, and she fucking killed it. Best mom ever," she trails off for a moment, more mist clouding her eyes.

I can't hold back anymore; I pull one of her hands across the table and take it in mine, lifting her palm to my lips. She shudders, a wild cry wracking her shoulders in response. I hold her hand with one of mine and trace calming circles in her palm, waiting for her to regain composure and continue. After a minute, she does.

"Anyway, she embraced me when I got pregnant, and we've raised Effie together. My mom is the best mom and the best grandma, seriously." Her bottom lip trembles, and all of me aches to slow that tremble with the press of my lips to hers.

"My mom has early-onset dementia. She had an episode a couple of years ago, and then... more and more. We went to the doctor, and I found out she'd had a few episodes prior, and she'd taken herself to the doctor and didn't tell me. She didn't want me to worry. But because of her earlier visits, her EOD became a pre-existing condition."

"When I took the job at Globo-Fitness, I was really real with the owner. I said; I looked up the insurance to cover the generic meds she needs—she's on five daily—and when I realized there were only two places in town, I applied to both. Then I begged the owner not to just hire me but hire me and help me do the impossible."

I cock a questioning brow.

"Normally, you can only insure your kids on your health insurance. It's not open to extended family members. Not usually."

I didn't know that. Then again, I don't have a kid or a parent that needs me. Hell, I don't have anyone that needs me, and here she's been, a mile away, a million things needing her.

"The man who owns Globo-Fitness happens to be, surprise, surprise, health-obsessed. When my branch manager contacted him and explained my issue–that I needed to get my mom on my insurance so she could get the meds she needed—he agreed to personally reach out to the insurance company himself." She smiles, adoration in her eyes. I don't know who owns the Globo franchise, but I fucking like the guy.

"So I'm able to support her with my health insurance, which feels great. Because without those meds... she's almost completely gone." She winces a little. "She actually needs them adjusted, but the doctor won't adjust the meds without a new brain scan. But our insurance won't order or cover the scan because of her pre-existing condition. If we want the scan they say we need, we have to pay for it."

Now it's my turn to wince because what an absolute shit show. The American healthcare system is a joke. They'll pump Elsie's mom full of meds, but then they won't give her the test that would help her potentially reduce her meds? Fuck that. I'm heated for her. And I'm heated that she's gone through all this alone for so long.

"So," she pushes out a breath, leaning back like she's just unloaded the world's heaviest backpack. "That's what my life is like. Raising my four-year-old and taking care of my mom, who is steadily declining."

"You have help?" I ask, remembering that she spoke with someone else on the phone at my place last night.

"Our neighbor, Fanny. She and my mom are friends. Not just because mom's sick, either. They were friends before, too. Her son came last night to help look for mom. Fanny's good. She's saved me so many times. Effie loves her."

Effie. Her daughter's name still trips me up. "I can't believe you're a mama." I look down to where I'm still smoothing circles on her palm. "You're so strong, Elsie. You amaze me. You've been handling this life on your own, and I'm in awe of you."

I look up to find tears dripping from her dark lashes. "Th-thank you," she sniffles.

"What do you want from life, Elsie?"

She stops my circling and closes her hand around mine. "A partner. An equal who will go through life with me. Someone to love us unconditionally. I want happiness, and everyone says they want that but watching mom's decline, I've really realized... happiness and love, it's all I want."

Nerves wrack my gut as I stare down at her hand tenderly closed around mine. "Do you want that with me?"

I get the courage for my eye to come back up to her face. "I think I have the beginning of it with you. I just didn't let either of us get lost in it." She amends nervously, "I mean, that is if you want me, too. If you want this, too. Or, you know what I mean." Her cheeks are pink, and it makes my chest ache with pleasure.

"I've never dated anyone with a kid," I admit, "until now."

Our gazes idle. "You want to be my boyfriend?" she asks like she doesn't know the answer.

"Fuck yes, I do," I answer quickly and easily. "Stand up," I say, knowing we have things to discuss, but the pertinent shit—are we together and are we okay—has thank fuck been ironed out.

"You're my girlfriend now, yes?"

She nods breathlessly, resting her hands against my pecs.

"Then I want to kiss you as Elsie, my girlfriend."

Another breathless nod from her. I waste no time curling my palm around the base of her neck, tight enough to drag her close to me with just one hand, loose enough so that her blood still flows and it won't leave a mark. Her hands wrap mine on her throat, and she sucks in a delighted breath as I pull her close.

"I can be Dominant, too," I tell her as I sink my mouth down on hers, still holding her by the throat. Her fingers curl around my hand, back into her own skin as she moans into my kiss. Our tongues clash together, frantic and fearless. She opens wide for me, so I kiss her deeper, nibble her bottom lip, stroke her tongue with mine—I kiss her in all the fucking ways I know how to kiss, and after a minute, we break apart, smiling but gasping for air.

"What else can you be?" she asks, her chest heaving in her dark hoodie. I smooth the blonde hair away from her delicate features and kiss the end of her nose.

"You've only ever seen *me* unravel," I whisper down to her. "But I can be the one who pulls the thread. I can and will unravel you, baby."

She fishes her hand between us and takes mine, waffling our fingers together. "Show me now."

34

Elsie

That's all I want with you. Experiences.

"Is she still asleep?" I ask Fanny over the phone. I've only been gone forty-five minutes–between my trip to Paradise and the time with Bran at the park–but still, I have to check in, knowing how quickly calm can turn to chaos.

"She's up, actually, and..." Fanny cups her hand to the receiver. "Doing good. Doesn't seem to want to talk about last night, if she remembers. Ate some pancakes and asked to go to the park with Effie."

"I can come back; we'll go together," I say, disappointed to not stay with Bran but eager to get to my first priority. Because I'm falling for Bran, but my mom and my girl have to come first. I've always been first to them.

But Fanny won't let me. "No way, missy. You need to de-stress after last night. My son's here, came by to see how we're all doing after last night. The four of us will go to the park, get some lunch and be back in a few hours." Her voice dips to absolute privacy. "She's had her meds, she's dressed and hydrated, and she's okay. Now you get yourself okay, Els. Alright?"

Tears burn my eyes. "Thank you, Fanny. For everything. I love you."

"Oh, stop. I love you all too. That's why I'm here. Not as a favor, but because of love."

I ask her to make sure Effie has sunblock on her ears and nose, to make sure she wears socks, to make sure she keeps her eyes on mom, and to tell her son thank you. She agrees to it all, and after we end the call, I turn to see Bran standing off near a large oak tree, trying to give me privacy.

I realize that I want him to hear. I want him to know. Because he's a part of us now, whether he's met them or not, I can feel it in my bones that Bran is here to stay. And I want to show him that I want him here to stay, too.

"You could have listened," I say, snaking my arms around his waist after ducking under his arm, propped against the tree. He drops to his elbow, pinning my back to the bark, and lowers his mouth to mine.

Fishing my fingers into his beard as he kisses me, I have never felt so good. My troubles with mom, the burdens of her illness–when I'm with Bran, they seem manageable. And that's how I think you're supposed to feel with your partner– the two of you against the world.

"Trying to give you privacy," he says into my spread lips as we kiss lazily, my lower half burning with need.

"I don't want privacy from you anymore. I want you to know it all."

"Hmm," he groans appreciatively against my throat as his mouth works me over. The grate of his barbed beard hair against the soft skin of my neck makes me crazy.

"Bran, let's go to my house. Now."

He steps away, our hands linked. "No."

Confused, I tip my head. I want to fuck his brains out now that we've figured stuff out. Isn't that make-up sex? I've never had make-up sex and with Bran, I bet it's heavenly.

"I don't want the first time I go to your place and be in the space you share with the people you love to be sneaky. I want the first time I go to your place to be because I'm entering your life, out in the sunshine, not sneaking."

Well, fuck. He was going to get laid before, but the romance in that thought process turns me into a molten, horny monster.

"I want to tell you how fucking sweet that is, and normally that would make me swoon but Bran..." I step into his space and cup his face in my palms; my fingertips draped over the edges of his eyepatch. "I need to be *with* you."

He blinks. "I drove your car here and parked it at your house. Let's go get it." He fishes my keys from his pocket and drops them into my open palm.

Twenty minutes later, we're standing in the entryway of Bran's house. On the drive over, his hand stroked up and down my thigh tenderly. So yeah, I'm absolutely drenched. Like, wring my panties out.

Of all the things he and I have to discuss—like our future; namely—we both seem at a loss for words. At the same time, we grip the hem of our hoodies and lift.

On the floor, a pile begins.

Beneath his sweatshirt is a white t-shirt, like mine. We lose those, too, and the pile grows. After three more passes, we stand in front of each other in nothing but our underwear. My white cotton panties and no-nonsense wireless bra tell a story of a woman not expecting to be fucked by the hottest man ever.

He reaches out, stroking his calloused fingers down my arm, leaving needy bumps in its wake. "Fuck, baby, this is hotter than a corset and heels."

I tip my head, giving him an exaggerated and disbelieving eye roll.

"Seriously." He steps in, the hard ridge of his cock connecting with my lower belly, making my insides seize. "Because it's you–no role, no act, just you."

Then, before I can really melt at how fucking swoony my man is, he sweeps me into his arms and carries me down the familiar hallway, straight to his bedroom.

It looks different in the morning, sunlight littering the space in stripes, courtesy of the opened shutter over the window. His bed is thrashed, blankets a sleepless heap in the center. The room smells like Bran, musky and sweaty, woodsy and clean. A dog bed and dog toy sit untouched in the corner. It's not really decorated, and it's empty, and I'm so glad to be here filling it. With him.

He doesn't bother closing the door. Bracing his hands on my elbows, he leans down and kisses me, slow and sweet. Our mouths open and close together as we discover how we tenderly kiss, unhurried and with purpose. This kiss is leading to something big.

Leaving a hot trail of kisses down the column of my throat, he works his way between my breasts, cupping them over the cotton bra. Tugging the cup down to expose my hardened nipple, he seals his mouth over it, sucking it in hard and deep. My piercing twists with the torque of his tongue, and instinctually my hands go to the sides of his head, where I hold him as he teases and suckles.

Groans and whimpers, our music is made of longing and desire, and it's the best fucking thing I've ever heard. Abandoning his face, one of my hands falls between us, aching to discover the hard ridge that pushes against me.

Dropping to his knees, my disapproval at the loss of his hard dick from my palm comes out in a whimper.

His laugh drips with promises of everything I want and how easily it will be mine. I lick my lips as he smooths his way down my belly, circling my belly button with his tongue.

"Don't worry, Elsie, we have time for everything." His vast palms spread down the sides of my thighs as he looks up at me. An urgent flutter tears through me, starting in my pussy and ending in my chest. My hands fall to his shoulders, find his muscles taut to the touch. He feels so good in every way. "But you've had your hands on me as my Goddess. Now it's my turn to touch you."

"We have time for everything," I repeat back to him with a coy smile. Then I shut up because he slips a broad finger under the crotch of my panties, tugging them aside.

He stares there at the place I'm soaking in want for him. When he kisses my swollen, pink folds, releasing a sigh of ecstasy into me, I feel it.

The emotion.

It starts building, knotting at the base of my throat, low and tight. I blink, not wanting to get emotional. I've been crying all morning. This is not the part where I cry. This is the part where I test my vocal cords and moan, moan like my orgasm depends on it.

For some reason, my body has other plans. I want to moan and I want to tremble. For each sigh of contentment, there's a tear for my happiness. I've never felt so many things at once. And instead of covering it up, I decided to embrace it. Give myself over to this experience, to us, to whatever we're building together.

His chin juts forward into my cunt, his tongue delving between my lips. Curling, he makes long, deep passes through me. My entire body burns from my seam up, an ombre of tingling gratification. Slowly, he kisses my clit before sucking it into his mouth, one of his fingers circling my open and dripping greedy sex. A ribbon of white-hot need sways down my spine, winding tight at my seam where his mouth takes me like a meal.

"Bran." It's all I can muster. My head is growing groggier by the minute as everything between my legs grows fuzzy and warm, so fucking warm. I don't think I've ever been this hot; this turned on.

I've seen him naked. I've watched with torturous delight as he lost control of himself and orgasmed, rocketed shamelessly everywhere.

Yet, my heart slams to my ribs as a bead of sweat follows my sternum down my chest. Moisture pools in my palms as hairs rise on the back of my neck.

I want to tell him I can't take this much longer. That every single part of Elsie Francis has been waiting for a man like him, and now that his sinew and sex are in my life, I need him inside me.

Releasing my clit with a wet pop, he peppers quick kisses on my glistening cunt. Standing up, we share a slow, inebriating kiss.

"I know." And he does because the next thing he does is lie me down in his bed, in the center, dragging my damp panties down my hips. Raising to my elbows, I unhook my bra, and his eye pins me to the pillows as he pulls it down my extended arms.

Hopping off the bed, he hooks his thumbs beneath his briefs and steps out of them. His forearms bracket me against the bed, our mouths fusing in dense, emotional kisses. I feed my fingers through his beard and relish the moan he feeds my mouth. I stroke the elastic running through the side of his hair, my other hand wrapped around his back. His cock scrapes my seam, thick and heavy with everything he's been wanting to give me this entire time.

Only now I'm smart enough to take it.

"Bran," my legs tremble as he grabs each, wrapping them tight around his trim waist. I look between us at our bodies, sweaty and eager. The weeping head of his cock brushes my mound. Reaching between us, choking himself at the base, he guides his veiny erection to align with my center. I want it. I want it like I've never wanted dick before.

"Please," I pant, and then he's over me again, his body bracketing mine.

"*I know,*" he smooths curls back from my damp face. Our sweat seals our torsos together as he moves his hips forward, slowly entering me.

He's big, but I didn't realize how meaty and generous he

really was until now. I hiss as my pussy spreads, sending a burning down my thighs. The pads of his thumbs smooth across my forehead and cheekbones, his hips stalling out as I struggle to adjust.

"I'm sorry," he says because there's not much he can do about his size. I wouldn't want him to. My kitty just needs to adapt.

"Don't stop."

He kisses the end of my nose before crashing his lips against mine, hips feeding me more of his cock. My legs tighten around him; one of my hands crawls to the back of his neck, the other clawing at his swollen bicep.

He feels so good.

I don't just mean where we meet, either. His sculpted figure beneath my palms–it's a wild turn-on, one I've never felt before. I always thought meatheads couldn't fuck, but this—this is life-altering heat between my legs. I didn't know I could burn so bright, and this man is the accelerant.

We kiss, and we rumble words of praise to each other. We roll over, and I ride him, his fingers never leaving my piercings alone, twisting and pulling as my hips wiggle and grind into him. We flip back, with him between my legs, mine looped around his waist above me.

I want to come. I want him to feel me tighten, feel me spasm, feel how my body drinks his body in. I want him to see how much I want him and what he does to me. How good he makes me feel.

I'm close, and with his hands in my hair and our noses nearly touching, I'm headed towards the edge.

The shadows of mid-morning fall against the window, throwing shade over one side of him. Darkness falls across his eyepatch, and I blink up, taking in the erotic silhouette of my tough, beautiful man.

"I like you," I say, a tear slipping out, getting lost in my curls. He shudders a breath, and the noise of his happiness makes my pussy clench around him. Then I realize his eye is moist.

"God, do I like you too, baby. *So much.*"

And that's the cheese that sends us over the edge.

He rolls his hips, the tingly scrape of his pubic hair against my groin driving me wild.

"Do you," he pants, struggling through a sentence. Then he stops his hips with my orgasm nearly tipping off the edge. "Do you want me to touch your clit?"

Oh my God.

He doesn't want to come unless I come, and he wants to know that I'm *actually* going to come. Jake never once made me come, and he never asked about it either.

I shake my head. "I'm there. *I'm there.* Are you?"

He begins moving his hips again, and my eyes struggle to focus. Blood rushes through my ears as I summit my peak, my orgasm hungry and greedy.

"I like you," he says again right as the first wave of my orgasm crashes down, tightening hard around his swollen cock. "Oh my God, yeah baby, come, *come,*" he coaxes, low and sweet, his eye focused on my expressions. While watching my mouth open and close, screaming silent cries of intense relief, he begins to thump and pulse inside of me.

Then I feel him. *His* warmth spraying my insides. *His* come flooding my abdomen.

His come inside of me. My cunt grips his shaft as I

continue to come, long and deep pulses still flooding me as I do.

"Oh my God," he pants, but he's still moving his hips, warmth still leaving him to enter me. The feeling of him over me, pushing into me, fucking me soft while he shudders with his orgasm... it was so hot. The best sex of my life. Easily.

"Bran," I pant, wrapping my arms around his neck. "Oh my God. That was like..." I trail off. "I don't even know."

He sucks my earlobe into his ear, the thrumming in my belly finally starting to subside. "Mmm," he groans, licking. My fingers play in the sweaty wisps of hair on his neck.

I snicker a little, and he pulls his head from me. "What?"

"We told each other how much we like one another during our first time having sex *and* cried." I bring a hand to my forehead, with just my thumb and pointer finger out.

He barks out a laugh, the trained muscles of his chest pumping against me as he does. God, I love that feeling. "Yeah," he laughs, "I guess we kind of are losers." He kisses me. "There's no one else I'd want to be a loser with, though."

I wrinkle my nose, straining up from the pillow long enough to kiss his nose. Still inside of me, he slowly pulls out.

"But we'll be everything, Elsie." His expression slides to something sinister, and he shoves his hand through his hair, sweat keeping the waves of dark from his face, slicked back. He grips the base of his dick, which is fattening up again. His cap is slick, and I want to wrap my lips around it. I've only given him head once. And not even to completion.

He knees his way over my torso, and I tremble when his heavy, warm sac drags over me, leaving goosebumps in its wake. Every part of him is so masculine and substantial. All the strong DNA arm-wrestling the weak traits, and born from that was Bran. All freaking man, and all fucking mine.

I'm practically whimpering when he gets to my mouth, sliding the salty bulbous head of his cock onto my tongue. I've never had a man put himself in my mouth after sex, and I'm pretty sure if Jake had tried that or anything like it, I'd have ripped his balls off. Clean off.

I moan as his length slides down my throat with ease, and I fight the gag wracking my lungs. Because I want him there, and just as much, I want him to know what *belonging* feels like.

Because I know with all certainty, he's exactly where he belongs.

But then he jerks back, hollowing my throat, emptying my mouth, tripping up my senses. Now I want him again; how could I not? I peer up and find him grinning down.

"Fuck, look at you," he says, smiling wide beneath the darkness.

"I want you again."

He shakes his head, swinging a curled leg back to get off of me. He wiggles his hands, and I give him mine. Once I'm standing—no doubt with a questioning look on my face—he weaves our fingers together.

"Let me make you lunch. And then we can do whatever you want until you want to go home."

I take care of mom. I take care of my daughter. I remember what it felt like to be taken care of. Not in the way that mom sometimes cooks here and there but to be thought about ahead of time, day in and day out. To know that someone's focus is always on your well-being.

I missed that. I don't need it, but it feels good anyway.

"Thanks." We get dressed, Bran insists I wear an oversized Paradise t-shirt that looks more like a dress than anything. But I get it. Seeing your girl in one of your shirts is hot. And truthfully? I feel fucking hot in it. Because it's a small way he can tell me that I'm his in these early stages of dating.

I get it, and I like it.

I watch him scramble eggs while I sit on the floor, legs outstretched in front of me but crossed at the ankle, rubbing Stoner's ears. Bran occasionally glances my way, smiling, but his brightness has dimmed for some reason.

"You know," he says, interrupting my worried train of thought. "I like being a Submissive. I like giving up control and testing my willpower. I like having those choices made for me."

I quirk a brow, the conversation unexpected. "Oh yeah?"

He purses his lips, then nods. "Yeah."

"You...." I trail off, drag out the word, and stall until I can say the words without feeling embarrassed—in case I'm off base and he's just making conversation. "You want to keep doing that, maybe like... a day or two a week?"

His spatula stops mid scramble. He turns, and his mussed-up dark hair and gray sweats make me flutter between my legs. So hot. So stereotypically, unapologetically, utterly, manly hot.

"Hell yeah, baby." He amends after a moment. "But only if you do."

I'd be his Dominant, the Goddess to his Stray, every night if it weren't for one thing stopping me.

"Would you ever want me to be your pet?" I ask shyly, edging around the topic. The spatula hits the counter with a

Stray

resounding thud. Stoner's head lifts from my palm, where he'd had me trapped in a perpetual scratch.

"Elsie." He pushes the pan from the stove and waves me up to him. Abandoning Stoner, I go to him. Gripping my shoulders, he speaks low and serious in a way that makes my muscles go molten. "I would literally do anything you wanted to do, not because I don't respect myself or any of that shit." He gets closer, his hands tighten. "I would do it because it's with you. And even if we try something and don't like it, we had that experience together." He smiles, leaving a chaste kiss on my lips. "That's all I want with you. Experiences."

He returns to the eggs as I find my way to his kitchen table, a bit wobbly after all that romance. I didn't know romance gives you sea legs, but then again, my man has an ocean tattooed across his chest. Should've known his heart would make me wobbly.

He slides a plate of eggs in front of me and pulls out a container of fruit from his fridge. With the addition of two bowls, two spoons, and two glasses of water, he finally takes a seat next to me.

"Elsie," he says seriously as I chew through my first bite of creamy, hot eggs. His jaw ticks like he's approaching a scene he doesn't know how to handle. I put my fork down.

"I know you aren't ready for me to meet Effie. I get it. We've only been seeing each other for a little while. But I want you to know, my intentions are permanent, and I want to meet her as soon as you're ready. Same with your mom." He scoops up a bite of eggs and winks at me. "I'll be here forever, so no pressure."

I'll be here forever.

Daisy Jane

The night Jake dumped me, I thought I'd never hear anyone say that to me. That no one would ever want to take me on.

We finish breakfast while teasing ourselves about crying during sex. I love being able to laugh at ourselves but be intimately raw, too.

There isn't anything about him I don't love.

I sincerely hope Effie girl feels the same way.

35

Bran

Once she gets to know you, she'll know a real hero.

Bran: *WYD*
  Van: *Jack shit, why?*
  Bran: *Pump?*
  Van: *It's Friday*
  Van: *It's 8 on Friday night, in fact*
  Bran: *You got plans?*
  Van: *No*
  Bran: *Then wtf*
  Van: *Fuck*
  Van: *Fine*
  Van: *When?*
  Bran: *I'm already here*

Van: *Of course you are*
Van: *Be there in ten*

ELSIE, Effie, and Elaine were going to the movies tonight, followed by a round of bowling, and then, according to Effie (which I heard from Elsie), out for ice cream.

I'm on my own tonight. That's fine.

But now I'm in my head again, a place I thought I'd broken the lease with. But apparently not. Only this time, it's not about my eye.

Well, okay, it is about my eye but not in the Arizona Robbins and "the leg" way that it used to be.

It's about Effie.

I'm head over heels for Elsie, and I know that over time, Effie could come to understand my injury and my disability. But initially... I'm concerned. She's not just a kid, but she's at a young age where you're frightened of seeing things new to you. I'm afraid that my eyepatch will scare her.

It's not like I'm Mr. Fucking Rogers walking in there with a soft voice, a nifty story, and a goddamn cardigan. I've spent my whole life being a meathead. My hair and beard are dark, and my ink is visible even with clothes on. To a beautiful four-year-old girl like Effie, I could very well be the fucking boogeyman.

On cue, fifteen minutes later, Van slides into Paradise in a black ringer and basketball shorts, spandex to his knees underneath. People always think we're brothers, mostly because we're both shredded with dark hair and dark beards.

Stray

As much as Sammy is my sister, he is my brother because family doesn't require a blood share.

We slam pre-workout and start our lifting. Van seems distracted, but I called him here for advice because of all of my friends; somehow, Van is the most level-headed. If you can overlook his stalking his current girlfriend, that is.

"So, what do you think?" I ask him, hands on my hips as I edge closer toward him. "You think it's too soon?"

He lifts his head from where it's hanging over his knees and swipes over his face with a towel. Neither of us needed another leg day, but if I didn't do this, I'd be at home worrying like a goddamn old lady.

And I'm trying not to do that. Because now that I've grown through some of my issues, I realize they were really fucking self-indulgent. People have far worse issues than missing an eye.

"What?" he asks, clearly not focusing. I can't blame him—he's had a lot on his mind. Gossip Girl (fuck, why isn't that his nickname?) told me that Van and his girl had a fight. They're... going through things. I'm not sure what they're going through, but I respect the sore heart. I know what that's like.

But I need his advice, so I soldier on.

"Do you think it's too soon for me to meet her daughter?" I ask, patiently waiting for his focus because this matters to me so much. Instead of arguing that he wasn't listening, I simply want his advice.

Returning the bar to the rack, having just finished his last set of box squats, he turns to face me, clapping a hand over my shoulder. "I think it's pretty cool you're worried about if it's too soon or not," he admits. "You care."

Daisy Jane

I scratch at the side of my cheek, a thousand-yard stare into the empty gym.

He tightens his grip on my shoulder. "What are we worried about here, Bran?"

The real concern is something he probably hasn't even considered. "Brian," he says, using my real name, I can't honestly remember when he last used it. My eye goes to his because real-naming is serious. Everyone knows that.

"She's four," I tell him, with vulnerability in my voice. Raising my hand to my face, my fingers trace the edges of my eye patch. "What if she's scared of me, man?"

He nods. "Very valid concern. But I think there's a way you make it cool."

My good eye rolls instinctively. I'm used to pushing away the idea that one eye is okay, that one eye is not that big of a deal. "There is nothing cool about losing your eye unless you're like an Army vet or something."

He guides us toward the bench in front of the free weights, and we fold into the seat. He massages his quads as he talks.

"Kids are cool, man. They're a blank slate. They don't have all these predisposed ideas of shit. They see something, and they're willing to learn whatever. You know?"

I nod but feel no more secure in meeting the girl.

"If she's scared of me, her mom won't see me."

He clasps my shoulder again, this time using his hand to force my head his way. Being partners with Mally is making him soft.

"Stop. Okay?" he says firmly, and goddamn, now I'm emotional.

Stray

Apparently, Bran in love is a lot like Sammy on her period, only with one eye and a penis.

"Brian, you're a good fucking dude. This chick really likes you if she wants you to meet her kid. Okay?" He thumps his closed fist to my chest. "She really fucking likes you, man."

I blink. "I love her."

He smiles at me. "It looks good on you."

"But her kid." I adjust my eyepatch without even knowing it.

Still holding my neck, he talks and gives the advice I came for. "You explain you were in a situation with a bad guy and that the bad guy hurt you, but you won."

"I don't know," I sigh.

"You don't need to know. I do. That story is absolutely true, and the kid will think you're a hero. Then all you gotta do is bring books that have like, good pirates in them and shit like that. Then all she'll associate with an eyepatch are heroes." I peer at my friend, catching his emotion as he continues. "And once she gets to know you, she'll know a real hero."

I turn forward again. We sit in silence for a moment. "I meant every word I said."

* * *

WE FINISH OUR WORKOUT, and when I ask Van if he wants to share with me about things happening between him and his girl, he declines. That's the thing about us—we'll open up, but we have to be ready.

Daisy Jane

When I get back to my place, I take a long shower and think about what Van said. I could try and make it cool. Explain to her–in simple but truthful terms–how I lost my eye and be prepared to talk about the surgery. That's something Van told me before we left Paradise. He said kids love gore and shit, and even though she's a girl and she's four, have the surgery story handy. At least a PG version if possible.

To help me sleep, I made a list of things to do tomorrow while Elsie is at work. We'd agreed on having dinner tomorrow at my place because Elaine is going to Fanny's house with Effie. Fanny's son has a daughter Effie's age, and twice a month, they play at Fanny's.

Hearing all these nuances of Effie's life makes me so eager to meet her. Elsie talks about her non-stop now that I know, and I feel like I know her almost, too.

How she loves chocolate but hates fudge and refuses to accept that they are indeed the same thing.

She has a favorite actor (that made me snort because what four-year-old has a favorite actor?) ,and it's (get ready for it).... Nicolas Cage. After I got done crying actual tears of hilarity from that information, I asked Elsie why on Earth was he her favorite and how the hell did she even see anything he was in? Not only is Nic Cage kind of um... past his prime... but also Nic Cage?

Whenever I need to get a quick hit of happiness, I think about what Elsie said. "Mom was watching her once and fell asleep with the TV on. A Nic Cage movie came on, and Effie watched it. There weren't any bad words because TV, but the movie? *Ghost Rider*. She's been in love with him since. Is begging me to let her watch *Con Air*, which unfortunately also happens to play on cable TV often."

Stray

That sweet little thing loves *Ghost Rider*. It always makes me smile.

I can't wait to meet her.

To help with my nerves until I've earned that moment, I continue making my list of things I'd like to get Effie.

I add to that list a few times a week, and it helps get me through the next six months.

36

Elsie

I'm in love with him. Like, so fucking hard.

We've been dating for six months.

Six months!

Longer than I've ever dated anyone, even Effie's dad– who was just under five months before we decided to go "all the way." I'd do it again because it brought me my girl but wow, what a loaded choice that was, huh? All for less than a minute of poking between my legs.

Speaking of that, that's another thing to check off my list. Worrying about good boyfriends being bad in bed.

Bran is *next-level boyfriend.*

I force myself to ignore our eight-year age difference because I don't like thinking of any other women having their hands and mouths on my man. I've also never considered myself someone to say "my man," but holy hell. Bran brings out this primal; *I'll club a hoe* mentality whenever we're out together. I never act on it, obviously, but all the women always checking him out is foreplay.

Not in the way you'd think.

He's so fucking humble and gentle but equally complex with rough edges. He whispers dirty things into my ear with a voice so low and deep it makes me gush, but then he softly feeds his hand through my hair, tenderly holding my head while we lie together.

We're still Stray and Goddess once a week, and in those times, the way he hands himself over to me with no questions or hesitancy, giving me every ounce of trust and vulnerability in him? Fuck. It's... He's...

I'm in love with him. Like, so fucking hard.

I haven't said it yet. Because we're approaching a big step today, and my focus is all on that.

Today, Bran and I have decided to host a barbecue at my place. Bran and Sammy are coming over to meet mom and Effie.

Since I'd already met Sammy at Paradise in the first stop of my grovel tour, she and I had swapped numbers shortly after that and have been text friends since.

I like Sammy a lot. She loves her brother so much and her immediate acceptance of me in their lives... It meant so much. More than she'd ever know, considering I'd never been asked to meet anyone's family before, and here we were, texting almost daily so that we could have a serious, permanent bond, too.

I've been talking to Effie about Bran over the last two months, and had been telling her that mama met someone special and that I really, really like him and I want them to meet. Effie is a kid that likes everyone. Children's hearts and minds are unmarred and free from judgment, and in my gut, I know she'll like Bran.

But he's nervous.

Even his nerves turn me on because it means I really matter to him—that his impression on Effie is extremely important.

Last night, we FaceTimed after mom and Effie were asleep. Excitedly, I said, "tomorrow's the day!" with a squeal because our world's finally colliding means we can spend more time together... all of us. The last six months have been the best ever, but once Bran can freely come to my house and we can go to his, our relationship will be serious.

I mean, I know it's serious now. Because I know how I feel, and I'm pretty sure he feels the same way. We're constantly telling one another, "I like you," and I'm almost certain like has become an unspoken code for love. But I think we both know we need our loved ones to meet before we put that word into the universe.

More so, he and Effie need to meet.

He'd gotten emotional on FaceTime, chewing his cheek to abstain from tears. Finally, one broke free as he admitted his fears to me. "I just want us to work so bad, baby, that I'm worried she won't see me how you do. That she'll be scared of me." He even mentioned regretting all of his body tattoos, all because he was worried they could scare my baby.

It was then I knew, without a doubt, I was head over heels, there will never be another, ink his name on my wrist, change my Facebook status, wear his sweatshirts just to smell him, fall asleep with a smile on my face *in love*.

"Hey you," I answer as Bran's number lights up my phone. We've talked a few times today, but now that it's barbecue o'clock, he's calling again. "Ready?"

He swallows thickly, and I get a vision of him on his knees in front of me, hands cuffed at his back, mouth gagged, cock in a leather harness attached to my leash. Even though we're a real, light-of-day couple, we are still fully enjoying a Dominant and Submissive relationship one night a week.

We're also other things.

I'm his pet some nights, and fuck do I love that. I love being man-handled under those vast palms; the feel of his grip stretched tight against my jaw as he holds my mouth open and commands me to hold his come on my tongue–masturbation material, seriously.

Sexually, we're so many freaking things. I didn't even know this kind of sex life was possible. I kind of assumed once you were in "the relationship," sex is tender and romantic missionary and not much more.

We have that, too. And don't get me wrong, the way Bran makes love is hot. He keeps our chests together as he ebbs his hips between mine, holding my jaw, nipping my lips the entire time. He whispers into my mouth, dirty, beautiful things, like how perfect my pussy feels around him, how right it feels fucking me, how much he likes me. And he always slows his thrusting before he comes—holds himself still deep inside of me, his eye piercing my gaze. And that's how we come–gazes locked, bodies together so tight that our sweat seals us.

It's intense, and it's perfect, it's Bran.

We do it all, and now it's time to see if we can have it all. And I'm pretty sure that we can.

Thankfully, mom is having a good day today. We were actually going to have this little barbecue last weekend, but mom was on a string of bad days, the last of those being a day where she didn't even speak.

The non-verbal symptom is showing up more and more, and it cracks my heart. I've been calling into Globo more and more or taking Effie with me. Bran went with me to the pharmacy, where I convinced them—after an hour—to please call my mom's doctor and adjust the milligrams dosage of one of her meds. Finally, they did, and it's helped some. But the truth of it is... she is progressing, and she needs a brain scan. I'm contemplating opening a few credit cards and seeing if the hospital will split it between them because if the scan shows us a progression, maybe we can get new, better meds. Or something.

But I put those worries out of my brain today.

"Yeah," he says, "I feel like I've been ready since I learned about Effie. At the same time, though, I don't know if I'll ever feel ready."

I know he's battled with Effie's reaction to his appearance. According to Sammy he's been so much more accepting and loving of himself since we've been together—and I'm so proud of him. I know it was a lot to work through—seeing yourself for who you are instead of who you've told yourself you've become—that's a feat.

"You're ready," I assure him, wishing I could be with him to smooth my fingers through his beard in the way he loves that makes his eye close and his chest relax. "Bran, everything is going to be okay, alright? Mom's having a good day. Sammy's excited. Effie is insanely excited. Fanny brought over cupcakes. The sun is shining. Our hearts are beating." I smile at the fact that it's the truth, the things I've said. Finally, life is turning around. And I know as soon as I get those credit cards opened and get that scan done for mom, a meds readjustment will help.

I also know I need to start wrapping my mind around the fact that help is all there is for us now. Good days are what we have; meds are what we lean on. But the fact of the matter is, mom will not be cured. She will not improve; she will only decline.

Even so, I will try my hardest to advocate for her meds adjustment and stay on top of it, despite the fact that her pre-existing condition has basically put her last in line for care. Still, I'll fight for her, for the upcoming physical therapies to maintain her motor control—all of it. I'll fight. Bran will fight with me. And while I wish we didn't have to fight at all, it's better not to do it alone. I know that now.

"Okay. Well." He pauses, and I can feel his nerves buzzing through the receiver—my sexy, sweet man.

"Baby," I say, free with my terms of endearment now. "You're going to do great." *I love you* is right there, practically falling from my lips, but he's nervous, and I want him to know I mean it, that I'm not saying it because I'm trying to soothe him.

"Sammy just pulled up, and she's standing at the side of my truck. We'll be there in ten, okay?"

"Okay." I say, then add, "Hey, it's going to be good, okay? Effie will love you." I want to say *because I love you*, but again, I stifle it. "I can't wait to see you guys."

"Same."

* * *

EIGHT MINUTES LATER—HIS nerves made him drive fast, I'm sure—Sammy and her brother, the love of my life, wait on our doorstep.

Bran is wearing a long-sleeved black button-down with faded black jeans and black boots. His hair is combed in that "did I comb it or does it just look this fucking perfect on its own because I'm a hot guy and hot guys always look good" type of way. From his hand hangs a large gift bag, pink and glittery. He didn't tell me he was bringing anything, but I forget about it quickly because I'm so freaking excited they are here.

After gushing over my man privately through the peephole like a creep, I open the front door with a smile on my face so big that my eyes squint.

"Ee!" I squeal, stepping onto the porch to pull Sammy into a hug. She smooths her hands down my back, and I stroke the long, silky dark hair on her head as we embrace. "I'm so glad this is happening. Finally."

Sammy, the ever sarcastic, sassy but sensitive badass, rolls her eyes when Bran pulls us apart, needing to get his arms wrapped around me. "Yeah, damn you being a good mom and wanting to wait until you were sure about us before introducing us to her," she deadpans in a dry joke.

Bran's arms swallow my body as he pulls me to his chest. My pussy flutters at the familiar sexy scent of his cologne, his toothpaste, and his laundry soap. "She's sure about me. I think it's *you* she's unsure about," he says to his sister after pressing a kiss to the top of my head. He loosens his arms just enough to peer down at me, not afraid to be gooey in front of Sammy. His voice is quiet and soft when he says, "thank you for letting us all the way into your life. You look fucking beautiful, and I'm so glad we're here."

Then he kisses me, nothing fancy—no tongue, just his lips pressed to mine for a quick second. But it's like it seals those beautiful words straight into my heart. My eyes get misty, but I'm able to blink them away when he turns his focus to Sammy, who has her hand over her heart.

"You two," she says, shaking her head. "Are so cute that I kind of hate it."

"Sorry," I say unapologetically as Bran releases me, smoothing his hands down his shirt. I don't have the heart to tell him that four-year-olds do not give a single shit about clothes or wrinkles, but he's nervous enough. I let him fidget.

"Okay, so mom's having a good day; she's out back with Effie right now."

Sammy has been clued in about mom's condition, and when I say clued in, I mean I definitely had an emotional breakdown to her on the phone once weeks back after mom had a series of really bad days. Since then, Sammy has taken an interest in mom's care. I mean, I'm still just her brother's girlfriend. They're good people.

Bran grabs my hand as we enter the foyer, Sammy closing the door behind us.

"How about I show Sammy the house," I say, not because the house is a mansion but because I grew up here, and so has Effie. And... I think he needs to do this part on his own. If we're given a crutch, we'll use it and take longer to walk. Without the crutch, he'll walk on his own. "And you go out back and meet Effie girl."

His chest shudders; he nods quickly but pushes out a long, deep breath. "Okay."

I rock up to my toes and kiss his lips. "I told her you're coming over. I told her you're very important to me. I told her you're going to be around for a long time, okay?" I pat his chest, clenching my thighs at the tight muscle beneath my palms. Even on the cusp of a big emotional moment, he still turns me on. Can't help it.

Sammy and I give him one last encouraging smile before he heads to the sliding door.

I link my arm through hers, whispering, "I'll show you the house later. We may be acting all noble by not going out there, but we're totally eavesdropping on this."

She scoffs. "Uh, duh."

Bran slides the bag from his wrist, lowering it to the concrete. Effie is on the side yard, no doubt retrieving something she kicked or threw over there. Mom turns from her spot on her chaise lounge, sees Bran, and slides up to her feet.

"You must be Bran," she smiles warmly, and my chest tightens at how much of the old her I see and feel at this moment. Sammy's hand sifts through mine, and she waffles our fingers together, giving me a squeeze.

"Elaine, it's so good to meet you finally," he says to mom, their hands meeting in a shake. She shakes her head, waving a hand down between the two of them.

"From what I know about you and Elsie, I think we should be hugging hello," she says with humor, wiggling her fingers up at him. He nods with a smile, meeting her in a slight crouch for a hug. She pats his back before releasing him, looking him up and down.

"Well, aren't you a tall drink of water," she says, batting

her eyes playfully. "My daughter said you are the most handsome man she's ever met, and I'll have to agree."

"Ahh," he says somewhat uncomfortably, which makes Sammy push an elbow into me.

"It's true," I whisper to her from the privacy of our place, tucked behind the mini blinds like two creeps.

She nudges me again, more gentle this time. "He hates compliments."

I shake my head. "He better learn to love them because Elaine is the queen of thoughtful compliments. The kind that make you like, see things in yourself you never saw before."

Sammy's head falls to my shoulder as we continue to watch the movie of what I think we realize is both of our lives playing out. Because if Bran and I are as serious as I hope we are, Sammy will become my sister, too, and moments like this will be ones we will both want to reflect on, not just me.

"She seems like a really wonderful woman."

I shush her. "We're bad spies. Spies don't talk."

"You started it," she says before falling into silence next to me. Her arms tighten around mine as Effie jogs happily through the lawn, the sun illuminating her fair curls, making them practically glow.

In pink leggings and a red, white, and blue Captain Marvel t-shirt (she clearly chose her own outfit), she runs right up to my mom, grabbing her leg. "Gramma, I can't get the ball, there's a bug next to it, and it could jump on me."

"Ohh, that's silly," my mom says, wiggling free from Effie's gentle grip. "I'll get it. Now's a good time for you to meet your mom's friend."

Mom wanders to the side yard, leaving my girl and my man standing on the back patio alone together. I'm pretty sure neither Sammy nor I are breathing.

"Hi, Effie, my name is Bran; it's nice to meet you," he says, lowering his height to a crouch in front of her. My heart is beating uncontrollably as I watch, and I wonder if Sammy's is too, or if it's just the mother in me, nervous for them both.

"Hi, Bran." Effie's little hand flies to her tangle of curls—she refuses a ponytail or bun—and she digs at her scalp a few times, head cocked. "Bran like the brown muffins Gramma eats to help her poop?"

Sammy snorts. I choke on a horrified laugh. Bran controls the humor that ripples through his lips, leaving him with a twitchy smile.

"Spelled that way, yep." Then, unexpected to both of us, Bran launches right into his absolute deepest anxiety, his greatest fear, the thing that's been holding him back for years. "My real name is Brian. Do you know how to spell Brian?"

Effie shakes her head.

"You spell it B, R, I, A, N."

"B, R, I, A, N," Effie parrots back.

"But my friends are super silly, and they started to call me Bran—spelled B, R, A, N," he says.

"B, R, A, N," Effie repeats again.

"Do you know what letter is missing?"

Effie taps her chin as if she's actually considering it.

"B, R, I, A, N and B, R, A, N. There's a one letter difference. Bran is Brian without the I."

Effie's little brows pull together like the Pythagorean

theorem is up to her, but her eyes pop when she adds, animatedly, "Yeah! It is, huh?"

Bran grins at her, and it melts both my heart and my panties. "Yep. And do you know why my *du–*" he catches himself and corrects course–"*silly* friends started to spell my name without the letter I in it?"

She shakes her head, and I can see she's genuinely curious.

He brings his large hand up, tapping his pointer finger directly to the center of the eyepatch. "I lost my eye, so my friends thought my name shouldn't have the letter I, either."

Though it's kind of a complex joke for a four-year-old, Effie seems to understand, tossing her little head back in a wild laugh. The corners of her mouth are stained blue from an ice pop, and the sun pours over both of them in a way I wish I could remember forever–olden, happy, perfect.

Then, without missing a beat, Effie edges closer to Bran —stepping between his crouched legs–and reaches up. What feels like, in slow motion, she smooths her tiny hand over the edges of the patch, then leans over his thigh, resting her other hand against it to steady herself, and touches the elastic buried in his dark hair.

Dropping her voice to a childish whisper (which is still loud enough for eavesdropping creeps because, let's face it, children do not know how to be quiet), she asks, "what happened?"

I swallow hard, nerves pumping through my eardrums. Sammy's arm tightens around mine so hard that my shoulder burns. We grip each other for dear life.

"Eight years ago," he starts, and he stops when Effie positions herself comfortably between his legs, resting one of her hands on each of his thighs.

"Oh shit," Sammy whispers, "her immediate comfort is going to break him. He's going to cry."

"I was hanging out with some friends, and we met some bad guys, and they were being mean to my sister."

Effie scrunches her nose, her fingers mindlessly fanning out on his thighs. "It's not nice to be mean."

Bran nods. "I know, so I told them that, and they hurt me." He reaches up and holds his hand over his eyepatch. "I lost my eye, but the important thing is that my sister was okay."

"You saved her, huh?" Effie asks, raising her hand to place it on Bran's, over the eyepatch.

He swallows. Sammy nudges me. "He's gonna break."

I'm breaking, tears streaming deliriously down my cheeks. I can't even say anything because I'm one moment from a vagina-exploding, ugly sob fest.

"Yeah," he finally says, his voice a little raw. "I saved her."

"You're a hero," she says, "and you're my mama's boyfriend."

"I am her boyfriend," he says, voice still rocky. He nods to the pink bag he brought with him. "I brought you some things. Do you want to look at them together?"

She nods but doesn't run for the bag like she usually would when she gets a gift. Normally she'd already have the entire gift torn open by the time the person giving it to her had even sat down. But when Bran rises to his feet, she holds out her hand, wiggling her fingers.

"Oh, Jesus Christ," Sammy sighs. "You're going to be

pregnant in no time."

Love burns through my chest, searing the backs of my eyes, sending a fresh set of happy tears down my cheeks.

Bran slides onto the picnic table we have on the patio, and Effie hands him the bag before climbing up onto the wooden bench, sitting right next to him.

"What's in the bag?" I whisper to Sammy, who I'm pretty sure is crying, too.

"He's been collecting stuff for her." She sniffles, but I can't risk taking my eyes off the two of them to look at her. "Stuff to make her comfortable with him."

Yeah, if I had it my way? I'd be pregnant tonight.

My heart swells against my ribs. I'm so full of love for him.

First, he pulls out a book. The way he talks to her so that she understands but doesn't shy away from adult truths, I love it. "I got you this book about all the good pirates in history," he says, sliding the rectangular "PIRATE EXPLORERS" book across the table.

"Do you like pirates?" she asks, blinking up at him.

He smiles. "I like the good ones. Do you think I look like a good pirate?"

She studies him for a minute, considers the question, and then focuses on the book. Flipping through a few pages, she looks back to Bran. "Yeah, you do." She grins broadly up at him, his dark eye glistening. "A good, hero pirate. Mama's good hero pirate."

He reaches into the bag, pulling out another item, and that's when Sammy pulls us back from the window. "Okay, it's going really well, but maybe we should let them do this on their own now. I know you want to know, and Bran will

Daisy Jane

tell you, and so will Effie. But if they're going to have their own relationship, we should probably let them be."

I whimper, but I know she's right.

"Hey," she says softly as she physically turns me away from where two of the most important people in my life are bonding. "Show me your mom's med regimen, I mean, while we wait?"

We'd gotten a new set of meds just two months back, and I'd already seen the early signs that maybe they needed to be adjusted again. But I was waiting to get my shit together for the scan. I'd told Sammy all of that.

"Yeah," I nod, realizing she's right. If Effie and Bran are going to have their own relationship, I have to let it bloom.

In the kitchen, out the front window, I notice Fanny and mom sitting in a lawn chair with glasses of iced tea in their hands. I tap the window, they look back, and we wave.

"Was the plan always to sneak off to let those two talk?" Sammy asks, waving at mom and Fanny with me.

"Mom told me she was going to get lost for a bit." I smile as I lower my hand, loving the sight of my mom having a nice day with her friend. "So she planned a little front yard rendezvous with Fanny."

"Nice woman," Sammy says as she starts spinning the row of amber-colored bottles to reveal their labels.

I tap the lid of each, telling her exactly what the doctor said each is for, leaving out nothing. Then I pull out my notebook–the one I keep hidden at the top of the pantry–and tell Sammy what meds we used to be on that stopped working. She's a nurse, so even if she can't write a prescription, maybe she can at least tell me what to bug the doctor or pharmacist for.

"Mind if I write these down?" she asks, already pulling a piece of paper from the back of my notebook.

"Please do. I'm all ears for anything you can offer in terms of med switches or med changes." Sammy scribbles like a doctor, filling the lined page with complicated names as well as small notes as to what I was told they'd do.

Then, as if we're in a doctor's appointment, she asks, "tell me how it's gone since you switched meds."

Glancing to the window, I see Bran and Effie thumbing through yet another book, this time one about art. Smiling, I turn back to Sammy and take a deep breath before giving her a concise synopsis of the meds struggle. "What she really needs," I end the speech, "is a brain scan, but the insurance won't cover it. So until I can figure out how to charge it to multiple cards, figuring out if there are other, better meds for her would be so freaking helpful."

Sammy writes and nods, then looks up at me. "How many cards would you have to open for the scan?"

I swallow. "The scan is forty-grand."

"The fucking healthcare system," she shakes her head, "that's a crime."

I nod. "Anyway, I appreciate any of the light you can shed. I was iffy about this one," I say, laying my hand over one of the bottles, "but really, what do I know?"

We share a warming smile. "I'm going to start making the salad for lunch, okay?"

I nod. "Poke around when you need something. You're welcome to everything."

Sammy nods. "I won't tell if you wanna eavesdrop. Hell, I'll even cover for you. Enough of the whole, *letting them bond* thing. I'm nosey, damnit."

I smile at that. "Thanks, because I'm legit dying to know how it's going out there."

Sneaking back to the window– tiptoeing, so my ankles don't pop and give me away– I peer through the blinds to see Effie standing on her knees, hands on Bran's shoulders. They're facing one another, Bran speaking slowly, softly.

"That's right. And it's about the size of those rubber bouncy balls you get from a quarter machine. Have you ever gotten a ball from a quarter machine?"

Effie shakes her head, and Bran smiles, holding up a finger to her. She watches him as he digs around in his pink, glittery bag. A moment later, he produces a rubber ball–the kind you get from a quarter machine at a pizza house.

He slides his open palm towards her. "Like this."

She looks at the ball then up at him. When I think she's going to snatch the ball, instead, her head tips to the side. Her hands are still steadying herself on his shoulders, and the way it makes me feel brings more tears to my eyes. But I wipe them away, not wanting to miss this moment.

"Can I see the scar? The pink one you told me about?" Her little fingers pinch and smooth, fidgeting on his black shirt as she holds onto him. He's so tall that she could stand on that bench and still probably not catch up to him.

My breath catches as Bran's hand raises, covering the patch. "Are you ready?" he asks her, then amends, "if you get scared, that's okay. It's normal to be scared of things you've never seen. If that happens, you'll tell me to put it back down, right, Effie?"

She nods, holding her chin high when she says, "I won't be scared."

He smiles. "Okay."

Slowly, he flips the black patch covering his eye. I've never seen the scar streaking his eyelid. I've never seen the glass eye he wears, either. Granted, I've never asked to see it, and since we haven't been spending the night together or showering together—separate houses and all—I've never been in a situation where I'd expect him to take off the patch.

But he's showing my baby because she wants to know. Because he wants to give her as much comfort as he can. My hand falls across my heart as I watch my daughter reach up, tracing the jagged, marred skin running from Bran's eyebrow to beneath his bottom lid. With his eye closed, I can see it must've been a bad cut—the edges of the eight-year-old scar are still purple and raised, and truthfully, the scar is bolder than I thought it would be.

My heart aches for him and everything he went through and continues to go through, wearing that badge of honor silently every day. No one knows he saved his sister to earn that eyepatch.

Effie's fingers trace the scar over and over, and my mom-brain is screaming at me to tell her that that's enough, she got to touch it, she got to see it, don't make him feel uncomfortable. But I don't. Because something tells me that this isn't *just* for Effie.

"Can I see under?" she asks, stroking his eyelashes tenderly. Her other hand still clings tight to his shoulder.

He nods, and for the first time since I've known him, he opens his eye.

The glass eye—which he said he still wears so that his eye socket doesn't lose shape—from here, looks passable as a real eye. With a dark iris featuring a medley of chocolate browns, it looks good. Bran's told me, though, that when it comes to conversations, people can focus more when he's got the eyepatch than the glass eye.

"It's beauty-full," Effie says, putting her face so close to Bran's that I'm pretty sure he can smell her afternoon snack on her breath.

"Yeah?" he asks quietly, not to talk loudly right in her face. Or maybe because he's touched by how accepting she is and how she sees his flaw as beautiful. Bumps rise up on my arms and neck, my stomach floating up as my pulse quickens. This is a moment I will always remember.

"Yes. It's beauty-full." Tenderly, she strokes his eyelid near the eyebrow, then flips his eyepatch back down, covering the glass eye and the scar. "But I like you as a hero pirate instead."

Bran winks with his good eye and nods. "Me too, Effie."

Turning to put my back to the window, Sammy and I lock eyes. Both of us have red-rimmed eyelids and pink noses.

I just shake my head at her. "How am I supposed to get through this barbecue now?"

Sammy laughs with a nod, then winces when she realizes it's her brother that I'm dying to jump. "Keep it in your pants, Elsie. This is a family barbecue."

We share a laugh; out front on the lawn, mom and Fanny are chuckling over something, and behind me, in the yard, my girl and my man are bonding.

I hadn't been nervous about how it was going to go, but I can't deny how absolutely fucking thrilled I am that it's going good. We're having a good day, all of us, and it's quite possibly the best day I've had in years.

37

Bran

We don't let go of the ones we love.

I really want to say that the last nine months of my life have been the best—because that's how long Elsie and I have known each other now... it's been nine months since she wore that silver trench coat into Paradise, looking to find her power.

But honestly?

And don't get it twisted—it has been a fucking glorious nine months.

The last month, though, of spending time with Effie every day? Fuck. I'm essentially always one adorable thing away from crying because my heart is so overly full. I don't just have my crew and my sister, but I have my girl and her little girl.... Things I'd started to believe I may never have.

Daisy Jane

Effie has got to be the fucking coolest kid ever. She loves everything. Princess stuff? Check. Superheroes? Check. Barbies? Check. Action figures? Check.

I have come over to her house every single day since we met at that barbecue a month ago. The first time she cried in front of me over the movie *Encanto*, I sobbed like a fucking baby. Not because of the movie, either. The raw, pure, sweet emotion that oozed from her had my heart in a vise. She owned me.

Last week, the three of us went to my house together because I wanted to show Effie my garden and cherry tree. In the privacy of the hallway, when Effie was getting her shoes on, Elsie warned me that when we got to my house, Effie may no longer be interested in the garden because of Stoner.

I guess she'd been asking Elsie for a dog for quite some time. With the stresses of Elaine's declining condition, Elsie didn't feel like she could take care of a dog, and she knew Effie wouldn't. That's when I had a harebrained idea that maybe Stoner could start having sleepovers with Effie. Elsie agreed and said I could break the news to her.

Once we got to my house, I asked Effie if she wanted to meet one of my best friends. First, she asked if he was a hero pirate too, and I laughed at that. When I opened the door, and she saw Stoner passed out on my couch, head hanging off like a drunk, she cried.

Actual tears of joy over my owning a dog.

I may or may not have wiped away a stray tear or two.

Now when I come to Elsie's, I bring him. And tonight is his first sleepover with Effie. She's very excited.

Stray

And I'm excited, too because it's also *my* first sleepover.

Dating the woman of my dreams for nine months and building a life together is wonderful. But when you have to go home to your own lonely house each night and leave that warmth and love… leave your life… in a different house across town? It's a fucking drag.

Tonight, though, Elsie asked me to sleepover. She thinks Effie can handle seeing me there at night and in the morning. Even though I trust Elsie, Effie and I have grown to be something of buds. I asked her if I could sleepover with her mama when I brought Stoner, and she said yes.

Now here I am, parking my truck in Elsie's driveway, Stoner fogging and snotting up the window of the passenger door. A year ago, my greatest aspiration was a date that didn't end in being called a cyclops, and today I have everything I've ever wanted and more.

I just want to make sure those people know exactly what they mean to me.

But before I can do that, Mally calls.

"What's up, man? I'm at Elsie's. About to go in."

Mally sighs. "What can we bring tomorrow?"

Another big step? The boys are coming to Elsie's tomorrow. They've already met my girl a ton of times, but they're meeting Effie and Elaine. Because they're like my blood brothers, it feels like my family is meeting her family. But because they can also be idiots, Sammy's coming along to keep Mally in check. Batman's bringing his two kids and wife, and Van is bringing his new girl, Violet.

Fuck, it's all just coming together, and I feel like I won the lotto.

Daisy Jane

"Uh, I'll ask Elsie and text you later. I don't know."

Sammy calls over Mally's shoulder in the background. "Don't make Elsie do everything. Help her!" I roll my eye privately, but inwardly I listen because my sister has never steered me wrong.

"Fine," Mally says, "I'll text Elsie. Have fun tonight."

"Thanks. See you tomorrow for leg day?"

"Yep. Van and Sammy say hi and bye."

"Hi and bye."

Ending the call, I grab my bag, Stoner's bag (Effie was adamant that he has a bag of his own) and head inside.

"Stoner!" she squeals, running full stop toward my dog, who has laid down in the first two seconds of being in my girl's house. She drops to her knees, and wraps her arms around him, peppering kisses on his head. He lifts his snout, licking her cheek once, then submits to her smothering. He's a grouchy, lazy old bag of bones, but he loves Effie.

"Hey baby," I say to Elsie, who comes around the corner in a floral baking apron smeared with flour. Her blonde hair is balled up on her head with a blue scrunchie, making her eyes shine like a lake in summer. My heart flexes every time I see her. *They're mine.*

"Hey you," she says, feeding an arm around my waist. Pressing a kiss to the top of her head, we stand hip-to-hip, grinning like lovesick fools as we watch Effie put a unicorn horn over Stoner's head.

"When is dinner?" Effie asks, adjusting the horn as it slips down Stoner's head, over his eye.

Elsie looks at her watch and shrugs. "An hour tops. As soon as grandma gets back," Effie stands, and surprisingly, so does

Stoner. That motherfucker doesn't budge when it's negative degrees outside, and I'm waiting with my balls in my throat like a jackass for him to take a leak. But for this girl, he'll do anything.

And I get that.

"Don't get dirty, Effie!" Elsie calls after her daughter. The dynamic duo trots off down the hall toward her room, giving me all of Elsie's sweet, sexy attention.

Our lips meet in a sizzling kiss, Elsie's fingers finding their favorite spots on my cheeks as she drags them down through my beard. I groan into her mouth, the gentle stroke sending electricity up my spine.

"I'm excited for our sleepover," I whisper against her lips, and they pull into a wide smile.

"Me too."

***

SOMETHING I'VE LEARNED about healthy relationships through dating Elsie is that she likes having me, but I'm under no dissolution that she needs me.

She made an entire dinner—and a batch of chocolate chip cookies that low-key made me question my interest in health and fitness—and put everything away when I took Effie out front to catch the ice cream truck.

When they did bath time, I cleaned up the kitchen and had a cup of coffee with Elaine, who'd just gotten home from a late matinee with Fanny. Elaine and I have bonded pretty well too, which I had been worried about. I mean, I don't have a daughter, but I imagine Sammy introducing me to a guy who lost his eye in a bar fight, who's covered in tattoos, and whose dog is named after the condition that comes from doing too many drugs?

Elaine waved that all away when I'd told her I thought she might not like me for those very reasons. And in one of her very lucid states, I'll never forget what she said to me.

"You're young. You still look in the mirror and see what your brain tells you are your flaws. Once you have some more years and life under your belt, you'll see how freeing it is to see the good in yourself over the bad. You're smart, patient, kind, generous, and handsome. You have people who love you. You own a business, and you like animals. And the part that really seals your fate on being part of this family? We love you, and we don't let go of the ones we love."

I'm sure she meant that "they" love me in the same way a person says they love a pet or a place, not that Elsie had told her mom she's in love with me or anything because she and I hadn't shared those words. Not yet. Still, however she meant the compliment; I took her advice and let myself grab it with both hands, eager to digest the sweet compliments.

"Elaine," I say to her now as she pulls the ticket stub from her cardigan pocket, tossing it in the trash under the kitchen sink.

"Yeah?" she pats her curls that are in a neat bun atop her head. "More coffee?"

I shake my head. I asked Effie, but I hadn't asked Elaine, and now seems like the time to talk about it.

"I'm spending the night here tonight." I swallow around the awkward knot in my throat. Elaine may have early-onset dementia, but she's lucid tonight, and she knows what spending the night means.

Slowly, she smiles, sitting back down across from me.

She puts her soft hand over mine, squeezing. "I'm glad. I'm glad you guys are serious."

Because when you have a kid, Elsie having a guy over in itself is serious. She'd never introduced Effie to anyone before me. But waking up in their home makes me part of their lives in a personal way that dating from separate houses doesn't allow.

It *is* serious.

But before the conversation gets too deep and wild, Effie escapes from her room, freshly bathed, wet hair dripping onto the floor as she beelines for us. She hugs Elaine first, then me, hanging on my arm after.

"Storytime. Since you're sleeping over, Mama said I could ask you to read the story. But she also said," she pauses, tapping her little finger to her chin. "I think she said don't bug ya about it." She blinks up at me, those wide blue eyes sparkling just like her mama's.

Elaine gives me a smile that says, go, and takes our mugs to the sink. I tell her goodnight and follow Effie down the hall, using my socked foot to wipe the droplets of water she's left behind from her wet curls.

She races into her room before me, and when I turn the corner, I find Elsie sitting on the edge of Effie's bed, folding clothes from a circular blue basket. Her white tank top is damp from leaning over the tub; the dark outline of her braless nipples and metal piercings are visible in the muted bedroom light.

Before I can pass her a private and nasty look full of promises, Effie slides in front of me, gripping a book to her chest.

"I've been saving this all week."

I pry the book from her arms as she giggles, and I see it's the pirate book I brought for her the first day we met.

She drags me by my wrist to her bed, where she climbs into my lap before I've even sat down completely. I catch Elsie smiling at us, her eyes so full of joy that I'd do anything for her to stay this way. To keep her so happy forever.

With Effie comfortably in my lap, Stoner waltzes in and helps himself to a spot on the foot of Effie's bed. With Elaine's soft humming in the distance as she knits in her recliner, I read a bedtime story to one of my new very favorite people in a room of people I love.

* * *

THE DOOR CLICKS SHUT, and a moment later, Elsie appears in a white terry bathrobe. I reach under the comforter and find my cock stiff as fuck against my belly. I got hard the moment I got into her bed and her smells were all around me. But seeing her all casual and content–not dressing up to be the Goddess, not donning an apron to be the mom–I'm practically dying to get inside her. To tell her how amazing she is. To make sure she knows how good she should feel. To make her feel that fucking good.

I pat the bed as she smooths lotion down the column of her neck.

"How was your shower?"

She shrugs, tugging the clip from her head. Curls sheet down her shoulders as she finger combs, smiling coyly at me. "Could've used company."

I groan because I would love nothing but a tiny, steamy

shower stall with Elsie. My cock is getting fat at the thought. But I know that won't be until we live together.

The fact that us living together is a thought in my mind? Fucking exciting as hell.

But I know I'm on Elsie's timeline, and I'll wait patiently until she's ready.

"I'd love to get my big, dirty hands all over you in the shower," I rasp, keeping my voice low. It's my first sleepover, and already, I know how shitty it will feel to sleep at my place tomorrow.

"Oh yeah?" She smiles, and as she tugs at the tie at her waist, I wiggle my brows.

"You taking that robe off reminds me of you taking off your sexy detective jacket."

She giggles, a noise that wiggles through my chest. "Sexy detective jacket?"

I nod. "Sexy Carmen San Diego, gray version."

She giggles again at that, and I pat the bed again, a bit more aggressively. She frees the loop at her waist, and the robe falls to the floor.

She's naked, her skin pink from the pelting of hot water. Her nipples are hard, metal shining, and when I eye my way down to her pussy, I see faint traces of blonde hair growing in. The last time Elsie and I had sex was last week, and she was bare then.

She sees me hovering and smooths her hands over her body, sending a delicious curl of heat through my core.

I pat the bed again, jerking forward to fully sitting.

"I like it," I say as I wrap my fingers around the back of her thighs as she knees toward me across the mattress. She sifts the tips of her fingernails through my hair, grating gently against my scalp, sending a shock down my neck, raining through my shoulders. Over and over, I press my lips into the short, faded curls springing up on her mound. I make noises softly into her warm skin, noises to tell her I needed to have my mouth on her like this, that I'd been waiting for this.

Finally, I tug her down, and she falls easily into my lap, looping her arms around my neck. Her slender legs bracket my hips, our hot seams grinding. My cock, suffocated by briefs, rigid and thick, presses tight to her damp slit.

"How do you want me tonight?" she moans the question into my ear like she needs my answer to breathe. "How?" She grinds down on my cock again, seeking friction for what I knew was her very wet and eager little cunt, as I suck one of her nipples into my mouth. The metal barbell clanks against my tooth, and blood rushes to my dick at how good she feels in my arms, lap, and mouth.

"Loaded question," I grit out, a charcuterie of sexual positions filling my head. There isn't a single way I don't want her. The way her ass jiggles in my palms as she straddles my lap–hell, I could take her like this. My cock flexes against her center, and she sighs dreamily. God, if that doesn't feed my ego.

"I want you in every way imaginable."

Pulling her hair together in that dreamy fucking way women do, she holds it behind her head as she worms in my lap. "Maybe tonight, we could take a page out of the Goddess's book," she breaths, still holding her hair like a pinup. I lean into her, filling my mouth with her breast, moaning from the honeyed taste of her.

"You feel like taking control of him," I thrust up against

her hot core, the warmth and wetness of her smeared against my thinly veiled erection. "By all means. You own him."

Her hips stop rolling as she drops her hair, bringing her hands to my face. Thumbs smoothing through my beard, she says, "I own you."

Three words. I know they're true but hearing them is *really fucking hot*, like, majorly. My dick jumps a little, spitting out some arousal—how could he not? Looking down at our laps, she smiles. "I felt that you know?"

I shrug. "Kind of thought it may go unnoticed," I say against her sternum as my mouth travels to her other breast. "Since it's already pretty wet down there."

Her fingers curl into the hair at the back of my neck as she moans, my tongue flicking over her piercing. "I want you so bad," she exhales the words, her voice empty of her confidence from a moment ago.

I lift my face from where I'm suckling her tit and find her blue eyes moist, staring down at me.

"I'm so happy you're here," she rasps, the moment thick with emotion. Smoothing my palms up her back, her spine rolls to meet my touch. I curl my hands over her shoulders, holding her down tight in my lap. My dick spears through her lips, still trapped by soaked nylon.

"I'm so happy to be here. I'm so happy you're mine."

She nods, biting her lip in a valiant effort to stifle the clearly unexpected rush of emotion. She strokes my beard as she talks.

"I thought I'd be alone forever, you know. I never imagined I'd find someone who wanted me, care about Effie like she was theirs, and be patient with mom and everything going on with her." She rolls her lips together; blue eyes focused on the ink across my chest. The lost ship at sea. Eventually, her eyes come to mine.

"I felt like that. Lost."

"Me too."

Something powerful ping pongs between our bodies, invisible but omnipotent, and I know this is the moment. Right now.

"I love her, Elsie. And I love Effie." I take a small breath and study her. "And I love you, too."

A sigh rushes past her trembling lips, and she fuses our mouths together in a passionate, feral kiss. I reach between us and find my cock, freeing it from the damp mess of fabric. Gripping it, I smooth it between our slickness. Sliding inside of her, she keens as her pussy swells around me, accepting me with wet ease.

Acutely aware of her hands gripping my face, her cunt tight around my cock, she tastes my lips subdued and slow. Spit ribbons between our lips as she pulls back just enough. Lodged inside of her deep, balls to her bare ass, fingers gripping my beard, she whispers, "I love you, too. So much Bran. I love you so much."

Then the room fills with our music; slow grinding of hot skin, teeth sinking into flesh, fingers dragging through tangled, damp hair. She matches my groans with plea-filled whimpers, tears fall all around, and I growl into the nape of her neck.

When I thrust up, she sinks down, our bodies falling into orgasmic sync while the words we spoke swirl through us. I fucking love her, and feeling her body needy, thriving for me... "I love you," I repeat as my orgasm chokes my willpower, winning out.

Her hands slide down to the column of my neck, her thumbs digging into my clavicle. Her face cinches up tight, and her grinding slows, and I know she's there with me. Letting one hand fall to our connection, I use the fat pad of my thumb to stroke her pert little clit.

"Oh my God, *yes*," she keens, hands tightening on my throat. "Now," she pants, her body shuddering, drawing closer as she spasms around me. The best goddamn feeling is that tight little pussy drinking me down.

On cue, more from poor willpower than excellent listening, my cock pulses, my orgasm rocketing from me with force. She grinds down on me with each spurt, her pussy clenching in response.

"I love feeling you come inside me," she pants as she peels herself off my chest. Her curls are damp, sticking to the nape of her neck, on her forehead too. She smooths her thumb along my bottom lip before kissing me, hot and quick. "I love you. You know, now that I've said it, I want to say it all the time."

I kiss the tip of her nose, then bring my thumb to my mouth, sucking off all of the flavor from her. She watches me do it, her eyes darkening. "See? How can I watch you do that and not tell you that I love you?"

She dismounts, and my cock slides out of her, hitting my belly with a wet slap. Standing at the side of the bed, body glistening from our passionate session, she steps apart, grabbing her inner thigh. "Watch," she says, her voice smoky. A trail of my come appears at her open, swollen pussy, slowly journeying down her thigh.

"That's fucking hot," I admit, always knowing it would be hot but never having had the chance to witness it until now. Most women are eager to towel off, clean up, and get rid of all traces of the Elmer's Glue-like substance.

Her thighs snap together and my focus returns to her beautiful face. She opens her mouth, no doubt to say something supremely sexy and seductive, but before she can speak, a piercing howl comes from the hall.

Effie.

I've grown to adore that sweet voice, so I know when I hear it in distress. The hairs stand up on my arms, and I jerk out of bed, scrambling through my open bag to find clothes. A soft hand falls across my forearm.

"I'll be right back; it's probably just a nightmare." Elsie's already tugging on a pair of sweats, a tee shirt waiting for her on the foot of the bed.

She *can* go.

She's been handling everything alone since Effie was born, so she certainly doesn't need me to go. But when I said I love Effie, I wasn't just saying that. I do love her. And I don't take this love I have in my heart for these women lightly.

I want Elsie to see that I'm not just here for sex during this sleepover. I'm here for all of it.

"Can I go?" I ask before she can leave the room. She stops, her hand on the doorknob, her brow knitted. "I'm prepared for her not to receive me well, and I'm sorry if it makes it harder for you to get her back to sleep if that *does* happen." I smooth a hand down my beard nervously. Effie's crying continues, and my body fills with nervous energy, and I can't stand still on my feet. I move to Elsie and take her by the shoulders, speaking low.

"But I'd like to try because..." A lump of emotion appears

in my throat, and I talk around it because, damn, what an emotional ride it's been. I used to ignore emotion, run from it really. But the rainbow of things I get to feel now, on a daily basis, is fucking amazing. Makes me feel alive, which I know now is different than just living. "I want her to know when I'm here; *I'm here*. I'm not just here for this," I move a finger between us as she releases the door handle.

Rocking to her toes, she kisses my cheek, wisps of blonde hair sticking to my beard as she pulls back. "Thank you. I love you."

"I love you, too," I say, then rush out the door and push into Effie's room.

Flicking on the light, I see a concerned Stoner tucked under her arm, Effie's face buried in his neck. She's gripping him tightly, and he looks protective of her already. The Ursula and Scar plush toys lie motionless on the floor. Stoner has replaced them already.

"Ef, it's Bran. What's the matter, baby?" I ask, sliding onto the foot of her bed.

Reaching up, I tuck some of her unruly hair behind her ear. "You in there, Ef?" I whisper.

Slowly, she peels herself from Stoner, who nudges into her lovingly as she peers up at me. "I had," she sniffles and snorts. "I had a b-bad dream," she stammers, and the tears on her cheeks feel like daggers in my heart.

She looks to her side then up to me, blue eyes rimmed with red. "Can you s-sit by me?" she asks, and that one question makes me feel embarrassingly good. She didn't call out for me, but even so, *I make her feel safe*. And it feels like my life's greatest accomplishment.

Forcing myself to the top of her twin bed, Stoner gets

comfortable between my spread ankles, and without a word, Effie drags her blanket over my chest, the end held tight in her curled fist and snuggles into me. With my arm draped around her back, her breathing starts to normalize, and with each second that passes, she becomes more relaxed.

"You better? You talk about the nightmares with mom or not?" I don't know what's normal, but I know we don't have to do it how Elsie does. It could be better if Effie and I have our own ways of handling things.

She nuzzles her face against my pec, her hand now gripping both her blanket and my t-shirt.

"I had a dream I was home alone," she whispers, "and I couldn't find anyone, and it was real, real scary."

The night Elsie got the call that Elaine had wandered off comes to mind. Effie had clearly internalized that since she's having nightmares about being left alone. Smoothing my hand into her curls, I kiss her head. "You won't ever be left alone, Ef, okay baby? Don't you worry about that. If mama isn't here," I say, feeling a strange surge of confidence. "I'll be here."

"You don't live here," Effie says. "When mama goes to work, I'll be here alone."

I know I shouldn't promise things to Effie without talking to Elsie, but this little girl's worry is strangling me from the inside out. "I promise you; you will not be home alone again until you're a teenager and you're begging to be by yourself."

The answer seems good enough because she snuggles into me, and moments later, she falls back asleep. Around that time, Elsie tiptoes into the room.

Her eyes meet me after taking in the scene, a broad smile on her face. "She loves you too, you know."

Stray

I don't respond because now I only have one thing on my mind. "I want all of us to live together." I kiss Effie's head as Stoner drapes his head over my foot, readjusting mid-snooze. Elsie takes in the sight.

"Me too."

38

Elsie

I just know how to make donuts, that's all.

The flesh between my thighs burns, but I don't tell him to stop. Because I'm so close, and it feels so good.

Beard burn spreads up my thighs.

I want to pull his hair, grab at his shoulders, and feel his ropy muscle flex beneath my touch as he buries himself between my legs.

But I have to hold a pillow over my face, so I don't wake up the entire house.

It's 5:43 in the morning. And Bran is, apparently, an early riser in more than one way. After waking as a little spoon with his steel rod splitting my ass, I found myself on my back with him sucking on my panties, making my pussy clench.

Stray

When I asked him to take my panties off because I couldn't take the vague teasing anymore, he winked. My Stray can torture me just as well as I can torture him, and I love that the Dominant role is passed like a baton between us. "Come on my tongue, baby, come on, give it to me."

His dirty talk always takes me there, always, but somehow having us wake up together is a strange sort of aphrodisiac. Like oysters or something. Because he only needs to urge me the one time before I'm gasping and sucking into the down pillow, thighs locked around his head as his tongue abrades my clit in short, wet flicks.

My belly tightens, my groin trembles, the world goes black, and I'm coming, I'm coming as I bear down on his face. He roars into me, a groan of pleasure and eroticism that seriously makes me feel like the sexiest woman to ever exist. Gripping my waist, he kisses my clit, inner thigh, and sticky and swollen lips. He just keeps kissing me as my orgasm shudders through.

"Good morning."

"Good morning," I tell him when I lift the pillow off my face to see the man who eats pussy like I've never experienced. Ink, tousled waves of dark hair and tanned clumps of hard muscle stare back at me from between my spread, shimmering legs. I'm wet everywhere; his beard glistens, too.

"You're so hot," I tell him, "I'm just staring at you, wondering how the hell I got so lucky to score you because that's how I feel. Like I scored huge."

He keeps his eye on me as he presses his lips to my thigh, kissing me slowly. Then he crawls his way up to me, tugging me into his chest. His chest is hard against my lips as I give him a soft kiss, settling into his nook. Peering down, the sheet tents from his weeping, heavy erection, a dark spot on the sheet where it drapes over his cockhead.

My mouth waters for him. When I reach for him, he grabs my wrist. "I'm close," he says somewhat bashfully, which renews the heat between my thighs. How hot is that?

"From going down on me?" I ask, surprised, turned on, and drunk from everything that is Bran.

He nods. "You made me come on my desk from spanking me, so this shouldn't be surprising, baby." He sighs, reaching down to adjust the pole of dick straining against the bedsheet. "It's you. You *ruin* him. Literally and figuratively."

"Well, then, why is my hand in Bran-prison?" I ask, wiggling my fingers, wrist still in his calloused, firm grip. A grip that ignites my insides and makes me imagine myself round with our baby. I could lie beneath him and have him spear into me, his hand at my throat, his dark eye pinning me to our bed... *for the rest of my life.*

"Because there's something specific I want," he says, the words slow and lazy... comfortable. His comfort warms me, somewhere deep, like inside my bones.

"Tell me," I whisper, knowing there's nothing he could say that I'd deny. Because watching him flourish, giving him confidence, handing him pleasure... It's brought me a new understanding of love.

His fingers move through my hair as his raspy voice floats above us, the room still darkened by early morning. "I want to sit on the edge of your bed, not a scrap of clothes on either of us, and I want to hold your face, hold your hair, and watch my dick disappear into your mouth. I wanna watch you take me, Elsie, and I'm gonna come watching you."

Wetness pools between my legs as his words make me

hazy. Fuck, that's so hot. "See?" I ask, my voice torn to shreds, all of me disarmed. "You practically force me to say I love you by saying things like that."

He laughs, dark and soft, and it rumbles through my insides like loose gravel on hot asphalt. "That's the dirty thing I want."

"Yeah," I say, interlocking our arms. "But it's beautiful."

We fall silent because it's true. His sexual want is a tender, intimate, deeply personal connection. So I say what must be said.

"I love you."

And then we move around the room until his long legs are off the bed, feet firm against the floor. My hands rest on his knees, and he cups the underside of my chin with one hand, holding his monster cock with the other. He feeds himself to me, nice and slow. My lips seal around him greedily, my pussy clenching at the sight of the bulging veins erupting down his length, thick and purple.

He's heavy in my throat, salty, too. His fingers feed through my hair, exposing my bare face to him. I watch his eyelid go heavy as his gaze tapers on me, his hips giving a single thrust when I bottom out on him. His thumb traces my cheekbone.

"You're so fucking beautiful," he grounds out, keeping his voice quiet and controlled through his straining need. His stomach knots up, muscles coming alive everywhere as he tenses and flexes, his cock pulsing in my throat.

I breathe through my nose, and his thumb swipes away the water pooling in my eyes. He's so deep; I struggle to breathe but force my nose to work because I don't want this to end.

His balls are warm and full against the underside of my chin. He smoothes a finger down the bridge of my nose, sawing his hips slowly into my open mouth.

He's standing now, gripping my head with tenderness and possession as I suckle at his hefty cock, my fingers buried in the dark hair on his thighs.

"Baby." His thumbs and forefingers cradle my jaw, and he dips his head down, dropping intimate eye contact onto me. "Thank you," he whispers, teeth gritted, cock starting to harden even more against my tongue. Pulling out, he leaves just his cockhead in my mouth, and I seal my lips around his crown, giving him a long, soft suck.

"Oh fuck, yes. Thank you," he groans, "thank you for making me come. Thank you for this."

His cock spasms and I know he's about to blow. Slowly, I sink back down onto his length, letting him lose himself as deep as he can. Thick heat splashes the back of my throat, his masculine grunts making me almost dizzy. Tenderly, he cups my cheeks and watches my expression as he orgasms in my mouth, directly down my throat.

I swallow him down, every last drop, loving the warm glide of it down my throat and into my belly. Looping his hands under my armpits, he lifts me to my feet and tastes my mouth in a salty, sexy kiss.

"Thank you," he repeats, wrapping his arms around me in a wonderfully naked hug.

I want to tell him he doesn't have to thank me, but before I can do anything, he's grabbing our sweats–the ones we peeled off in the middle of the night so we could sleep skin-to-skin–and tossing them on the bed.

"I was thinking I'd get an early start on breakfast." He

smiles, shoving his hand through his messy dark hair. "Effie told me she's never had a homemade donut, so I thought maybe I'd get the dough going, let it rise an hour then when she wakes up, we could make them. Together."

My lips twitch with a smile. "You're sweet."

He shrugs it off. "I just know how to make donuts, that's all."

* * *

TWO HOURS INTO THE MORNING, Bran is armed with a rag and a bottle of spray cleaner as he attempts to de-sugar the kitchen.

Turns out, Effie loved making donuts. Also turns out that donuts are a huge fucking mess. But Bran wouldn't allow me to clean it up. Even mom, who seemed a bit groggy and lethargic this morning–which sometimes happens–offered, and he refused.

Effie is out back with mom, playing with a full belly in the sun, and I'm watching the show of Bran with a kitchen towel tucked into the waist of his joggers, stretching his torso across my counter as he cleans.

Drool.

A knock comes at the front door, and Bran gives me the "who is it?" look that everyone gives another person in their presence when anyone comes to the door. Then we hear a familiar voice. "Hey, guys, it's me."

Sammy.

I waste no time in letting her in.

"Is everything okay?" I ask because her eyes are wide,

and she seems kind of... frantic. My question brings Bran into the entryway, by my side, concerned.

She nods, peering around me out the sliding door where Effie spins around on the lawn.

"Listen," she says, her voice strong and determined, eyes tamped down on mine in a way that makes me almost scared to look away. "I got Elaine in for the brain scan. I'm really good friends with the technician and neurologist... Well, he owes me one." She looks up at her brother and winks, then finds me again, slack-jawed and silent. "Consider it pro-bono but don't tell anyone. And like I said, we need to go now." She looks down at the digital watch on her wrist. "Our window is limited."

Bran squeezes my shoulder. "You help Elaine get ready; I'll get Effie ready."

Sammy nods. "Text me the minute you're there. Park in lot A, come in the doors that say radiology, and we'll go from there."

"Radio—" my mind is spinning, I'm struggling to keep up.

"Got it, we'll be there in twenty." Bran takes over from here, and I do what he says, grabbing mom and telling her we forgot about a doctor's appointment, and we need to move quickly.

Thankfully and sadly, she's a bit bleary today, and the world is slightly out of focus for her at the moment, so she agrees easily. As Bran promised, we're at the hospital just shy of twenty minutes.

Bran carries Effie on his hip to speed things up because kids tend to walk slow when you're rushing to get an unreported brain scan off the record. Sammy is exactly where she said she'd be and quietly ushers mom and me into a room where a short, light-haired doctor stands clutching a clipboard to his chest.

"Hi. You're Brian's girlfriend, right?" The man outstretches his hand to me, and Sammy takes mom from my arm, talking softly to her about changing into the medical gown. They go to a room adjacent to this one, where the large tube machine rests.

"Yeah, I am. I don't exactly think I know what's going on here, but thank you," I say nervously.

He chuckles. "Probably better if you don't know but let's just say I had Sammy up my ass about doing this scan."

"I'm sorry," I say, knowing that she was doing that on my behalf. Warmth threads through my chest, though, because knowing people love you never feels bad, even when it's awkward.

He waves a hand down, gesturing like it's nothing. "Eh. I was going to do it for her no matter what." He smiles. "She has that way about her, you know?"

I nod, knowing just what he's talking about. "Oh yeah, I know. Dating the male Sammy, remember?"

He laughs again, and Sammy returns with mom, who is now covered head to toe in a floor-length pale blue medical gown.

"Cinderella has arrived," the technician jokes. And then he ushers us out, closes the blinds, and Sammy and I stand on the other side of the glass, waiting for the machine to stop whirring. Waiting for the doctor she's finagled into this to come read the scans.

Effie had a sugar crash, falling asleep in Bran's lap in the waiting room. His eye is closed when I go to check on them, and the sight is so fucking adorable; I take my phone out and snap a picture of the two of them. Sammy interrupts me.

"Dr. Gleason's ready for us." Her eyes are wide, and her lips are drawn together like she already knows something but won't let on to anything. No matter what the outcome, she put her ass on the line for us to get this scan. This would have financially fucked me for the next foreseeable future if I would have had to pay for this.

I squeeze her arm. "Thank you. I know the cost of this to you." I swallow the hot lump of emotion in my throat. "Thank you."

She touches my hand and then tosses her head back towards the door. "C'mon."

A man called Dr. Gleason is with the blonde technician, who clearly has a little crush on Sammy. They're speaking in the weird, quiet way people do in the background of TV shows where you're not sure if they're whispering or just moving their mouths. Their heads pop up when the door closes with a whooshing seal, facing us.

"Where's my mom?" I ask immediately, noticing the room is empty but for the four of us. I turn to Sammy. "Where's my mom?" Panic throttles in my veins, but Sammy's hand over my forearm immediately calms me, just a little.

"She's okay. Another nurse took her to the lab. For bloodwork."

Oh my God. If they took her straight to the lab, it must be really fucking bad. My head begins to spin, vision blurring as Sammy snaps somewhere above me? Near me? Arms fish under mine, and I realize that the Dr. has lowered me into a chair. Sammy smooths her hand down my thigh,

Stray

talking to them quietly as if I can't hear. "She'll be okay; just give her a second."

The words give me the energy to fight the fear. I swallow thickly and shake my head. "Sorry, just lightheaded."

"Listen, listen to Dr. Gleason, okay?" Sammy's eyes are still wide. But I'm confused by her because mom is in the lab, and Sammy almost looks... eager.

I turn my attention back to the Dr. with the clipboard who is doing the favor.

"Your mom has an abnormal buildup of cerebrospinal fluid. It's hanging out in all the little cavities of her brain." He flips the metal clipboard around, showing a medical illustration of a human brain, tiny black ink pointing to different areas. I can't make my head focus as much as I want to follow.

"Okay. So, fluid building up in the folds of her brain?" I repeat, committing it to memory. I take a deep breath, and the Dr. nods pleasantly at me. *He has to be pleasant, do not be offended.*

"Let me tell you what's going on. Somewhere in her spine or brain–and we have a very promising lead on the initial scan leading to her neck–the flow of CSF, the cerebrospinal fluid I mentioned earlier, is being blocked." He gently presses a curled fist into his flattened palm, as if I didn't understand "blocked."

I nod.

"When the ventricles are stressed, they enlarge, which puts additional pressure on your brain. Some symptoms of that are memory loss, headaches, fatigue, aphasia..." He smiles and steps toward me while folding the clipboard back to his chest.

"Do you see what that means?" Sammy asks, shaking my arm.

The Dr. hands me paperwork, and I look down at it, scanning it. I see the word *shunt*. I look back up at him, Sammy still clinging to my arm.

"She doesn't have early-onset dementia, Elsie. It was a misdiagnosis. She's got fluid in her brain, and once they figure out where her nerves are damaged, blocking the flow, they can put in a shunt." Her eyes are welled with tears and my bottom lip trembles, hollowing my chest with the most powerful happiness.

Life-changing.

"I mean, there are details here and there, and she will need to taper off the medication she's on now; she can't just quit cold turkey. And she'll have to go through a series of tests, including a few more scans and bloodwork. It won't be immediate. You won't have her back in a week." He takes a deep breath, then exhales, finally smiling. "But you'll have her back. Soon."

Sammy pulls me into her chest, and I'm glad she does because my knees go wobbly, and I feel like I could faint. "I'm so happy for you," she says, laughing through a cry, her hand in my hair. "Oh my God," she breathes, "this is everything, Els."

I peel myself from the woman who made this possible and take her face in my hands, tears running down my cheeks. Laughing and crying maniacally from happiness, I give her face a little wiggle. "*Thank you, thank you, thank you, Sammy.* You did this. You did this. You saved her."

She's crying and she's laughing, and then we're hugging. And to an onlooker, we may be overly emotional and completely spinning out over this news, but... this changes the trajectory of our lives. This means Effie gets to grow up with the world's best grandma, and I get to keep my mom. My hero.

"Does she know?" I whisper as Sammy, and I blow our noses and pull it together. Because Effie and Bran still haven't heard. And I want to tell them. But mom needs to know first.

Sammy looks up at Dr. Gleason. He shakes his head. "No. She's..." He trails off, but I nod.

"I know. It's not a good day."

"Don't worry," Sammy says, "we're on the road to only good days."

And for the first time in my life, I really think that's true.

39

Bran

She moans her love for me as she kisses over every piece of damaged skin.

What a fucking insane day.

I kind of feel like I'm living in a movie. Because Elaine getting better? Recovering fully and not deteriorating like was expected? It's like getting a second chance.

Kind of like waking up *after* you're stabbed in your fucking head and could've easily died. I had a second chance this entire time, but until Elsie, I'd wasted it. And I completely saw that now.

Elaine's groggy from the commotion, but after the lab draws this morning and another scan, too, she's close to a shunt consultation. And that's the thing Elsie can't even believe. I keep catching her staring off into the distance, her eyes fixed on nothing, just in awe.

Elaine is asleep now, and even though my sleepover was only supposed to be one night, Effie asked me to stay. She asked me to stay, and after she and I spent all day at the hospital together, she clung to me like glue.

And I fucking love it.

I'm not entirely convinced her reasoning isn't tied to the hope of getting more homemade donuts for breakfast, but she's getting me in at the place I want to be, so I can't fault her.

Effie went out easy, falling asleep in my lap while I read her more of our pirate explorer book. I tucked her in, Stoner protectively next to her. I scratch his ear. "Good boy." I pat his butt. "The best boy."

Back in Elsie's room, she's waiting for me, perched on the bed, completely naked. Well fuck. There is not a better way to be greeted.

"Would you like to be naked with me?" she whispers, grinning, the excitement of the day still on her face. But I know she's tired too, so after I fuck her right, I'll make sure she sleeps good and deep.

I lock the door and strip off my clothes faster than necessary, stumbling on the bed to make her giggle. Then I smile, slow and sizzling, and she scoots closer to me on the bed. Her smirk falls away, and her eyes grow serious. She shifts until we face one another, with her legs crossed, mine out in a V encompassing her.

She cups my face, and I lean into it, kissing her palm.

"I want to be completely naked with you," she whispers, rocking up to her knees, legs still crossed behind her. Her fingers trace the elastic hiding in my hair, and my pulse quickens.

"I love you so much that sometimes I can't believe you chose me." Her voice is so gentle, yet my dick twitches, coming to life at the fingers grazing my temple. She slides her fingers along the edges of the patch.

She's never seen me without it. Effie, yeah, because she's a kid, and honestly, sometimes kids are easier to deal with. I know Elsie loves me, but my stomach clenches regardless.

With a nod from me after her eyes hover on mine, she flips up the patch, sliding it over my head, then tosses it on the bed.

Wrapping her hands around my temples, my hands go to her waist as she brings my head to her. Her lips move over the jagged magenta skin. Her bare tits heave against the bristled hair on my chest, erotic electricity between us. She moans her love for me as she kisses over every piece of damaged skin. My fingers knead into her as she does, my cock growing tall from the intimacy.

"I love you," she whispers, putting distance between us as I look up at her and open my eye. She studies the glass eye for a moment, touching the side of my face as she does. Facing me again, she says, "I'm so in love with you; it hurts to think of life without you."

My dick thrums, strengthening with each of her words. I press my fingers to her lips to quiet her. Reaching down, I free myself, and like she knows, her lids grow heavy, and she leans back.

I slip inside of her easily. I bite my lip when she presses her hands to her lower belly and aches from the fullness as I sink inside. Hands twisting the metal on her tits, she clings to my forearms to steady herself as she rides me in long, deep grinds.

Because we have time together, I now know what she needs. When I'm her Stray, she needs me to hand over my control and will and give myself up to her, which I greedily and easily do. But when it's just us, no roles other than two people who fucking thrive off and hunger after each other, she needs to feel kept and secure.

I smooth my hand around her ribcage and up her back, pulling the loose ends of her hair to jerk her head back. She inhales a happy noise that makes me pulse inside her, and I curl my other hand around her breast, hard.

"Quiet, baby. Shh," I warn her, very aware that we are not alone in the house. It's only my second night sleeping over–I kinda feel bad being such a fucking horn dog on both of them. But I can't help it.

She grabs the back of my head, pulling me to her breast until I'm sucking her pierced nipple onto my tongue, and she's whispering dirty, fucking filthy things down at me. My hips bounce into her as her words saw at the thread tethering my orgasm to the ground.

"I'll be quiet for you. I'll be quiet because my mouth will be full; your cock will be so deep in my throat that I couldn't even whimper if I wanted to."

Then she spins around, saddling her legs over my face.

She grinds her clit over my mouth, and I know she loves what my beard leaves behind, so I make sure to pay attention to her warm, sticky thighs, too.

Slowly, she traces the edge of my very hard cock with the tip of her tongue. Then she takes me into her mouth, finding the back of her throat with ease. Bobbing on me, she uses one hand to knead my inner thigh and the other... I jerk my hips slightly when the tip of her finger slides up my ass, nudging inside the hole.

Circling, poking in, sliding out, she teases my ass as she sucks my cock, and I moan my enjoyment straight into her pussy. Holding her ass, I pull her apart and slide my tongue up and down the slippery skin, prodding her opening before sealing my mouth over her clit again.

She whinnies, making noises of intense pleasure, and her thighs braced around my face begin to quiver.

My tongue floods with her sweet taste as I feed on her, knowing she's close. I can sense it in how her mouth slows on my length, how her finger stays buried deep inside me, pushing against my prostate. Her sexy, unfocused brain adds fuel to the fire burning deep inside me to feel her come on my face.

"Mmm," I murmur praise into her, squeezing her supple ass that fills my palms. "Mmm," I continue as she bears down on me hard, my mouth and nose completely buried in her.

The deterioration starts with her spine, wiggling and writhing against my body. Her mouth is chaotically skirting my length, sometimes sucking me hard, other times just kissing the tip. She's coming, but she can't let go of me because playing with my cock is part of the turn-on that got her here.

She contracts, waves of pleasure holding her captive as she bucks and throbs, her pussy doing it all right over my mouth. Goddamn. So fucking hot. Feeling how fast she came for me, tasting her orgasm while I hold her ass on my face... *fuuccking good.*

Too good.

"Put your mouth on it," I rasp out, feeling out of control. A second ago, I was holding her ass open to watch her come, licking to feel her come. Now I'm dripping, hard, a throbbing mess bobbing against my groin as she kisses my balls. "Fuck, baby, I need you to suck me."

She turns, giving me one blue eye from the top of her sloped, soft shoulder. "Say that again," she whispers calmly like precome isn't starting a lake between my ass cheeks.

"I need you to suck me."

She tips her chin over her shoulder, exposing the lower half of her face. One sexy grin, and she's sending my cock down the tight channel of her warm throat, resting her wet cunt over my mouth and nose, inundating me with the woman I love.

When I suck her clit again, I know she's going to try and wiggle away because she's sensitive and swollen from her orgasm.

But she lets me bury my face in her wetness and groan through my orgasm, which comes urgent and fiery up the shaft of my cock as she sucks the crown.

"Mmm," she moans a little as the first spurt floods her tongue. She sucks my head, letting me empty myself completely. Her diaphragm moves against my belly as she swallows but doesn't choke. And when I've groaned and come for what feels like an entire minute, she slides off me.

"See? Like right now, I want to tell you I love you because that," she points at my softening cock as she slips off the bed, grabbing her robe. "That was so hot and a turn-on, and *ah*," she gushes, pressing her palms to her cheeks. When she's cinched the robe and is ready to use the bathroom connected to her room, she gives me the most contagious smile.

"All I did was come," I say, but I know what she's talking about. It wasn't that I came. She and I both know that her coming all over my face had me milliseconds from turning into a water hose. Elsie's never had a man react to her the way she deserves. She didn't know until me that she really is a Goddess.

"Yeah," she nods, "except everything you do is the ultimate aphrodisiac."

I lift a brow. "Feed me chili, and you'll be singing a different story, baby."

Her cheeks pinken, but she rolls her eyes playfully. I hop out of bed, and we take turns going pee, washing up, brushing our teeth, and the rest of our pre-bed rituals. The air is thick with a hot buzz, though, because there's something strangely bonding about seeing someone's everyday rituals. Like she and I are further linked, closer because I've seen that she is someone that rolls the end of the toothpaste tube and double checks the lights are off.

It feels good to have more of her, and it feels good to share a routine.

I do not want to think about going back to my place tomorrow night.

Hell, I won't even have Stoner now since I'm pretty sure Effie wants to sleep with him.

Somehow, though, I drift off to sleep with my girl in my arms and a smile on my face because... I don't think I'll have to sleep alone again. This feels too good.

40

Elsie

Taking him this way makes him mine

I knew before he slept over, but truthfully, I'd lost focus after everything that happened with mom. But a few weeks post-good news about mom's condition, I am awakened.

I'm asking Bran to live with us.

Now, I don't know how long it will be an "us," considering mom's lucid days consist mostly of complaining about how I folded her laundry (the shunt is working, but the process can be frustrating) and griping that she wants space from my hovering. Hovering, me. Can you believe it?

Okay, I admittedly hovered. But just some. I mean, as she awakens inside of herself, sometimes the harder it is for me to believe how lucky I am.

I really thought Effie and I were going to lose her, but not only did she come back to us, but she's getting back parts of herself she used to stifle. She's really living now, and I'm so happy for her. Sometimes I do just stare, I admit because I'm still so in awe of it all.

But for now, Effie and I are asking Bran to move in with us.

I'd asked her about it a few weeks ago–and she'd happily and easily agreed. But I told her I wanted the time to be right, and then everything happened with mom and... well, it doesn't matter. Here we are now.

Mom's onboard, itching to hatch a plan with him about a house swap of sorts. I told her she's not going anywhere until she's done with her current treatment plan, and she begrudgingly agreed.

Originally, I thought just a private moment between the two of us would do. But now, that doesn't quite feel right.

And that's why I have one grouchy four-year-old and her sleepy grandmother sitting at the kitchen table at seven in the morning. Bran, who I had to coax back to sleep with a blowjob–poor me, huh?--will be out here any minute. I know because I set an alarm. I couldn't wait.

Too excited.

"Okay, so Effie, you start it all off, okay?" I nod, flipping the last pancake onto the plate. Mom and Effie have cut fruit and assembled Greek yogurt parfaits–one of Bran's favorites. Mom said she didn't need to be here for this since she knows she won't live here one day, but I essentially told her to kindly stuff it.

"I know, mama," she yawns, dropping her head to her bicep on the kitchen table.

The alarm pings, echoing faintly from my closed

bedroom door. I know Bran. He will wake up, immediately see I'm not in bed, go straight to Effie's room to see if I'm there, then head out to find us. He's been here a handful of nights already, but it's not a habit or familiarity thing. I know who he is, and that will be the order of operations in his heart.

Moments later, the bedroom door whirrs open, and then Effie's door creaks, too. I smile, the edges of my heart feeling blurred, like all of the love once kept in my heart is bleeding out all through me, filling me with the hottest, fuzziest feeling.

He appears at the end of the hall, looking relieved when he sees the three of us. I lower the plate on the table and tell him to take a seat, a cup of coffee already waiting.

"Do I snore so loud that we're already having a family meeting, just a few weeks in?" He asks, raising his hand over his head in an erotic, elongating stretch. He could scratch his ass, and I'd probably still like it, seriously.

I take a seat across from him as Effie twists in her seat until she's facing him. He pats his lap, and she kicks her legs over. He always rubs her feet, and she's a sucker for it, and I'm a sucker for them.

"I made you this card."

He lifts a brow, adjusting his eyepatch before taking the folded piece of printer paper from Effie. "What's the occasion?" He smiles down at her, focusing intently. I love how he pays attention to her, waits for her answers, and takes time to listen. He isn't doing it for me; he's doing it because he cares about her.

"Just cuz," she shrugs, grabbing at a pancake from the plate in front of her. She takes a bite, and I don't scold her for using her hands because I'm lost in the exact moment his eye met the front of the card.

I see the slide of his shoulders, dipping down with the hollowing of his chest as he sighs. Deep, full of emotion, he exhales. I swallow against the clog of tears forming in my throat, working their way up to my eyes. He tips his head to her.

"I like your card, Ef," he says, his voice husky, emotion bubbling over.

I'd seen the card.

It's Effie and Bran holding hands with Stoner on the ground. Above it says "best friends." I know she means it too, and that's what makes me so proud. I picked a good one, the best one, and it's his reaction that tells me how fucking right I am.

He wipes his cheek, hugging her tightly. "You're my best friend, too."

"And Stoner," she adds, and it always makes me chuckle hearing her sweet voice say such a platonic yet questionable word.

"And Stoner," he adds, sliding her back to her own chair, helping her to some pancakes.

She takes a bite, and mom and I still sit quietly across from them. He still hasn't opened it.

"Open your card," Effie says, earning a rush of relief from me. She bites into her pancake with a squeal of delight, and I know we've lost her to sugar. But it's okay; I can take it from here.

Bran reads the inside of the card, which I've written and Effie and I have signed. Bran's eye goes to mom, silently sipping her coffee.

"With your blessing?"

She nods. "I hope I'm not in your hair too long, but of course, Bran, with my blessing." She rests her mug on the table. "You're the blessing."

He tips his head back to exhale a rush of air, clearly a grab at controlling his emotions. I love how I always know just how he feels because he never tries to hide it. Attention back on us, he smiles.

"Yes. And honestly, I was starting to stress out about not being here with you guys."

"Girls," corrects Effie.

"Girls, right. Sorry, Ef."

I smile. I move my foot up the length of his calf under the privacy of the kitchen table. "Now it's time to eat because we have a lot of rearranging in this place to do before you can even move in."

He lifts his fork, winking at me first. "Eat; you don't have to ask me twice."

* * *

"Oh fuck, yes, right there, right there." Hands full of Bran's silky hair, I hold him against me as he eats me. My orgasm pounds down my back, surging through my hips and rushing to a ball of heat between my thighs. "I'm coming," I whisper-moan down to him, my thighs clamping around him as his fingertips sink deeper into my sides.

I spasm, tremble, and hold him there until he's licked me for the last time, and I'm too sensitive. He tips up on his elbows, a wet grin on his lips. "God, I love doing that," he says, looking more sated than me.

But when he pushes up to his knees, wiping his mouth on his discarded t-shirt, I see he is in fact, not sated. Between his legs, veiny and eager, his cock bobs heavily, pink tip swollen.

"Now it's time to return the favor," I say, clambering to my knees, practically drooling for him. He takes my hand before I can reach for him and pulls my knuckles to his lips for a stalling kiss.

"I want you to be the Goddess tonight." His tongue smears across the surface of my palm, making my skin tingle.

"Yeah?" I ask, the idea of controlling his orgasm making me pulse from the inside out. "Anything specific?"

He shrugs. "I trust you..."

I tap my chin, trying to remember where I stashed my bag of goodies after the last time we used a toy. Lifting three shoe boxes and a garment bag, I find the hidden bag and search until I find exactly what I need.

He eyes the harness and the dildo strapped to it. "You game?" I ask without specifics.

He studies the length of the shiny toy and then nods. "You always make me feel good."

A few minutes later, we are on the bed on our knees, me behind him. With half a bottle of lube between the two of us, I wrap my arms around him as my hips work the toy inside of him. He winces at first, and asks for his Goddess to move slowly, and I do. With one hand, I twist his nipple, rock hard and responsive. My other palm wraps around him, jerking him torturously slow. He writhes somehow without moving–erratic breaths and wild grunts, occasionally sighing out *fuck yes*.

I roll my hips, stroke him, and tell him everything I feel.

"God, you're so sexy, Bran." I grip his muscled chest tightly, letting his nipple have a break. He moans when my nails drag down the ropy knots of his abs. "You're so beautiful, so perfect." My groin goes flush with his smooth cheeks, the toy filling his ass completely. I know it's just a toy, but something about the vulnerability he's giving me. Taking him this way makes him mine, in just another way. "You make me feel so lucky, do you know that?" My lips carve a hot trail across his shoulders.

My hips find a pattern that makes him push back against me and makes his hands reach back to pull me in closer, deeper. "You're so strong; you're so fucking masculine that just smelling your shampoo makes me wet." I drag my tongue across his warm skin, eating up his musk. He groans, his fingertips pushing into my ass. I drive the cock in and out of him with more force.

"Your tits feel so good against me. The metal," he groans, tipping his head back as bliss crawls up through his core, devouring his resolve.

I return to the praise because my good boy needs to hear it. And God, he is so good.

"You're such a good lover, Bran, and a good boyfriend. The best." I slide out of him only to sink in harder, finding the spot that sends him over the edge.

"Oh, baby, fuck, I love you," he groans as his fingers sink into my bones; he's holding me so tight.

Pumping him faster, I kiss his shoulder and give him the relief he deserves. "Come." I drop my voice to a smoky whisper, like my inner Goddess. "You're such a good boy. I'm going to make sure you know how good you are." I jack him quicker as I sink all the way inside of his tight ass, my grip on his cock constricting. I enjoy the soft curling of his spine and the quickening of his breaths.

"I'm going to make you come so hard every day because you're such a good boy."

I bite into his shoulder again as his cock pulses in my curled fist, his orgasm looming. "You're my good boy. Forever, aren't you?"

He nods, both of our bodies coming to a sweaty stop. I twist my hands around the slick edge of his cockhead, smoothing my thumb over his slit just as he erupts. Twisting my fist down his cock, I jerk him as he drives toward my hand while bringing me with him, still reaching back and holding me tight.

"Elsie," is the last intelligible thing he utters before his orgasm breaks free, ropes of come landing with a heavy thud across the bed. My pussy clenches at the noise, and I lick my lips against his back. "Good boy."

He breathes through the rest of his orgasm, coming hard, making a beautiful, hot mess. And when I peel myself from him and empty him of the toy, he falls forward onto his forearms, panting.

I unclip the harness at my hip and both on my thighs, then give each strap a hard tug, tearing it from my legs last. It falls to the bed, and I knee it away, sitting between his still open thighs.

Peppering kisses over his ass, I smooth my hands everywhere I can–down the trunks he calls thighs, around his hips, up the small of his back. I kiss him everywhere. He let me have him so fully tonight; I've never felt more loved. More connected.

"God, I love you," I tell him, finally clambering to my

feet to get a towel. I was in a daze–forgot about after. Now I kind of understand how that can happen. It's not that you don't care; it's that it still feels so good.

"I love you too. Shit, baby, that was hot." He pushes up to his knees, his cock still thick but hanging lower. "You own me; you know that?"

I smile at him because it feels like the opposite. "Mutual ownership," I offer from my place in front of the sink, talking to him through the open bathroom door. "How's that?"

"Perfect." He smiles as I drag the towel up the split of his perfect ass, making sure he feels okay. I change the sheets while he gets us water, and when I curl up next to him, finally ready for sleep, he turns to me in the dark.

With his lips against my forehead, beard rousing my skin, he says, "Thank you for your love and for bringing Effie into my life. I love you." He kisses the top of my head, and just a few moments later, he's out.

With my palm on Bran's chest, the rhythm of Bran's peaceful heart is the soundtrack to my sleep.

To my life.

Epilogue: One Year Later

Bran

From lonely and lost Stray to this, this perfect life blooming on the horizon.

"Dude, you said I was going to get to push this time," Mally says, stepping next to me behind Effie's swing.

"You can push, but she has to want you to push," I tell him for the millionth time.

Elsie is back at the house, preparing a barbecue for everyone. Sammy's there helping, of course, because my sister is pretty much always at our house.

Our house.

Mally takes over once Effie squeals his name, and I take a seat on the empty bench, my head and heart a bit overwhelmed with how much things have changed in the last year.

Epilogue: One Year Later

My guys came and met everyone at Elaine and Elsie's not long after Elaine got her correct diagnosis. Mally and Effie hit it off, and it makes sense because Malibu's maturity level is on-par with Effie's. Henry and Robin–eh, now that Elsie is friends with Robin, she won't allow me to call Henry by his nickname of Batman. Robin hates it, and the women always stick together, so now he is Henry.

Which feels fucking weird.

Anyway, Henry and Robin are thrilled that Elsie and I are together and serious–they want more kids in our friend group. And Van? Well, he's happy with his wife Violet– they got married shortly after I moved in with Elsie.

I moved into Elsie's house so I could help take care of Effie as she and Elaine went through the medical appointments pretty heavily there for a while. It was kind of perfect, though, because it gave Ef and me a solid chance to bond, and I'm lucky. So fucking lucky because Effie accepted me right away. She's such a good kid. Smartest kindergartener I've ever met.

About six months ago, Elaine was tired of living with us. More so, I think she felt like she didn't want to cramp the growth that the three of us were experiencing. The comfort we'd grown into. We didn't want her to leave, but we came up with a plan when she said she'd spent the last few years being less active because of her condition and that all she wanted was to get back to things she loved.

She moved into my house, tending my garden and taking care of my cherry and peach trees. She and Fanny had their bridge club there and even bingo. The garden kept her busy, but the small size of the home wasn't too much that she couldn't maintain.

Epilogue: One Year Later

That put her just ten minutes from us, in a place where I could change or fix anything that she wanted because I owned it.

Things were fucking great. Perfect, even.

But it's not enough.

Call me greedy. Maybe I'm a glutton. But when it comes to this happiness that I finally have? I want to know it's mine beyond a reasonable doubt.

"Still thinking about popping the question soon?" Van asks as he flops down next to me on the bench.

"Yo," Mally calls from behind the swing, a grin on his face. "I got here before you!"

Van holds his thumb up, turning his mouth towards me. "God, he needs a girlfriend. He texted me this morning saying he was going to watch me on Find Friends and leave at the same time as me since we're *equidistant* to your new place—"

"He's still using the word-a-day calendar?" I ask, biting back my grin.

Van nods. "He texted me thirteen times today already." Smoothing his hands down his thighs he turns to face me. "I'm afraid he's going to be living above our garage in some weird, homemade apartment, and my future kids are going to call him Uncle."

I snort at that because at one point I was worried that guy would be me. Looking back at Mally, the tall, muscular blonde man who has no problem getting women but, for some damn reason, has yet to get one to stick.

"Dude, I gotta work with him all day, and Violet never turns him down. She always feels bad for him, so he's at our house half the week."

Epilogue: One Year Later

I wince. "Damn, that sucks."

His eyebrows drift up. "Yeah, man. We haven't even been married for a year, but we can't be *careless* because Malibu could be in another room, and I don't even know it yet."

I pat his back. "Well, this has been a nice diversion away from my shit, but that sounds more like a Van problem than a Bran problem."

"You think so, huh?" He rises, stretching his arms above his head. "Wait until Violet has Elsie and Sammy feeling bad, too. Then you'll be singing a different tune."

I stand, too. "Nah, you're forgetting; Malibu's idiot charm doesn't work on Sammy. And Sammy and Elsie are tight."

Van's displeasure fades as a smile curls his lips. "Dude, so, you really want to propose soon, huh?"

Nervously, I smooth my hands through my hair, then touch the elastic of the patch. I still wear it. After all, a hero pirate is one of the best things you can be.

"I do. Fuck, I'd do it today if I could."

I've had a ring since the week after our sleepover. But with everything happening with Elaine, there was never a time just for us.

Six months ago, I thought it was the perfect time. Elaine was moving into my place, Effie had started kindergarten... things were good. But Elsie, who'd been working at Paradise as a trainer since we got together, decided her interest in training came down to her interest in muscles and helping them.

She started massage school, and now she's a certified massage therapist with her own place inside Paradise.

Epilogue: One Year Later

Watching her grow her career in a field she loves—and to have it be at my gym? So fucking cool. My girl is so badass—proposing went rightfully to the backburner. But after she graduated and set up shop in Paradise, Stoner had a small procedure, and I couldn't do anything but worry about him until he was well again.

And that brings us to now.

"Do you really want all of us there for your private moment?"

Before I can answer, Van's phone rings, and he abandons our conversation. "Hold on," he says, putting a finger up. "Violet was going to drive her car to your place since I have to head to work after." I nod.

"Hi, sweetheart," he says, his voice dropping low, sounding sweet. I mime, sticking a finger down my throat, which earns me an eye roll from the Bodfather. He gives me his back, taking some privacy for a phone call with his wife.

I don't blame him.

In fact, I'm jealous he gets to use that title. *Wife.*

"Ohhh, really?" he drags out, happiness thick in his voice. I guess Violet's giving him some good news, and it occurs to me she could be filling his head with some dirty shit, so I face Mally and Effie, so I don't have to hear that.

"How's he doing?" I ask Effie, whose little fingers are clinging to the chain as she slices into the sky; Mally's pushes are powerful but controlled.

She grins, blonde curls covering her face as she whooshes back to Mally's waiting palms. "Good! He's good, Bran, he's really good!"

Mally shakes his head, giving the swing another shove. "From your lips to God's ears, my girl."

Epilogue: One Year Later

Van slaps his hand down over my shoulder and motions something to Malibu, who stops the swing. He lowers his mouth to her ear. "It's time, Ef."

She turns, giving a proud nod to one of my best friends.

"We don't have to go yet," I protest, "Elsie was gonna text me when the house was picked up."

She and Sammy wanted us out of their hair, and the guys wanted to come early since they have to work later, so we met at the park for Ef to get her energy out.

"Violet's at your place, Elsie says to come back."

"Bran," Effie calls, standing on the edge of the cement, toes brushing the bark of the playground. "Can you help get my sweatshirt off?"

Turning, I see Van and Mally are standing off near the bench, checking their phones, both of them. "Just a sec, guys," I call to them before jogging over to Effie. One of her arms dangles free, and the rest of her tangled in the sweatshirt.

Fishing my hand into the sleeve, I carefully take her wrist and slip her arm free from the sweatshirt. I pat the top of her head. "Now close your eyes; I'm gonna lift."

She nods, squeezing her eyes shut as I lift the sweater off her. "All done," I tell her as I pull the sleeve right-side-in and begin to tie it around her waist for her. She likes wearing her sweatshirts like that, and even though the look is not good on me, when she asks me to do it to match her, I always do.

"Bran, guess what?" she asks quietly as I align the knotted arms of her sweatshirt to the center of her outfit.

"What?"

"Mama got me a new shirt for the barbecue today."

I smile at her, tucking a blonde curl behind her ear.

Epilogue: One Year Later

"Well, be careful, barbecue can stain, and I know Mama likes to keep your clothes stain-free."

She giggles, and I do too because you try not to laugh when an adorable little girl clings to your forearms and wiggles her way into your heart. For a second, she looks at Van and Mally, then back to me. Dramatically, she clears her throat.

"Bran, I am wearing the shirt that Mama got me."

I nod. "Good for you, baby."

She grabs my face, her hands so small they sink into my beard. Bringing our faces together, I can hear Van and Mally burst out into a raw chuckle. I'm confused. "Bran," she says, her strawberry breath hot on my face. "Look at my new shirt."

Letting go of me, she leans back and pinches the fabric, pulling it taut. She smiles, proud and broad, and my eye moves over the shirt.

I read the words in my head.

I read them again. I look up at Effie, who's still grinning like a fool. I read the words on the shirt again. I put my hands on Effie's shoulders, my breath trapped in my chest.

"Ef," I say, and her head bobs, curls bounce.

"Just like it says." She beams, literally beams. "I'm going to be a Big Sister."

I rise from my crouch, dizzy as shit, and look at my brothers. Rather than checking their phones, they were videoing this. Van was. Mally was... he slides his phone into his pocket, and from behind the slide, in the opposite direction that we'd been facing, Elsie appears.

"It's lucky you're so in love with Van when he talks to you, or else sneaking her behind us would've been tough,"

Epilogue: One Year Later

Mally says, smiling at me from somewhere deep in his heart. He's waited for me to be happy; all of my brothers have.

I don't know if that's why Elsie included them at this moment, but I'm glad she did.

Scooping Effie up against my chest, Elsie and I split paces to meet.

"Let me hear you say it," I whisper, so happy I'm shaking. I hold Effie closer to me, and she strokes my beard, nuzzling her cheek to my head. "Elsie, tell me."

Elsie's cheeks are stained with tears. "I'm pregnant." She smiles, looping her arm around her daughter, the three of us hugging.

"You're gonna be a daddy," Effie says, still petting me. "With my mama."

I nod. "I am. The three of us, Effie, we're going to have a baby together."

"Me too?" she asks, looking surprised as her blue eyes widen.

"Yeah," Elsie says, smoothing her palm up Effie's back. "You'll get to help us, and you'll be the big sister, just like I told you. And you'll teach your brother or sister all sorts of things."

She wrinkles her nose, one hand gripping my neck. Her heart beats against my chest.

"Are you excited?" I ask, sensing she's caught on something.

"What's the matter, baby?" Elsie asks, brows pinching. "When we talked about this at home, you were happy." She tips her head to the side, lowering her voice to this soothing, *mama can fix anything* tone that makes me both love the fuck out of her and want to fuck the shit out of her.

Epilogue: One Year Later

She turns to me, our faces close from the way I'm holding her... but really, she's holding me. "You're gonna be the baby's daddy, but you won't be my daddy."

From off in the distance, I hear Mally and Van.

"Oh, *okay*, so we're cutting onions today."

"Oh my God, Violet's going to be so pissed she wasn't here for this."

I lower down to my knees, putting Effie on her feet in front of me. This isn't anything that Elsie and I haven't discussed. Adopting Effie is something that I want to do, but Elsie wants us to be married first. Now that she's pregnant, I can almost guarantee that the wedding is going to happen soon. Stressing if the proposal is too soon? Glad I didn't waste too much time on that.

"Effie, I want to be your daddy so bad that I asked your mama. Did you know that?" Tears rain down my cheek, and now is a time I wish I had my other eye. Not because not having it takes anything away from this, but because I want another way to capture this beautiful, life-changing moment.

"I asked her. I said, *I love Effie so much.*" I pause, swallowing the sob in the chest. I can sob to Elsie later about this moment, but right now, for Effie, I gotta keep it together. Effie and I had exchanged I love you's early on in our relationship because she's an open-hearted extrovert, and I loved her the moment I saw her in her SpongeBob pajamas, stomping her foot for mac n cheese.

"But I wanted to ask you if I could be your daddy. That means you wouldn't be Effie Carlisle. You'd take my name, Ef. You'd be legally my daughter." I swallow, the impact of the words making my body ache; I want it so bad. I want this girl to know that I'd die to be her daddy and that I'll take care of her and her mom and her grandma and whoever else comes along for my entire life. "Effie Edwards."

She smiles and falls into my arms as she cries. Over her shoulder, I look at Elsie. "She's crying, so can I sob like a baby now? Her crying gives me a free pass, right?"

Elsie giggles, crying. Mally is sniffing, and even Van is struggling.

"I love you, Effie. And I would be honored to be your daddy. Can I be your daddy?"

Her answer is quick. "Yes." She peels her face from my neck and turns to her mom. "I said yes!"

It's not a yes from Elsie to a marriage proposal, but it's a yes to a lifetime of love and happiness. From lonely and lost Stray to this, this perfect life blooming on the horizon.

I used to wish the night of my accident away, praying to return to a time before it happened. And now? I wouldn't change anything, not for the world. Because without my injury, I may not have found my Goddess. And without her...

I'd still be just a Stray.

If You Liked This Book

Hello beautiful.

I hope you enjoyed the book. Equally, I hope you enjoyed your time snuggled up reading. If you liked the story and feel like sharing your opinions and thoughts, I'd love to hear what you have to say and what brings you to my books over in the reviews on Amazon.

Thank you again for taking a chance on me. I hope you liked the book.

Daisy

Also by Daisy Jane

Series:

Men of Paradise (1 Book So Far)

Where Violets Bloom / a stalker romance / MF / Book 1

Stray / a femdom romance / MF / Book 2

Oakcreek (2 Books So Far)

I'll Do Anything / a bully femdom romance / MF / Book 1

After the Storm / an alpha MM romance / MM / Book 2

The Millionaire and His Maid (3 Books)

His Young Maid / an age gap boss/employee romance / MF / Book 1

Maid for Marriage / an age gap romance / MF / Book 2

Maid a Mama / a surprise pregnancy romance / MF / Book 3

The Taboo Duet

Unexpected/ an age gap Daddy figure romance / Book 1

Consumed / a Daddy kink romance / Book 2

Standalones:

The Other Brother / dual POV / MF

The Corner House / single POV / MFMM, MFM, MFM with an HEA

My Best Friend's Dad / age gap instalove novel / MF
Waiting for Coach / age gap novel / student teacher / MF
Hot Girl Summer / a taboo step sibling romance / MF
Pleasing the Pastor / an age gap virgin romance / MF
Release / a taboo MMF, MM, MF romance

Made in United States
Orlando, FL
23 July 2024